Midnight Nocturne

To Susan Vassi,
What would the Grove be's without you? Some of my first and happiest memories (of the grove) are of working on plays with you.

Cameron
Byrne

Midnight Nocturne

Cameron Byrne

Copyright 2010 Cameron Byrne

Hard Cover ISBN 978-0-557-67978-2

Paper Back ISBN 978-0-557-67977-5

Contents

Chapter 1. Prelude 1

Chapter 2. Gypsies In The Night 7

Chapter 3. Until Death 17

Chapter 4. Leigh Bryant 33

Chapter 5. Masquerade 37

Chapter 6. Remembering How To Dance 43

Chapter 7. Paper Crosses 49

Chapter 8. Crowd Surfing 53

Chapter 9. The Anxious Guest 59

Chapter 10. The Mistress 69

Chapter 11. Special Invitations 75

Chapter 12. The Jewel 85

Chapter 13. Forgotten Depths 103

Chapter 14. Cloak And Dagger 109

Chapter 15. Chaos 115

Chapter 16. The Newborns 121

Chapter 17. Discreetly 127

Chapter 18. Alucard 131

Chapter 19. According To Plan 135

Chapter 20. Awake 139

Chapter 21. Insight 143

Chapter 22. A Price Paid 147

Chapter 23. Chase 151

Chapter 24. Peculiar 157

Chapter 25.	Dead On Arrival	161
Chapter 26.	Last Ride Home	165
Chapter 27.	Threshold	169
Chapter 28.	Curious Dreams	177
Chapter 29.	The Gift	183
Chapter 30.	Daydreams	187
Chapter 31.	Jesse Bryant	193
Chapter 32.	Lung Shot	201
Chapter 33.	Curio	205
Chapter 34.	Blood In The Nile	211
Chapter 35.	A Small Sacrifice	219
Chapter 36.	Unwelcome Guest	225
Chapter 37.	Purpose	229
Chapter 38.	Uncertainty	239
Chapter 39.	False Dreams	243
Chapter 40.	Play It By Ear	247
Chapter 41.	Leap Of Faith	255
Chapter 42.	Dark Corners	261
Chapter 43.	Erased	267
Chapter 44.	The Means To An End	275
Chapter 45.	One Final Dream	285
Chapter 46.	Broken Promise	289
Chapter 47.	Requiem	297
Epilogue		301

CHAPTER 1
PRELUDE

The rain fell all around him in soft, cold sheets that whispered through the night. Always, it seemed, the rain came with his melancholy moods, but still he loved the crystalline showers. Each drop of rain felt like a kiss from an angelic lover on the pale skin of his cold, immortal body. In his imagination, she would descend from the heavens, shrouding him in her wings, heedless of his damned soul and transgressions. On nights like this, Kehl Sanrla's craving for love overcame even the blood lust that had cursed his kind from the beginning of time.

An unaccustomed chill shot its way through his body as the rain grew heavier. He let a smile play its way across his lips as he spread his arms to welcome the oncoming storm. Another chill ripped across him. His muscles tensed as his body shuddered in a visceral reaction that not even vampirism could extinguish. A shuddering sigh of pleasure exploded from his lungs as the rain continued to fall in drenching sheets. The deluge forced him to his knees with his senses reeling. His eyes blinked open just in time to see a bright arc of lightning streak across the night sky.

As he admired the glittering plasma in the skies, he wondered if he'd tempted fate just a little too much tonight. The thought excited him even more as he silently willed the weather to turn even more aggressive. As though in response to his wishes, the temperature dipped suddenly and the rainfall seemed to redouble in intensity. Craning his neck back, he parted his lips to let the rain run over his fangs and into his mouth.

The storm grew in its fury as Kehl gathered himself together and regained his feet. Sudden gusts of wind whipped around him through the rainy night. Silently he thanked whatever god was responsible for the storm, grateful for the temporary respite it offered him of his undead life. Lightning glimmered once more in the heavens as it rushed down to strike a lightning rod barely fifteen feet away from where he stood. With a heavy heart, he realized he must take shelter inside his lonely home.

He had been standing alone on the large rooftop patio of his darkened mansion. Having existed for hundreds and hundreds of years, living in such a building became not so much a luxury but more of a necessity. The course of an immortal life brings with it not only wealth, but also a never ending collection of items. And although vampires are undead, they occasionally possess a certain sentimentality. Eventually they must acquire more and more space to store their collected clutter. Luckily, the old addage that Time is Money applies to no one more keenly, than to the vampire.

Large glass doors led the way back inside. Swinging them open silently, Kehl made his way into the library. The only illumination in the cavernous room was a single candle standing alone on a nearby table. His library, while not huge, was packed with books. By Kehl's logic, there existed no knowledge that was not power, and through his many years, he had kept all but the most frivolous of books. He had found that unlike many of his former companions, books remained true. Only the books, like him, remained immortal, and so he held them very dear.

Just inside the entrance sat a small pile of towels and dry clothes. He'd sensed the storm coming some hours ago and prepared accordingly. He peeled off his soaking wet pants and laid them carefully off to the side so that the sun would dry them in the coming day. He then dried himself off before pulling on a set of fresh clothes. Only the slightest dampness clung to his long dark hair as he made his way across the cool tiles that led further into the cavernous room.

The upper chambers connected directly to the second story of the library. He favored it this way; they were his favorite rooms in the house. It only took him a few moments to pick up the candle and make his way across the library to the spiral staircase that led up to the second level. Had he so wished, he could have turned on the electric lights and illuminated the entire room. Instead, he often left them off, for on nights like this he preferred the candlelight for its companionship. In reality, he had no need of any light whatsoever; being a creature of the night he could see perfectly in total darkness.

Entering his quarters through a small door, his candle cast shadows throughout his expansive bedroom. Dim golden light touched upon dark blue silk as he made his way to the dressing room. The room brought a smile to his face. Dracula's patron color in Hollywood always seemed to be a dark blood-like crimson. Kehl found that in times of great thirst, the simplest shade of red would almost immediately launch him into a thirst-driven frenzy. When surrounded with blue, he could fight his hunger for a longer period of time, almost to a point where he could suppress the urges entirely.

Swiftly, he made his way to a large dresser where he kept knickknacks and trinkets. Standing amid the junk and relics of the past sat a rather large invitation. The surface of the card appeared to be completely black upon first glance; but then, upon closer inspection, a dark blue raised ink lettering seemed almost to appear out of nowhere. The handwriting, graceful and meticulous, was beautiful hand-painted calligraphy. The words read:

You are invited to

The Midnight Nocturne,

An exclusive nightclub experience …

Kehl knew of the Midnight Nocturne only through media and gossip. It was relatively new on the nighttime scene but had managed to make quite a splash. The invitation was a mystery; he had seen celebrities and the like entering and leaving the club on the television, but he himself tried to remain a rather secretive individual. Even though he'd received the invitation days ago he still could not decide whether or not to go. Lifting the card, he opened it to see what appeared to be a hand-painted moon silhouetting the figure of a voluptuous woman beckoning to the viewer.

Your presence is required by order of

The Mistress.

Come, enjoy the many pleasures of the Solstice

The fact that the invitation said that he was required and not invited intrigued him; he wondered who else would be "required" to arrive and what purpose their presence would serve. He felt desperately lonely after having isolated himself in his mansion for the past several years, only interacting with the outside world through investments and business associates. Perhaps it was time for him to venture out once more into society and sample what little he could of a normal life.

He looked to the furthest wall of his room where an elaborate oil painting hung. In it stood a tall slender woman shrouded in a dress that seemed to change color from every angle. The lady was not quite as exotic as the one portrayed in his invitation but was instead borne of a more sinuous sensuality. Her emerald eyes were downcast, and despite their vivid color, they were somehow clouded. Pulled back, the brown silk of her hair hid little of her face in a simple yet elegant arrangement. Showing a mastery of detail, the artist had painted the two faintest traces of white two inches below her earlobe.

Kehl took his candle and walked to the painting, speaking softly as a dreamer would in the deepest of sleep. "Rana Alexander."

There came a slight whirring noise from behind the wall followed by a click, like the sound of a surreptitiously opened door. With a hiss the portrait, and a large portion of the wall, slowly sank back to reveal a spiral stone staircase that led deep down into the darkness. The light from his candle did little more than illuminate a few feet ahead as Kehl began his descent. This secret place, concealed deep within the core of the manor, had only this single secluded staircase as access.

His feet eventually found the rough stone landing at the bottom of the stairs. The room was made from materials far predating the manor, most of them shipped from deep within Europe. Set into the stone to the right rested a small reservoir of oil. Touching the dark pool with his candle, Kehl ignited the small bowl and sent a blazing streak of fire shooting across the room as it lighted similar reservoirs. It seemed that the room burst into an inferno as the flickering flames licked the walls. They bathed the room with a reddish orange glow that brightly illuminated its contents. As before, the light was not necessary, but it was exactly the way the chamber would have appeared many years before.

Every wall was covered with all manner of different torture devices: thumb screws, meat hooks, vices, wracks, and barbed wire, all arranged into neat lines. Devious devices, meant to sever both the flesh from the body and the sanity from the mind. None of the instruments or contraptions had seen use in centuries, and many of them looked brand new despite their age. Kehl glanced thoughtfully around the macabre room. Created centuries before, the devices had one purpose: the torture of Kehl Sanria. His feet moved of their own volition as they carried him to a massive iron maiden that dominated the room.

Kehl bowed his head and knelt before the massive cast-iron beast. How long he had languished in its innards, stabbed from every direction. The pain had only redoubled every time he tried to escape. His vampiric gift of regeneration had manifested as a curse when new perfect flesh would quickly grow to replace the damaged. The pain never lessened. No scar tissue ever formed to take the edge off the thousand needles burying deep into his flesh.

Kehl tilted his head back and looked up to read the harsh words chiseled into the iron: **"In Memoriam Rana Alexander."**

Ancient dried blood caked the maiden around the seams, a testament to the efficiency of the horrible device. Reverentially, Kehl touched the blood as softly as he could; it was many centuries old and now crystallized. Memories flashed through his mind like a hot poker jammed suddenly and violently into his brain. In his mind, the suffering he had endured was justified for what he had done as well as for what he had become.

Far above, a clock deep in the manor solemnly tolled off the hour. It struck nine times, and it felt as though each toll decimated his soul. Tonight marked the winter solstice, and, by fate, the very night of his birth. It was long held as legend that a child born on the winter solstice would be born different, evil and twisted. The hour, often referred to as the Dark Hour, brought many things both wondrous and horrible into being on its zenith. Every toll of Father Time's bell brought that hour closer.

Centuries ago the Sanria family had been gypsies, traveling throughout Europe in a modest enclosed wagon that the family had built themselves. Covered in carvings from stem to stern, the craftwork told the history of the family, as well as legends of the Dark Hour. When the time for Kehl's birth had grown near, the family was forced to find a midwife in a nearby town. Kehl's father, Matthias, had reluctantly obeyed to wait outside the wagon while a pugnacious woman had scornfully volunteered for the delivery, and only after having her pockets lined with silver.

Gypsies in those times were rarely accepted into closely knit villages. Most often they were viewed as thieves and vagabonds and were turned away. Even when fortunate enough to have found a friendly place, they could not find the trust and camaraderie that an established townsperson would enjoy. Such had been the case on the night of Kehl's birth. After finding the midwife, Matthias found himself forced to bargain and plead with the woman.

In the end, it took nearly all of the Sanria family's meager savings in order to persuade the reluctant lady. Matthias despised the stranger who grunted and moaned her way all the way back to the family wagon. By the time they arrived, Matthias had begun to wonder if having this person present during his wife's labor would make things easier or more difficult. He watched in silence as the midwife cautiously climbed in to tend to his wife, Elaine, as though the wagon itself threatened her in some way.

Through most of the ordeal, Kehl's father had fought his urges to be by his wife's side as she screamed with the labor of childbirth. Many long hours passed with only the briefest of pauses in her pains. At first, Matthias thought that perhaps the midwife would pull through for him and his wife, but as more and more time passed, he started to notice more and more cursing coming from inside the wagon. The woman eventually burst through the doors of the trailer, screaming with an insane fire in her eyes.

"For all my efforts I cannot bring this child into the world! The Dark Hour is fast approaching, and if the child is born on the solstice, we must destroy it! Otherwise we may bring one of the damned onto our living earth!"

Kehl would never know it, but his father had been the only reason the midwife did not destroy him at that very moment. Matthias knew that the death of his son would also be the death of his dearest wife. He acted quickly, literally carrying the hysterical woman back out of the wagon before locking her out entirely. Matthias joined his wife inside the wagon and preformed the rest of the birthing. He was glad that they could not afford a clock to announce the hour. It weighed heavily on his mind that he might be bringing a thing of evil into the world.

He had indeed brought one of the damned onto the planet, and yet for the first twenty-one years of his life, Kehl lived as a normal boy. No abnormalities whatsoever presented themselves, none of the strengths or weaknesses given to his kind manifested in him. Even the sun held no sway with him. For during most summers his skin would tan to a deep brown. His young mind was fiercely intelligent. His hair was long, black, and attractive. One color alone could never quite describe his eyes, as they were a curious shade of gray that never seemed to be quite the same from moment to moment. He seemed completely normal even when under the most scrupulous of inspections. Unfortunately for him, he was doomed to be something far, far more than normal.

CHAPTER 2
GYPSIES IN THE NIGHT

Thirteenth century, Europe.

High in the mountains, in one of the forgotten countries of the Old World, rested the small town of Braunburg. It was a tightly knit community, with perhaps two dozen or so families. Positioned in a small valley, shrouded by seemingly endless trees and bordering by a mountainside, it could not have been more secluded. Several small families managed to remain mostly self-sufficient between hunting and farming. Occasionally traders or merchants would come through, allowing the villagers to barter for the things they lacked.

Frederick the Second was the current Holy Roman Emperor and sovereign of the realm. Having returned to Europe after a somewhat successful crusade, he was now excommunicated and at war with the Papacy. So far, Braunburg remained untouched by the ensuing religious wars. The residents of the town, however, were split almost evenly between either supporting the Pope or the Emperor. Frederick represented a new, almost scientific, view of the world, while the church remained true to their religion.

Several soldiers who lived in the town managed to maintain a peaceful environment among the population. Their leader was a man who had served under Frederick during his crusade into the holy land. His name was Rallos Alexander, and though Braunburg retained no official mayor or governor, he was unmistakably the man in charge. He, along with several former knights, defended the town whenever necessary. He was unprepared, however, for the night that the gypsies stumbled upon Braunburg. That fateful night would change his family's destiny forever.

The evening gloom had already settled in around the town. Morning rains had brought with them a clinging fog that became trapped in the valley throughout the day and into the night. Above, the sky was clear and the moon full. Its light illuminated the fog just enough to lend the entire area a hazy, ghostlike aura. A cool breeze brought a chill to the skin of anyone venturing outside at such a late hour.

When Rallos heard the banging at his front door, he was already laying in bed. Dressing himself quickly to answer his comrade, he accidentally banged into a corner with his muscular frame. He was a well-built man who was more accustomed to being outside or in his forge than being in the house. Cursing softly under his breath, he made his way to the front door and pulled it open. The man waiting outside with a torch was not a small man but nonetheless stood a foot shorter than Rallos.

"What is it?" Rallos asked, calmly, his low voice seemingly hushed by the fog.

"Gypsies, sir, and mounted raiders, coming through the pass, almost at a gallop. I had to push my horse as hard as I dared to make it back here in time."

Rallos stepped outside and quietly shut his door before he spoke again. "How many are there?"

"Perhaps two or three in the trailer, not counting the driver. The wheels weren't sinking very far into the ground. As for the raiders, there were ten, heavily armed with swords and bows."

"We shall have to act quickly. Gather up the other men, I will ride out and meet them head on."

"Yes, sir."

Rallos's bright blue eyes narrowed as he watched his subordinate rush off into the fog. Turning back toward his house, he was startled to find his teenage daughter standing in the doorway watching him intently. Her eyes were a bright emerald, her hair cut almost boyishly short. He had expected the knocking would have woken her up, but she was already dressed, save for her shoeless feet. Rallos couldn't help but smile softly. His daughter grew more and more beautiful every day. But the thought of suitors coming to call quickly made his smile vanish.

"What's going on, Daddy?" She asked simply.

"We have a few visitors," he replied briskly as he set off for his horse. "I don't have any time to talk about it right now, Rana."

The moon provided enough light for him to make his way to his stable.

Undaunted, Rana followed after him though the grass, barefoot. "Are there bandits?"

Her father turned around suddenly and looked her directly in the eyes. "Yes, there are bandits. Right now, I need you to go back inside. Shut the doors and windows and warn your mother."

"Yes, sir," she answered.

Rallos noticed the fear that crossed Rana's face; she knew that it was real. He had warned her long ago that this might happen one day. Word came from all across Europe of the senseless killing that was happening in the name of faith. Rana immediately rushed back to their home to warn her family. Rallos watched her proudly; she'd not questioned the order he'd given her. For all he knew, it might be the last time they ever spoke.

His corral sat just a short distance away from his home. Making his way quickly to the single stable at its side, he swiftly saddled his horse. He rarely had need of his sword and normally kept it either in his forge, as he was also the town smith, or with his saddle. Today it was with his saddle, and luckily so. His forge was a bit further away from his home, and it would have taken more time to retrieve the blade.

As he rode away through the village and into the forest beyond, two men joined him on either side. One was the scout who'd reported to him earlier, the other a heavyset bearded man in his late thirties. Both carried torches even though their light barely penetrated the fog. The two were brothers who'd served as knights under a fallen king. They'd found peace in the town of Braunburg under the command of Rallos.

"Three against thirteen," the heavyset man said to Rallos in greeting. "My kind of odds."

Rallos smiled distantly; his thoughts were still on his home. He had three children, counting Rana. A young son named Scott who was not yet old enough to lift a sword, and another daughter named Trysta who was nearing adulthood. He also thought of his wife, Marie. She would doubtlessly scold him when he returned home for rushing off to battle and leaving them alone.

Pushing such thoughts from his mind, Rallos began thinking about the situation at hand. The natural formation of the valley that Braunburg lay in had only one entrance. It was well hidden, and visitors were few and far between, usually limited to the random traveling merchant. He and his men would arrive there in only a few moments.

He heard the commotion before he saw it; there were shouts and yells coming from just beyond a bend in the trail ahead. Slowing their horses to a calmer pace, Rallos and his men slowly took the corner. The wet forest floor muffled their approach, only the light of their torches would give them away. A single gypsy wagon came into view. It was brightly illuminated by lamps hanging at all four of its corners. Surrounding it in a rough ring were ten armed and mounted raiders. One of the wagon's two horses lay on its side heaving, an arrow protruding out of its bloody flank.

As they grew closer, Rallos picked out the driver of the wagon. He wore colorful gypsy clothes and stood perhaps only a few inches shorter than himself. The man boldly held his ground with a scimitar drawn. One of the raiders drew back his bow and sent an arrow screaming towards the gypsy. Rallos spurred his horse forward, fearing that he had arrived too late. In a masterly show of skill, the lone defender turned his scimitar sideways and blocked the missile easily.

"Halt!" Rallos roared.

For a split second eleven pairs of eyes turned to gaze at him, the most surprised of which belonged to the lone gypsy.

"What has this man done to offend you?" he demanded.

The only reply was a battle cry as the raiders turned their attention to Rallos and his men. Badly outnumbered, Rallos kept his allies close as the fight began. In the confusion, he noticed the gypsy launch himself at the bowman, dismounting him with a single strike of his long, curved blade. The riderless horse bucked up into the air before running off into the darkness.

Rallos and his men drew their swords and engaged the enemy. Their opponents seemed to be inexperienced at best, but their superior number gave them a great advantage. One on one, Rallos would have dispatched them easily. With so many attackers, however, he barely managed to defend himself. His blade lodged in his foe's body as he ran one of the raiders through.

The dead man took Rallos's sword with him to the ground as he fell from his horse. Without his main weapon he would have to use his hunting knife. A new opponent struck at him as he drew the smaller blade. It was a savage downward slice, meant to cleave him in two. Holding the knife firmly with both hands, he blocked the blow. The force of the impact jarred him badly and knocked him out of his saddle.

He hit the ground hard, knocking the air from his lungs. Experience had taught him to roll quickly away from the horse, lest the beast trample him. As he gasped desperately for air, he scarcely noticed the raider about to strike him down. The fatal stroke stopped just inches away from Rallos's neck. At last catching his breath, he looked at his would-be killer. The curved point of the gypsy's scimitar protruded from the bandit's chest for an instant before being torn back out. Kicking the man from his feet, Rallos then retrieved his own sword.

"Thank you," he called to the stranger.

"You are welcome," The gypsy replied with a strange accent that Rallos couldn't place.

He was almost as tall as Rallos and probably around the same age. There was little doubt that he fought to protect his family inside of the wagon. His eyes were hazel, and his hair came down to his chin in short waves. It was clear that the gypsy had seen his fair share of fights, which was demonstrated not only by his skill but also displayed by his haggard visage.

A loud commotion behind them both drew their attention back to the battle. Three of the raiders had separated from the group and were trying to break their way into the wagon. To Rallos's great surprise, the door burst open from the inside as though kicked. The raider closest to the door was knocked completely from the wagon while the next one was impaled cleanly on the blade of a curved sword.

A young, rakishly handsome man with long, very dark brown hair burst from the wagon and engaged the third bandit. Rallos had no doubt that this was the gypsy's son. Both combatants were very skilled, although the young gypsy seemed to have the upper hand. Unbeknown to him, the bandit he'd knocked off the wagon had regained his feet and now tried to attack from behind. Rallos felt a sinking in his gut, even as he and his newfound ally rushed to the younger man's aide. They would never make it in time.

An arrow sailed through the mist, piercing clean through the flanker's neck. As the raider turned to look for the source of the attack, another arrow slammed through his chest, spearing him through the heart and killing him instantly. On the wagon above, the young gypsy heard the body fall behind him and made short work of his opponent, killing him in just two more strokes of his blade.

The young man's gaze turned further up the trail. Something had caught his eye that made him lower his sword. Both Rallos and the older gypsy followed his line of sight to where Rana sat on her horse, the mist swirling about her, making her seem ethereal and ghostly. Everyone stopped what they were doing for the briefest of moments as they watched her ride slowly forward. The young gypsy, still standing on the wagon, seemed to be the most captivated of all.

Rallos's brow furrowed as he turned to look at the older gypsy. He would have to address his daughter later. For now he had a responsibility to the village to find out exactly what was going on. He kept his blade in his hand as he addressed the stranger.

"Now, tell me what was happening here," he said slowly.

"We were part of a caravan," the older gypsy answered as he sheathed his weapon. "The raiders have hounded us for more than a month, picking off the other families in our group until only we remained."

"We?" Rallos asked, as he looked to the wagon.

The slightest burst of anger rose up in Rallos chest as he noticed that the younger gypsy was still gazing at his daughter. As he looked back over his shoulder, he noticed that Rana returned the strangers gaze firmly. It made her father proud that she also kept an arrow knocked in her bow.

"Yes, the young man defending the wagon is my son, Kehl. My wife, Elaine, is still inside," the gypsy answered.

"And who are you?"

"My name is Matthias Sanria," the gypsy answered, offering a welcoming hand.

Rallos took his hand and shook it firmly. "And I am Rallos Alexander. The archer on the horse is my daughter, Rana."

"I thought as much," Matthias replied with a smile, "judging by her skill with that bow."

A wide smile spread across Rallos's face as Matthias turned back to the wagon and called out to his son.

"Kehl, bring out your mother, it is safe now."

Kehl bowed his head slightly before ducking into the wagon. A few seconds later, he emerged with a strikingly beautiful woman dressed in the finest of silk. Made in Italy, the silk was distributed throughout the known world by both traveling merchants as well as the gypsies. The fact that this woman wore such an expensive garment meant that she was either royalty, which Rallos doubted seriously, or highly skilled in making garments out of that rare material.

"This is my wife, Elaine. We were on our way to sell my wife's dresses in one of the large cities," Matthias said. "She is considered to be the best dressmaker in this part of the world."

Elaine was tall and slender. Her raven hair cascaded down her shoulders and back in long flowing strands. Her eyes were an odd sort of hazel that lent her gaze both a kind and penetrating quality. With her son standing next to her, Rana could see where he got his looks from. Her heart thudded in her chest as she found herself trying to avoid the young man's gaze for some reason. She felt flushed and wished that her hair was as long and as beautiful as Elaine's.

"I believe them," Rana said, riding closer to the wagon and addressing Elaine. "That dress you're wearing is beautiful."

"This is my daughter, Rana," Rallos said, introducing Elaine to his daughter. "And I am Rallos Alexander."

Elaine smiled in a friendly way. "I'm thankful you came along when you did. I was afraid that I would lose both my husband and my son. I must repay you somehow."

She disappeared back into the family wagon and returned seconds later with a simple yet incredibly gorgeous dress. It was like nothing Rana had ever seen before in her life. She felt that Kehl's gaze still fell upon her, and as she looked up to meet his eyes, a shiver shot through her like lightening. Her heart skipped a beat, and she felt lightheaded.

Only moments before, they'd caught sight of one another across the battlefield, but now they were much closer together. Something in the young man's eyes made her feel like she was dying slowly, willingly. Not wanting to be rude to Elaine, Rana reluctantly tore her gaze from Kehl. She sighed slowly to hide the fact that she'd been holding her breath.

Elaine had noticed everything that was going on. "I think this dress would look very nice on you Rana. Don't you agree, Kehl?"

Kehl nodded. "Yes, absolutely."

"Then, if the dress suits you, Rana," Elaine said with a smile, "I shall give this to you in thanks for helping save both my husband and my son."

"And for you and your men, Rallos," Matthias said. "I will reward you with silver. But first, I must attend to my horses."

Rallos watched as Matthias gently coaxed the wounded horse to its feet and released it from its harness. Its wound appeared to be fairly shallow, and the bleeding had slowed down considerably. The raiders had most likely shot the horse while it was struggling to pull the escaping wagon. Blood loss, combined with exhaustion, had no doubt taken its toll on the poor beast.

"Would it be too much to ask for the use of a stable?" Matthias asked. "Only until the horse has recovered enough to pull the wagon."

"I don't think that would be a problem." Rallos said, taking into consideration that Matthias had saved his life. "In fact, you would be welcome to use mine."

"Thank you," Matthias replied. "I know it may sound strange, but this horse is like a member of our family."

"It does not sound strange at all." Rallos replied kindly.

"Kehl," Matthias called, "lead the other horse into town with the wagon please."

"Yes, sir," Kehl replied before jumping from the wagon as his mother vanished back inside.

Kehl walked over to the remaining horse and carefully took hold of its reigns. Without hesitation, the lone horse started pulling the heavy wagon along the path through the woods. Rallos and his men took up positions in front of and behind the wagon, just in case more raiders should happen to attack. They would come back later to bury the bodies, after the family was safe. Rana drew her horse close to Kehl as she tried to think of something to say. A simple question finally sprang into her mind. "Where are you from?"

Kehl chuckled a bit, in a not unkind sort of way. Rallos noticed the laugh and turned to look back from his lead position with an agitated look in his eyes. The young gypsy quickly cleared his throat and made the most serious face he could muster. Rana saw all of it happen and barely managed to not burst into laughter.

"That is ... hard to answer," Kehl said as Rallos returned his eyes to the way ahead. "I suppose you could say I'm from the wagon."

"What do you mean?" Rana asked, her voice barely a whisper.

"I was born in the wagon," he answered. "My family never stays in one place for too long."

"You have such a strange accent. I thought perhaps you were born in some strange land."

"My family comes from all over the world," he said, looking up at her with a smile. "And yes, you could say that some of those places are strange."

"I would love so much to hear more about you and your family, but I'm not so sure that my mother will take to you," Rana said softly before returning her eyes to the trail.

Ahead of them, Rallos called out to the town of Braunburg, letting the inhabitants know that the threat had been eliminated. Several of the townsfolk opened their doors and peered out, while Rallos's own family rushed out of their home to see if he was okay. His young son, Scott, and older daughter, Trysta, were both very happy to see him. Marie was every bit as furious as Rallos had expected.

"Rana!" Marie cried, walking forward, "How dare you!"

Rana remained silent as she rode back towards the stables. Her mother looked much like her, with darker hair and eyes. Her visage, however, was much more harsh and cold than her daughter's. After spending years without her husband during the Crusades, she'd grown independent and forceful, almost to the point of being cruel.

"She did well tonight, Marie," Rallos said in Rana's defense.

"She saved my life," Kehl added with a grin as he brought the wagon to a stop just several feet away from Marie.

Marie was slightly taller than the young gypsy, making it easy for her to look him down. The smile quickly vanished from his face. A sudden chill raced up and down his back as the feeling came over Kehl that someone had just stepped on his grave.

"And who are you?" Marie demanded of the young gypsy.

Kehl looked over at his father and then at Rallos before turning his gaze toward Rana, where it lingered.

"I am the man who intends to marry your daughter."

CHAPTER 3
UNTIL DEATH

Several years passed, and although the Sanria family left the small town of Braunburg occasionally, they always returned after a short time. Matthias and Rallos became fast friends, though Marie would never fully accept Kehl and barely socialized with Elaine. Kehl and Rana, however, were nearly inseparable. Most times, Kehl would stay in town when his parents traveled to other places to sell their stores of silk.

The young gypsy had made good on his words. He only had eyes for Rana, and she reciprocated his feelings. Among the villagers, their names were nearly synonymous, for one would rarely be seen without the other. Kehl's stories of foreign lands enchanted Rana, just as her strong, warrior-like spirit captured his heart. After their first year together, he formally requested her hand in marriage, and she happily agreed.

The day of their wedding was set into stone with the whole village planning to attend. Each person had contributed individually to the ceremony, in keeping with the local customs. There was food and drink everywhere, and nowhere could be found an unhappy face. Even Rana's mother seemed to have finally released her resentment of her future son-in-law and seemed to be enjoying the celebration.

It was winter, which was an odd time of year for a wedding, but the year was unseasonably warm, so no one minded terribly. Flowers blooming long into the warm winter decorated the town; they were of the most delicate pink and vibrant blue. Little children won small prizes for collecting the blooms, and afterward the flowers became even more rare than before, hardly to be found anywhere except the farthest reaches beyond the town's boundaries.

Kehl wore neatly cut formal clothes that had been custom tailored by Rana's mother. Rana herself wore a white silken dress that Elaine had once worn to her own wedding. Marie had at first been reluctant to make Kehl's wedding clothes but complied when she saw the beauty of

Elaine's dress. The couple had spent three days apart, as was the tradition of Braunburg. Led separately down to the temporary outdoor alter, they couldn't keep their eyes off of one another once together. It was all their parents could do to keep them from running to each another. In the past, they had never been apart for more than a day.

The happy couple had hardly exchanged their vows and said their I-do's before Kehl lifted his new wife into a white, horse-drawn wagon. Jumping quickly to the reigns, Kehl snapped them confidently. Their new home lay some ways beyond the village, but the journey would not take too long. Even after traveling for some time, they were still able to hear the merriment in the town. Reaching a clearing, Kehl looked back down at the village and then back over at Rana with a grin on his face.

"Sounds like they're having quite a bit of fun down there."

"Not as much fun as you and I are going to have once we get home," Rana said. "In fact, why wait?"

She immediately scooted herself closer to him on the wide bench seat and nuzzled up against his neck. Her hot breath tickled his ear for a brief moment before she kissed his earlobe. The sensation sent shivers down Kehl's back. Rana felt the muscles of his shoulders tense and took it as a signal to plant a small kiss on his neck.

Kehl gasped as he wrapped an arm around Rana's slender shoulders, holding her tightly to him. The both of them had changed so much in the brief years since their fateful meeting. Rana was now, easily, the most beautiful woman in the town of Braunburg. Kehl counted himself lucky to have found such a perfect woman.

Kehl had taken to working with her father in his forge, eventually taking over most of the workload. His body was now chiseled as if from stone. The mere sensation of her lips gently brushing his tan skin excited Rana in ways that she'd never known possible.

Her lips moved slowly back up his neck and chin before finding his lips. Kehl turned his head and they shared their first truly private kiss. Rana wrapped her arms about his broad shoulders, pulling herself closer to him. This was the first time they had ever been alone together. As with the customs of not only Braunburg, but most of Europe, they were never allowed alone without a chaperon. During that time, they'd been allowed to flirt, but never allowed to touch. It was the most horrible, yet rewarding form of torture that the young couple could imagine.

Now that they were together and allowed to freely touch one another; the years' worth of oppression manifested itself as pure intensity.

A simple touch, or kiss for that matter, contained its own explosive burst of sensation that it otherwise wouldn't have possessed. The couple felt such sensations throughout their entire bodies. As their lips parted and their kisses deepened, the two young lovers quickly became intoxicated by the mere presence of one another.

Kehl was the first to reluctantly part from their embrace. "If we keep this up, then we aren't going to make it to the cabin."

Over the years, Rana had picked up a bit of Kehl's sometimes cocky, always carefree attitude. "Would you really mind if we didn't?"

"Well, I wouldn't, not at all. I love you with all of my heart, and if I had to, I would consummate this marriage down there on the grass."

"Consummate?" Rana said, laughing brightly. "Kehl Sanria, I don't ever want to hear that word come from your mouth again."

Kehl chuckled a bit before they kissed briefly again.

"I prefer to say that we are 'making love,'" Rana said softly as she nuzzled up against his neck once more.

"Oh, I can think of a few more things we could call it," Kehl said, as a broad grin spread across his face.

"Don't let the thought even cross your mind!" Rana said with a light laugh.

They rode along in comfortable silence for a few minutes, content merely to be alone together. Rana looked about into the darkening woods. Evening would be upon them shortly. In the sky above, the stars were already becoming visible in the perfect sky. Even the breeze, for so late in winter, bore only the slightest of chills. It seemed to the young couple, as they arrived at their cottage, that it would be the perfect evening.

Months ago, Kehl and Rallos, along with several of the other villagers, had come out into the forest and picked a level spot for the new home. After clearing enough trees for a house and a modest garden, construction began. It was a simple, comfortable three-room cottage, more than enough room for two people. A nearby spring provided water, and the location was not more fifteen minutes away from town by wagon.

"It's wonderful," Rana murmured as Kehl pulled at the reigns and brought the horses to a stop.

Kehl grinned a bit. "Why don't you go on inside and have a look around? I've got to put the horses up. We built a coral and stable in the back."

Rana smiled before giving Kehl a lengthy kiss. "I'll be inside, waiting for you."

Being careful not to harm her dress, Rana climbed down from the wagon and made her way to the door. As she neared the entranceway she noticed that the entranceway bore intricate carvings and designs in the same style as Kehl's gypsy wagon. There were miniature carvings of both of their parents, as well as of the young couple. A soft smile crossed her face as she noticed two areas of untouched wood next to her likeness, doubtlessly left there for future members of the family.

As her eyes traveled further down the doorway something strange caught her eye. On one side of the doorway there was a strange clump of mushrooms growing. They seemed to be giving off the faintest hint of blue light. She reached down to touch the strange growth. She brushed the cap of the mushrooms lightly with her fingers. They felt as cold as death, yet somehow still strangely alive. The sensation sent shivers up and down her spine and threatened to spoil her mood.

As she straightened back up, Rana tried to put her discomfort at the back of her mind. She then carefully opened the door to her new home and stepped through into the main room. It took a moment for her eyes to adjust to the darkness inside. The dim evening light filtering in through the doorway and provided just enough light for her to make out a large table and some sparse furniture around the room. It wasn't much, but to her it didn't matter. All that was important to her was that it was a place for herself and her new husband to start their lives together.

A shriek escaped her lips as a pair of strong hands wrapped about her waist from behind.

"Kehl," she gasped, turning around slowly in his hands. "You know I hate it when you …"

Her voice trailed off for a moment. For a split second, she would have sworn that she had seen a faint light coming from Kehl's gray eyes. Her thoughts quickly returned to the odd mushrooms growing outside of their door. Their light had seemed similar. The light in Kehl's eyes vanished so quickly, however, that Rana decided that it was simply her imagination.

There were no more words as they quietly embraced. The strange thoughts inside of Rana's head vanished quickly beneath a wave of love, pleasure, and contentment. As their lips met, the world around them vanished. Laughter rang out through the dark cottage as they tried to make their way to the bedroom and stumbled on random bits of furniture.

Time passed from that moment on, regardless of how much the young lovers felt that it stood still in their private cabin. The hour grew late, and the revelers in the village finally went home, many stuffed with food and filled with drink, but all of them content. It was the night of the solstice, the longest night of year, a night that brought many a superstitious thought to minds of Braunburg. And yet, even as dark storm clouds crept sluggishly into the valley, no one seemed to notice.

Before long, a light rain began to fall from the heavens, soft and peaceful at first but then growing in intensity. Inside their warm cabin, Kehl and Rana slept peacefully, Rana lost in a deep dreamless sleep. The rising storm outside seemed to have come bearing a nightmare for Kehl, as his dreams turned dark and troubled. As he tossed and turned, he moved farther away from Rana, almost to the very edge of the bed.

In his dreams, Kehl found himself in a dark barren landscape where everything was withered, black, and dead for as far as the eye could see. The ebony-colored grass beneath his feet crunched with the sound of dry bones as he walked alone in an endless field, the barren monotony broken only by jagged rocks and the mangled, twisted corpses of trees. In the dark skies above, the clouds boiled in a tempest that seemed to be the very wrath of a god.

Kehl had no idea where he was. It seemed that just moments before he had been lying in bed with his arms curled around Rana. He had no idea that this was a dream, and when the chill wind blew and the leaves in the dead trees clicked together like the knuckle bones on a long-dead skeleton, the dream seemed all too real. The only thing he was able to think about was getting back to Rana. He cast his gaze all around in panic, trying to decide which way to go.

Choosing a desiccated tree close to the horizon, he set out toward it, running as fast as his legs would carry him. He avoided the jagged rocks that he encountered and quickly reached his destination at a pace only possible in dreams. The tree sat isolated on top of a small mound that rose to a height of some thirty feet. Climbing up the deceptively steep slope, he stood next to the tree and surveyed his surroundings.

To his dismay, the landscape appeared no different than before. In fact, it looked even more desolate from this vantage point. Kehl then turned around and examined the tree behind him. Its massive trunk was four feet in diameter. Although unable to discern its height through his dream eyes, the highest branch seemed to be impossibly high.

Slowly stretching out a hand, Kehl touched the dead, blackened bark. The sensation that met his fingers made the tree feel cold and dead, yet somehow alive beyond all possibility. Kehl's brow furrowed. This tree was huge, yet the intensity of the sensation of life seemed even fainter than that of the smallest insect. Surely it must have been very close to the verge of death.

As he looked up through the branches, Kehl felt and saw the tree shudder momentarily from its roots all the way to its top. Seconds later, the sensation of life beneath his fingertips vanished suddenly and completely. In real life, Kehl would have had no way to know that what had died was the last remaining living thing in this wasteland. In his dream, however, the knowledge was all too absolute, all too clear. He knew now that he was completely alone.

After turning around, he leaned up against the partially decayed trunk. The bark scraped his back as he slid down into a sitting position. His mind started to work furiously. He wondered how he found himself in this strange place. The idea that this was a dream was still far from his mind. He wondered where Rana was and why he couldn't find her. Sadness filled his thoughts, and he looked off into the empty distance, unable to make sense of it all.

Within moments he felt an unfamiliar chill work its way across his body. Shivers ran all across his body as he rubbed at his arms in an attempt to warm himself. Instead, the sensation intensified to the point that it felt as though the entire core of his being was incased in ice. His heart suffered most of all, feeling as though it were being gripped by an infinitely strong and deathly cold fist.

Kehl was quickly growing numb in his extremities. With his little remaining strength, he pushed himself to his feet, trying to ignore the icy, prickly pain washing over his skin. It proved difficult for him to maintain his balance as he looked down from the hill desperately in search of shelter. Taking one step forward, he failed to keep his balance and fell forward painfully onto his knees. Unable to catch himself, he then tumbled forward and down over the hill.

Anger surged in Kehl as he rolled to a top at the bottom of the slope. Adrenaline pounded through his veins and renewed his strength. Leaping to his feet, he clenched his fists and screamed to the heavens. "Why am I here!" he roared.

As though in response, deep booming laugher echoed down from the skies like thunder. Lightning crackled through the clouds and struck nearby, followed by a strong and chill wind. Looking around, Kehl sought out the source of the voice. The laughter continued.

"Welcome to your new home," whispered a voice directly behind him.

When he turned to see who it was, his eyes met only the horizon. Most strange of all, the voice seemed so very familiar. More familiar than he could have possibly expected. It was his own.

Kehl was more confused than ever by these strange words. "My new home? I would never call this cursed place home!" he yelled.

"It is the only home for once such as yourself," the voice whispered.

"One such as me?" Kehl laughed, growing wary as he turned slowly to look behind him. Once again, the only thing that met his eyes were dead empty fields. The voice remained silent until Kehl finally ventured a question. "And what am I?"

The answer was immediate, blunt, and concise: "Nosferatu."

Kehl was dumbfounded. He had only heard of the Nosferatu in old wives' tales. They existed only in stories that parents used to keep children in their beds. According to legend, they were bloodsucking monsters—their very souls damned by heaven. He knew little more than that they were supposed to be evil, wretched things that prowled through the night in search of victims.

"How could I possibly be one of the damned? I don't have fangs. I have never done an evil deed in my entire life."

Once more the laugher thundered through the air. "You were born into this world already damned by God, for he, in his infinite mercy and grace, has overlooked you. Your curse has lain hidden deep in your very soul and your blood ever since the day of your birth, waiting to manifest."

This time it was Kehl's laughter that echoed out across the wasteland. "This is all just a dream," he said. "I remember now. I am actually just asleep in the cabin next to Rana."

"Unfortunately," the disembodied voice answered. "You are only partially correct."

"What?"

"Your physical body is indeed lying in your bed, but this is far, far more than a mere dream. This is only the beginning of your descent into darkness."

As if to assert the reality of the situation, the sudden urge to vomit erupted inside of Kehl, forcing him to double over with his hands on his stomach. He heaved and choked, but nothing would come out. His body ached in a way that was all too real. Nausea and dizziness swept through him as he gagged once more.

"Tonight is a special night, is it not?" the voice queried, heedless of Kehl's condition.

"What ... do you mean?" Kehl asked as the nausea momentarily abated.

"This is your wedding night, isn't it?" Kehl remained silent, and after a moment the voice spoke again. "And not only that, it is also the night of your birth, correct?"

"Yes ... yes!" Kehl growled through his nausea. "Why does it matter that it's my birthday?"

"It matters because that same hour that you came screaming into this world now approaches. It is bringing with it your destiny. It will change you from what you are now to what you are doomed to become. You see? The hour is drawing nigh."

Seemingly summoned by the voice, a single clock hovered in the air in front of Kehl. Suddenly, the single clock multiplied into millions, surrounding Kehl on all sides. He whirled around, looking from clock to clock as they all ticked in unison. They all read the same time: midnight. The solstice was only moments away. His veins seemed to flow with ice water as he started believing what he was being told.

"Think too of Rana; her fate will be worse than yours. It will be her blood that *christens* you in your new life." The voice seemed to drip with sarcasm.

Kehl started laughing, quietly at first, but then growing louder. His eyes gleamed with a mild insanity. He found himself unable to move from the intense mixture of sensations. Barely managing to put his hands up to his forehead, he pressed the palms of his hands hard against his temples.

"What is so funny?" the disembodied voice questioned, sounding slightly amused.

Kehl had to restrain his laughter long enough to reply, "I would never harm Rana. It's ridiculous to think that her blood would transform me into one of the damned."

"It's not her blood that is going to turn you into a vampire," the voice replied. "That part of your fate is already inevitable. Instead, you will feed upon her lifeblood. She will be the first victim of your unholy hunger. Her essence will awaken such powers within you that you can scarcely imagine."

"I don't want any powers!" Kehl screamed. "All I want to do is live out the rest of my life with Rana. I would never do such a thing to her."

"You would never do such a thing," the voice agreed in a somewhat sympathetic tone. "If you ever had the choice. But you *don't*, and it is going to happen no matter how much you fight it. The less you struggle, the easier this will be. It doesn't have to be difficult. You will find that your natural instincts will take over, sweeping your mortal concerns aside. It is so easy when you give in. I am going to show you something now that you have never seen before," the voice continued. "You should consider this a privilege; most humans pass their entire lives without ever seeing this. It should help you realize just what you truly are."

"What is it?" Kehl screamed as he whirled around.

"Your soul," the voice whispered.

Kehl felt a shockwave wash down over him from above and blast outward around him. The clocks that still surrounded him were all transforming quickly into shattering glass. He threw his arms up and closed his eyes, trying to protect his face. An unseen wind swept the glass toward him, encircling him. He screamed as the gale whirled about him, licking him with its razor tongues. Soon it felt as though the glass had flayed every inch of skin from his body.

The pain stopped suddenly, leaving him with the fear that there was no flesh left on his bones. As he cautiously opened his eyes, he saw an incomprehensible number of shards of glass suspended in a shifting and glimmering cloud directly in front of him. The pieces then flattened out into a single flat layer as they gradually formed a disc. Each piece then slowly turned ever so slightly to align with its neighbor. The seams became invisible as a perfect round sheet of glass formed.

Liquid orbs of quicksilver dripped onto the top of the formation from some unseen source in the heavens. The fluid spread out slowly on the backside of the glass as the disc slowly became reflective.

"Look now into this mirror, look at who you truly are. This is what you are when you've been stripped down to your very soul."

Kehl had no choice but to meet his own gaze in the mirror's surface. His eyes were now a more shocking color of gray, the empty shade of a drowned man's eyes. His skin was charred and blackened; as though it might flake away if the slightest breeze. To his surprise, his flesh remained pliable as it moved with his expressions. As his gaze moved further down his face, he spotted the two massive fangs pressed down near the sides of his lips. As he opened his mouth, he saw them elongate as though in preparation to bite.

"What trickery is this?" he whispered in disbelief.

"There is no trickery, Kehl. This is the true manifestation of your soul. Tell me, is it not true that you have seen glimpses of this when looking into your reflection? The black hair, the grey eyes that always seemed to be a different color?"

Kehl shook his head. "With all my heart, no." He looked deeply into the surface of the mirror and raised his hand to it. He found that at the ends of his fingertips ended in long talons that seemed to rip the very air asunder. They clicked softly against the mirror as he touched it, still unbelieving that this could be the true form of his being. The ticking of the clocks resumed once more. The icy blood flowing through Kehl's heart began to burn.

"What's happening to me?" he stammered, falling away from the mirror.

"Your blood is beginning to turn to the cold ichor that flows through the veins of the undead."

"Who are you?" Kehl demanded, casting about to find the source of the voice.

"I am part of who you were, and a part of who you will become. I am the attempt made by your hidden mind to soften the horrible blow that is about to be dealt to you." The voice carried with it a twinge of remorse.

Somewhere deep in his dreams, a bell began to toll slowly. The hour had arrived, bringing with it the solstice. Each time the bell rang, it ripped through him, tearing his soul asunder. A scream burst through his clenched teeth as his muscles convulsed and twisted in spasms. Then came the hunger, an unbearable, gut-wrenching hunger that made him sick to his stomach. He sank to his knees and drove his fist into the ground in an effort to stem the pain. The earth shook all around him as his new, inhuman strength surfaced.

"I must leave you now…" the voice said, with a measure of pity. "Hold these words to heart: cherish these last few moments with Rana, even though the memory of their passing will curse you for the rest of your immortal life."

"Wait," Kehl murmured, leaning his head back to look toward the tumultuous skies as if the voice had resided there. "What's going to happen to Rana?"

He received no answer.

"Kehl …" came a familiar female voice.

The sound of the words alone seemed to echo back and forth across the dreamscape, bringing life wherever its soft sound touched. It seemed even to warm the chilled wind. At once, dead trees filled instantly with brilliant green leaves. Barren fields burst to life with rich brightly blossomed flowers that filled the air with their scent. Off in the distance, something disturbed the fields, sending waves of petals drifting lazily up into the air.

Kehl knew Rana was bringing life to the wasteland. As he looked out into the distance, he saw her slender form moving toward him through the fields. The clouds above suddenly burst apart, allowing bright rays of sunlight to penetrate through. One such beam of light fell directly on Rana, setting her figure ablaze. Dressed once more in her wedding dress, she put to shame the beautiful flowers around her with her brilliance and beauty.

As she came closer, Kehl called out to her. "Rana, no! Please, don't come any closer!"

Even though she remained some distance away, her soft voice carried easily to his ears. "Shh … do not worry, my darling."

"No, you don't understand," he cried as he covered up his face. "You don't understand what I am!"

"Yes I do, Kehl," she answered.

Rana now stood only a few meters away from her husband. Kehl reluctantly took his hands away from his eyes. His young bride was as radiant as ever. Her green eyes sparkled with a deep love, a love only for him. Her wedding dress sparkled with angelic light as the wind played with her hair. He would remember the smile that crossed her lips then for the rest of his life. It seemed both morose and pleased at the same time, filled as always with her love for him.

"Don't be afraid, Kehl," she whispered as she drew close to where he knelt. "Only my blood can stop your pain."

The wind once more caught her hair, and as if by the hand of providence, and swept it away from her neck. His pain immediately ceased, and in its stead came a feeling that he hadn't felt for years. It tugged at him the same way it had on that first day, the irresistible pull that he had felt the first time he had seen Rana. His body moved of its own accord. He rose with a grace that he had not hitherto possessed. His mind kept screaming that this was something he shouldn't be doing but also that what he was doing was meant to be.

"Remember Kehl," Rana whispered as he cupped her neck with one hand and wrapped the other arm about her waist, "I will always love you. No matter who or what you become. Do not forget that."

Her last words were barely audible as the bell tolled its final stroke, proclaiming that the hour had come. Kehl opened his mouth. His fangs elongated even as Rana tilted her head slightly to the side. She made not a sound as the two pearly spears plunged deep into her throat. Her eyes closed softly, as if from a pinprick, and then opened again with a deep sadness welling up behind them. She wrapped her arms about Kehl and softly caressed his back as he drained the life from her. Her blood filled him with the deepest ecstasy—his love for her only magnifying the sensation. A sigh escaped Rana's lips as her head lolled back and her arms dropped from Kehl's back. He immediately drew back; the hunger was gone.

"Rana?" he asked, shaking his wife softly. She made no response and hung in his arms like a limp doll. He was unable to fully comprehend what had just transpired. "Rana!"

He shook her again and held her tightly in his arms, and it was then that his dream ended. He awoke with a start, drenched in sweat, glad that it had only been a dream. In fact, he was convinced it could only have been a dream. A red line crept across the room where the clouded moon peered into the room. The sheets fell aside as Kehl swiftly got out of bed and went to the window, throwing open the shutters. The cool night air rushed in to the warmth of the cabin as he gazed out at the horizon. The moon was low in the sky, just above the mountaintops. As its light filtered through the surrounding clouds, it changed into a crimson hue. Kehl felt as though the moon was the baleful eye of God, staring down at him and judging him harshly.

His hand rose to his mouth to stifle a yawn, but he immediately withdrew it. Something warm and slightly sticky clung to his lips. He looked at his hand; his fingertips were coated with blood. Now that he saw the blood, he could also taste it in his mouth. To most humans, the taste would have been bitter, but to Kehl it tasted sweet.

He felt for the fangs and pricked his tongue on the edge of one. It was impossible, Kehl thought. He shook his head, not wanting to look back at the bed, for he knew what he would see there. Instead, he searched for some proof that the dream was not real; perhaps he had only been the victim of a nosebleed in the night. Reluctantly, he turned his head toward the bed and nearly lost his legs at the scene that met his eyes.

Rana lay in a crimson sea of her own blood, her essence leaking through twin puncture wounds in her throat. It was then that Kehl knew the dream had been reality, and that he had indeed been the instrument of Rana's death. Tears clouded his vision as he stumbled forward to the bed. His tears mixed with the blood on his lips, filling his mouth with a sweet salty flavor. Blood spilled from the edge of the bed as he knelt beside it and reached across to his dead lover.

An inhuman and heartrending scream ripped from his lungs. Far below in Braunburg, the people began to stir. The unnaturally loud and long roar woke them from their sleep. They gathered with lit torches in the courtyard of the town, fearing the unknown, afraid of what lurked in the dark. They feared for Kehl and Rana, as the two young lovers were far from the safety of the village.

It was decided that a group of only the strongest and bravest men be sent as a search to check on the newlywed couple. Rallos demanded that he should be the one to lead. Even though it was Kehl and Rana's wedding night, he could not deny his concerns. Rallos and his men went armed with long swords sheathed at their sides and bows slung across their shoulders. Many strange things dwelt in the mountains, and they had to be prepared. If need be, they would fight to the death to protect the young couple.

Rallos pushed his horse harder than his companions, fearing the worst had already happened. He arrived several moments before any of the others and quickly rushed to the door. The sounds of sobbing stopped him short. Holding his torch with one hand and drawing his sword with the other, he made no hesitation in kicking the door in. No sooner had he walked through the door then he dropped his sword.

His beloved daughter Rana lay dead, surrounded by her own blood. At her side sobbing uncontrollably was Kehl. Rallos's face fell slack as he stumbled forward; she was obviously dead, yet still so beautiful. In some dark macabre way she looked like a flake of snow, freshly fallen on the most crimson of roses. Rallos bowed his head and knelt at the foot of the bed. Of all the things that could have happened over the years, of all the grisly deaths he could have suffered as a knight, he would rather have endured them all instead of seeing his own daughter dead before him. Tears fell from this mighty man as his strength failed him and brought him crashing to the floor, sobbing desperate prayers.

The rest of the men came in soon after, aghast at the grisly scene. They first questioned Kehl as to what happened, trusting him to tell the truth, but as he spoke of his dreams their attitudes changed. Anger replaced worry, and they were soon beating him. Rallos, half mad with grief, made feeble attempts to protect his son-in-law. Somewhere deep in his heart, he found that he could not blame Kehl; something had happened here that was beyond his or any mortal's control. His anguish made his efforts to save the boy impossible as all strength left him. His still-flowing tears clouding his vision. They beat Kehl and cut him, and when his wounds healed they beat him and cut him again. The strange supernatural occurrence of his regeneration only fueled their fury. Rallos couldn't stand the sight of what was happening.

The last thing Kehl would remember of that night was being dragged from the cabin. He only struggled once when he lost sight of Rana and fought his way back into the cabin. Before he could make his way to her side, one of the villagers knocked him out cleanly. Taken far away from the town, they chained him deep in the bowels of an abandoned castle and left him for dead. He had no way of knowing that his fate rested not in the town that he had once called home but rather in the hands of a single woman.

The decision to leave his fate in the hands of Rana's mother was nearly unanimous among the villagers, with only three people defending Kehl: his mother and father, and, oddly, Rallos. No one, not even Rallos himself, could understand why. Maria asserted that the death of their daughter had driven her husband insane. She also demanded that she alone had the right to do whatever they wanted to with Kehl. The town agreed with Marie. With relatively no opposition, Kehl's destiny lay firmly in her hands, whether it be his execution or something far worse.

Oblivious in his underground prison, Kehl languished the hours away, oblivious to all except the picture that stayed forever in his mind. The image of Rana lying lifeless in her own blood would not leave his consciousness. He had destroyed the one thing in his life that he held most precious, a sin that would forever mar his conscious. Hours turned into days, and the days turned into a week, and all too quickly the hunger returned.

The craving seemed to rend him to pieces and was far more painful than any torture that he could imagine. Soon, time lost its meaning, and without his knowing, a full year had passed. Even when the hunger had driven him ravenous and mad with lust he did not struggle against his bonds or prey upon the creatures dwelling in that forgotten dungeon. With the lack of nourishment, his body soon atrophied to the point where he was little more than a skeleton covered in parchment-like skin. He felt that he deserved this fate, but death proved elusive no matter how deteriorated his body became.

On the anniversary of Rana's death, Kehl had a visit from the last person he expected to see. He came bearing a torch. Kehl couldn't see who it was at first, as he was blinded by the light. His years underground made what little remained of his eyes overly sensitive. He could only discern the outline of a powerfully built man. By the time his visitor had drawn near, the light seared his eyes. The torch came so close that he could feel the flames licking at his cheek.

"Happy birthday, Kehl," the voice chanted with a malicious edge.

Kehl squinted at the newcomer; his eyes struggled to see past the brilliance of the torch. It was Scott, Rana's younger brother. It seemed like only a minute had passed from the wedding to the present, and it took Kehl a moment to take stock of the changes in his brother-in-law. The loss of his sister had chiseled the young man's soul into a sharp, jagged-edged stone. His eyes no longer shone with the pride that he bore for his sister but instead burned with a crushing hatred that transformed his face into a mask of pure spite. As soon as he had seen that Kehl recognized him, Scott shoved the torch into his face, laughing as Kehl made feeble attempts to scream.

Scott pulled the torch away and saw that both of Kehl's eyes, along with most of his face, had burned away. Scott knew that Kehl was weak and suspected that his vampiric restorative powers would not be able to soak up so much damage. Indeed, Kehl's healing powers were, at best, nonfunctional, and his burnt flesh looked like little more than charred paper. Kehl tried his best to say that it wasn't his fault, that he hadn't been in control of himself, but he only managed to make a weak hissing sound.

"No use begging or making excuses," Scott said. "There's no one here to protect you now. We drove your parents from our town a long time ago. Even my father, your staunchest supporter, has been exiled."

Somewhere deep in his mind, past the hunger and pain, he took note of the happy news that Rallos had defended him. The thought barely had enough time to register before a boot smashed into Kehl's midsection, crushing his ribs. In turn, the shattered bones punctured his badly deteriorated organs. The pain was more than he could bear, and it only took a moment for Kehl to black out.

Scott looked down at what had been his brother-in-law. He could barely hear the breath coming from Kehl's parched lips and delighted himself with kicking him again and again. The sounds of Kehl's bones crunching pleased his ears. And yet, Scott found that it wasn't enough. He couldn't wait to bring Kehl back to the village. He felt that death alone was not enough for this monster. With his mother's approval, he had invented an almost infinite array of torture devices in the past several years. He was now eager to test them out on such a deserving subject.

"My mother and I have plans for you." he growled down at Kehl.

And so it was that Scott took custody of the dungeon's sole inhabitant and carried the near-corpse back to the village. He had been busy for the last year and had dug a small dungeon under his home. Scott filled the bowels of that deep cellar with the most diabolical of man's creations. For many, many years, the unfortunate Kehl Sanria endured while Scott and his mother force-fed him the blood of vermin and tortured him until the day the vampire outlived them.

CHAPTER 4
LEIGH BRYANT

Present Day

The streetlights barely managed to sparkle across the mangled black and red 1967 GT500 as it roared its way through the nighttime streets of New York City. Having paid a small fortune for the damaged remains of a once magnificent car, the owner had spent the remainder of the money armoring its frame and body rather than having the exterior restored. Bullet-resistant glass and heavily armored body panels offered much more protection than a shiny paint job or sparkling rims. Underneath the hood, it was a different story; the engine was massive and immaculate, heavily tuned and modified beyond the bounds of legality to allow the weighty car the agility it needed. The only things that it could be said to lack were handling and good gas mileage.

A bystander would expect to see a muscular or dangerous-looking man climbing into the beast of a car. Instead, they saw a lithe young woman with a supple torso and graceful, powerful legs. Many were the men who made the mistake of tangling with her, for little did they know that she was one of the most dangerous human beings in New York. Her name was Leigh Bryant, and she could be recognized by her shoulder-length brown hair and the reading glasses she often wore to accentuate her sky blue eyes.

She was a hunter, born and bred, trained from the earliest stages of life in the ways of combating foes that were many times more powerful than herself. Her father, Jesse Bryant, not wishing for her to become a mindless killer, had also taught her that although a human can view a thing *as* evil, it doesn't mean that the thing necessarily *is* evil. To him the loss of all compassion was the absolute evil. Judgment must be tempered with understanding.

Several years ago, Jesse retired and left the family business to her, choosing instead to live out the rest of his days in a rather humble cottage somewhere in Europe. Although promising to visit, Leigh found herself guilty of not making the journey. It was not for lack of wanting to, but rather of not having the time or the money. As time passed, she found herself missing her father more and often reflected on their memories together.

She had her first assignment with her father at the age of ten, hunting down a werewolf in New England. She compared her experience to other fathers taking their children on deer hunts but would often joke that deer don't bite back. During the hunt, she had been separated from her father and was attacked by the wolf. Her quick reflexes had saved her that moonlit night, but her body still bore faint, barely visible scars across her torso and back. She kept a memento of the encounter tied to her keychain: a shimmering white fang from the beast she'd slain.

Twelve years and more hunts than she could remember spanned the time between then and now. The only creature that she'd never before encountered alone was a full-blooded vampire. Something deep inside of her felt uneasy about her appointment tonight. She couldn't help but wonder if tonight she would face this final, most deadliest of foes without her father by her side.

Sometime several days ago, someone had managed to slip an invitation into her car without setting off the alarm. This was no small feat, as her car was not only equipped with an alarm, but several homegrown threat-deterrence devices. The invitation greatly piqued her curiosity. It was a potential business proposal. The invite itself was black, save for the raised navy blue ink proclaiming "The Midnight Nocturne" across its front. Judging from the clandestine means in which it had been delivered, she felt that it would be in her best interest to attend. Whether the letter meant a trap or a new employer was yet to be seen, but the sender obviously knew how to find her. The ramifications of either outcome made ignoring the invitation an impossibility.

She took the back roads to the nightclub, through the dangerous parts of the city where she could avoid unneeded attention until absolutely necessary. It also let her unleash her car, for the police rarely patrolled the areas of the city that were owned by the night. Already she could see the beams of spotlights throwing bright shafts of light into the air above the nightclub off in the distance. They were intended to draw people in during the night, like moths to a flame, and the lights served their purpose well. She was only several blocks away when her ears met the thumping bass that reverberated through the darkness from the club.

She'd found the invitation in her car two weeks earlier, giving her valuable time to research the club and its surroundings. A quick Internet search had brought up its history, which wasn't much to speak of. It had originally been a factory with its own attached warehouse, operating somewhere around the time of the depression, only to be abandoned in the early fifties. Much of its past had been lost to the mists of time, but it seemed that the building had, until recently, been the rather prized possession of a historical foundation. Their Web site stated that they were sad to lose ownership of the building, but with the amount of money offered by an anonymous buyer, they were able to fund their other endeavors for many years to come.

The Web site also retained a basic floor plan of the facility but warned that many renovations were underway. This meant that the map of the building would probably be useless. There was also mention of a lower level and a subbasement on the site, although there were no further details. Still, the information helped Leigh to feel a little bit more prepared. Running over the map in her head, she tried to think of any applicable strategies and tactics in case of an attack. Few came to mind, given what little information she'd gleaned off the Web; she would need to see her surroundings first-hand in order to make viable offensive or defensive plans.

Lost in her thoughts, Leigh didn't notice when a jet-black motorcycle rocketed out of an unmarked alleyway just ahead of her. Catching sight of the bike, she immediately hit her brakes as the rider lit up in her headlights. For a moment, time seemed to stop as Leigh gritted her teeth in anger and fear. Her car was quite heavy, and there was no way she could come to a stop without hitting the motorcycle. The life of the biker certainly would have been lost if not for the rider's own incredible reflexes. Leigh barely noticed the sight of his thumb flipping a small switch on the handlebars. The motorcycle instantly kicked back onto one wheel and accelerated as the rider shot a glance her way.

The glare of her headlights on his helmet prevented Leigh from seeing the rider's face, but she knew for certain that he was looking directly into her eyes. With the sudden burst of speed, the motorcycle managed to safely avoid a collision. Missing the rear wheel of the motorcycle by mere inches, Leigh's car finally skidded to a stop. Her heart felt like it was about to beat its way out of her chest as she realized she had been holding her breath, and she gasped for air.

Leigh turned quickly to look out her side window, watching as the bike screamed down the opposite alleyway. Blue and black leather—she committed the biker's appearance to memory. There was some kind of patch on his arm, but she hadn't gotten a good enough look at it to identify it. Despite her intense anger, she felt some admiration for the biker; it had taken skill to pull out and avoid the crash, and she respected that. Her car remained undamaged, as well, and for that she couldn't help but be grateful. If she ever saw the biker again, though, she would let him have a piece of her mind for being so careless. Throwing the car back in gear, Leigh resumed her course, admitting to herself that maybe she had been driving a bit too fast as well.

CHAPTER 5
MASQUERADE

The club was not far away, only a block or two, evidenced by the increasing number of cars parked along the side of the street. Leigh hoped that her invitation would grant her a reserved parking spot, as it said that her presence was "required." She felt slightly embarrassed that the exterior of her car was in such bad condition. Although the rough exterior helped make the car less conspicuous under normal circumstances, under the bright lights of a nightclub parking lot it would put her vehicle into sharp contrast with the opulence surrounding it.

As she rounded the last turn and arrived at the club, she found her eyes assaulted by colors. Leigh was unprepared for the transformation the building had undergone from the faded, poorly scanned pictures on the Web. The building itself was roughly L–shaped, with large cathedral-like windows. Where once there had been only dirty windows, there were now magnificent stained glass conglomerations of random colors. Modified to look almost like a gothic church, the structure was painted black, with gargoyles lining the rooftop and buttresses flying out over the entranceway. Wave upon wave of bass poured from the building from a popular fast-paced dance song.

Not usually having time for what she would consider a leisurely nightlife, Leigh seldom paid any attention to such venues. This club, on the other hand, was truly a thing of wonder and managed to captivate her. It was hard for her to appreciate just how huge the building was until she found herself driving underneath the buttresses. The towering stained glass windows were only mere feet away, and Leigh couldn't help but gaze at them in wonder. Out of nowhere, a sense of disbelief tore into her amazement and left her agog. Who, powerful and rich enough to build this club, could possibly have business with her?

The line of cars waiting to let their passengers out was quite long, and the line of people waiting to get in looked to be even longer. Leigh always prided herself on her punctuality, but the queue of would-be guests moved at such a sluggish pace that she started to grow anxious. She felt even more uncomfortable as she realized how out of place she was. In front of her sat a double stretch limo and behind her an exotic sports car that was so low to the ground she could barely even see it in her rear view mirror. Everyone and everything surrounding her car exuded beauty and perfection, making her feel inadequate.

Her body could have hardly been in better shape, but with her conditioning came muscle, and she felt that her legs were slightly disproportionate to her slender torso. Her breasts filled her dress nicely, but she worried that her exposed shoulders were too toned and would look mannish. A blush burst across her cheeks as she neared the entrance. Walking up the red carpet were women that would have put supermodels to shame. She hastily checked herself in the vanity mirror as the valet made his way to her car.

"Damn," she said.

The curse seemed out of place coming out her lips as she looked herself in the mirror. She had remembered to do her hair and put on her earrings, but it had been so long since she had spent a night out on the town that she had completely forgotten to put on any makeup. All too soon the valet was knocking impatiently on her window. Huffing out an irritated sigh, she opened the door and nearly knocked him off his feet. Biting her lips in embarrassment, she suddenly remembered an old trick that her mother used to use when she ran out of makeup. Biting down a little harder on her lower lip she then did the same to the other, flushing them into a slightly brighter shade.

"Quite a car, ma'am," the valet said snidely as he looked her vehicle over with disdain.

Leigh retrieved her invitation from the door pocket. She then turned and gave the young man a polite smile from the darkness inside of the car. After handing over her keys, she climbed out onto her feet and made her way up the carpet. Leigh didn't pay the valet enough attention to notice that he was standing jaw askew as he watched her walk away. What she did notice was that the other people waiting in line were watching her intently and whispering quietly to one another. Under the bright lights of the entranceway, her natural beauty radiated brilliantly and dazzled everyone around her.

Conversations lowered themselves to near-mute hushes as she walked past. Leigh felt her blush deepen as the club goers scrutinized her body. Perhaps, she thought, it was because she'd forgotten her jacket. In her mind, the dress that she wore seemed like nothing more than a rag. She had bought it years ago intending to wear it on the first date of her life. The date was unfortunately a trap, and she had instantly sworn off the whole dating scene. Despite her misgivings, the dress she wore was truly a thing of beauty. Tiny silver butterflies seemed to flap their wings across its dark blue shimmering fabric as she made her way to the doorman.

"Ah, Miss Bryant …" The man spoke to Leigh as if she were a regular to the club, even though she was certain that she had never met him before. He was a tall, well-balanced man with a military-style haircut and deep brown eyes. His appearance was immaculate, with a bright and shiny name tag buttoned to his jacket that told the world that his name was Terrance. Standing next to him was the typical velvet rope guarding the doors. The thick, wooden doors looked like they could defend themselves, as they appeared to be taken off some old abandoned cathedral.

"Hello … Terrance," she said, trying to feign the same familiarity with the bouncer and failing miserably.

"You are expected, ma'am," Terrance said in a surprisingly kind way.

Leigh feigned a knowing smile and nodded at him as he unhooked the rope and led her to the doors. Another bouncer took Terrance's place as he pounded his fist against the door's massive birth three times. The slightest moment later she could hear the scraping sound of a deadbolt being unlocked. The doors were just slipping open when she heard the high-pitched whine of a familiar motorcycle pull up behind her. She turned to look back and saw a powerful figure of a man dismount the motorcycle. His jacket was well worn and trimmed with blue as were his pants. The patch on his shoulder was clear now—it sported a brilliant blue letter S encircled by sapphire roses.

The man also seemed to be receiving the royal treatment, just as Leigh had. Leigh examined his bike, quickly picking out the small canister of nitrous the man had activated earlier to escape colliding with her car. To control the bike during such an intense burst of power, the man would have to be a very skilled rider. Leigh's heart picked up its pace as the strange man began pulling off his helmet. She was about to walk over and confront him when her train of thought was interrupted.

"This way, if you please, madam," the polite voice of Terrance said as he ushered her into the club.

Leigh looked over her shoulder as the doors closed behind her. She could only see the back of the rider's jacket as he tended to his bike. She cursed silently that she hadn't gotten the opportunity to see the face of the mystery rider. Why was he here? Had he been sent to follow her? Or had he been invited as well? In either case, Leigh decided that she would have to investigate further to find out if he was a threat.

Her suspicions moved to the back of her mind as her attention turned to the main entrance and coatroom of the club. The lighting in the small chamber was subdued and dusky, but not so dim as to lose its elegance. It was not as grandiose or flashy as the exterior of the building but was every bit as striking in its presentation. Nearly every surface of the room, save for the floor, was covered with black velvet. The floor tiles were black and white, with the lighter tiles set in the shade of the full moon and the dark tiles the color of the most pitch-black night. On the opposite side of the room sat a pair of bloodred doors that were only slightly smaller than the exterior entranceway. She could now clearly hear music. An attractive girl appeared behind a nearby counter.

"Hello, Miss Bryant, and welcome to the Nocturne. Do you have any items that need to be held for you?"

Leigh blinked in surprise. The girl could obviously see that she didn't have any items, but was instead delicately asking her to check any weapons. Reaching into her small handbag, Leigh pulled out her tiny Berretta. With only the slightest hesitation, she dropped the clip and emptied the chamber, handing the small gun over. The check girl then took the gun and clip and knelt behind the counter, stowing the weapon in one of several numbered lock boxes. Leigh also handed over her handbag to be held, as there was nothing else of any importance in its contents.

"Here is your mask, madam. Please enjoy your evening at the Nocturne," the girl said as she resurfaced from behind the counter and handed over a mask.

Leigh had no prior knowledge that the dance this evening was going to be a masquerade ball and felt slightly embarrassed that she hadn't had the forethought to have realized. Looking down, she gazed for a moment at the mask. It was handmade of feathers and sequins, crafted with exquisite mastery. It would elegantly cover the top half of the face. She was about to put it on and head for the door when she thought of something. "Do I get a ticket or something for my gun?" she asked.

The girl at the desk only grinned slightly and said that she never forgot a face or the items that went with it. Leigh nodded slightly and walked to the doors. She would have felt better if she had some kind of receipt for checking her firearm. She wondered what talent the cloak girl had that would allow her to remember a face when it would be covered by a mask. A sigh escaped her lips as she walked on; she was in someone else's world now and must abide by their rules. But it was yet to be seen whether this was either an elaborate trap or a genuine business opportunity.

CHAPTER 6
REMEMBERING HOW TO DANCE

As Leigh approached the doors to the main section of the club, she found that they suddenly, albeit slowly, began to swing open on their own. The scene that waited on the other side would have fulfilled even the most decadent of clubber's dreams. Alive with music, the room pounded with the beat. On the spacious dance floor writhed a sea of bodies, entranced by the rhythms pulsating through the air. High above, some thirty or forty feet over the heads of the dancers, a massive glass canopy let in the night sky. All of the catwalks and railings of the factory remained in place, and Leigh could see people walking up and down them. Many were dancing, some were socializing as they looked for their next partner, and some were just enjoying their drinks. Massive speakers and clusters of lights hung from chains that fell from the ceilings at seemingly random intervals.

The main floor of the club was almost as long as a football field, and it stretched out beneath the high stained glass walls. In between each window sat what looked like a rather large painting. All around the boundaries of the room were deep overstuffed social booths, set out to allow for comfortable mingling. Leigh lost track of her bearings as she walked further out onto the floor. She could see that certain parts of the club offered other services, with signs and ropes dividing them off. What appeared to be an old machine shop now served as a rather large and decadent dining area, while another area seemed reserved for card games.

As Leigh pulled her mask down over her face, she found that it fit very comfortably. Unfortunately, it slightly impaired her peripheral vision by a few degrees. Despite the slight inconvenience, she could still look about at her surroundings with ease. Surprisingly, the basic floor plans she'd studied online remained basically the same, with few minor changes. The biggest change was merely the removal of the old machinery that once covered what was now the dance floor. She couldn't help but wonder if the lower levels still remained intact.

The faintest hints of a smile brushed her lips as the tension across her shoulders started to melt away. Except for the open area in the middle of the floor, there were plenty of areas where she could find cover. If things went bad, she would simply stick to the walls. The catwalks would also provide a good way of getting an edge on her opponents if she needed to. Content with her preliminary plans, she let herself relax a little bit. So long as there wasn't a threat present, she might as well enjoy herself for the first time in ages.

She found herself pleasantly disoriented by the beautiful masks surrounding her. She half hoped that the man who rode the motorcycle would confront her. Laughing, she dismissed the thought. She didn't even know what he looked like without his gear and helmet. But perhaps he would recognize her, she mused, having felt the sensation that he was looking directly into her eyes before that intense split second passed.

Walking around the dancers in the center of the floor, Leigh felt the urge to join them. The only problem was that she didn't really know how to dance. Having trained for combat for almost her entire youth, the freedom of dancing seemed alien to her mind and body. Without an opponent or forms to guide her limbs, how would she know what to do? She wondered, sardonically, if she wouldn't accidentally punch someone in the kidneys if nudged the wrong way.

After edging as close to the outermost fringes of the floor as possible, Leigh started to step slowly from side to side. She gently swung her arms with the beat and joined the dancers as nonchalantly as she could manage. Everyone seemed to be more interested in their partners than to a lone girl who could not dance. Still, Leigh was unable to shake the strong feeling of inability gnawing at her self confidence.

All at once she caught a glimpse of a rather tallish man staring at her through the crowd. A strange gray light seemed to be shining off of his mask. At first she looked away, thinking he was only a figment of her imagination. Giving the area a second glance, she found that the strange man had vanished. She shook her head and decided to keep on dancing. She wasn't the best dancer, but she was starting to enjoy herself, at least a little.

"You've never done this before, have you?" a male voice called to her, easily heard, even over the volume of the music.

Leigh jumped, as the comment came seemingly from out of nowhere. Turning around, she saw the man who had been looking at her. It was surprising how fast he had been able to make his way through the tangled dancers. He was a tall, well-built man with slightly tousled black hair that hung down to his shoulder. Somehow he seemed strangely familiar to Leigh, despite his mask. Her heart thudded in her chest as she tried to make herself talk. Just as she was about to start, the subtle scent of the man's cologne caught her senses and brought her up short for words once more.

Leigh narrowed her eyes and gave the man a sideways glance. "Do I know you?"

He smiled the scoundrel's smile of someone hiding a secret. Instinctively, her attention was drawn to his teeth, but she found herself unable to separate herself from his gaze. His eyes seemed to be a deep hue of hazel that she couldn't avoid looking at. A strange, otherworldly sort of intensity seemed to burn deep beneath inside of him, drawing her in. The strange gray light that she'd noticed earlier was gone now, but his visage was no less mesmerizing in its absence.

"We've met before, but only very briefly." He laughed softly as Leigh stopped dancing. "Do you want me to show you how to do that?"

"Do what?" Leigh asked, desperate to get her defenses back up against this charming man. "Oh, you mean dance? No, I ... I don't think I have any rhythm so I would probably just waste your time, or embarrass you."

She suddenly felt herself blushing behind her mask.

"Bah!" the man replied. "You wouldn't embarrass me. In fact, it would be a pleasure if you would allow me to give you some advice. You weren't actually doing a bad job of it to begin with. You just looked uncomfortable. Dancing is not completely about looking good; sometimes it's simply better to look like you're having a good time. I only want to show you a way to dance that will make you feel more comfortable, if I may." He indicated that he wanted to put his hands just above her hips.

"Oh ... um ... okay," Leigh said, feeling slightly foolish as she raised her arms to give him room.

His hands were firm but oddly cold as they wrapped about her body. His fingers also seemed to be slightly longer than normal and extremely strong. She cursed herself for letting the man get so close but still found the experience exciting. Nightclubs, no matter how refined, normally contained a few people who were only looking for brief encounters of one kind or another. Leigh would indulge this mysterious stranger for a while, if only to ascertain the root of his strange familiarity with her.

"Now, you can hear the beat, right?" he asked.

Leigh smiled despite her misgivings and started nodding her head slightly in time with the music.

"That's right," the man said. "Keep nodding with the beat. Now, do exactly what you were doing before."

Leigh did as she was told and suddenly found herself bobbing up and down with the stranger's hands about her waist, feeling rather goofy and more than a little embarrassed. She had not been aware until now just how stiff and uptight she was before he'd arrived. Although his hands were cold, they still made her feel more comfortable about what she was doing. She soon found herself rocking from side to side more easily and more in time with the beat.

"Almost done," he said, giving her a pleasant smile. "Now, this may feel a bit weird, but I want you to sway your hips."

Leigh laughed and stumbled as he gently applied pressure to one side of her waist.

Still smiling, he reassured her. "That's okay; let's try it again. If at first you don't succeed—"

"Try, try again," Leigh finished for him.

Her thoughts immediately turned back to her first failed date. An odd feeling spread throughout her mind and body as Leigh looked up into the stranger's eyes. It was a feeling that she had not felt in a very long time. She found herself wanting to know more about her new dance partner. Perhaps she had finally met someone who could convince her that it was time to try dating again.

Starting over once more, the stranger placed his strong hands around her waist as she again found the beat. She moved her hips from side to side, letting his strong hands guide her body. She was surprised to find that dancing felt natural and that the motion he was showing her felt good. It felt even better having his hands around her waist. But he soon removed them. Leigh was no longer merely stepping from foot to foot but was instead moving her whole body in time with the music.

"See? Now just do what your body tells you to and you'll be fine." He grinned at her and started dancing himself.

Leigh laughed playfully and continued dancing; soon she felt her self-consciousness start to vanish completely. Her enigmatic partner danced in a lithe manner that seemed different from those around him. His movements were sensuous and inviting, and Leigh found herself drawn to him. A slight dizziness seemed to settle down on her thoughts, and she could not resist starting a conversation with him.

"You taught me how to dance so easily, and I don't even know your name yet," she said, edging closer to the man.

"My name is Kehl Sanria, and I didn't teach you how to do anything. Your body already knew how to dance. All I did was merely remind it."

The thought of using an alias was a fleeting thought in Leigh's mind as she smiled happily. "My name is Leigh. Leigh Bryant."

No sooner had Leigh given her name than she almost fell over as a noisy female dancer who collided with her. "What the hell are you doing?!" spat a catty voice.

Regaining her balance, Leigh turned to see a couple who were obviously drunk and, most likely, under age. The girl wore a skirt that was so short that you could see her ass when she moved. Oddly enough, she also wore a scarf, which seemed rather old fashioned. Her partner seemed to be less irritated at Leigh and more preoccupied with admiring his companion's posterior. Leigh's eyes narrowed as she looked him over. He was sloppily dressed in a high-collared shirt that looked like something out of the '70s.

"Don't mind her," Kehl said to Leigh as he wrapped an arm about her waist and tugged her away. "I feel like she wouldn't even be a match for you," he continued, after they were out of earshot.

Preferring for the moment to follow Kehl's advice and avoid confrontation, Leigh followed him silently out into the middle of the dance floor. After several moments, they were dancing again, surrounded closely by the bodies of other people. A short while later, Leigh's irritation from the encounter vanished completely. Leigh smiled sarcastically as she thought about Kehl's strange choice of words concerning the matter.

"What exactly did you mean when you said you 'feel' like she wouldn't even be a match for me?"

She could tell that Kehl was embarrassed even through his mask; it only served him right for saying something like that. His arm was still around her waist, though, and she didn't know why she let him keep it there. Ever so slightly his grip tightened in a pleasant way in response to her comment. His fingers felt both frighteningly strong and oddly comforting at the same time as they pulled her the slightest bit closer.

"You have a strong body," he explained. "I could feel it in your waist."

Leigh smiled and for the first time in a long time felt good about her body.

"Can we dance closer?" she pleaded softly, leaning up close to him and whispering it in his ear. "Can you show me how to do that?"

"Of course," he answered smoothly with a grin.

They stayed close this time as they let their bodies move to the beat. Leigh fantasized that Kehl had been the one to invite her due to some secret crush on her. Her body was moving in ways that she never knew it could as she tried to draw him in. Dancing closer to his body, she stepped in and slid up against his chest. She could feel herself start to sweat as Kehl took hold of her just below the small over her back, pulling her closer still. His body was firm and toned underneath his clothes, but unlike her, he seemed to give off no heat whatsoever.

They danced closely for several minutes, their bodies entwining more and more. She wanted to pull back, but she was afraid that Kehl had been the one to send the invitation; that the mistress in her invitation was only a figurehead to disguise Kehl as the true proprietor. She also found herself getting excited and did not know how to deal with it. Her head was spinning, and the room seemed to be flipping end over end. So far she'd managed to keep herself fairly collected, but this was all new to her. She was falling head over heels for this stranger. She finally decided that she needed a break.

"I'm not used to all this dancing," she said with a laugh. "Do you want to grab a seat?"

CHAPTER 7

PAPER CROSSES

With the dance floor behind them, Leigh led the way to one of the nearby plush booths. She slipped gracefully into the seat and pulled her mask off. Kehl paused beside the booth momentarily to gaze upon her features. Her face was strong yet delicate, in a way that made the color of her eyes a brighter blue than any he had ever seen. After taking off his mask, he tossed it on the table and sat down across from her.

"You don't wear any makeup?" he asked as he got comfortable in the seat.

She laughed nervously. "I kind of forgot to put it on. I don't usually come to places like this."

Kehl smiled. "You don't need the makeup, anyway."

"Thank you," Leigh said, not wanting to meet his gaze after the compliment.

"I don't usually come to these places either," Kehl continued.

"Please," Leigh replied with a grin. "You probably come here every week and leave with a different girl every time."

"Oh, of course," Kehl said with a sarcastic wave of his hand. "And I sometimes even leave with several girls."

Leigh laughed lightly, though she noticed a distant flash in Kehl's features for the briefest of moments. He was a very handsome man, and in the dim light she could see the pale remains of a fading tan across his angular face. Little did she know that Kehl had not seen the light of day for many, many years, and that the slight tan remained in his skin was because he'd had it on the night he turned.

"I could believe that," Leigh responded. "You're pretty good looking without your mask on."

"Would you believe me if I told you that I've only ever been with one woman?" he replied, somewhat seriously and with a rather sad smile.

Leigh smiled. "I would have believed you if you hadn't just swept me off my feet out there on the dance floor."

Kehl laughed and smiled at her playful jab.

"No, seriously," Leigh continued with a pleasant smile. "I'm always on guard. The last time I was with a guy he turned into a monster, literally. Ever since then I guess my training just seemed to take over." Biting her lip she suddenly felt as though she may have let this stranger know a little too much about herself.

"I was starting to wonder if you were involved in some sort of martial art," Kehl said. "You carry yourself like you are constantly on guard. And, like I mentioned earlier, you seem to be in excellent physical shape."

Leigh quickly spotted a cover for her earlier slip. "I do a little kickboxing and mixed martial arts. I also work out several times a week, at least."

"It shows," Kehl replied.

"You said we've met before, but I don't recall …" Leigh started to say, only to find herself interrupted by the waiter, who appeared suddenly.

"May I get you anything to drink tonight?" he queried cordially while serving them two tall wine glasses of ice water.

Leigh looked at Kehl and then back at the waiter. She was just about to tell him that she didn't have any money with her when Kehl piped up. "It's on me. Get whatever you want," he said, looking over to Leigh.

"Just a soda please," Leigh said.

She didn't normally drink, and she definitely didn't want to before she knew what tonight was all about.

Kehl ordered a soda as well and the waiter left to get them their orders.

"So what brings you here tonight?" Kehl inquired.

Leigh frowned slightly as she pushed her straw from its wrapper and stuck it in her water. "Work."

"What kind of job do you have that brings you here?" Kehl asked as he looked around the club. "It must be nice."

"It's not all it's cracked up to be. I have to live from contract to contract, and I can barely keep my car running." *Plus, it's dangerous,* she thought. "On top of that, I don't have time for a love life." Her irritation with her vocation compelled her to start twisting the empty remains of one of the paper straw wrappers.

"A gorgeous girl like you, and you don't have a love life? Now, I find that hard to believe," Kehl said as he watched her twist the paper into two odd bits.

Leigh turned red but continued talking. "Most people do. They would rather believe that I have slept with fifty men than believe the truth." *That I haven't slept with any,* she thought, grateful that Kehl seemed uninterested in prying.

With the shorter of the two halves of twisted straw paper in her fingers, Leigh absentmindedly wrapped it about the longer piece. Tied together, the two pieces formed a rudimentary paper cross. She grew quiet and distant as she twirled it absentmindedly between her fingers.

"Want to see a magic trick?" Kehl asked softly, checking over his shoulders to make sure no one was watching.

Leigh smiled brightly with curiosity as her attention returned to Kehl. "So long as it doesn't involve my clothes disappearing, sure."

After checking over his shoulder once more, Kehl reached slowly across the table to the small cross that Leigh had made. Ever so slightly his finger touched only the very tip of the small paper crucifix and that was all it took. Leigh's hand recoiled as the small cross ignited and disintegrated in little more than the blink of an eye. To anyone else, it would have been an amusing trick, but to Leigh it could only mean one thing: Kehl Sanria was a vampire.

Leigh grit her teeth, grabbed her mask, and slowly started edging from the booth.

"Are you sure we've met before?" she demanded quietly of him. A deep sadness she couldn't explain started building in her heart. Was this man one of the vampires who had escaped her father in the past years? The more she thought about it, the more she started to believe that it was a trap just like before.

"Yes, but it's not how you think," Kehl said, pleadingly, as Leigh got up from her seat. "Please, wait."

Leigh only shook her head as she stomped off. Her father's words kept echoing through her mind. Even though Kehl was a vampire, maybe he wasn't evil. He couldn't have exactly just popped up next to her on the dance floor and said, "Hey, I'm a vampire. Want to dance?" There was no way he could have known she was a hunter. Now that she knew the truth, it put her ill at ease. The mere fact that he was a vampire could mean that she would be hunting him one day, and she couldn't deal with something like that. Seeking to escape the situation and to forget that she ever met Kehl or developed any burgeoning feelings for him, Leigh made her way up to one of the catwalks above the dance floor.

She was most surprised as a painting met her at the top of the stairs. It was a vivid painting of a chill autumn day; it seemed almost a bit too bright to be real. Leigh looked around at the surrounding catwalks. There were at least a dozen identical frames hanging about. These were the posters she'd noticed earlier. From a distance she'd thought them to be only paper images that were lighted from behind, but up close she realized her mistake. She touched the edge of one of the frames absentmindedly, trying to tear her mind away from Kehl.

"Digital picture frames," said a kind male voice behind her.

"Don't—" she said, stopping short as she whirled about, expecting to see Kehl.

"Patronize you? I wouldn't dare offend a guest in the Mistress's establishment."

Leigh was taken aback. The man standing before her looked to have the physique of a twenty-year-old while his dark brown hair showed streaks of grey. His hands were long and slender but showed calluses and other signs of hard labor. In short, his entire presence seemed to be a walking contradiction. Even his eyes, which were dark brown, seemed to be flecked with gold, the same color as the two glasses of champagne he carried. Leigh thought he was good looking but nothing more. He had the air of society, and she had little use for his people other than for writing her paychecks.

"The frames are expensive, aren't they?" she said in a more forceful tone than she intended. "I hope I didn't leave a smudge."

"I wouldn't worry too much about a smudge," the man answered pleasantly. "It's really only a computer monitor turned sideways with a fake wood finish. In the size that these are here, they are only, oh, I'd say around two thousand dollars."

"Ah, that's not too expensive." Leigh said, although she could definitely use two thousand dollars for something other than a picture frame.

"They are also easily cleaned," the man continued. "Like I said, don't worry about it too much."

The man grinned pleasantly and turned to leave. Leigh was surprised that he had not offered her his extra drink or even properly introduced himself. She went to call him back, but the man interrupted her just as she had drawn breath.

"The time will come for introductions," he said without turning back. "Enjoy your time at the Nocturne while you can."

CHAPTER 8
CROWD SURFING

"We don't have invitations!" A small group of young women were outside, desperately waiting in the cold to get into the Nocturne. One of them in particular was actually too young to even get in. She was not planning on entering legitimately, however. All of her friends believed she was twenty-one. They had no clue that she'd only just graduated from high school and turned eighteen shortly after.

"You never said anything about needing invitations," another of the girls shouted.

"It's okay, it's okay," the teenager announced nonchalantly as she stepped to the front of the group. "They know me here, for real."

"Oh, stop lying, Anne, you don't even look old enough to get in here. You look like jailbait for crying out loud."

Anne looked down at her own slender, petite frame, and knew that her friend was right. She was dressed fashionably in a short skirt with leggings and a hand knit v-neck sweater that showed some of her lingerie and the cleavage beneath. It still wasn't enough. Even though Anne felt much older than her actual age, the way she was built seemed to scream her true age. A heavy sigh of exasperation escaped her lips as Anne returned her gaze to her friend. In a moment her appearance would no longer be an issue.

"You know how old I am," Anne replied flatly as she reached out with her thoughts.

The reply from Anne's friend came as through from a dummy, a hollow sounding, "Yes, you're twenty-two."

A brilliant smile crossed Anne's face, but the smile was short lived as she turned back to look at the entranceway. Her friend, Elizabeth Rose, was making her way up the red carpet leading into the club with a strange young man. Elizabeth was being treated like royalty, while Anne was forced to wait in the cold. Anne had her suspicions as to why her friend was receiving such a reception but would have to make it further into the club to find out for sure.

"Come on, girls," Anne said loudly. "I've spotted my man."

The small group of girls followed her obediently up to the bouncers standing at the rope. In truth, Anne had never been to this club before, nor had she met any of the bouncers. It wouldn't make any difference—she'd only picked one at random anyway. As she stepped up to the unsuspecting guard, she made a show of adjusting her clothes as well as her assets. The group of girls behind her giggled profusely as she did so. A wicked grin spilled across Anne's lips as she began working her own brand of magic.

Normally, the thoughts of others would come into her mind like whispers. It was not until she opened her mind that she could understand what was coming and going through other peoples' heads. It took only a second's worth of concentration. After closing her eyes for that short time, she cleared her own thoughts and listened with her mind.

The physical world around her seemed to grow dull ever so slightly as her attention focused on the thoughts. To the unaccustomed, the combined noise of both mental and verbal noise would be overwhelming, maddening. To Anne, it was the sweetest of music. For only a moment she let her mind wash back and forth over the heads of the club goers. Their thoughts carried her own presence of mind away from her body, washing her back and forth like the waves of the ocean.

She often thought to herself that if she ever wanted to pursue a career in psychology, it would be triumphantly easy. After finishing high school, however, she'd decided to not ever follow that path. Firstly, she'd never be able to explain her insight into the mind to anyone else who wasn't sensitive or talented like herself. And secondly, she'd seen far too many ugly things in her brief eighteen years. Some things that she'd encountered in the minds of others she could never share; there were thoughts too horrifying or disgusting to even grace with remembrance.

Anne's thoughts hovered for a moment over the minds of her 'friends.' She quickly remembered why it was so impossible for her to have real friends. She was not yet able to dismiss every mean idea or thought that any potential friends might have about her. In addition, friendships with members of the opposite sex were out of the question. She found that most guys were thinking about the prospect of sex almost constantly. Her friends were currently thinking that she was lying about knowing anyone here at the club. Of course, they were right, but the thoughts that followed, the mean, shallow opinions about her body and dress, were uncalled for. After tonight, she would never socialize with these girls again.

As she locked onto the thoughts of the bouncer she'd picked out, she reached out with her mind. Using her psychic abilities, she burrowed into his thoughts and memories. She learned his name and discovered his deepest, darkest fantasies, all without giving him so much as a hint as to her activities. Throughout all of her life, she'd never found anyone capable of resisting her powers. Several sensitives managed to detect her a time or two, but she'd easily found ways around even the best defenses.

Her mark tonight was an exceptionally easy one. The bouncer's name was Barry, and he was enjoying himself this evening. Sexual thoughts were foremost on his mind, as most of the club goers were young, attractive people wearing tight clothing. She would exploit this angle to its fullest advantage. After a seconds of reading his simple thoughts, she found what she was looking for: the still-fresh memory of an erotic dream. Anne latched on the fantasy and dove deeper into his mind, slowly and carefully taking control over it.

Anne was not an unattractive young woman, but her body did not match what was in Barry's fantasy. She was slightly shorter than her friends and petite in build and endowment. To Anne, even her hair seemed normal. Instead of trying to hide her body, she instead dressed to magnify what she had. but none of this would have any impact on what she was about to do. She could make herself appear to be anyone in a subject's mind. If she chose, she could even make herself seem invisible by cutting off all visual and audible cues to the conscious mind.

It was easy enough work to copy the image of the woman from Barry's dream, whose name happened to be Victoria. Anne overlaid her own identity in the bouncer's mind. He clearly did a double take as Anne made him notice her alone in the crowd. Her character of Victoria was obscenely dressed and her jacket hung loosely open to expose as much of the ample breasts beneath as possible. Her hair was long and widely styled in dirty blond curls that came to the small of her back.

Anne cocked her hips to the side, and her image of Victoria did the same. She made sure that Barry noticed her illusory low-riding jeans and the apparent lack of undergarments. Barry's eyes went wide.

The sexual energy poured from his mind and was nearly intoxicating. Anne could feel his thoughts of discomfort as he quickly became excited. The one thing that she didn't change about her true self was the color of her eyes, which were still a very deep shade of brown.

"Hello, Barry," she said, giving him a wink.

The group of girls behind her grew silent as they saw what was going on. To them, Anne looked completely normal, just as she had several minutes ago. Barry stuttered several times and couldn't seem to come up with anything to say. Anne looked back at her friends and gave a nod that said "I told you so." Her plan was working well. It was taking only a small amount of her energy to influence the bouncer, whereas making the whole crowd and group of bouncers think she was invisible would have been exhausting and nearly impossible.

"Hello, Anne," Barry finally said aloud, even though in his mind thought he'd said Victoria. "Right this way, please."

Barry unclipped the rope separating Anne and her friends from the entranceway. With a simple trick of the mind, Anne kept Barry's attention locked firmly on her illusion. She then made her friends invisible to his mind. Her small group then crossed onto the carpet quickly, amazed at the purely natural influence that Anne seemed to have over the bouncer. Barry acted as though Anne was a long lost flame or a celebrity or anything other than the somewhat mousy girl that she actually was.

"I will see you in your dreams tonight, Barry," Anne said with a seductive voice before vanishing into thin air.

Barry smiled absentmindedly, and then frowned deeply, convincing himself that he had only imagined letting a guest into the club. Shaking his head in an attempt to clear his thoughts, he refastened the rope and returned to this duty. Anne made sure to plant the seeds in his mind for some very interesting dreams. The bouncer was only doing his job, and Anne had intentionally used his own ideal woman against him. She hoped that his dreams later that night would be enough to compensate him for the trouble.

As she made her way into the club, a strange feeling of foreboding wrapped around her like a fog. Her friends didn't seem to notice as they commented on the way the coatroom was laid out, gasping at every little detail. Anne felt like she was trespassing on someone else's territory, as though the entire area was controlled by some dominating force of will. She decided that it would be best to keep her abilities low key this evening while trailing her friend Elizabeth.

As her friends checked their coats and nonessentials, Anne took a moment to cast her mind out over the dance floor. The pulsating flood of emotions nearly overwhelmed her. She'd never before experienced such a thrillingly intense feeling of vitality and life. At the same time, she noticed that something was different here. She was unable to lock completely onto one person's thoughts, nor could she process all of the information coming to her.

Something, or someone, seemed to be blocking her attempts to explore the club mentally. It took her considerably longer to find her friend Elizabeth than it should have. Even once she'd located her friend, she was unable to properly enter her thoughts. She returned her mind back to her own body and gave the girl at the front desk her jacket before entering the club proper. As she steeled herself for what was going to be a difficult night her, her hand absentmindedly made its way up to her neck. Her fingertips brushed carefully at the two pale scars hidden beneath her hair. Anne had no doubt now that something was wrong with not only her friend, Elizabeth Rose, but also with this strange night club.

CHAPTER 9
THE ANXIOUS GUEST

The limousine seemed to slither its way through the damp and dirty New York streets. It was a stretch crimson Hummer; the vehicle could most accurately be described as decadence incarnate. The wheels each sparkled with encrusted diamonds, rubies, emeralds, and sapphires in the ultimate show of wealth. Although there was room for nearly twenty people in the bowels of that luxurious beast, only two people rode in the passenger compartment. One was a massive man of dark complexion, whose muscles writhed like eels under his perfect skin. His bright brown eyes were currently admiring the single jewel that he currently wore—a brilliant insignia ring with a flawless jet diamond inlaid in its center. His teeth, white as pearls and sharp as daggers, suddenly glimmered as a smile crossed his lips.

"Why are you so happy, my love?" asked the second passenger. Her voice carried a faded accent that many centuries ago would have found its roots in a poorer section of Edo Japan. The dark man turned his eyes to his companion, noting to himself that the cognac diamonds he had dressed her in set off her deep brown eyes brilliantly, especially when framed by her long jet-black hair. Her name was Kitsu, her name partially taken from the fox demon.

"There is but one thing in this world that I have craved more than yourself," he said, turning his eyes back to the black diamond on his finger.

"Is it another jewel?" Kitsu asked with only the slightest hint of feigned jealousy in her voice.

A grin played its way across the man's face, revealing his fangs. "Yes."

Sincerity found its way into her voice. "I'm worried about you, Drake," Kitsu said, taking a delicate hand and caressing the back of his neck. "Ever since I brought you into the night you've had a fascination with jewels, and it only grew once I released you from my control."

"This one is special, and you already know why I am so interested in jewels," he said in an affectionate way. "You know, my story is almost cliché. Suicide wasn't uncommon during the depression."

Her voice was soft with compassion as she spoke. "But your wife taking your two children with her was unnecessary ..."

Kitsu must have heard his story a thousand times in their many years together, but she never chided him for repeating it.

"Yes," Drake whispered, looking deep into the jewel on his finger.

He could still remember that night, so long ago. It had been an inky dark night, one that could only be found in the slums of Boston during the Great Depression. His then-living heart had pounded in his chest as he ran home that evening. After months of unemployment and near-starvation, he had finally managed to find a job as a metalworker. But his joy was short lived as he threw open the door to his home only to be greeted by a crushing silence.

Under normal circumstances, his wife would have been waiting up for him to come home. Fear mingled with his reborn pride as he sought out a candle and some matches; he refrained from calling out his wife's name for fear of waking his two young daughters. Finding the matches and candle, he carefully lit the wick. The odor of sulfur that drifted up and stung the inside of Drake's nose might as well have been born of the fires of hell when it combined with the sight that greeted his eyes. His daughters sat cold, blue, and motionless at the kitchen table, their heads lying in their dinner plates, obviously poisoned. Off at the other end of the room, in front of the apartment's only window, his wife had hung herself.

All of the horrors of that night were little more than an unpleasant memory now. He could remember finding the small vial of poison, of hunting down the small oriental medicine shop where his wife had purchased the substance to confront the owner. The anger, hate, madness, fear, and remorse that coursed through him at that time were gone now. When Drake finally burst into Kitsu's drug store and threatened to end her life, she had offered him an escape. At first, he suspected that she was offering him the release of suicide. Instead, she offered him something much more tempting than death: the fulfillment of all of his mortal desires through an immortal life.

Half insane with grief, Drake decided to accept Kitsu's offer. She then introduced him to the hidden back rooms of her establishment where she kept the servants that she fed upon. Kitsu had later explained that she had no prior knowledge of Drake's wife's plan to commit suicide. His wife had bought the poison with the false intention of dealing with some troublesome rats. Although, when Kitsu later looked back on the unfortunate business, she realized that even had she known the woman's true intentions, she still would have sold her the poison. Her desire and love of Drake was covetous. She would gladly give up her own life before parting with him.

"Ever since those days in the tenements, I have fought to distance myself as far as possible from poverty," Drake said. "It's the one feeling, the one emotion that was left from my past life. The jewels represent my power and wealth. The one that I am after tonight, the real Midnight Nocturne, can bring me more power than anything I've ever dreamed of."

"Don't you think it's rather arrogant, or foolish for that matter, for this 'Mistress' person to name her club after the jewel?" Kitsu questioned.

"Not really," Drake answered. "Practically no one alive today would know of it or remember its discovery. The only reason I ever knew about it was because I was *alive* when it was found. Even if someone did know where the club got its name, I doubt that they would believe that a mere nightclub owner would actually possess the single most unique jewel on the planet. It is a priceless artifact."

"Do you think she really has the jewel?"

"When she first contacted me she told me amazing, unbelievable things about it. At first I did think she was lying and that the stories were nothing more than a small part of an elaborate con. Then I did some digging and managed to track down the original notes from the jewel's discovery."

"How on earth did you find those, after all of these years?" Kitsu asked, making herself a bit more comfortable in her seat. Her fingertips still gently caressed the back of Drake's neck.

"There is an Egyptian curio shop in the rich part of town. The owner, a woman named Aja, said that her family was tied directly to the jewel. I didn't believe her story, not until she produced the notes from its discovery. She also told me of a way to destroy the jewel and unlock our true powers."

Kitsu rolled her eyes slightly before returning her gaze to Drake.

"So you believe in the legends, then? That in an attempt to bring order to the world, the Egyptians sealed all things magical and arcane away in that single jewel?"

Drake spoke with conviction. "Its destruction would free our full potential as the children of the night. It would renew the times of old. We would be as gods among common mortals."

Thoughts of power and wealth filled his mind as he imagined a new world, his world, a world without poverty and with a lover by his side who would never die. His control of the world and all things in it would be absolute. The mere thought of it made his mouth water. If the legends were true, then tonight he would have everything he'd ever desired.

Kitsu distracted him from his serious thoughts as she gently ran a fingertip around the two very jagged scars on his skin of his neck. She thought happily to herself that she'd done a good job with turning him. There were many ways to turn a human into a vampire, both slowly and quickly. The slower methods were relatively free of the risk of failure, taking sometimes as long as months. Faster methods were, however, much more dangerous and stood the chance of either outright killing the victim or dealing such a harsh system shock that both the physiology and mental state of the victim could be damaged permanently, rendering them little more than a ghoul or zombie-like creature.

The slightest smile touched her lips as Kitsu remembered turning him successfully in a single night.

"But why are you calling yourself Alucard? Isn't it a bit silly?"

Drake deeply enjoyed the somewhat odd concealment of his name and laughed slightly before answering her question.

"Actually, yes, it is, but for right now I want to keep my real name hidden from the Mistress, just in case our deal tonight turns out to be a trap."

She smiled, and without another word leaned in close to him, kissing him deeply on his lips.

"Enough talk about this jewel," Kitsu murmured with a coy smile. "I'm starting to get jealous."

Kitsu remembered how much she'd pitied him that night so long ago as their lips touched once more. Once turned, she'd quickly established in him a sense of not only her dominance, but also of her needs as a woman. Her appetite was voracious, and when the pain of his wife's death had finally dulled, Drake had become a much more willing and obedient lover. Kitsu's own feelings had surprised her, growing over the years into the familiar feelings she remembered from her time of being human.

The luxurious seating of the limousine allowed the couple ample room to wrap themselves up in each other's arms as their kiss deepened. Drake's powerful arms pulled Kitsu's slight frame closer as she laid her arms over his shoulders. Kitsu brushed her fingernails ever so slightly against the back of Drake's neck, savoring the sensation of his shivers. Their embrace would have continued, if not for the sudden stop of the vehicle that nearly sent them sprawling on the floorboard.

After regaining his composure, Drake angrily pushed a button and activated the intercom to the driver. "What's the matter?" he asked, making no effort to hide the irritation in his voice as Kitsu checked her makeup in a convenient vanity mirror.

"It's a roadblock, sir," came the voice of the driver. "There are several men in front of the limo. I wouldn't have stopped, but they're armed and motioning for me to get out."

"Stay where you are, I will handle this," Drake instructed, carefully taking off his ring before opening his door to step out into the waiting street.

Snow had begun lazily drifting down to the grimy street as Drake made his way to the front of the limo. This particular stretch of the road was darker than most, a perfect place for an ambush. Indeed, Drake could already make out a half dozen people blocking the street. He also noticed there were at least two others waiting in the darkness and acting as lookouts. Five of them had pistols leveled at him; two of them also held flashlights. One member of the gang seemed larger than the rest and appeared to be unarmed. He stepped forward to meet Drake as he approached.

The man's face was angular with a strong brow that shadowed his eyes. His light brown hair was cropped close to the scalp. Drake could tell from the broadness of the other man's shoulders that if he himself were mortal again he would have a fight on his hands.

"That's going to be my ride," the stranger called, the sound of the streets thick in his voice. "After I take care of you and your driver."

There was no emotion in Drake's voice as he replied. "I am going to make you an offer, and keep in mind that I don't usually do this. Tonight is a good night for me, so if you drop your weapons and clear the street I will spare you your lives and you can all go home and live out the rest of your existence."

Drake assumed the men were either hunters or common robbers. In either case they would have to be dealt with decisively. If they did not accept his deal, he would be forced to use violence. The thought clicked into his mind that someone must have tipped them off as to his plans tonight. Deep inside his gut he wished with all his might that it was not the Mistress of the Midnight Nocturne.

"I am afraid you don't have any leverage to negotiate with," the leader said, jerking his arm up and signaling the rest of his group to take the vehicle. The gesture may as well have been the signal to an executioner for his men to be slaughtered.

Drake looked over his shoulder and back at his driver, giving him a short nod. He and his driver were no strangers to this type of situation, and his servant knew exactly what do to. In the amount of time it took to turn off a switch on the dash, all of the exterior and interior lights on the Hummer winked out of existence. In the passenger compartment, Kitsu smiled. She knew it would be a good fight, but she did not intend to soil her beautiful dress in the struggle.

Every bit as quickly as the light vanished, a crushing silence washed over the alley. Six sets of eyes watched as the silhouette of the man that was supposed to have been their victim vanished into the darkness. It was now obvious that they were dealing with a problem. Only a fool would ambush a vampire in the nighttime, at the peak of its power. One of the men holding a flashlight jerked it back and forth, casting the beam around the alley seeking to find his foe.

"What the f—." His final words were cut short as the flashlight fell to the ground.

His companions heard a faint gurgling sound as the flashlight died. It was then violently crushed underfoot. The night around them fell deathly silent again, enveloping them all with an absolute sense of impending doom.

"Over there!"

Immediately the remaining people with guns emptied their weapons in the direction where their friend had been standing, their fear outweighing their concern for their ally. A weighty meat-like thud soon followed. The only other man carrying a flashlight rushed forward. What he found nearly made him vomit. A headless corpse lay on the ground, looking like little more than shredded meat. The head, however, remained in perfect condition in its death mask.

"Oh god. Oh god. Save me," the man begged as he dropped his flashlight and gun, falling to his knees.

"Not tonight," a voice whispered in his ear.

The man started to scream but an immensely strong hand grabbed him around the neck and lifted him from the ground. He gasped, bringing in enough air to scream, only to have an incredible pain explode into his lower back. He knew there was air in his lungs, but try as he might he couldn't make a sound. The pain continued to burn throughout his body as he was tossed almost casually into the trash lining the side of the street. The last thing his eyes saw before his vision blacked out was the glare of light coming from his own flashlight moments before it was shattered into a million pieces.

Kitsu cracked her door open. "Try not to get any blood on yourself, darling!" she called.

"You're going to make me late!" Drake hissed at his adversaries as he swiftly found and dispatched another enemy. Off in the distance he could hear the lookouts making a run for it, each in opposite ways down alleys on either side of the street. A moment passed as Drake decided whether to eliminate them or let them be.

In the space of that instant, one of the hunters finally managed to locate Drake and thrust his pistol fiercely up against the back of his head. The icy metal pressed against Drake's skin brought back distant memories of mortality.

"Got you now, you bastard," the gunman said, pulling the trigger.

Drake lunged to the side as the gun went off. The shot missed him by millimeters. The muzzle flash burnt his ear and deafened him on one side. He was a vampire, and an exceptionally strong one, but he was not invincible. Dazed and off balance, he looked around to see Kitsu standing directly behind the man, driving a dagger deep into his neck. If not for Kitsu's quick intervention, the devastation of such a wound would have easily ended his existence just as easily as a stake through the heart.

Drake could see the disappointment spread across Kitsu's face, even through the pitch black night. "I barely saved you," she said with scorn in her voice. "Don't be so cocky next time."

Kitsu let the corpse fall limply to the ground. It still held the gun. She immediately stepped forward and picked up the weapon, whirling about to fire two rounds into the last gunman, killing him before he could return fire. Quickly readjusting her aim, she fired two more rounds off into the darkness, killing one of the lookouts before he could run to bring reinforcements. Without bothering to look, she leveled the gun in the opposite direction and shot the other lookout in the same manner. Now all that remained was the leader of the group, who, despite the carnage and death that had just erupted around him, somehow managed to remain calm.

"Do you think you can handle the last one?" Kitsu spat, offering Drake the gun.

Drake nodded as he pushed the gun away. The burning and ringing of his ear was swiftly fading, becoming little more than a slight annoyance.

"Get back in the car," Drake said, refusing to look at Kitsu as he walked up to the last remaining member of the group. This was his night, and his alone. To him, the legends were an absolute truth, and the thought that he had almost allowed himself to be slain while so close to his objective made him sick to his stomach. He would allow nothing else to stand in his way, no matter what the cost.

Still, Drake found himself impressed by his opponent. The man he approached was cool and defiant, even though fear shone clearly in his eyes. On any other night, Drake would have considered turning the man into one of his servants. But tonight he could feel only the rage from having disappointed Kitsu, and he did not want to fail her again.

"It's not a very fair fight," the man said to Drake, even though it seemed he could see reasonably well through the darkness.

"Light!" Drake called to his driver.

Instantly the lights on the hummer flickered back on, silhouetting both men in bright illumination.

"Thank you," the man said.

"It won't change anything," Drake growled as he prepared himself to fight. "Not a damn thing."

"Then I'm going to die, aren't I?" the man asked, not allowing his fear to creep into his voice.

Drake made no reply as he shifted his stance ever so slightly.

"I won't make it easy for you then!" the man screamed defiantly, pulling out a long knife that he kept hidden at his belt.

The hunter leapt fearlessly at Drake, slashing viciously at his gut. This time there was no arrogance, no wasted movements as Drake slapped the knife hand in such a way to utilize the man's momentum, turning him slightly. It took only a single step for Drake to get behind the weak mortal. In one fluid motion, he wrapped his arm about his neck. With a violent jerk of his arms, Drake broke his foe's neck, ending his life. Dropping the body to the ground, he made his way back to the Hummer, hoping that nothing else would go wrong that night.

Before he could open the door, a sleek exotic car roared up behind the limo. The driver stuck his head out the window and addressed Drake.

"Is everything okay, sir?"

"Yes," Drake answered, taking a moment to check his suit for bloodstains in the headlights of the car. "Only a minor complication, continue along with the plan."

"Yes, sir," the driver replied as Drake opened the door to his limo and pulled himself back in.

Kitsu immediately pounced on him with a towelette from the bar inside the limo. She gingerly wiped away the powder burns on Drake's ear and cheek. He immediately felt like a small child under the care of his mother. Flinching away, he grabbed the towel away from her and dealt with the unsightly marks himself. As he gazed back at Kitsu, he saw no hint of her earlier disappointment at all, only an all-consuming expression of love.

"Please," he murmured, smiling in spite of himself. "Do not use your dominion over me to make me feel better."

Kitsu edged closer to him and laid her hand on his thigh. "You should know better than that, darling. I no longer have any power over you whatsoever," she whispered, laying her head down on his shoulder.

"I love you," she continued, "and I only want for tonight to be perfect for you."

Drake sighed and bowed his head slightly, knowing that her words were true. He felt Kitsu's comparatively small hands wrap about his own. The sensation of her touch sent shivers up and down his spine as he leaned closer to her. His anger seemed to be fading very quickly under the warmth of her loving smile.

"I love you too," he answered, throwing away the towel and wrapping his arm about her shoulders.

Several moments of silence passed as the limo slowly grew closer to the nightclub. For some reason, Drake could not shake his feelings of self-doubt. Nor could he shrug off a growing fear of further problems awaiting him at the club. The fact that someone would be willing to sell such a unique and powerful item seemed much too good to be true, and despite his optimism, he suspected some hidden sort of treachery.

As drake looked down at Kitsu once more, he felt a pang of guilt run through his chest. Why did he have need of the jewel when he already possessed immortal life and a lover who would never die? Would the jewel drive a wedge between himself and Kitsu as his lust for power grew? And then the most troubling question of all slipped into his mind: If forced to choose between the jewel and Kitsu, which would he choose? His eyes widened as the shock of his own thoughts reverberated though his mind. Guilt swept through him as he pulled Kitsu closer and tried to push such thoughts from his mind. She could sense in him that something was amiss even though his embrace brought a smile of contentment to her lips.

Seeing Kitsu smile seemed to drive all of his dark thoughts away. Never again would he allow himself to entertain such thoughts. He leaned closer to her and kissed her gently on the forehead, suddenly wishing he could make love to her there in the limo and banish all memory of what had just transpired in his mind. Pushing the intercom button once more, he spoke to the driver.

"How much longer till we arrive?" he asked.

A moment passed as the driver made a rough estimate in his mind. "Perhaps another ten to fifteen minutes, sir."

Drake smirked and looked at his watch. The would-be ambush had delayed them, but hardly enough to made a difference in their schedule. "Make it take twenty, and do not interrupt us again unless it is urgent."

"Yes, sir."

Kitsu could not help but laugh. "Want to continue what we started earlier?"

"Yes," Drake said softly. "I want to thank you for understanding me so completely."

"There is no need for you to thank me," she answered quietly.

Drake's genuine, slow spreading smile was all the thanks she needed. She tilted her head up and kissed him tenderly on his lips. For Kitsu and Drake as creator and creation, truly loving one another required a complete abandonment of such roles. Thus far into their relationship, they had been completely successful.

"Another kiss would be nice," Kitsu murmured with a soft smile.

Reaching over to a conveniently placed knob, Drake dimmed the lights down to only accents. The interior softly glowed with a candle-like illumination. Beside him Kitsu twiddled with the controls of a stereo receiver, which soon filled the cabin with soft romantic music.

When they both finished, they fell back into each other's arms.

"We don't have much time," Drake sighed as a strange chill touched the back of his neck.

"Then we will have to make the most of what we have left," Kitsu replied happily.

CHAPTER 10
THE MISTRESS

*W*ho am I?

Some distance away in the nightclub, far away from the dance floor, in the private chambers of the owner, stood a nude woman in front of four mirrors. Innumerable candles surrounded her, brightly illuminating the features of her body. Her hands loosely laced together as she held them just below her navel. She gazed deeply into her reflection, searching for the inner calm that she would need for her plan to succeed. What she saw in the mirror was a cold, calculating, and, putting narcissism aside, very beautiful woman. When she closed her eyes for a moment she could not recognize the woman staring back at her when she reopened them.

I've changed so much, physically and mentally. Yet, still, I do not know if I am ready to go through with this.

Her lack of recognition in herself dealt a crushing blow to her confidence. It had taken her years to plan and prepare for her masterpiece, and soon it would be complete, yet she was having trouble dealing with the face in the mirror. Taking a hairbrush with a handle made of bone, she ran it through her long hair. A smile spread across her lips as she saw a man slowly approaching her from behind through the mirror.

"All is in preparation, Mistress," the monotone male voice said from behind her.

She watched his reflection as he knelt behind her. With her moment of doubt dispelled by the appearance of her most trusted servant, the Mistress turned and looked down upon the obedient form. He was strongly built, even though his age was clearly advanced. Such a physique could only be maintained by a lifetime of training and discipline. Contrary to his conditioning, his short hair lay unkempt, a clear sign that he regarded other things as more important.

"Good," she said as she reached down and tangled her fingers in his hair. "Now look at me."

The kneeling man was confused. "Mistress?" he asked.

"I want you to look at me," she repeated, slowly pushing his head back and forcing him to gaze upon her.

His blue eyes welled up with tears, though no emotion shone through them. A twisted grin tore its way across the Mistress's face when she saw his reaction. Commanding such complete control over this man sent shivers through her core and filled her with a consuming sense of ecstasy.

"Why are you crying, servant?" she asked in a cold, self-pleased voice.

"I, I do not know, Mistress," the man stammered as the tears continued to roll down his cheeks.

She continued to play with his hair. "Am I not beautiful? Am I not your every desire?"

Silently, the man nodded.

She then lowered her voice until it was barely a whisper. "I know why you are crying, my pet, and perhaps one day, if you serve me well, I will tell you." She took her hand from his hair. "Now, bring me my dress."

Her servant vanished into the darkness as she turned back to her mirrors. He returned silently after a few brief moments. After kneeling once more, he extended his arms as he offered the Mistress her clothing. Along with dress there were several undergarments, which the Mistress took first. She dressed silently as her servant stared blankly straight ahead.

"Now," the Mistress said without thanks. "you may return to your other duties."

Several minutes later, the Mistress left her quarters and made the short walk to the security room of the nightclub. The room was illuminated solely by the cold harsh glow of computer monitors. In a chair in front of the monitors sat a black-haired man. He had long ago abandoned his birth name in exchange for the alias of Rastis. Only the Mistress knew his real name, and she kept it well hidden. Like the rest of the staff of the Nocturne, he would gladly lay his life on the line for her. Rastis was once on the verge of being caught as a hacker and charged with high crimes when the Mistress appeared to him, offering salvation.

"Have our special guests arrived yet, Rastis?"

The Mistress stood so close to him that he found it almost unbearable. She was excruciatingly beautiful, with long reddish brown hair that flowed in waves to the small of her back. Her voice was deep as she spoke but not as deep as her eyes, which were an unfathomable pale blue. Rastis struggled not to take his gaze from the monitors as he made his reply: "Yes, Mistress."

Rastis motioned to two monitors where Kehl could still be seen sitting in a booth. In the other screen, Leigh seemed to be lost in one of the large picture frames.

"Switch to the thermal cameras," the Mistress commanded.

Rastis flipped a switch and the screens all exploded into vibrant shifting colors. If there were any inhuman visitors to her club, she wanted to know. Most of her invitations were to carefully selected guests, but a few invitations had also found their way to random patrons in order to generate interest. Several counterfeit invitations had also turned up; some were even crudely crafted with construction paper.

"I can't make him out now. Where is he?" she asked, taking a step closer to the monitors.

"Here," Rastis said, indicating a dark blue silhouette of a strongly built man surrounded by the brighter colors that represented warm humans. "He's been sitting there for some time now. He is almost invisible on the thermal cameras. He is obviously not human. Is he a vampire?"

"Yes," she replied. "And a very old one at that. What of Leigh? What is she doing?"

Rastis changed the screens around as he spoke. "She actually seemed to be doing some reconnaissance earlier, but other than that she has done nothing suspicious. Last time I saw her she was talking to Richard up on the catwalks. Here she is."

The Mistress looked to the screen and saw a sunburst of color in the shape of an athletic young woman.

"Switch the cameras back to normal," she said, watching closely as the screens turned back to the normal spectrum.

Even on the computer screen, the Mistress could see that Leigh had a natural beauty about her, and a supple, powerful body. A hint of jealousy crept into her heart as she gazed at the girl. Her plans could potentially be jeopardized by Leigh's comely appearance. Even more alarming, she felt herself strangely attracted to the young woman.

"They actually happened upon each other out on the dance floor earlier. It seemed like he tried to show her how to dance."

"What!" the Mistress growled, pressing her fist down on the security desk.

Rastis did not understand her sudden outburst, but wisely decided not to dwell on it.

"They took a table together, but she stormed off suddenly," he continued.

In the blink of an eye, the Mistress regained her composure. It seemed that Leigh and Kehl's brief encounter may have played out exactly as she would have wanted. Her eyes remained locked firmly on screens as she thought through the many possible reasons of why they may have split up.

"Have they talked since?"

"No, not at all. Oh, by the way, here is your earpiece," Rastis said, successfully changing the subject as he handed the Mistress a very small earpiece radio.

"Is this the one you've been working on?" She immediately took it from him and slipped it carefully into her ear.

"Yes," he answered. "It uses the bone-conducting technology that I borrowed from the military."

The Mistress smiled slightly at his use of the term "borrowing." "So you've worked out all of the kinks, then?"

"Yes, they should function properly now. If you need help, just ask for it like I was right next to you, and I will hear you no matter what is going on around you."

"I shouldn't need any help."

The thought of the Mistress needing help sent shivers down Rastis's spine. Her very presence dominated all those that she met. She was powerful, rich, and attractive, and though her staff bore absolute loyalty to her, they could not help but feel intimidated by her presence. Rastis turned to watch as she walked away. Underneath her sparkling stardust dress he could see her sensuous form glide against the fabric.

An almost painful wave of guilt tore its way through his mind as his eyes moved below her waist. He turned his eyes back to the monitors and tried to force the blooming daydreams out from his head. He needed to concentrate on the job at hand. Death would find him before his Mistress would find him failing her. Rubbing at his eyes with his hands, he attempted to clear his mind.

The Mistress paused at the door. "Do you have a girlfriend, Rastis?"

"No, I don't, Mistress," he quickly replied, unsure of where this line of conversation would lead as he turned to look at her. Had she noticed him looking at her body?

"Have you met the girl running the reception area?"

"Brittany?" he said with the hint of a smile. "Just in passing."

"She has a crush on you," she said as bluntly as possible.

Rastis's jaw dropped as he gawked and tried to think of something to say. "Are you sure?"

"Quite. No offense, but she has a thing for geeks, and you are quite the example."

All Rastis could do was grin happily. He'd secretly wanted to ask the girl out as soon as he'd laid eyes on her, but thought himself hopeless. Now that he knew a glimmer of hope did indeed exist, he would waste no time. He immediately decided that on his first break he would go to the lobby and ask her out. The Mistress, seeing Rastis's mind racing, took the opportunity to exit. Her actions may have seemed like kindness, but in reality she had indeed caught him staring at her body. While it was true that the coat check girl had a crush on Rastis, the Mistress only saw fit to tell Rastis as a means to an end. She did not want the burden of his affections weighing her down.

CHAPTER 11
SPECIAL INVITATIONS

After leaving the security room, the Mistress made her way through the winding halls of the Nocturne. Tonight was the night of her public debut. Right now, her confidence in her plan was now absolute. It had taken so much work and careful planning to bring these events to bear that even through her elation she almost felt weary and ready for the long-sought conclusion. Tonight would change everything for both her and her two unsuspecting guests.

Ever constant in her club, the bass pounded louder as she made her way to an inconspicuous door. This was it. Her hand paused at the doorknob; all the pieces were in place, and it was now up to her to set them in motion. Her masterpiece was almost ready, and the time had come to complete it. A smile crossed her lips as she gripped the doorknob firmly, opened the door, and stepped through.

A sea of living bodies met her eyes as she stepped into the deejay's box at the head of the dance floor. The deejay noticed her entrance and instantly lowered the volume of the music. With a wave of his hand, he signaled for all of the house spotlights to focus on the Mistress. Silence gradually fell upon the surprised dancers as all eyes turned to look up at her. She found the experience both exhilarating add slightly arousing with everyone waiting eagerly for her to speak.

"Good evening, ladies and gentlemen!" she shouted, throwing her arms up into the air. "Welcome to the Midnight Nocturne! I, as you may have guessed, am the Mistress of the Nocturne. You have all been invited here tonight to celebrate the passing of the winter solstice, a night long surrounded by mystery, intrigue, and romance!"

The crowd roared in agreement as the Mistress took advantage of the brief moment to scan across the crowd and find her special guests.

"Now now," she said, hushing the crowd with her hands. "Don't get too rowdy yet. The night is still young, and the real party doesn't begin until the stroke of midnight."

Once more the crowd erupted in applause, but this time the Mistress let it die out on its own.

"Several of our guests have received special invitations requiring their presence. If those of you would please make your way to Terrance." A spotlight panned to light the bouncer up in one corner of the dance floor. "He will be most glad to lead you to my private chambers. As for the rest of you, enjoy your evening at the Nocturne and remember," the Mistress said with a wink, "it's the longest night of the year, so make the most of it!"

Throwing her hands up once more, the music immediately resumed at its full volume, and the club was once more alive with the rhythmic motion of hundreds of bodies. It was only a short walk back from the deejay box back to her chambers. Again she paused in front of the door. She could sense that someone was waiting for her on the other side. A slight smirk crossed her lips. She only allowed two people free access to her chambers, and she knew for a fact that one of them was currently on an errand.

"Hello, Richard," she chirped as she opened the door and stepped into a luxurious leather-clad entrance chamber.

The man who Leigh had met earlier stood in the center of the room waiting for the Mistress. His mask lay abandoned, discarded onto one of several coffee tables spread about the room. He had a handsome, careworn face that showed not only his great wealth but also the struggle that it had been to acquire it. He smoothly offered the spare glass of wine he had been carrying to the Mistress.

"I'm afraid it's grown a bit warm," he warned with a bit of an ironic grin.

The Mistress grinned slightly and waved the glass away.

"I actually prefer my drinks a bit on the warm side, but I must regretfully decline, Richard. We have business to attend to tonight."

"As you wish, Mistress," Richard replied, not sounding in the least bit disappointed as he downed the extra wine in a single gulp.

In the five years that he had done business with the lady standing before him, Richard still didn't know much about her past. She had appeared one day while Richard had been preparing his bankruptcy papers. She had presented him with an irresistible deal: he would have complete control over several large companies and handle all of her substantial finances. If the companies were to crash and burn, he would take sole responsibility and accordingly go down with the ship. In reality, he was little more than a puppet, but he could conduct business regularly and have use of a private jetliner. The puppet enjoyed his role.

"The guests should be here any moment," the Mistress said as she moved further into the room. The words had hardly escaped her lips when there was a soft tap at the door.

"The first guest has arrived, Mistress," came a soft voice from the other side.

"Show them in, Terrance," the Mistress called in greeting.

As ordered, Terrance opened the door and showed a tall, handsome man with long dark hair through the door. It was Kehl. His precisely cut suit was still slightly wrinkled from his earlier motorcycle ride. As he removed his mask, he looked over the room appraisingly. A pang of anger shot through the Mistress as she caught sight of his gray eyes. Something in their depths made her want to fly across the room and rip his throat out.

Masking her anger, she introduced him to Richard instead. "Richard, I would like you to meet Kehl Sanria."

Rather than flinching at the use of his proper name, which under normal circumstances was well hidden, Kehl crossed the room in a few strides and took Richard strongly by the hand.

"Nice to meet you, Richard."

"We have heard so very much about you, Kehl," the Mistress said with a sly smile.

"Then that must mean that you are the Mistress," Kehl replied, his expression giving away no hints as to his true emotions.

"Call me Olivia, please," she said in a neutral tone.

Kehl's hand snaked out almost faster than the eye could see, but as it touched her hand, it was so soft a touch that it was more of a caress. Gently, he lifted it to his lips and kissed it, subtly inhaling her scent of roses and barbed wire. Deep down and hidden in his mind, his thoughts turned to Leigh, although he didn't know why. He'd only met the girl a short while ago. In an immortal life, such immediately developing feelings seemed irrational.

"You won't bite, will you?" Olivia asked, biting at her lip in a wry grin.

Instead of dropping her hand in shock, Kehl rather kissed it once more and let it go easily.

"So you know," Kehl said, somewhat unsurprised. He glanced back at Richard before returning his eyes back toward Olivia.

"Yes, I do. It seems a man named Rallos Alexander founded a small monastery on the outskirts of Braunburg following the death of his daughter. He spent the rest of his natural days praying to his god for answers."

A frown clouded Kehl's brow. "For his sake, did he ever find any?"

"None whatsoever. His efforts to record the events surrounding his daughter's murder did answer some of our questions about you, however. Many of his records still exist to this day in the ruins of that place."

Kehl's heart sank as he realized that this woman seemed to know more about him than even he did. His gaze lowered in thought as fresh waves of guilt broke upon his conscious with the mention of murder. Images of Rana laying dead in her wedding bed flashed into his mind. And what of this new girl he suddenly found himself interested in? Would the same happen to her if he were to lose control?

"I know how you were tortured," Olivia continued in a soft voice. "I know how you bore the suffering until the day there were no more of the Alexander family to bring you pain."

Compassion was no stranger to Kehl, even though his heart was cold and dead. It surprised him, ever so slightly, to hear such a tone in this strange woman's voice. His eyes instinctively met hers, and he saw something deep and hidden in their depths. A slow moment passed as Kehl watched Olivia deftly conceal her emotions beneath an icy gaze. Her tone carried its playful lilt once more as she continued.

"It seems that despite the fact that you were responsible for the death of his daughter, Rallos bore you no ill will. In fact, he tried to save your life, petitioning his estranged family for your freedom. In return, they disowned him and cast him from their home."

Anger and sadness boiled up inside of Kehl. He had come tonight in hopes of forgetting his past and maybe of forgetting that he was even a vampire for the briefest of moments. It seemed though that the past proved to be a vicious, pugnacious foe that would not easily be vanquished.

"Is this why you have brought me here?" he hissed. "To raise up the demons of my past? If so, then I believe I must ask your leave."

Olivia acted as if he had never spoken and ignored him as he walked to the door.

"What if I told you that Rana still drew breath?" she called with a businesslike tone.

Kehl's fangs bared in the blink of an eye as he threw his gaze over his shoulder. He stopped just short of the door."What?" he exclaimed.

Kehl was suddenly furious at the thought that he had suffered and secluded himself for centuries when all along Rana remained alive and well. His hand crept up to his forehead as a million thoughts and memories rushed past his mind's eye. Most confusing of all was the presence in his thoughts of the girl he had just met in the club. The night had just turned very, very unpleasant.

"How is that possible?" he asked, knowing that the question was futile. He could see the triumphant rise of Olivia's eyebrows and the keenness in her expression. He had more than taken the bait and would now have to hear her out.

Another soft knock came at the door, interrupting Olivia before she made any reply. Once more she bade Terrance grant the guest entry. The door swung open silently to allow Leigh entrance. She had only taken a few steps into the room before she stopped short, as if having run into a brick wall. The mask she wore hid her expression as she glanced back and forth between Olivia and Kehl.

Tearing off her mask and throwing it away, she jabbed a finger at Kehl,

"Wait—" she growled as she realized that he was the other special guest who had been greeted so royally at the entrance. "You were the one on the motorcycle, weren't you?"

She couldn't believe it. He had said that they had met before, but *briefly*. The encounter had been brief indeed, and he'd been wearing a helmet at the time. The edges of Kehl's lips turned up in a smile that completely masked the maelstrom of emotions that were currently at war inside his skull. Here was this girl, thrust into his affairs against all odds for the second time that night.

"I'm sorry, Leigh, I found myself running late for an appointment. *This* appointment in fact, and I must confess that I have a slight affinity for speed."

"Yeah, yeah, whatever. Your *slight* affinity almost *slightly* wrecked my Mustang! And don't call me, Leigh," she shouted. "It's Miss Bryant to you."

The thought that she was shouting at such a gorgeous man made Leigh feel queasy to her stomach. In fact, she had admired the speed of his reflexes at having escaped the collision. Even through her current fury, she was still curious about his motorcycle. She locked her eyes on Kehl and noticed that he was about to reply before he was suddenly interrupted.

"My, my, my," Richard murmured as he bent over and retrieved Leigh's mask. "You were gorgeous with your mask on, but with it off you are simply stunning."

Leigh's eyes, already narrowed with her agitation at Kehl, now turned towards Richard. She inadvertently fixed on him with a malicious look that was a little more intense than she had intended. Her deepest desire for that split second was to punch one of them, but which one? Her anger at Kehl was intense, even though it felt strangely empty. In reality, Richard had just paid her a compliment, even though it made him seem a bit sleazy due to his timing.

"Mistress," Richard said, without taking his eyes from Leigh, "would I be correct in assuming that this is Miss Leigh Bryant? The only child of the legendary vampire hunter, Jesse Bryant."

"Yes, she is," Olivia chimed in pleasantly. "My name is Olivia, and this is my business manager, Richard."

Richard bowed slightly before Olivia continued. "I do hope you don't mind me calling you by your first name, but it feels like we already know you."

"I don't understand," Leigh said with a mistrustful look at the strange woman standing in front of her.

"I had the pleasure of employing your father in England," Olivia answered. "In fact, he is still working for me now."

Leigh mentally recoiled as Olivia stepped forward to her. In the rare and brief occasions that her father called, he never once mentioned having taken on active jobs. Was it possible that what was going on might be something more than a purely professional situation? Olivia was a very attractive woman, and with her father being single, how could Leigh blame him? Reluctantly, she decided for the moment to assume that it really was just a job. She still couldn't grasp what possible reason would be important enough to bring her father out of retirement.

"He told me to tell you that, 'Just because we perceive a thing *as* evil, that it doesn't mean that it necessarily *is* evil.'"

"So he *is* working for you?" Leigh was surprised by the quotation but still suspicious. "How did you find him?"

"It was a chance meeting in the Queen's Rose Garden. I was there on business, and he merely seemed to be sightseeing. We started talking and soon after we had a business deal."

This information only made Leigh trust Olivia less. Her father was a well-traveled man who'd seen many foreign lands. It seemed odd that he would be so interested in sightseeing in his adopted country, especially having already seen many of the wonders of the world. Even so, how could anyone deny sightseeing in one of the most beautiful, historic countries in the world? Sometimes Leigh envied her father in his retirement.

"He doesn't usually make acquaintances with strangers," she interjected.

Olivia grinned in a coy way. "He had his reasons … Would you like to speak with him?"

Leigh raised an eyebrow and looked at Kehl, who seemed lost in his thoughts, and then back at Olivia. "Yes, I think I would."

"Richard, if I may borrow your cell phone?" Olivia said without ever taking her eyes off Leigh, even when Richard handed her the phone. She flipped it open and pushed one of the speed dial buttons.

Leigh could hear the numbers swiftly dial themselves on the phone as Olivia put it to her ear. After a few rings, Leigh heard a voice answer, although she couldn't understand the words.

"Hello, Jesse," Olivia said in a casual, familiar tone. "There is someone here who would like to speak with you."

With little hesitation, Olivia took the phone from her ear and tossed it to Leigh. Leigh caught it and slowly raised it to her ear. This all seemed too easy, too quick. Maybe she, herself, was too green to truly know what was happening.

"Daddy?" she asked cautiously, disbelieving that her father was actually listening on the other end.

"Peepers!" came her father's gruff voice over the phone with his nickname for Leigh.

"Why haven't you called me? It's been at least two months since the last time. You've even picked up a bit of an accent!" she exclaimed as softly as possible as she moved away from the others. She couldn't remember the last time they'd talked and could hardly contain her joy.

"I've been busy, baby. I imagine the Mistress has already told you I'm working for her."

"Yes, Olivia has filled me in," Leigh replied while trying to hide the suspicion in her voice. "I thought you were retired."

"You know how it is," he said with a chuckle. "It gets a little boring just sitting around the house with nothing to do but watch TV."

"You could try reading," his daughter answered.

"I do read," he replied in a silly way that made Leigh laugh.

"Have you at least kept up with your training?"

"Are you kidding me?" He chuckled. "I'm retired ... Of course I have! Wouldn't want anyone catching me getting soft—especially you. Remember, we were supposed to spar the next time you visit."

Leigh felt herself blushing, even over the phone. "You mean the *first* time I visit."

"Meh," her father grunted. "Don't worry about that right now."

Leigh suddenly realized how much she missed having her father nearby. After taking a few steps away from the others, she decided to try and find out what her father was up to.

"So what exactly are you doing for her?"

There was an odd silence on Jesse's end that went on for several moments. Leigh couldn't stop the suspicions that suddenly burst into her mind. There was something that her father could not tell her, and she found herself wondering if her earlier assumptions were true. Not once had her father kept a secret from her before.

"I'm afraid I can't tell you that just yet, Peepers. I'm under a contract of sorts, and you know how it goes with confidentiality and such."

"Yeah, I know how it can be sometimes," Leigh said, slightly irritated that her father had blown her off twice now.

"Anyway, baby, I have some work to finish up and I will be there in a few hours." Leigh heard some scuffling in the background.

"A few hours? Are you back in the States?"

The odd silence returned to the conversation once more. "... Yes, no one is really supposed to know that, though, not even you. Please don't be upset. I am sure that once you accept Olivia's offer you will understand why."

"I don't know if I can do that, Dad, I don't even know what her offer is yet," Leigh answered. "How long have you been back?"

The silence that followed made Leigh's heart ache, and when the answer came, she knew what it would be.

"A while," Jesse said.

Leigh sighed heavily, feeling more uncertain about this strange situation than ever.

"You can trust the Mistress," her father said suddenly.

"Okay," Leigh answered after a moment's pause, but not without misgivings. "I love you."

"Love you too, baby. See you in a little while."

"See you soon, Daddy. And be careful out there. The forecast is calling for some snow tonight."

"I will be on the lookout," he replied before hanging up.

Leigh took the phone from her ear and looked at it in mild disbelief before closing it and tossing it back to Olivia. She was now slightly miffed not only with Kehl and Richard but with her father as well. How long was he going to be back in the States before letting her know? It irritated her to no end, but it seemed there was no choice left but to see what Olivia had in store for her.

CHAPTER 12

THE JEWEL

As Leigh turned her eyes toward Kehl, she had to wonder if Olivia had used the knowledge of his vampirism as leverage to force her proposal. It seemed very plausible, even though she didn't really know all that much about the man. What she did know was that the two of them both seemed firmly snared in Olivia's web. There now seemed little left for either of them to do but play along.

"Anyway, back to business," Olivia said. "This is the waiting room for my private chambers. I rather enjoy getting the introductions done here before proceeding to a more comfortable area. Now, if the both of you would please follow me."

"Mind if I tag along?" Richard asked Olivia, with a sideways glance at Leigh.

"You may," Olivia answered.

She then led them away from the small sitting room to a dark hallway adorned with several paintings and lit only by concealed lights. The floors were made of a black marble that had been polished and shined to a mirror shine on which not a speck of dust dared trespass. As they walked further down the hall, one particular frame made Leigh pause. Instead of a painting, the frame had been adapted to hold bladed weapons.

"These are … interesting," Leigh commented as she eyed the half dozen blades in the case as the rest of the group moved on.

All the weapons bore a jet-black finish and displayed several inlaid jewels. Two fighting knives had emeralds laid into their handles, while beneath them sat a long blackened katana with a red and black grip with inlaid rubies. Three throwing knives fanned out at the bottom of the case—in each of their centers sat a massive sapphire.

"These are beautiful," Leigh murmured to herself. "Though I don't see how they would ever be very tactical with the jewels and all. And I don't understand why the blades are black."

"Oh, those things," Olivia said dismissively as she too came to a stop. "They are merely decorative relics. Come, come now."

Leigh took one more glance at the blades before rejoining the others. She noted that there was little need to keep show pieces sharpened, but she could tell with just a glance that the weapons were surgically honed. They were a little flashy for her tastes, but she definitely liked them and wondered if they would become part of her assignment.

"Where exactly are we going, Mistress?" Kehl asked as Leigh caught up.

"To my inner sanctum," Olivia answered darkly before flashing them all a mischievous grin.

Richard narrowed his eyes as Olivia laughed merrily and turned her eyes forward. She was not usually in such a mood.

"Just kidding," she continued. "It's nothing quite as sexy as all that. It's more like my living room."

The hallway ended abruptly at two massive hardwood doors stained so deeply a shade of red that they looked black. Richard stepped forward to take hold of the two intricate brass knobs before pushing the doors open. Leigh half-expected to see a decadent waste of money as the doors swung open but instead saw a continuation of the same theme. Black marble floors with black walls, illuminated by the same concealed lighting .

In the middle of the room, centered around a moderately sized coffee table, there were several deeply cushioned crimson chairs as well as a medium-sized flat-panel television. Functional or Spartan would have been the best words to describe the arrangement. Leigh was surprised to see it was nothing more than a simple loft apartment. Olivia's permanent lodgings must have been located elsewhere, in a more spacious and luxurious location.

"Please, take a seat," Olivia said as she motioned toward the comfortable-looking furniture.

They all did as they were directed. Kehl took an easy chair to himself while Leigh sat on one end of a loveseat. She felt slightly uncomfortable as Robert immediately made his way to sit down right beside her. Olivia walked over to stand directly in front of the television. Her higher position naturally gave her the appearance of command and an air of authority.

"Now that we are all comfortable, Olivia, would you please explain yourself and tell us what business you have with us," Kehl said.

His voice was calm and controlled, allowing no room to doubt his seriousness.

"Of course," Olivia replied.

"I have brought you here because I have a problem," she continued. "And it is no simple affair that would affect only myself. Rather, it is far more important than that. You see, I have come into the possession of a certain jewel, the very one after which my club is named."

Kehl's eyes narrowed briefly in thought and then widened considerably. Leigh, on the other hand, listened neutrally, having no idea of what jewel Olivia spoke of.

Kehl's voice carried a slight note of disbelief as he questioned Olivia further. "You actually have the Midnight Nocturne?"

"I do," she answered simply.

"What is the Midnight Nocturne?" Leigh asked.

"It is perhaps the most sought after jewel on the entire planet," Olivia answered. "As well as the most flawed."

"I've never heard of it before," Leigh said quietly.

"Then tell me," Olivia queried, "how familiar are you with the diamond industry?"

"Not at all really. I don't have time or the money to really have any interest in it," Leigh answered.

"Then let me explain the basics of the industry as briefly as possible. The jewelry dealers of the world would have you believe that diamonds are the rarest commodity on the planet and that flawless diamonds are the most valuable of the lot."

Leigh nodded.

"To the contrary, diamonds are actually one of the most common gems on the planet. It is only their regulation and presentation that makes them valuable. And since diamonds are so common, sometimes it is the flawed examples that are that much more valuable."

"I don't understand," Leigh said.

"Imagine if humans were each identical and flawless like diamonds. Everyone would be exactly the same and things would become very uninteresting and boring in a short amount of time. The same holds true for rare jewels. Just like individual people stand out in a crowd, so too do unique diamonds. Speaking in those terms, the Midnight Nocturne is truly one of a kind."

"The Nocturne is said to be the most flawed diamond in existence," Kehl reiterated. "Some also believe that it has special, supernatural properties."

"I can assure you, Kehl," Olivia said, effectively cutting him off, "that both of your statements are indeed true. But tell me, how much do you know of its history?"

"Not much," he answered. "Only that it was discovered in the tomb of a forgotten pharaoh in the early 1930s. There was some scandal as to who was the rightful owner. Obviously, it should have been considered one of the historical treasures of Egypt. Its discoverers felt otherwise. After changing hands several times and becoming the subject of several scandals, it vanished into the black market several years into World War II."

Leigh's eyes turned to Kehl as she began to wonder just how old he was. "You were alive during the thirties?"

"Yes, though I don't know if 'alive' is the proper term."

"How old are you now?" she pressed.

"Old enough to remember that the jewel interested me greatly. Some of my kind even suggested that it may have been the key to curing our ... condition."

A distant look crossed Kehl's face as he suddenly grew silent.

"Regardless of how old Kehl might be," Olivia interjected, "he is correct about the discovery of the jewel. Can you remember in which tomb the Nocturne was found?"

Kehl remained quiet for a few more moments as he tried to remember. "In the tomb of Amenhotep, I believe."

Olivia smiled in a most patronizing way. "You are only partially correct. The tomb was indeed that of the pharaoh Amenhotep IV, but that is not the name he chose for himself in life. He chose instead to be known by the name Akhenaten. He was the first pharaoh to try to convert all of Egypt from a polytheistic religion to a monotheistic one under a single god. He nearly succeeded. His legacy is directly tied to the history of the Midnight Nocturne and its creation."

"Its creation?" Leigh asked. "Like I said before, I don't know much about the diamond industry, but isn't it impossible to make a true diamond?"

"Yes, but this one is quite different. Keep in mind though that the Midnight Nocturne is completely indistinguishable from a natural gem."

Kehl found this last bit of information to be the most unbelievable piece yet. "If it was man-made, how could you possibly know how it was created? It dates back to the time of the pharaohs."

With an enigmatic smile, Olivia bent over and placed her hands carefully on the sides of the coffee table. With a single fingertip, she pressed a hidden catch, opening a hidden drawer. She then slid it slowly open before reaching inside. What she retrieved from its depths appeared to be the laminated remains of an ancient document. Carefully closing the drawer with one hand, she gently laid the artifact on the surface of the table before sitting down.

"What's this?" Kehl asked as he moved up onto the edge of his seat.

Leigh's curiosity was piqued as she mimicked Kehl in trying to get a better look. Many of the creatures that she dealt with on a fairly regular basis were things that were known only in ancient myth and every bit of information she could acquire might one day be lifesaving. As her eyes fell on the deteriorated piece of parchment on the table, she felt as though she were being pulled deeper into something that she had little hope of fully understanding.

"This," Olivia answered, "is a document that has been handed down through my family for generations. It is one of the few remaining scrolls to have survived the destruction of the Library of Alexandria."

"How can you be sure it is legitimate?" Leigh asked. "The world is full of counterfeit artifacts."

"Unfortunately, my family history is the only proof that I can provide. During the Crusades of the middle- to late-thirteenth century, one of my ancestors served as a British spy. He was a master linguist and eventually secured himself an important position among the ranks of Frederick II. Frederick, at the time he started his crusade, was the current Holy Roman Emperor. His crusade was both a success, in that he secured Jerusalem, and a failure in that he was excommunicated from the church for his disagreements with the Pope."

Kehl was reluctantly starting to become interested in the tale. "Is Frederick tied to the jewel as well?"

"Only in the fact that he sent my forbearer on missions that carried him throughout Egypt and its surrounding areas."

Leigh also found herself being drawn in. "What was his name?"

"He kept his true name very secret. The alias that he traveled under during those times was Berenger. On his last mission before returning to Europe, his team became lost in a sandstorm out in the Egyptian desert. They somehow stumbled upon the ruins of what had once been a fortified complex. The storm forced them to take refuge inside. What they found when the maelstrom subsided was a treasure beyond imagining."

"Was that where they found the scroll?" Kehl asked.

"Yes," Olivia said with a nod, "along with many others. Someone managed to save them during the destruction of the Library of Alexandria and spirit them safely into the desert. Berenger took several of the scrolls that they found there as proof of the discovery. His role as a British spy mandated that he keep the most important information for his true king and crown. Before returning to Frederick with the information, he translated the scrolls to the best of his abilities and uncovered this treasure." Olivia motioned to the paper sitting on the coffee table.

"What happened to the rest of the scrolls?" Leigh asked.

"Unfortunately, the rest of the complex was buried by another sandstorm before Frederick or the English could ever plunder its stored knowledge. For all anyone knows it may still be intact, buried somewhere under the desert. Berenger handed over several of the retrieved scrolls to his false master and several to his true masters in England, but he kept this one here for his own family to take advantage of one day."

"So what does it say?" Kehl asked.

"It is a record that has survived since biblical times. It follows the life of the third son of Adam and Eve, Seth. He created the Kauket Stone, the jewel that we know today as the Midnight Nocturne. This scroll tells the story of his life and death and chronicles the most important thing he ever accomplished."

"I'm not so sure that I believe all of this," Leigh said as her eyes narrowed a bit.

"Why not?" Olivia replied. "The Bible chronicles the lives of many important figures, and many people believe it to be the absolute canon of Christianity. Why would it be so surprising that the life of Seth would not be important enough to garner attention? Many people find it odd that he is not mentioned more in religious texts. The Bible pretty much just says that he went out and lived his own life, worshiping God and leaves it at that."

"Also," Kehl added, "some scholars believe that the original writings contained in the Bible were stored somewhere along with the many thousands upon thousands of scrolls destroyed along with the Library of Alexandria. If those scrolls hadn't been burned, the Bible would probably be a much different book. Thousands of years' worth of knowledge literally went up in smoke with the destruction of the library."

"I've heard of the library," Leigh snapped at Kehl. "And I have heard of that particular theory."

"Then why would it be so odd that several documents survived?" Olivia suggested.

"It's not," Leigh answered calmly. "I'm just a little skeptical. I didn't mean for you to stop telling us about the scroll."

Olivia smiled slightly. "Then I shall continue, starting at the beginning. And I must ask you not to debate any of the theories surrounding its creation, if only for the sake of better understanding its importance."

Kehl nodded immediately, followed somewhat reluctantly by Leigh.

"Adam and Eve had three children soon after leaving the Garden of Eden: Cain, Abel, and Seth. It is also assumed by some historians that there were many, many children omitted by the Bible. Both Adam and Eve, along with their children, were said to have lived hundreds upon hundreds of years. Our scroll picks up with Seth about halfway through his life.

"Now, whether you choose to believe that the earth was populated solely by the children of Adam and Eve or that there were perhaps other people already here, Seth somehow found a wife, Azura. The scroll states that together they started not one but several of the ancient civilizations together. Their children were initially raised to believe in a single god and, like their parents, enjoyed incredibly longevity."

"It almost sounds like they were immortal, though in a much different way than me," Kehl said softly.

"And like you," Olivia said with a strange note in her voice, "they were different than normal people today. They were blessed with miraculous and almost superhuman abilities.

"The scroll says that as more and more time passed, Seth and Azura took to the deserts of Africa after starting the tribes that would eventually come together to form the Egyptian empire. Centuries later and after the death of his beloved wife Azura, Seth emerged from the desert alone to find a world changed. Without his and Azura's influence, many of their children and several of the other children of Adam and Eve had fashioned themselves into gods. The small tribal communities he remembered were now grown into the bustling civilizations of the ancient world.

"He was greatly saddened to find that many of his children now warred among themselves. Word reached his ears of great battles in which a great many of his offspring had killed one another. It brought to his mind memories of his brothers, Cain and Abel. Immediately trying to set things right, Seth made his way to the capitol city of the largest civilization on earth at that time."

Kehl now saw the connection to Akhenaten. "Egypt?"

"Correct," Olivia replied. "The scroll even provides proof for itself in a small bit of information that is widely known today. It mentions briefly that his after his departure into the desert that Seth was deified by his children and followers."

"I've never heard of the god 'Seth'" Leigh said, although with perhaps a little less skepticism than before.

"Oh, but you have," Olivia answered. "His name was originally pronounced with a sharp T on the end. It was not until much later and in a different language that the softer *th* was added. His name to the ancient Egyptians was Set, the Egyptian god of the very desert in which he made his home with Azura."

Leigh's eyes widened ever so slightly. She had indeed heard of the god Set.

"Ironically, the scroll says he was unrecognized by his people upon his return and was unable to gather any followers. After an unspecified amount of time, he spirited himself into the private chambers of the then newly appointed pharaoh Amenhotep IV."

"How did he manage that, I wonder?" Kehl mused as he rubbed at his chin. "The pharaohs were some of the most jealously guarded monarchs of all time."

"The scroll describes Seth as having the same almost-superhuman abilities as his relatives," Olivia answered. "Perhaps being among the first children of Adam and Eve magnified his talents even more. I'm positive he had a keen intellect as well. Regardless of how he gained access to the pharaoh, the scroll says that he quickly earned the trust of Amenhotep. Within the course of several months, he then managed to convert the pharaoh into believing in a single god. Amenhotep soon changed his name to Akhenaten and started to convert all of Egypt into the belief of one god. The name of the single god was Aten, and if you break down the two parts of Ahkenaten's name, it literally means the servant of Aten. Aten meant in turn either the sun or the disc, depending on how you translated it. Either way, it still referenced the same astral body as viewed by the ancient mind.

"During his reign, Seth and Akhenaten were largely successful in promoting this monotheistic religion. Even though it seemed similar to sun worship, Seth accepted it as a proper representation of his and his parents' god. Slowly, he and Akhenaten brought about the ideas that would make Aten an omnipresent deity nearly identical to the modern Christian god in twentieth-century interpretations. With the influence of the Egyptian empire behind him, Seth managed to stop much of the conflict between the descendants of Adam and Eve. Toward the end of Akhenaten's rule, both the pharaoh and Seth began to realize that with their passing, the world would soon return to the way it was before. Many of the older Egyptians still believed in other gods or godlike beings but were left no choice but to alter their practices when their pharaoh demanded a change.

"The strongest opposition came from the priests of the ousted sun god, Amun-Ra, who at one time had been nearly synonymous with Aten. Akhenaten argued that Amun-Ra was merely one of Aten's creations and could never be a true symbol of his glory. He then proceeded to ban all Amun-Ra worship. For years the former priests of the ousted sect plotted the assassination of both Seth and Akhenaten. Their attempts were never successful. There were also several other 'gods' ousted by the pharaoh who chose instead to bide their time. They knew that without Akhenaten, the new monotheistic religion would easily be overturned politically.

"In the document, it then says that Akhenaten's wife, Nefertiti, came forward with an idea that would ensure the survival of monotheism. For many years she'd worn an amulet that seemed to somehow weaken even the most powerful of her adversaries. Some of the people she mentioned encountering with the charm were some of Seth's own children. Seeing the connection of her amulet to his own bloodline, Seth immediately started investigating the jewel. It seemed that when it neared anything even remotely supernatural, it rendered the object or person completely normal. When he brought it close to either himself or his children, it seemed to render them completely human and ordinary."

"Sounds like Kryptonite," Kehl said in a sardonic tone.

"Did the amulet contain the Midnight Nocturne?" Leigh asked, ignoring Kehl's flippant comment.

"No, not entirely. What it had inside was a very fine powder composed of thousands of grain-sized rare gems. The scroll says that Nefertiti showed Akhenaten and Seth the mine where the powder came from but informed them cautiously that the only way to complete a working amulet was to sacrifice a human life. Sacrificing a more powerful person, however, would create a much more powerful amulet. At first the idea of human sacrifice disgusted Seth, and he refused to listen to Nefertiti. She argued that with a powerful enough amulet, he might be able to save countless numbers of lives throughout the endlessness of eternity. With a strong enough amulet, he would be able to suppress not only his own bloodline, but also nearly every other supernatural thing on earth.

"This concept weighed heavily on Seth's conscience, for he knew Nefertiti was right. Akhenaten offered to sacrifice himself, but he was a sickly man and Seth knew wouldn't give the amulet nearly enough power. Additionally, he would never allow it; the pharaoh was far too important to the reborn monotheistic religion to give his life. Unable to bring himself to choose a martyr for his cause, Seth decided to sacrifice himself. At first, Akhenaten refused to allow it. Seth was not only his mentor but also his ancestor. After years of private debate, Seth at last received a fleeting acceptance from Akhenaten. Before the pharaoh could stop him, Seth rushed to the temple of Aten. The scroll doesn't mention the particulars of the ritual, but it does say that the power released during the final ritual was so great that it illuminated the night sky. It seemed that Seth's very soul coalesced around the minute jewels provided by Nefertiti and crystallized with his final breath.

"Akehenaten and Nefertiti named the jewel Kauket. The name held several meanings and was actually the name of the first goddess of the night. The scroll says that perhaps the name was meant to commemorate the hour of Seth's death or to signify the coming of 'night' for the other 'gods' on earth. In ancient Egypt, this would signify their death or 'ending.' It also could be the physical description of the jewel, as gazing into its facets is often compared to looking into the night sky on a cloudless night when the stars are at their brightest."

"Where did the 'Nocturne' part of the name come from?" Leigh asked.

"That part I can answer," Kehl said. "At the time of its discovery, I remember it first being called the Kauket Stone. After it was stolen for the first time, the papers started calling the jewel the Nocturne because of the way it vanished so quickly, like music in the evening air. A short while later, a journalist with a knack for languages translated Kauket, and the name Midnight Nocturne was coined, even though the word *midnight* is probably not the most direct translation."

Olivia nodded once to confirm Kehl's statement.

"If all of this is true, then why are there still things like vampires and werewolves around?" Leigh wondered aloud.

"Some things managed to survive," Olivia answered, "though in a greatly diminished state. Given the virus-like transmission of both lycanthropy and most examples of vampirism, it's no surprise that the diseases mutated in order to survive. The creatures we see today, even as advanced as they may seem, are feral compared to what existed in the ancient world. Kehl here is an exceedingly rare example of his kind. He may even be like the old ones, from the time before the jewel was created."

"Why is that?" Leigh asked as she looked over at Kehl.

"He was born into the world as a vampire, weren't you Kehl?"

"I was born human," Kehl said sternly. "This curse manifested itself much later in my life."

A sudden wave of emotions washed through Leigh as she looked over at Kehl. He was a mystery to her, and this newest insight into his life only made him that much more of an enigma. Her heart began to race at the idea of him once being human. If only she'd met him then, perhaps there would have been some small chance for them.

"Enough about me, what happened to Akhenaten?" Kehl half growled, seeking to change the subject.

"Akhenaten's new religion quickly started to fail immediately following his death. His wife, Nefertiti, and young son, Tutankhamen, found themselves unable to maintain monotheism in the empire. Polytheism soon resumed, although in a weakened state, without the supervision of the once-many gods. In the case of Seth, he was supremely triumphant even after his death. His descendants were now completely human with absolutely no special abilities whatsoever. Their longevity was now also truncated to the span of a single lifetime. His sacrifice gave the jewel far more power than he could have ever imagined. Its influence spread instantly throughout the world in the blink of an eye."

"But there were still were religiously motivated wars," Leigh said. "There still are many going on today."

"That is because of the one thing that Seth or any god could never correct," Olivia rebutted. "Human nature. But Seth was still successful because the people fighting the wars since the creation of the jewel were only mortals. Could you imagine a world torn apart by the constant warring of thousands of godlike men and women? The wars that we have today would seem like children fighting in a sandbox in comparison. Imagine someone a hundred times more powerful than a vampire or a werewolf hell-bent on world domination."

"I understand," Leigh said quietly.

"As for Akhenaten, his existence was largely erased from the pages of history by his successors. Nefertiti and Tutankhamen did their best to preserve his legacy, although they did much of it in secret. Instead of having temples devoted to Aten or Akhenaten destroyed, they cleverly 'recycled' the masonry back into the renewed polytheistic structures. Much of the original artwork and hieroglyphics from Akhenaten's reign still survive to this day because they are on the opposite side of the stone, away from the viewer. Nefertiti most likely ruled Egypt for this short period, at least until Tutankhamen was old enough to ascend to the throne."

"And how are we connected to all of this?" Kehl asked.

"I need help protecting the jewel," Olivia answered plainly.

"From what?" Leigh asked. "Don't you have the jewel locked away safely in some vault somewhere?"

"It is in a vault underneath this very club."

Leigh was incredulous. "Why isn't it locked away in a bank somewhere?"

"The nature of the jewel makes it impossible to trust anyone with its possession. Do you remember how long it stayed in the museums after its discovery before it was stolen, Kehl?" Olivia asked.

"It was such a brief time in such a long life," Kehl answered as he tried to recall. "It couldn't have been more than a week, perhaps two at most."

"The jewel unfortunately provokes an irresistible feeling of covetousness in nearly all who lay eyes on it. Initially Seth planned to have the jewel buried deep within the desert after his death. Akhenaten was unaware of this wish and decided instead to keep the jewel as a trophy of their success. Fortunately Nefertiti was immune to the effects of the jewel, perhaps due to the protection of her own amulet. After the death of her husband, she spirited the jewel into his burial chamber where it remained hidden for all of those years."

Kehl posed a question. "If your ancestor Berenger knew of the location of the jewel, why didn't he seek it out?"

"While the scroll says that the jewel was located in the tomb of Akhenaten, it does not give the exact location of his burial. Also, you must keep in mind that Berenger kept the scroll a secret from both

Frederick II and the British. He could not launch a search for the Midnight Nocturne without giving away his true intentions."

Kehl wanted to know as much about the situation as possible. "If you don't mind me asking, how did you manage to come by the jewel?"

"Why does that matter?"

Kehl shrugged. "I was just curious. You mentioned that the jewel makes people extremely covetous, and I wondered what lengths you had to go to secure it."

Anger crept into Olivia's voice as she spoke. "Are you implying something, Kehl? If you are, then I can guarantee you that you will leave here without any compensation."

Kehl remained silent for a moment before apologizing. "I'm sorry, I couldn't help but be curious. I was actually wondering if it was another one of your ancestors who discovered the tomb of Akhenaten."

Olivia sighed. "It's all right, perhaps I overreacted a little bit. To answer your question, it was not one of my relatives, though I wish it had been. The jewel came to me from an estate auction that cost an unbelievably large sum of money. The men who discovered the tomb of Akhenaten were little more than grave robbers who masqueraded themselves as archaeologists and treasure hunters. They were murdered the night the jewel vanished from the museum. It surfaced again on the black market shortly later and was bought and sold by some of the richest people in the world."

"And now someone wants to steal it from you?" Leigh asked.

"Yes."

"Your club actually does seem rather secure," Leigh said. "Who could be powerful enough to steal the jewel from you?"

"I don't suppose you have ever heard the name Alucard?" Olivia said.

"Who hasn't?" Kehl said with a hint of laughter in his voice. "It's 'Dracula' spelled backward, and it has flourished as a name in literature, movies, and even in video games ever since someone thought it would be clever to reverse the letters."

"That is correct," Olivia answered. "The man who wants to steal the Nocturne from me has been living under this false name for some time now."

"Why would he name himself Alucard?" Leigh mused. "Is he just trying to make himself sound cool, or is he something else?"

"Yes," Olivia answered. "He is something else. A vampire to be specific. I have only met him a handful of times, and as farcical as his name seems, he is a most deadly enemy. At first I considered selling the jewel to him, as he is one of the most avid jewel collectors in the United States. It then came to my attention that he intended to destroy the jewel and free his own true power as an immortal."

"As if being among the children of the night doesn't make him strong enough already," Leigh muttered.

"He wants enough power to allow him to build a world of his own," Olivia continued. "When I told him the deal was off, he threatened to destroy the club. When I refused him once more, he started making threats on my life as well."

"Is he strong?" Leigh asked.

"Very. He also travels with his former master and creator, a woman by the name of Kitsu."

"Are they going to be here tonight?" Kehl queried.

"I do not know if they will be here in person tonight, but I do know for a fact that he plans to launch an attack at midnight."

Leigh frowned. "Why don't you just shut the club down for tonight?"

"Tonight's events have been in the planning for months and cannot be rescheduled. There are more people out there on my dance floors right now than there ever were before. If the club were to close tonight it would take almost a year to recoup the investment I've made."

"So it comes down to money?" Leigh asked. "You would risk all of those people's lives just to make a return on your *investment*?"

"No, I'm not going to risk anyone's life," Olivia answered coldly. "That's why I hired you."

Leigh rubbed her temple with her fingers as she thought about what that might entail.

"Are you usually in the habit of asking your employers such impertinent questions, Leigh? Your father wasn't nearly as difficult to enlist."

Leigh started to reply but couldn't find the words. She knew that Olivia was partly right about her comment. The reference to her father, however, stung like a slap to the face, and she felt that it wasn't entirely appropriate. But under the current circumstances, Leigh would have to play by Olivia's rules, at least until she found out what was going on with her father.

"Besides," Olivia continued with a sideways glance at Kehl, "part of the profits from tonight will help pay you and Kehl for your services. I do plan to compensate you."

Kehl locked a stern expression on Olivia. She knew he had no need for more money. Although he found the history and presence of the jewel intriguing, there was no doubt that something else was going on underneath the surface. Olivia had mentioned the possibility that Rana may still be alive, and the idea unnerved him. Most likely Olivia had dropped the name with the intention of snaring Kehl into her plans.

"Something wrong, Kehl?" Olivia asked.

"I'm just not so sure that I am convinced that I should accept your *offer* just yet," he said.

A slight smile crossed Olivia's lips as she spoke. "Would seeing the jewel convince you?"

Leigh and Kehl looked at one another for a moment in near disbelief. Kehl spoke first. "I think that would do nicely."

"Very well, then. If you will just follow me," Olivia said.

Olivia stood and waited as the others did the same. "I intended to show you the jewel after tonight, but right now will be fine. I should not have expected you to understand its importance without ever having seen it in person."

"Richard," Olivia called into the kitchenette, "I am going to escort Kehl and Leigh to the vaults. You may stay here for the time being or return to dance floor if you wish."

"Yes, Mistress," Richard replied. "I think I may have left a lady waiting somewhere out there."

Richard gave Leigh one last appraising glance before disappearing into the kitchen to prepare himself a drink. Olivia then motioned for Kehl and Leigh to follow her as she made her way out of the living room. Kehl hesitated for a moment with a vacant expression on his face, deciding whether or not to follow. Leigh followed her without pause, intent on discovering how her father was involved with all of this.

Olivia led them further into her quarters and down another dark corridor. The walls were lined with paintings that all seemed to be interpretations of a single great jewel. Kehl and Leigh glanced at the images until they reached a set of mirrored elevator doors at the end of the hallway. Olivia pressed a standard call button but left her thumb resting on its surface for a moment too long. Leigh watched closely as a bright light seemed to pour from inside the button and move up and down against Olivia's fingertip.

"Fingerprint activated call button," she said as she recognized the work. "My father was fond of those."

"He is a very sensible man. I've learned a lot from him since I met him." Olivia turned and gave Leigh an overly friendly smile that seemed completely out of place.

Leigh could hardly believe the intimacy to which Olivia hinted. A sudden anger rose up inside of her, but she directed it more toward her father. If he and Olivia were so close, why would Jesse hide her from Leigh? Why would he have spent so much time with this enigmatic woman and not bother to call his own daughter?

"When things were slow," Leigh said in quiet remembrance, "my father would do security work on the side." Leigh smiled slightly despite the range of emotions pouring through her. "Needless to say, he spent a lot of time doing security work. Vampires, werewolves, and the like are fairly rare."

Kehl looked over at Leigh with an odd expression on his face. She couldn't quite tell if he looked angry, confused, or charmed.

"Sorry," she said with a shake of her head. "I didn't mean any offense."

"None taken," Kehl answered with a smile. "If the story Olivia told us is true, it would easily explain why my kind are so few and far between."

"Indeed," Olivia added as the elevator arrived.

Their reflections in the elevator doors ahead suddenly split in two as they slid silently open. The inside of the elevator was surprisingly spacious and luxurious, with leather-clad armrests, bright lighting, and mirrored walls. Olivia stepped inside and immediately beckoned for Leigh and Kehl to do the same. Leigh hesitated slightly, but Kehl quickly stepped past her and into the elevator. Leigh couldn't explain why, but for some reason she had never liked elevators. Their close, confined interiors, no matter how refined, reminded her of a coffin. She always dismissed the feeling as a side effect of her profession, having often encountered coffins with her father that were still very much occupied.

Leigh sighed and accepted that this was one time when she wouldn't be able to take the stairs. After stepping inside, she positioned herself up against the far corner of the interior. She crossed her arms before taking a spot against the wall, trying desperately to calm her nerves. From her vantage point, the small box of the elevator seemed to be slightly larger, although it wasn't much help. At least she would be comfortable on what would hopefully be a short ride.

"You seem to place a fair amount of trust in us," Kehl said as the doors slid shut and the elevator began to sink.

Leigh glanced over at Kehl's handsome features as he spoke. He had used the word "us" as though they were already working together. Leigh briefly thought of their brief encounter on the dance floor and suddenly felt herself getting dizzy. Leigh could hardly believe the thoughts exploding into her mind. She imagined the two of them alone in the elevator together. Nightmares of being bitten flashed into mind alongside fantasies of tearing away one another's clothes. Leigh closed her eyes, trying to force such thoughts from her mind. The darkness only intensified the intensity her imaginings as a sudden image of Kehl standing shirtless in front of the doors burned its way into her mind. Leigh popped her eyes open and tried in vain to look off into an empty corner of the elevator. Unfortunately, all four walls were mirrored, and there was little else to look at other than Kehl or Olivia.

"I know enough about you two to know what you're capable of," Olivia said after a few moments.

Would you know that I was just daydreaming about having my way with Kehl, right here in this elevator? Leigh thought to herself.

Leigh's eyes widened slightly in disbelief of her own thoughts. Maybe it was just her nerves making her think naughty things because she was in an elevator. Perhaps she was merely experiencing the innate seductive manor of all vampires. There were also the many years spent with no male companions that weren't some sort of physical trainer. In any case, she would have to keep herself under control until she could find some time alone to sort out her emotions.

Olivia remained silent as the elevator made its descent into the depths of the building. Kehl turned and looked back at Leigh, wondering why she blushed suddenly under his gaze.

"Are you okay back there?" he asked.

"Yes," Leigh said quietly before momentarily biting her lip. "Just a bit claustrophobic is all."

CHAPTER 13

FORGOTTEN DEPTHS

Silence blanketed the interior of the elevator as time seemed to slow to a standstill. Leigh now felt overheated and crowded in the elevator, even though there was more than enough room for the three occupants. She could smell Kehl's dark cologne and Olivia's fragrant perfume mixing in the air. Combined with her anxiety over this new assignment, the sensation was nearly enough to make her sick on her stomach. On top of all of that, she found herself being pulled deeper and deeper into some plot that involved her father.

Out of the silence came a slight hissing sound as the elevator shuddered to a stop and the doors slid open. The air that rushed into the elevator was hardly fresh, but Leigh was grateful for the relief it provided. She almost preferred the natural earthy smell of an underground cellar to that of the chemical perfumes her companions wore. Her claustrophobia quickly abated as she gazed out into the seemingly infinite darkness beyond the doors.

"These are the old storage rooms," Olivia whispered as she stepped from the elevator and flipped a small switch next to the landing.

A dim row of dirty, incandescent lights sputtered and blinked to life.

The change in surroundings was shocking; all around them stood dark work shelves veiled in a shroud of cobwebs and grime, stacked high with old parts that looked so twisted that no human should have ever created them. Tables and shelves stretched on through seemingly infinite darkness, beyond what little illumination the ancient light bulbs gave. It was as though they had stepped from a world of refined elegance into what could easily be considered an industrial dungeon.

"Follow me, please."

Leigh subconsciously edged closer to Kehl as they followed Olivia down a dark path between tables and shelves. In some places the path was bathed in deep shadows and abject darkness lay only a foot or two away. A shiver ran up her spine as images of corpse-filled tombs materialized in her mind. She wondered, somewhere deep in her thoughts, if people could have died down here beneath the old factory, injured by one of the devilish machines and unable to find help.

"How deep are we, Mistress?" Kehl asked.

Six feet under, Leigh answered sarcastically in her thoughts.

"We are now walking along the second subterranean level of this facility. Directly below us is our destination. The old vaults from the days when this was once a factory. On the first subterranean level is the club for our younger guests. These two levels are sealed off from everywhere except my private chambers."

The three walked on in silence until they came to a stairwell that led downward. From what little could be seen of it, the structure looked to be just as ancient as the rest of their surroundings. In fact, the steps looked as though they hadn't been repaired in quite some time. Olivia took one glance down the stairwell before turning back around to address Leigh and Kehl. "I am about to take you to the lowest and most secure part of the club, where I keep my most precious belongings."

Leigh could scarcely believe the state of the structure. "Are these stairs even safe? You seem to have money enough to have them renovated."

To Leigh's surprise, Olivia laughed sincerely before she answered. "This was another one of your fathers ideas. He told me all about exploring old mansions and such, searching for supernatural creatures. It turns out that sometimes the best defense is a bad set of stairs, especially if someone is after you and they are in a hurry. One bad step on these rickety steps and the whole thing falls apart."

Leigh nodded silently as she clearly remembered her father warning her of such hazards in abandoned buildings. It seemed odd though that he should suggest using such a dangerous tactic. She could remember him telling her to step on the far edges of the boards, closest to the nails. Such a maneuver not only silenced creaky boards but also set the feet on the safest possible locations. But even then, things could still go wrong, and often fatally so. As far as Leigh could remember, her father had always seemed to detest such traps, saying that only someone with disregard for human life would stoop to such tactics.

Olivia noticed as Leigh frowned and could imagine what she must be thinking.

"It was actually my call to leave the steps the way they are. Although he suggested the trap, he was of two minds on the matter. He feared that someone might get killed if the trap worked properly or that I myself might get hurt. I managed to convince him in the end."

Leigh's eyes darted up to Olivia at this newest hint at some sort of bond between her and her father. Worry implied caring, and caring for someone on a job, as her father always preached, was taboo. Not only did it make things personal, but it made things risky as well. Leigh tried not to make assumptions based on the words of Olivia. If the implications were true and her father was breaking his own rules, then Leigh could only guess what would happen next.

A click of a switch broke Leigh away from her thoughts as Olivia turned on more of the ancient incandescent lights. Reluctantly, they glowed their way back from hibernation and illuminated the stairwell. The three made their way down, one by one, until they were all safely at the bottom. From high up above they heard what sounded like a gunshot, which was quickly followed by the tinkle of falling glass. It was little more than a burst bulb, but it was still enough to put them all on edge. Even Olivia appeared to be slightly shaken.

"This used to be where the old factory kept its prototypes and copyrighted tools," Olivia said as she flipped yet another switch.

High above in the ceiling, bright floodlights burst to life. Massive ancient vaults lined the walls of the cavernous chamber and took up most of the floor space. There were a dozen of the large cylindrical behemoths, each with a door large enough to easily allow three people to enter abreast. Every door also had a large wheel for entering in a combination along with an identification number.

"Why wouldn't these vaults be enough to protect the jewel from Alucard?" Leigh asked.

Olivia was silent as she began walking past the vaults. Past one, two, three, four of them, until finally she came before the fifth. There was nothing special or peculiar about the vault to separate it from its brethren. It was a construct of cast iron that looked like it could hold ten to twenty people comfortably inside. Leigh thought sardonically to herself that they would make excellent fallout shelters.

"If you would please turn your backs," Olivia said as she took hold of the wheel in front of her. Her guests did as she bid without question.

She gave the combination wheel a quick spin, sending it clicking toward the correct first number. Briefly looking back over her shoulder, she reversed the wheel, bringing it swiftly to the next number.

With one more turn of the wheel, the door would unlock, and yet, she paused.

"No peeking," she murmured over her shoulder, masking her momentary hesitation.

What lay in the vault was one of the single most valuable artifacts known to man. But Olivia's thoughts were not on the jewel, but rather on the two people standing behind her. A sharp grin turned up the corners of her mouth as she gave the wheel its final turn. Everything was going according to plan.

"All right, you can turn around now," she said as the door gave a loud, metallic click.

Both Leigh and Kehl turned to see Olivia pulling open the door with only minor difficulty, as though it weighed nothing at all. Kehl decided not to patronize his employer by offering her help. As the door swung open, several lights in the interior of the vault flickered on automatically. Blinding white light met their eyes. It was so brilliant at first that it was almost overwhelming.

"Please, take off your shoes," Olivia said.

Olivia led the way and slipped off her slippers while stepping partway into the vault. Kehl and Leigh followed suit and found themselves standing in the entranceway to the vault. Further back they could see a sliding bar gate like the type seen in prisons. Behind it stood a white pedestal that held something covered with a black sheet. Kehl watched Olivia closely as she produced a key suspended by a barely visible chain from her cleavage. With a turn of the key and a muffled click, the gate slid open. But before Leigh and Kehl could step through, Olivia turned and blocked their path.

"I want you to understand something. What you are about to see is priceless and one of a kind. Do not under any circumstances touch it or attempt to steal it, otherwise this vault will slam shut and we will all be trapped in here with it for the rest of eternity."

"Wouldn't one of your employees come looking for you?"

"Perhaps, although they have been instructed otherwise. Even if they did, I am the only living person who knows the combination to this vault."

Having said her piece, Olivia walked through the door and allowed Kehl and Leigh to follow.

"I present to you, the Midnight Nocturne."

Olivia grabbed the sheet and pulled it slowly away to reveal a massive black cat's-eye diamond the size of a wine bottle. It stood completely alone on a pedestal except for a jeweler's glass. Its every angle revealed only perfection, even though the diamond itself looked so murky that it appeared black. Leigh blinked. She no longer felt dizzy ,but she could swear she saw tiny sparks flying before her eyes.

"I must be seeing things," she whispered.

"No, I see it too," Kehl said, taking a step forward to get a better look.

Olivia smiled as Kehl and Leigh turned to look at her. She could easily see the wonder in their eyes. Leigh was mortal, and Olivia was not nearly as surprised with her reaction as she was with Kehl's. Having lived for many centuries, he would no doubt have seen many of the world's wonders. To see him taken aback by the jewel almost made her feel like laughing at him.

"No, you are not imagining things. What you are looking at now is the most flawed jewel ever discovered. If you would examine it, please." She picked up the glass and handed it to Leigh.

Leigh slowly stepped forward, taking the glass as cautiously as she could with her hands shaking. Tiny multicolored sparks of light were still dancing in her eyes as she put the glass to her eye and leaned even closer. She gasped and nearly lost hold of the small instrument as the sight reached her eyes.

"Oh my god," Leigh said as her mouth gaped open.

She felt weightless and lightheaded, for suspended in the diamond was a galaxy of other jewels. It was like floating in space amidst an uncountable number of closely packed stars. Even the most bright and vivid pictures of galaxies far away in outer space could not compare to what lay in this comparatively small diamond. Reds, greens, blues, and other colors that she couldn't even describe assaulted her eyes. Individual sparks shone in areas as though they were supernovas, while in other parts there were nebula-like gatherings of light. Leigh pulled back when she realized that she'd been holding her breath. Gasping for air, she pulled back and looked at the gem normally. She could still see small glints of light dancing from its surface.

"It's incredible," Leigh said as she handed Kehl the glass. "It feels like you're looking at the stars."

"Indeed," Kehl agreed as he too examined the jewel. "I'd have to say it's one of the most beautiful things I've ever seen."

"Can you feel it?" Olivia asked as she replaced the cover over the gem.

"Yes," Leigh said as she felt her gut clench.

"Feel what?" Kehl asked.

"The seduction of the jewel."

"No, I can't," Kehl said as he looked at Leigh.

"I can feel it," Leigh continued. "Although my father trained me to resist such false temptations. It feels almost the same as when a vampire tries to take control of your mind."

"I have never experienced that sensation before," Olivia said with a sharp look at Kehl.

"Don't look at me. I've never done anything like that before. I am starting to feel different though," Kehl said as he flexed his fingers. "I can't quite figure out why though."

"Perhaps it is just another one of the mysteries of the jewel," Olivia suggested.

"Perhaps," Kehl said as he looked over at Leigh.

"Try to resist the urge to touch it. Although its power reaches around the globe, it ironically seems to magnify the powers or abilities of whoever holds it in their hands or is in physical contact with it."

"Ah," Leigh said. "It's a loophole. The jewel cannot fully cancel out the supernatural without making its own effects null."

"Precisely," Olivia replied. "I take it that you are both convinced now?".

Their agreement was confirmed silently as Leigh met Kehl's gaze. Olivia had something both Kehl and Leigh wanted. For Kehl, Olivia held vital information about his possibly still-living love. For Leigh, she wanted to find out the exact reason her father was involved with this strange woman. There was also the prospect of money, and though Kehl had no need of it, Leigh could easily think of a few improvements she could make to her car.

"Yes," Kehl replied simply.

"I will accept the job," Leigh added.

"Good, now we can discuss your payment and duties," Olivia said with a friendly smile that vanished all too quickly.

Rastis's voice crackled to life in her earpiece. "Mistress, it's started! I have two of our guests starting to turn in the middle of the dance floor. We need you topside as soon as possible!"

"It's begun," Olivia gasped. "Quickly, back to the elevator!"

CHAPTER 14

CLOAK AND DAGGER

Kehl and Leigh were at a loss as to why Olivia was pushing them out of the vault, not having heard Rastis's message. Following her direction, they walked back outside of the safe and put their shoes back on. Olivia slammed the door shut behind them and gave the combination wheel a sharp spin. Slipping her shoes back on, she took off at a near run.

"What's going on?" Leigh asked.

"Come on!" Olivia shouted.

Kehl and Leigh looked at each other and immediately started out after her.

"What's going on?!" Leigh demanded once more as she caught up with Olivia.

"Two guests are starting to turn into vampires," Olivia answered.

"How could you possibly know that?" Kehl asked as he pulled up next to them.

"Thermal imaging. Their body temperatures are dropping quickly, and they will soon be in a frenzy for their first taste of blood," Olivia answered as she looked sideways at Kehl. "You should know how that goes."

"What does she mean by that?" Leigh asked.

Even though Kehl made no comment, Leigh could see that Olivia's comment must have stung him. She assumed it had something to do with his past life as a human. For a single moment, she found herself worrying about what must have happened to him. Would she ever have enough courage to dare ask him about his past?

"The stairs!" Leigh cried as they approached their base. "I don't think they can handle us running on them!"

"We will have to risk it," Olivia said sharply as she leapt onto the staircase.

The steps shook violently as the trio raced their way upward. Rusted steel and rotten wood groaning as they tested their fate. A sudden rumbling vibrated the boards underneath Kehl's feet. Kehl looked back down the structure and saw several pieces fall away into the darkness. He was the last of the three on the stairs, and as he looked up, he realized how far he had to go.

"It's going to fall!" he shouted.

They still had two flights to go, with the whole structure now shaking dangerously. Leigh and Olivia were one flight above him when the step beneath his foot snapped in two. Without a sound, he grabbed for the rail next to him only to have it pull away from the main supports of the stairs. He let out a groan as he fell; he could see Leigh and Olivia up above and knew that they would not be able to help him. Just as his mind had accepted that he was going to have a very painful fall, he jerked to a stop. Incredulously, he looked up to see the rail, that he still desperately clung to, wedged tightly between two of the steps.

"Where is Kehl?" Olivia gasped at the top of the stairs.

Leigh shrugged and shook her head as she gasped for air. She watched Olivia look back into the stairwell and couldn't tell if the mysterious woman's gasp came from exertion or from panic at Kehl's disappearance. Cautiously, Leigh edged closer to the stairwell, alternating her gaze to the stairwell and then back to Olivia. A horrible sinking feeling spread out through her body at the thought of Kehl's demise.

"There he is!" she shouted as Kehl rounded the last flight of stairs at blinding speed.

No sooner had they seen him than the entire stairwell gave out one last surrendering moan and collapsed. Kehl made a desperate leap as the flight beneath him plummeted. For a moment, it seemed like he would fall to his doom. Not a second too soon his hands found the edge of the floor as the debris made a deafening crash to the floor below.

Kehl gasped as he attempted to grin up at the two very surprised women. "Just made it."

Leigh clicked her tongue and offered him a hand up, only to have it denied.

"Suit yourself," she said as Kehl pulled himself up.

Turning away, Leigh cursed herself over worrying for the arrogant man.

Kehl gasped as he sat down next to the gaping hole. "Phew. I didn't mean to be rude. I just didn't want to pull you down with me if I fell."

Leigh turned to him, planning to say some quick and stinging remark before she realized what he'd said. He didn't want her to risk her life trying to save his. She bit her lip as she realized that he would make a fine match for her if he weren't a vampire. It took some effort to push thoughts of kissing him right there out of her mind. There were more important matters going on, and they were still standing next to a new, gaping hole in the floor.

"We're still in a hurry!" Olivia hissed tersely as she set off again.

"Right!" Leigh said, taking off after her without a second glance at Kehl.

Kehl dusted himself off and stood up. With one last look down into what could have been his grave, he set off after his two new companions. This was definitely turning out to be much more of an adventure than staying sequestered in his manor. As it turned out, he was the only one not out of breath when they made it back to the elevator. Leigh and Olivia both staggered in and leaned against the walls as Kehl stepped in and pushed the button to return them to Olivia's quarters.

"I'm guessing that since you hired me that you want them destroyed," Leigh said as she caught her breath.

"Unfortunately, yes, and I need it done discreetly."

Apprehension crept into Leigh's voice. "I'm going to need a weapon."

"I understand, but under no circumstances are you to use guns," Olivia said sternly. "I don't suppose you would like to try those blades you saw earlier."

Leigh was quiet for a moment as she calculated her chance of survival against a newborn vampire. They were an entirely different beast than older ones. They were by no means as powerful, but their newfound strength was explosive. Leigh nodded distractedly as she decided that the blades would do. It was going to be quite a challenge. In truth, she could not lay claim to slaying a single vampire on her own. While she had trained with her father to kill vampires, he'd also sheltered her in their actual encounters. Leigh did little more than watch as he dispatched them himself.

Kehl seemed grimly calm despite the request just made of him. In the course of his long existence as a vampire, it was not the first time he'd been forced to kill. A newborn vampire was no small challenge, but he had disposed of them before.

"I will require no weapons, I believe," he said. "I will only need my mask."

Olivia nodded her consent as the elevator reached its destination.

With a hiss, the door slid open once again, and the three rushed into the living room. Richard was nowhere to be seen. The only trace of him was a spent martini glass on the coffee table. They had no time to linger, and they made their way down the next hallway. Pulling the same key from her dress, Olivia slid it into a recessed slot in the sword display. Leigh was surprised as the frame hissed when it swung open.

"Be my guest," Olivia said as she motioned to the weapons.

The blades were all things of beauty, and Leigh was reluctant to take them from their airtight home. She first picked up one of matching fighting knives, awestruck as the emerald it contained glinted and flashed. Gazing down its blade, she could not believe its sharpness. The edge was so fine it was almost invisible to the naked eye. This explained the airtight case; such blades, sharpened down to microns, were indeed so sharp that given enough time the movement of air alone could slightly dull the edge.

"Hurry," Olivia said. "We haven't much time. You'll find the sheaths in the bottom of the frame. Please leave the katana. I trust that you will be able to keep the smaller blades out of sight."

Leigh nodded and set about strapping on the fighting knives and daggers. Kehl tried not to look as she pulled her skirt up and buckled the knives to her firm upper thighs. The sheath on her right leg also had a holder for the throwing knives built into it. Leigh cursed as the sheath tore a small hole in her dress. She actually felt more comfortable though now that she was armed. As she looked back into the frame, she cast one last longing gaze at the blackened blade of the katana.

Kehl made his way to the entrance chamber. After picking up his mask, he took a moment admire it. He had no idea what was waiting for him out there on the dance floor, nor did he have any idea what troubles were waiting in the days ahead. It didn't matter. He was tired of being alone and tired of being bored. As he turned and watched Olivia and Leigh walking toward him down the hall, something stirred deep inside him. He was suddenly aware of his own fangs and of the scent of the thousand-plus warm bodies suffusing the club.

"Follow me," Olivia said as she wasted no time opening the door to her chambers and making her way back to the security office. Kehl and Leigh fell into step behind her.

"Glad to see you again, Mistress." Rastis said as she swiftly entered the room.

"And the same to you, Ras," Olivia said in a friendly manner. "Show us our targets."

Rastis indicated a screen that was lit up in bright Technicolor rainbows.

"If you will notice, two of our guest's body temperatures are dropping much lower than that of normal humans. If it had been you or me, such a drop in body temperature would indicate hypothermia or death."

Kehl frowned at the images on the multicolored screen. "Have you identified them yet?"

Ras flipped a switch and the screen suddenly looked normal. Leigh immediately recognized the two people who were slowly changing into vampires; it was the same rude couple who ran into her on the dance floor. She now realized why the girl wore the scarf and why the man wore a high-collared shirt: they were hiding the bite marks. It was one of the first tells she should have recognized.

"They're so young," Kehl whispered as he looked at them on the screen. The bloodlust that had gripped him earlier suddenly vanished as he saw that his prey were barely more than children, infants compared to himself.

"Who are they?" Leigh asked as disgust edged into her voice.

Rastis's voice was calm and even. "Two wealthy youngsters that were on our guest list. The boy is Randolf Townsend, the son of the former real estate tycoon of the same name. The girl is Elizabeth Rose, daughter of Emily Rose, the famous horticulturist. Both Randolf and Elizabeth's parents vanished under suspicious circumstances several months ago. They were official guests on our lists. My guess is that Alucard got to them."

"No doubt he offered them power, immortality, and access to their parents' fortunes to lure them into his plans," Olivia said.

"They did seem rather drunk on power earlier," Leigh said. "I bumped into them when I came in."

"Be careful," Rastis said without removing his eyes from the screen. "The youngsters may only be a diversion for Alucard himself. It seems that Randolf is out almost in the very center of the main dance floor, while Elizabeth is making her way down into the rave room." He indicated a bank of screens to his left.

The group could see Randolf dancing in a much more animated fashion than those around him, throwing his arms about wildly. But unlike her compatriot, Elizabeth moved toward the ramp leading the rave room in a catlike trance. Their behavior drew more than a few glances, but it seemed that no one paid them much mind. Most of the guests were either drunk were in altered states of consciousness by their own means.

"Take these," Rastis said, handing Leigh and Kehl both earpieces identical to Olivia's. "They are miniaturized two-way radios, so you can call us if you need any assistance."

"As I said before," Olivia said, "I want this problem dealt with discreetly; backup shouldn't be necessary. Rastis, have a group of unarmed guards in staff uniforms ready to help if need be."

Leigh laughed softly under her breath. If she or Kehl failed, the guards would be of little use. The newborns would tear though the defenseless crowd, killing at whim.

"How much longer till midnight?" Kehl asked as he looked around for a clock.

"Just under half an hour," Olivia answered. "You must hurry or they will start killing my guests."

With that Olivia led them from the room, back toward the door that led to the main dance floor. She allowed them a moment of silence to steel themselves for the task ahead. To both Kehl and Olivia's surprise, Leigh took out one of her throwing knives and lightly drew it across the side of her neck. Working her neck back and forth she got the blood through her skin.

"I will take the male," she said, as a paper thin line of blood appeared across her neck.

Olivia looked at Leigh quizzically, but Kehl understood perfectly what she was doing. Bloodlust roared up inside him, and it took a conscious effort to suppress it. He moved his eyes from her neck down further and focused his attention on her cleavage, which only served to arouse a different sort of lust. Gritting his teeth behind tightly clenched lips, he turned to the door and tried to push the thoughts from his head, repeating over and over again in his mind the name of his lost beloved. Olivia picked up Leigh's discarded mask and handed it back to her.

"You have twenty minutes until midnight," Ras said over their earpieces.

"Right," Olivia whispered. "Here we go."

CHAPTER 15
CHAOS

As Olivia threw the door to the dance floor open, music crashed into the trio like a wave. The party had escalated in intensity, and even though everyone was nicely dressed, the guests were now dancing provocatively. Leigh pulled her mask on and stepped out of the doorway into a very different and surreal world. All around her people danced, grinded, and groped, everyone behind the protective anonymity of their masks. Jets of fog shot from black boxes set around the dance floor, and lasers burst to life. A roar of approval shot up from the crowd as Leigh wondered how on earth she was going to find her mark. She looked around for Kehl and Olivia, but both of them had vanished from sight.

There was some static as Ras's voice crackled over the radio. "Keep moving forward; you're close now."

Leigh lifted herself up onto the tips of her toes and attempted to get a better view out over the dancers. The wavelike motion of the dancers prevented her from seeing more than a few people deep. Sighing quietly to herself, she joined the giant mass of dancing bodies. If her tactic was successful, she would not need to find Randolf. The very scent of her blood would bring him slavering to her neck. It was a dangerous tactic, but Leigh could think of no better way to find her prey.

* * *

On almost the opposite side of the club, Kehl searched for the entrance to the lower level. It wasn't hard to find. He spotted one of the extravagantly dressed ravers make their way through the crowd. Following the dancer brought him quickly to the entrance of the rave room. At first glance its entrance looked like stairwell, but as Kehl drew near it revealed itself to be a long ramp.

The walls and ceilings were painted matte black, and the floor was lined with ultraviolet-reactive red carpet. Concealed black lights made the carpet glow red, and Kehl could see several people wearing reactive bits of clothing and glow rods. He could smell the pungent odor of sweat mingled with sweet fragrance drifting up along the slanted hallway. Further down the ramp, the edge of dance floor was extremely cramped with people.

Kehl suddenly felt the distinct sensation that eyes were on him. As he made his way down the ramp, he turned to see a group of female ravers leaning against a wall. They seemed to be sizing up his clothing, perhaps wondering why he would be making his way down into the rave. One girl in particular seemed to stand out. She narrowed her eyes as their gaze met, though Kehl could not tell if it was out of anger or curiosity.

The girl whispered something to one of her friends as Kehl passed by, and though his ears couldn't pick up what was said, he knew it involved him. When Kehl's gaze lingered a moment too long, she starting walking toward him. Her hips swayed with each step in a comely manner. She was petite in build, though her catlike face made up for her size, with large dark brown eyes and full, expressive lips. Her wavy shoulder length hair was a slightly darker shade of color that almost appeared to be black. Bright streamers tied into her locks framed her face and made it seem like it was glowing.

Her clothing would have been considered conservative were it not two sizes too small for her body. She wore a hand-woven sweater with a plunging V-neck that not only exposed her modest cleavage but accentuated it, exposing no less than two inches of her nearly see-through lingerie beneath. She wore an extremely small plaid skirt that was much too short for winter. To keep her legs warm, she covered them completely with full length striped stockings.

"Hey," she said, giving Kehl a nod as he paused.

Thinking the girl had something frivolous on her mind, Kehl decided to continue on his way. But he caught sight of an intent in her eyes that made him look at her again. She bit her lip and narrowed her eyes once more in a way that made Kehl feel as though he was being closely examined. All too quickly he felt sharp probing into his mind, almost as though the person behind it expected no resistance.

To a normal mortal, the probe would have gone unnoticed. Kehl had experienced such psychological attacks before in his life and knew how to repel them. He knew without a doubt that the strange girl beside him was the source of the attack. Kehl brushed her out of his mind easily, but was surprised to find the attack instantly redirected and renewed. A moment later, he shut her out of his mind completely. As he turned to look at her once more, he did so with a much more appraising gaze.

"Yes?" he said in a pleasant tone.

"I told my friends that I would come over here and ask you if you wanted to buy me a drink," she answered simply.

Kehl looked back over at the group of girls standing against the wall. Their giggling confirmed his suspicions that they were up to something mischievous. He shook his head before attempting to walk off. There was no time left for silly games. As he turned away, the young woman's hands wrapped about his elbow and pulled him to a stop. When he looked back in her direction, she had a completely different expression on her face, an almost pleading look.

"That's not the real reason I came over here," she said.

Kehl was starting to lose his patience with the strange girl. "Look, I don't know what you're up to, but it doesn't matter how appealing you make yourself look to me, I'm not going to fall for it."

The girl glanced down at her own body momentarily and then back at Kehl, looking totally confused. "But I didn't."

Holding a hand up, Kehl shook his head, indicating that he wanted her to stop.

"Do you know how rare the gift of telepathy is? I've encountered so many fakes that I almost lost faith in the few real ones, like you. You have this amazing talent, and you use it to pick up men. It's pathetic."

The way her eyes widened suddenly in shock told Kehl that his remark had stung.

"I think that I may have come across the wrong way," the girl said as she blinked away tears.

"Yes, you did," Kehl replied in a less forceful tone. "Now, what is it that you really want?"

"I was covering myself," she said as the tear rolled down her cheek. "A distracted mind is much easier for me to read. I caught you thinking about Elisabeth as you walked by and … I don't use my power to pick up men." An angry edge hardened in her voice. "I was going to try to help you, but now I think you can just go screw yourself."

This time Kehl grabbed her arm in an attempt to stop her from leaving.

"Leave me be," she whispered, sending out a crippling blast of telepathic energy.

Although relatively unskilled in telepathic matters, Kehl managed to withstand the brunt of the attack. More than a few vampire hunters through the years had been skilled in the art, so he had to learn the basics of survival and defense. Shaking his head, he cleared out his mind and shielded himself for the possibility of another attack.

"What do you know?" Kehl asked again.

"Let go of my arm and I *might* tell you," the girl said.

Kehl did as she asked and was surprised at the speed at which she managed to slap him. Normally he dodged even the quickest of attacks easily. His speed as a vampire allowed him more than enough time to counter all but the quickest humans. In a display of her skill, the girl had completely masked both her intentions and her hand from his perception until the moment just before impact. He would have to be more careful dealing with her. Cursing himself, he acknowledged that he had deserved the slap. "I think I owe you an apology," he said politely.

"No, really, you think so?"

"I'm sorry," he said, bowing his head.

"It's okay," the girl said as she wiped away her tears. "I did come across wrong. I think I may have been more upset about failing to get inside your head. I thought at first that I was dealing with a normal human."

Her eyes filled up with an almost painful sort of curiosity and longing as she looked back up at him. "What are you?"

Kehl sighed inwardly. If this girl knew anything about Elizabeth, he was going to have to work with her if he hoped to find his target in time. After clearing out his thoughts completely, he envisioned the word "vampire" clearly in his mind.

"Read my thoughts," he said quietly.

A split second passed before the girl's jaw dropped. "No way, you can't be."

He nodded silently.

The girl grew quiet for a few moments. "Why would you want to kill Elizabeth if she is one of your own kind?"

"If she turns in the middle of the club she will kill everyone within her reach, just for starters," he answered. "How does this involve you?"

"She used to be my friend," the girl replied. "My best friend, actually. Wait, you've already read my mind, haven't you?"

"No, I'm not that good at telepathy."

"You just blocked me out of your mind easily and you're no good at telepathy?" the girl said with a bright laugh that caught Kehl off guard. "I must really suck at it then. Anyway, how about we start over like normal people. I am Anne."

"And I am Kehl."

"And we are both here to stop Elizabeth, if at all possible."

"Yes."

"I still don't understand why you're helping me," Kehl said.

"Let's just say I tried to stop her when she killed her mother, but I couldn't. She's turned into a power-hungry monster, and I can only imagine what she'd be like as a vampire. I caught your thoughts as you walked by and thought you could help me. I … I don't know if I'd be able to kill her."

Kehl looked into Anne's eyes and found himself believing her story.

"I understand," He said softly. "Where is she?"

"She's on the other side of the rave floor."

An image as clear as the brightest photo burst into Kehl's mind. It showed the dance floor from above. The people moved and danced, and in one corner a single person was glowing. Kehl could recognize Elizabeth from her image on the security camera. He wondered if he would have ever found her without Anne's help.

"You know," Anne said, "you might not want to go down there like that. You'll stick out like a sore thumb."

"It doesn't really matter," Kehl replied dismissively.

"Oh, it will if you have to make your way through that crowd down there. They don't much care for the elite socialites. Lose the dinner jacket and unbutton your shirt."

Kehl raised an eyebrow but removed his dinner jacket and threw it to the floor against the side of the hallway. Reaching up, Anne started unbuttoning his shirt slowly as a glazed look came over her eyes. Kehl took the moment to look over her once more as his thirst surged inside him. Anne looked up into his eyes and a strange sort of tension ignited between them.

With an almost imperceptible tilt of her head, the girl drew attention to her neck. Barely visible, and only because of the ultraviolet light, two pale circular scars appeared. Kehl looked back into her eyes, wondering if she was a vampire. She shook her head, in a way that would look like exasperation to anyone looking on.

I'm something else, she said in his mind.

Do you work for the Mistress? Kehl queried in thought.

No. But Elizabeth is tied to this club somehow, I just haven't figured it out yet. Anne lowered her gaze, though her voice remained in his head. *She's about to turn. You'll have to hurry. I've got to get back to my friends now. You can worry about paying me later.*

Paying you? Kehl asked in his mind as she walked away.

Though no reply. He heard Anne loudly tell her friends how much he'd wanted to take her back to his place, but that she'd turned him down. Glancing back over his shoulder, he saw her standing there, grinning wildly as her friends laughed, not believing her story.

Go! she told him.

Looking back down the ramp, Kehl set forward with a brisk pace. As he neared the bottom, the dance floor came into view. The rave room was perhaps only about a quarter the size of the main dance floor of the club, but what it lacked in size, it made up for in intensity. Instead of popular dance music, the music here had more harsh and trancelike beats. Laser lights burst from every corner of the room in a sense numbing explosion of color.

Kehl was accustomed to the scent of his kind, but there were so many distractions down here in the rave: sweat, perfume, cologne, the confusing eroticism of a room full of bodies moving up and down and swaying like the tide. Biting down on his lip, Kehl struggled to keep from getting dizzy, and that's when he caught it. A scent that was slightly different from those around him. It was fragrant yet cold, like the perfume of a dying flower.

Following the image that still appeared vividly in his mind, Kehl started edging his way around the crowd to where Elizabeth should be. Without Anne's help, even his strong sense of smell wouldn't have been enough to find his quarry. As slow as he made progress, he still might not be able to find her. The rave moved at a much faster pace than the dance above, and Elizabeth's scent escaped him as the crowd roared with the start of a new song.

CHAPTER 16
THE NEWBORNS

Elizabeth Rose, privileged from birth, came from a prestigious family with old money. Her mother had been one of the social elite of New York, masquerading her shady business dealings as lucrative thousand-dollar-per-plate garden parties. Needless to say, Elizabeth was spoiled and thought that the world belonged to her. She had at first dismissed the strange visitor at her mother's door. However, the visitor had shown her things, things beyond her wildest imagination: eternal youth, eternal power, and an eternity to grow wealthier than any mortal. Feeling no love for any other living being except herself and her friend Anne, she had given herself over to vampirism and killed her mother in the same night.

But now, as her blood began to run cold in her veins, she was having her doubts. The bite had been the single most painful, yet sexually explosive, moment in her entire life. What she felt now, though, did not feel right. The club had been warm and comfortable when she had entered, but now it seemed sweltering even though she was shivering. Still, she could not stop dancing, for she felt that she needed everyone to be as close to her as possible, as if she were a wolf dropped into the middle of a flock of sheep.

And where was her companion, Randolf? Their orders were to stay together so they wouldn't be caught defenseless. He said he'd caught the scent of blood and then quickly vanished in pursuit of its source. But Elizabeth easily dismissed his absence. In the face of immortality, his momentary foolishness was not a concern.

The chill in her blood ran deeper as her fear mixed and mingled with a growing hunger. She grabbed a man who had been trying to dance with her all evening and pulled him into a violent kiss. He resisted for only a moment before wrapping his arms around her and sliding them down past her hips. Elizabeth gasped as he squeezed her ass. A moment later, she pulled back from the kiss and pulled him in tight, laying her chin on his neck. She could feel his heart pounding and it drove her wild. Saliva ran in her mouth as her fangs extended. Lips quivering, her mouth opened as she prepared to bite.

At the last moment, just before her fangs touched the man's skin, another man caught her eye. At first she thought it was Randolf, and she immediately pushed her would-be victim away. The new man was tall, well built, and sharply dressed, standing about ten feet away. Unlike the rest of the dancers, he stood completely motionless, his eyes trained directly upon hers.

"Hello, Elizabeth," the man said.

She immediately knew it wasn't Randolf.

"May I have this dance?"

* * *

Still alone on the main dance floor, Leigh had no help finding her prey. She knew that help wouldn't be necessary, or even beneficial, for that matter. She did hope that Randolf found her soon, for midnight was approaching all too quickly. She'd been dancing for more than ten minutes before a voice that was more hiss than whisper came from directly behind her.

"Excuse me miss, your neck is bleeding," it cooed.

Leigh ignored the comment at first. Without turning around, she started to dance more provocatively. She hoped her dancing looked as sexy as it felt—she wanted Randolf as close as possible before engaging him. All too quickly she felt his presence looming close behind her.

She whirled just in time for the masked Randolf to violently take her in his arms. It was like dancing with an aroused, vigorous corpse. His body moved with the music and pulled her close but gave off no warmth. Somewhat taller than Leigh, Randolf had to lean over to get closer to her neck. He sniffed at her blood like a curious puppy.

"No foreplay yet," Leigh said as she hiked up her shoulder and snapped his mouth shut just as he was about to bite. "There are too many people watching us."

Randolf's arms tightened instantly about her waist as he bared his soon to be fangs. The dancers remained oblivious around her as the song continued. Leigh had to come up with something quick, and though her mind contained a flurry of ideas, very few of them were practical—and even less of them were discreet. Just as she was about to draw a dagger and drop Randolf where he stood, she spotted her salvation.

Less than ten feet away was a bathroom with no line and, hopefully, no one inside. Pulling back from Randolf, she looked up as seductively as she could manage into his eyes.

"We need to find somewhere more private," she whispered. "Follow me."

Leigh slid her hand slowly down his back, hesitating a moment before pinching his ass. Though she despised touching him, it had the desired effect. Randolf's arms loosened just enough to allow for a quick escape. Unfortunately, it also seemed to excite him as well. His breath now came in lustful pants.

Hastily, Leigh turned and walked toward the bathroom door, cocking her neck at such an angle to make her tiny wound visible. She hoped the tiny bit of blood in this sea of bodies would draw Randolf along with her. With a look back, she saw that he had taken the bait. Leigh encouraged him more as she gave him a wink and beckoned him on. Randolf's lips curled back into a wicked smile. Leigh felt a chill of fear as she saw his two newborn fangs grinning back at her.

Slipping through the bathroom door, she checked if anyone else was inside. She quickly ran past all of the stalls and bent over to check the ones with closed doors. Thankfully, the bathroom was indeed empty; she just barely made it back to the door in time to intercept Randolf at the entrance.

"Lock the door," she whispered as she slid the strap of her dress down on the same side of her cut.

Randolf did as he was told before leaping toward her with his fangs bared.

* * *

Kehl felt torn as he danced with Elizabeth. The young woman in his arms had all of eternity before her. Compared to what he had seen and experienced in his many years, she was only a mere infant. What right had he to cut her young life short? She was growing strong and feral in his grasp, and it was taking more and more of his strength just to hold her still. With a glance toward the ramp, he tried to see if the telepathic girl was watching.

Elizabeth leaned close to him as her eyes barely kept from rolling back.

"I killed my own mother last night," she whispered.

Kehl's eyes widened as he suddenly found the resolution necessary to complete his task. Laying her chin against his shoulder, Kehl felt her move to bite and shifted his weight to one side as if dancing. He gritted his teeth and stifled a grunt of pain as her newborn fangs buried themselves deep into his shoulder. With his free hand, he cupped the back of her neck—an attempt to make it appear that they were merely embracing romantically. It did the trick, and the other guests around them continued to dance without noticing anything out of the ordinary.

Kehl discovered a way out in the form of an emergency exit at the edge of the room. Elizabeth's fangs tore from his flesh as he forcefully swept her off her feet and up into his arms. Wincing away the pain in his shoulder, he struggled to keep her still while at the same time avoiding her deadly attempts to bite his neck. Kehl kicked the door open like a newlywed husband and walked through. His stomach sank, for instead of carrying Elizabeth into a new life, he was carrying her to her doom. The door opened into a massive stairwell with an exit up some stairs at the other side. Kehl could barely hold Elizabeth as her strength grew. Rushing to the other door, he tackled it open and tumbled through with the newly turned vampire.

***

Leigh's leg appeared to be little more than a blur as she planted a kick directly underneath Randolf's chin. His teeth clicked shut over his tongue, and he shrieked as blood began to leak from the edges of his mouth. He flailed backward. Swiftly and silently, Leigh slid her hand up her thigh, took a throwing knife out, and sent it hurtling across the bathroom at her foe. Randolf desperately raised his arm in a vain attempt to block the projectile. He screamed as it buried deep in his arm. Even though the wound obviously hurt him, it did little to lessen his overall strength. Leaping forward with blinding speed, he renewed his attack.

This time Leigh wasn't quick enough. His attack caught her square in her chest, knocking her back into one of the stalls and smashing her into a toilet. She heard something crack; she wasn't sure if it was the porcelain or something inside her body. Violently, Randolf grabbed her hair and jerked her head to the side. Leigh panicked and whimpered as she lost presence of mind and began struggling erratically. Her chest heaved as he leaned in closer.

Vomit threatened to rise up in her throat when Randolf lurched in close and licked the blood dripping from her neck. He shivered with delight and grinned as the blood smeared his lips. Slowly he licked more of the blood away and looked down on Leigh with pale eyes. She tried to take his wrist as he grabbed the strap of her dress, but it was no use. His strength had grown exponentially. A moment later, the strap ripped away, leaving her dress hanging loose over her breasts, barely covering her at all.

No! a sharp voice said deep inside her mind. *I will not die here, not like this.*

She gritted her teeth so hard it felt like they were going to shatter. In one swift motion, she pulled her daggers from her thighs, flipped them around once to gather momentum, and rammed them up under Randolf's ribcage on either side of his chest. He tried to scream, but the blades had pierced his lungs. All he could do was gurgle as he stumbled backward. With a yell of triumph, Leigh surged to her feet and thundered a kick into his torso. The blow catapulted Randolf from the stall to the top of the sinks on the opposite side of the bathroom.

Leigh ignored the pain tearing through her body as she launched forward and rushed the newborn vampire. Using all of her strength and momentum, she smashed her fist against the side of his jaw. Years of training taught her to follow through with her momentum. Clearing his face with her fist, she brought her hand back in a staggeringly powerful backhand.

She reached down and pulled one of the knives from Randolf's body. She turned it around and smashed the wound with the grip. Flowing once more with her motions, she ripped the blade up over his sternum. She pulled the other blade free and brought both blades down deep into Randolf's chest.

Randolf tried to scream but instead only sent a spray of his own blood high into the air. Leigh stepped back, trying to avoid the crimson shower. Randolf took advantage of the situation, pulling both knives free. He threw them clumsily at his attacker. Leigh dodged them easily but was not ready for the powerful kick that followed. His foot caught her just under the ribcage and sent her flying backward, crashing through a different bathroom stall. Leigh struggled to catch her breath as she fell onto her hands and knees. This was more of a challenge than she had anticipated. Randolf was no longer human and could now sustain far more damage than any mortal. She breathed heavily and pushed herself back up onto her feet.

CHAPTER 17

DISCREETLY

A thin blanket of snow had settled on the ground outside. It accumulated to little more than an inch, but to the small, peach colored kitten making its way slowly down the street, it might as well have been a blizzard. Fleas plagued the poor animal so badly that they had given it an infection in both of its eyes. Still, something was driving it onward, something pushed it on from the inside, forcing it to trudge through the snow that was one-half of its height. It stopped in the snow and watched with what little sight it had left as two people came tumbling suddenly out into the street. As quickly as it could, the tiny creature scampered underneath a pile of discarded wooden shipping pallets.

Kehl managed to keep a hold on to Elizabeth only long enough to get her out of the building. Now she was loose, on her feet, and fighting like a wild tiger as she clawed her nails and flashed her teeth. Kehl winced as he felt the skin peeled from his face as her nails flashed past. He grabbed her wrist, but even as he did her other hand shot out and dug into the flesh between his ribs. With a roar of pain, Kehl head-butted Elizabeth hard, aiming for her nose but instead only catching her cheek. But it was enough to daze her and knock her back, allowing him precious time to regain his footing.

Elizabeth lowered herself down into a crouch before launching herself headfirst at Kehl with a bloodcurdling screech. He looked around for something to defend himself with. Grabbing one of the stacked pallets, he swung it about as hard as he could. The crude wooden structure exploded into hundreds of jagged shards as it collided with the young vampress. Splinters and jagged chunks of wood tore at the girls face, body, and clothing, and it ripped off most of her dress.

Undaunted by the attack, Elizabeth rushed forward once more. She slashed wildly at Kehl's eyes seeking to rip them from their sockets. Kehl moved as quickly as he could but still caught a ragged scratch across his cheek. He slapped away her next attack with ease and then, moving with preternatural speed, broke inside her defense and moved behind her. Using his advantaged position, he slammed a kick into her ribs, breaking at least two of them.

As if invincible, Elizabeth ignored the attack and whirled about, landing a straight punch directly against Kehl's chin. It was an inexperienced and poorly-aimed blow, but it carried behind it the devastating power of a newly born vampire. Kehl was unprepared for it, and his head snapped back to expose his neck. Elizabeth jumped onto Kehl before he managed to regain his composure. Her legs wrapped tightly about his waist, and her nails dug into the skin on his head. Elizabeth bared her fangs and prepared to bite.

Kehl's hands moved in unison, blurring as they rushed up and slapped Elizabeth's head on either side, boxing her ears. As her head and body lolled backward with pain, Kehl pried her legs from around his waist and pushed her off. Dazed, Elizabeth fell to the ground and could do little more than rise to her knees. Kehl circled her and looked for a suitable piece of wood among the wreckage of the shattered pallet. In a moment, he had a big enough piece to do the job.

Rather than look at her face, Kehl grabbed Elizabeth's neck from behind and lifted her up onto her feet. He didn't want her young image staring back at him in his memories for all eternity. With a moment's pause, he closed his eyes and rammed the long wooden fragment up under her ribs and into her heart. Elizabeth gasped once and then jerked. Kehl hoped with all of his heart that she would find some sort of repentance in the afterlife. Death quickly claimed the newborn vampire as her body turned to ash in his hands.

Kehl watched sadly as the wind picked up her remains along with the fragments of her dress and carried them away. There were now no remaining traces of their brief encounter. Olivia now had her discreet ending to Elizabeth's story; her death would be just another one of New York's many mysterious disappearances. He doubted that Anne would ever say anything about her involvement in the affair.

Kehl wiped away the blood oozing from his cheek as the first wave of guilt crashed into him. Olivia knew the whereabouts of Rana, and even though centuries upon centuries had passed, he still loved her no less. He was still surprised to find himself willing to kill to find her, especially when the victim was one so young, so close to his own age when he had turned. The solace that he found in knowing that Elizabeth had been a vampire proved fleeting as he turned to walk back into the club.

He winced as he felt a sudden biting pain just below his ankle.

Kehl whirled around. He wondered at first if Elizabeth had somehow tricked him into thinking she had turned to dust. The empty alleyway proved that she was indeed gone. As he looked down, Kehl saw a small peach-colored kitten. It's eyes had swollen completely shut, and could barely move. It mewed pathetically and turned its head upward as if to look at him. Slowly reaching down, Kehl scooped the kitten up gently in his hands. Although it had just bitten him, it now showed no signs of struggle. The poor animal had merely been trying to get his attention.

He decided then and there that he would atone for taking one life by saving another. The kitten mewed once more as Kehl gently put it down in the front pocket of his jacket. He hoped it would be comfortable enough until he could find a more suitable place to keep it. The thought crossed his mind that perhaps Leigh would like to have a kitten. A sudden noise from the door caught his attention as he looked up to see the young telepathic girl come through.

Is it done? Anne asked, using her voice instead of her mind.

Kehl nodded and watched her as she stood there in silence for a few moments. Anne's eyes remained bright even though they were now filled with tears. She looked around the alleyway, as though looking for any signs of Elizabeth. As her eyes fell upon the remains of the pallet, her gaze lingered for a moment. Kehl quickly realized that she wasn't looking at the debris at all.

"Is there nothing left of her?" She asked in a tiny voice.

Kehl shook his head, giving her a moment of silence. "Only ash."

***

Inside the club, the bathroom was now all but destroyed. Randolf bled from countless wounds, yet showed only the smallest signs of weakness. Leigh would have to end the fight soon if she hoped to survive. Although she bore no open wounds, her body was badly bruised from their encounter.

Leigh kept her back to the door, guarding it as she watched Randolf try to flank her in the close confines of the bathroom. She was cornered in her position but would not allow him to go back out onto the dance floor. Carefully freeing the last of her throwing knives from their sheath, she balanced it carefully in her hand as a plan formed in her mind. She drew her arm back slowly, carefully aiming at Randolf's heart.

Randolf's hunger and pain-addled brain remembered the last two daggers. Dashing across the room, he lunged at Leigh with the intention of smashing her back against the door. Just as he made to tackle her, Leigh seemed to vanish. A bright flash of light burst into Randolf's mind as he ran headfirst into door and another pain lanced deep into his back.

Randolf looked down as he noticed the smallest edge of something black jutting through the remains of his shirt. Leigh had spun out of the way just in time to avoid being caught. Instead of throwing the dagger, she'd driven it deep into his back. But she knew that the wound would not be enough to finish him.

Then, standing directly behind the vampire, Leigh drilled a kick into his back. Aiming for the dagger, Leigh hammered it further through his body. Randolf slammed up against the door from the force of the kick. She then walked calmly back through the room, looking around for one of the fighting knives she'd dropped earlier. Randolf growled through his clenched fangs as he struggled to free himself after being literally nailed to the door.

She found one of the blades lying in the middle of the floor. With a few rotations of her arm, Leigh flexed her shoulder as she made her way back to her prey. Without missing this time, she drove the knife up under Randolf's ribs and directly into his heart. The vampire shuddered once before his body slowly turned to ash. Leigh turned around to look at her blood-splattered surroundings. The ruined bathroom was the only trace of their battle.

"Good work, Leigh," Rastis's voice crackled over her ear-piece. "I'm sending someone over to lock the bathroom after you've left."

"Thank you," Leigh replied as she let out a long sigh.

Her respect for her father was renewed after her first solo fight with a vampire. Memories flashed into her mind as she dug through the debris and retrieved her weapons. How many vampires had her father slain on his own without her help? She knew for a fact that many of his former targets were very old and much more powerful than Randolf, which brought a question to her mind: why would Olivia even have need of Leigh if she already employed her father?

A soft knock at the door broke Leigh's train of thought. She walked over to the door and pulled her dagger free from the pane. After returning the weapon to its sheath, she unlocked the door and carefully opened it just enough to be able to peer through. She didn't recognize the person waiting on the other side, but he was wearing a nightclub uniform.

"Give me just a moment," Leigh said, shutting the door once more.

CHAPTER 18

ALUCARD

Leigh walked over to one of the bathroom mirrors and looked herself over. Her skin was flushed from the exertion of the fight. The lower half of her dress was badly tattered and frayed, so she tore it away. Bruises were beginning to bloom to life in the areas on her exposed skin. She was about to leave when she noticed the broken strap of her dress. After checking in the mirror, she reached over her shoulder and pulled the two pieces together, tying them back as best as she was able. The dress now hung slightly crooked on her shoulders, but it looked much more presentable than before.

Leigh made her way back to the door and walked out of the bathroom. Bowing in respect, the staff member quickly locked the door behind her.

"The bathroom is going to need some work," Leigh said with a sheepish grin.

"It was an acceptable loss, ma'am," the staff member said before turning on his heel and vanishing back into the crowd.

Rastis's frantic voice burst into her ear as Leigh was about to make her way back to Olivia's chambers.

"Leigh, Kehl, have either of you made contact with the Mistress?"

"No," Leigh answered as she cast her gaze around the dance floor.

"Neither have I," came Kehl's voice over the earpiece.

"She's completely vanished from my monitors. I'm going patch us in to Terrance," Rastis replied.

There was a sudden burst of static, and then Terrance joined them on the radio. "I saw her conversing with an agitated guest earlier," he reported.

"I noticed that as well," Rastis said. "She was close to the service entrance."

"Contact!" Terrance called.

"Where are they?" Leigh heard Kehl ask.

"They're coming your way, Rastis," Terrance said. "It's Alucard, and he has the Mistress."

"I'm going to try to stop him," Rastis said.

"No," Terrance answered over the radio. "You're unarmed, and you don't know what the situation is."

"I cannot fail the Mistress," Rastis replied somberly.

"Rastis?" Terrance called. "Rastis!"

Leigh caught sight of the staff entrance door opening over the heads of the dancing crowd. On opposite ends of the dance floor, she also noticed Kehl and Terrance trying to make their way to Olivia. Leigh was easily the furthest away and set off at a near-run as she skirted the dance floor. A sinking feeling crept into her stomach as she realized she wouldn't make it in time.

Kehl made his way to the door first and rushed through; he had left the kitten with one of the employees of the club so nothing would hold him back. Bursting through the door, he found Rastis convulsing with his back against the wall of the hallway. Kehl knelt by his side and wrapped a strong hand about the back of his neck, cradling his head. He tried his best to hold Rastis still, but one of his arms was clearly broken and something didn't look right about his abdomen. Kehl could only watch as blood slowly leaked from the corners of Rastis mouth. Seconds later, Terrance and Leigh burst through the door behind them as Rastis tried to gurgle out words.

"Mistress," he said as his eyes rolled back into his head.

"He's alive, but only barely …" Kehl whispered as he slowly let Rastis head fall.

"They must be headed toward her private quarters," Terrance said as he drew his gun and gazed coldly down at his associate's body.

"I agree," Leigh replied. "Let's go."

Leigh and Terrance set off down the hallway toward Olivia's apartments. Kehl stayed behind just a moment longer to look over Rastis before following behind. He couldn't be sure if the man would live or not. Kehl's thoughts turned morbid. Death was in the air tonight, and he wondered who else would be claimed.

Up ahead, Terrance and Leigh found the door to Olivia's quarters in splinters. Leigh's eyes widened as they passed the case that formerly held her weapons. The glass was broken and the katana was gone.

Up ahead the motionless body of Olivia came into view, lying still in the middle of her living room.

"Terrance, wait. It's a trap!" she screamed as she came skidding to a halt, but it was too late.

A man who Leigh had never seen before lunged out from around the corner. He had to do little more than lift the stolen katana as Terrance ran, full speed, into its tip and impaled himself. Leigh scrabbled for her own blades as Alucard smirked at her and rammed the katana further through Terrance. Gritting his teeth even as he coughed up blood, Terrance struggled to lift his pistol to Alucard's head. The gun fell to the floor as his arms grew heavy and his life slipped away.

Leigh looked into the vampire's eyes and found herself looking into a set of bright brown orbs lit with a devious and fierce kind of evil. Leigh drew her own blades as Alucard ripped the katana through Terrance, freeing it from his body. Bright quicksilver sparks flew as their blades collided mere seconds later. As Leigh drew her second knife, she flipped it over in her hand and prepared to stab. Leigh saw Alucard's next strike coming before she could halt her own momentum. A sudden twist of his hips brought a kick up into her midriff, which knocked all the air from her lungs and sent her smashing up against the wall. Alucard stepped forward and prepared to cut off her head. Kehl arrived just in time to grab the large vampire's arm and stop the fatal strike.

With a growl, Alucard whipped his left arm around into Kehl's nose. Kehl staggered back as his eyes instantly clouded up with tears. He now had Alucard's full attention. Alucard whirled and tried to disembowel Kehl with the sword. Kehl dodged the slice deftly but was far from being out of range. Barely able to see, Kehl managed to dodge a second attack and threw a punch. Alucard countered the blow by slamming the pommel of the katana up under Kehl's chin. Staggering back once more, Kehl would have been finished if two things had not happened at the same time.

Thinking it better to lose an arm than a head Kehl, raised his arm as Alucard tried to thrust the sword through his forehead. At the same time, Leigh threw herself onto Alucard, slamming her fighting knife deep into the shoulder of his sword arm. Kehl could feel the katana bite into his arm as it thrust forward and severed the thin layers of his clothing. He was surprised as the blade completely lost all momentum and fell to the floor with a loud clatter. Lowering his arm, he could see the knife protruding from Alucard's back. Leigh had just saved his life.

The small victory was short lived as Alucard turned back and backhanded Leigh so hard that it spun her around. In the same fluid motion, he spun on his heel and fired a kick at Kehl's head. It was a hastily aimed kick, and it missed its target but still smashed hard into Kehl's forehead. Both he and Leigh fell at almost the exact same time. They had been ill prepared for this challenge and had no idea that Alucard was so strong and skilled in combat.

"Pathetic," Alucard said as he turned away from the two.

Reaching over his shoulder, he winced only slightly as he pulled the blade from his body. Looking down at the still body of Leigh and the writhing form of Kehl, he decided to leave them be. He was growing tired of all of the death, having already killed several times tonight. Alucard doubted that either of the two would make it to their feet in time to stop him. Picking Olivia up by the back of her dress, he pulled her limp body down the hallway and to the elevators.

Kehl's vision remained blurry as he rolled onto his elbows and shook his head. He was disoriented and thought that his nose might be broken. Through his cloudy vision, he made out two bodies that weren't moving. There was also someone fading off into the distance, like they were being dragged away. Realization came slowly, and brought with it a throbbing headache. Olivia was being dragged away, at least one employee was dead, and now maybe even Leigh as well.

Somewhere deep inside of him, old memories stirred of another young woman having her life stolen. Kehl shivered with his silent fears as he pushed himself up as quickly as possible. He quickly made his way to Leigh's side and felt for a pulse. He was relieved to find her heart beating strong. As he turned his gaze to look across the living room, he caught a glimpse of the elevator doors sliding shut, far down the opposite hallway.

Lifting Leigh up gently into his arms, he carried her carefully to the couch in the center of the room. Laying her on the cushions, he tried to make her as comfortable as possible. Leigh murmured something incoherent as he adjusted the pillow behind her head. A sudden pang of guilt tore through his mind. With so much at risk, he would not be able to stay with her to make sure she regained consciousness.

CHAPTER 19

ACCORDING TO PLAN

Pain flooded Olivia's senses as her eyelids flickered open. She found herself sitting against one corner of the elevator and immediately saw her captor standing at the controls. The floor shuddered beneath her, signaling that they were moving downward. Despite her injuries, a crooked smile spread its way across her lips. It vanished in an instant as she started to speak.

"Hello, Alucard," she said, pressing her palm against one of her eyes that felt as if it were bruised and swelling.

"My name is not Alucard," he growled.

"I already know that, Drake."

Drake continued along, ignoring her use of his true name. "You lied to me, Mistress. You told me that when I arrived I would be treated as an honored guest. Instead, I found that I was not on the guest list at all. The guards were even instructed not to let me in."

Olivia laughed mirthlessly as she checked the corners of her mouth for blood.

"You also told me that if I came here tonight you would show me the jewel and offer me a price," he said, remembering the sealed invitation he had received, enticing him with a private viewing of the Midnight Nocturne.

When he had been turned away at the door, he was filled with an undeniable, burning sense of longing. His need for the jewel now even outweighed even his vampiric thirst for blood. Overcome by anger, he'd found a side entrance and forced his way into the club. Balked by Olivia's schemes, he now found himself having to kill to get what he wanted.

"I will not be denied," he said, anger radiating from him. "You had your chance to sell it to me and make some easy money." With a hiss the doors of the elevator slid open. "But now I will have to take it from you by force."

Drake grabbed Olivia by the arm and jerked her up onto her feet. Her head spun as she tried to focus on him. The massive vampire was insanely strong, and she had no doubt he would honor his threat. Olivia felt no fear, however, as a plan started to formulate calmly inside her mind. Even despite the current state of things her plan was going along smoothly.

"Take me to the jewel, or I will snap your neck right here in this elevator."

"Right this way," Olivia murmured with a sweeping gesture of her arm.

In their earlier rush, she and the others neglected to turn off the overhead lights. Taking her first step forward, she found that her ankle was badly twisted but would hold weight. The pain made her dry heave, and she quickly stepped to the other foot. Limping, she led Drake through the basement, following the dim string of lights until they came upon the collapsed stairwell.

"Well?" Drake asked expectantly. "Where is it?"

Olivia gave a pained grin. "Just down these steps."

Drake inched forward and looked down into the hole in the floor where there was once a flight of stairs. His sharp vampiric eyesight sliced through the murky darkness below. Dozens of meters separated them from the floor below. He took one step backward before looking over at Olivia. An evil grin spread across his face.

"Ladies first," he said, grabbing her arm and pulling her close the edge.

Olivia struggled against his grasp but to no avail. Seconds later, Drake threw her into the hole. She fell uncontrollably toward the wrecked stairs below. Drake smirked as the sounds of her screaming reached his ears. It was a long way down, and he savored the almost sickening crash of Olivia's body onto the wreckage. He immediately leapt down after her, not yet allowed the luxury of killing her.

Drake landed in a catlike manner next to Olivia's crumpled body. He immediately grabbed her dress and pulled her to her feet. She was barely conscious and bleeding from dozens of wounds, but she was still alive. Little more than a whimper escaped her lips as Drake threw her clear of the rubble with inhuman strength. Her body hit the floor limp as a ragdoll and slid across the dusty surface. The first of her silent tears had only just rolled from her cheek when Drake made his way to her.

He clicked his tongue. "Such a shame. You had such a perfect body. I would hate to see it damaged any more than it already is."

Drake's eyes raked over her tattered and torn body. Lust welled up inside of him; not for the broken woman lying in front of him, but for the jewel she hid. Nothing else mattered to him now. He knew he was getting closer to it; his greed was blinding him to what he otherwise would have recognized as a trap.

"Get up!" he barked.

Olivia closed her eyes and tried to use her left arm to push herself up. A sharp pain burst from her shoulder, preventing her from moving. Two of the fingers on her other hand refused to work, but using both arms she managed to push herself up into a reclined position. Pain arced up and down her side and back. A groan escaped her lips as she rolled over onto her knees; one of which was badly damaged. Much more damage and she wouldn't be able to walk at all.

"Get up!" Drake shouted again, kicking her hard in the ribs and clipping one of her breasts.

The blow nearly made her vomit but was not enough to knock her from her knees. With a great amount of struggle, she clenched her working fingers and pushed herself up onto her feet. Her ankle still throbbed, and now her other knee didn't want to bend. It was a struggle for Olivia to remain standing at all.

Drake's voice dripped with desire. "Take me to the jewel now and perhaps I will spare your life."

Turning away from him, Olivia gripped her dislocated arm and staggered off toward the vaults. Everything up until now went spectacularly well. She really hadn't planned on the stairs collapsing, although she had definitely been prepared to be thrown around.. Needless to say, she didn't let Drake see the grim smile that crossed her lips as she painfully led him away.

CHAPTER 20

AWAKE

Leigh's eyes snapped open. It was a moment before the sharp throbbing in her cheek and forehead reached her brain. She ignored the pain and instead concentrated on trying to remember what had happened to her. She recalled stabbing Alucard in the back, saving Kehl's life only moments after he'd done the same for her. But she had no recollection of landing on a soft comfortable couch after being backhanded. Kehl must have carried her there, she thought with a blush. A sudden clatter from behind her drew her attention down the hallway to the elevator.

Turning her head, she saw Kehl pounding against the closed doors of the elevators, trying to pry them open. The world spun as she sat up on the couch and tried to regain her feet. She managed to keep enough control of her body to remain balanced as she stood up. Leigh knew it would be best to have a weapon. Returning to where the fight had erupted earlier, she retrieved her fighting knives as well as the katana. She then ripped another section off of her already-tattered dress and wiped away what remained of Terrance's blood off the long blade. With her mind still very fuzzy, it took her several tries to return the weapons to their respective sheaths. She took off at the swiftest pace she could manage to join Kehl at the elevator doors. She knew that he deserved the thanks for carrying her to the couch.

"They're already downstairs?" she asked, feeling stupid for asking an obvious question.

Kehl spared her only the briefest of glances before he returned to his task. "It's good to see you're all right."

Leigh nodded slightly, even though Kehl wasn't looking. "Thank you," she murmured softly.

"Ha, for what? I didn't manage to stop Alucard from knocking you out. He nearly did the same to me."

"Well, you saved my life when he was about to chop my head off. And then you carried me to the couch when I was down and out."

Kehl remained silent for a moment as he continued struggling with the door.

"How about you? Are you all right?" Leigh asked.

It felt odd to be asking a creature as unnaturally powerful as a vampire such a question.

"Yes," Kehl replied.

"Good," Leigh said as a sudden wave of dizziness forced her to catch her balance on the elevator.

As her vision cleared, she noticed that the heavy elevator doors showed signs of impact. Tiny spatters of blood rested inside small craters in the metal lining their surface. Taking a moment to focus, Leigh looked at Kehl's hands. Both his fingertips and knuckles were bloody and ragged; it seemed he had been trying to get into this elevator for some time.

"You'll never get in like that," she muttered, shocked at how much the concussion was slowing down her thought processes.

Pulling up her skirt, she took one of the throwing knives from the sheath at her thigh.

"Like I said before, my father favored these kinds of elevators," she said, starting to dig around the fingerprint reader plate with her knife. "He was well aware of their considerable strengths." She twisted the knife suddenly, brining the faceplate apart. "As well as their potential weaknesses."

Pulling out a mass of wires, Leigh now had access to the small circuit board that controlled the doors. On the back of the board, surrounded by capacitors and wires, was a very small chip. Closing her eyes for a moment, Leigh tried to concentrate. How many times had her father made her break into one of these things for practice. Reopening her eyes, she swiftly and expertly sliced through one wire and arced it directly into the small black chip.

Sparks flew, and she took a step back and examined her work. Small black spots of melted plastic fell onto the floor as the chip melted away. Slowly the doors jerked open, with the elevator waiting behind them. The elevator would now return to the first floor instead of retaining its position, but at least they now had access to it.

"Nice," Kehl said as he stepped in and pressed the button for the lower floor.

Leigh looked Kehl over before following him inside. The lacerations on his fingers and knuckles were already almost fully healed. If Alucard hadn't knocked her unconscious, she might have been able to spare him that pain. Just as Leigh was about to step into the elevator, she heard the door to Olivia's chambers quickly open and close.

"Go on without me," Leigh said as she glanced over her shoulder. "I think something else has come up."

Kehl followed her gaze and noticed what Leigh was talking about. A very beautiful and very agitated woman was swiftly making her way toward them. She fit the description of Kitsu and possessed an other-worldly aura. Kehl could tell the vampress was easily as old or perhaps even older than himself.

Kehl was worried that Leigh would be vulnerable in her current state. "Will you be able to handle her?" he asked her.

"Just go," she replied, "I'll catch up with you."

Leigh would never be able to make sense of what she did next. Leaning forward, she quickly gave Kehl a quick kiss on the cheek. Maybe it was the remnants of the slight concussion, or maybe it was the fear of the approaching vampress. Whatever the cause, she would remember it until the day she died—the sudden range of emotions washing through her heart, the deadly foe approaching her back, and the very confused look on Kehl's face as the elevator doors closed. She almost wanted to laugh.

CHAPTER 21

INSIGHT

Kitsu had not planned on this happening tonight. All that she'd desired was to come out and enjoy a nice evening with her lover. She should have called things off when they were ambushed on the road but instead decided to let things take their course. After being denied entrance to the club, Drake asked her not to follow him inside as he forced his way in. Instead, Kitsu shadowed him closely, following him without his knowledge, watching him carefully to see where he went. After Drake grabbed the woman that Kitsu guessed was the Mistress, she decided to hang back for a while.

After spending the last fifteen or so minutes at the club bar, she had grown impatient and decided to follow Drake. She easily slipped through the staff entrance, and was halted by the sight of a dead body. She was relieved to find that there were no hints of Drake's demise. But the relief was short-lived as she spotted a woman quickly approaching her. Her mind instantly flew to the worst case scenario. Blood coated the sword that the woman carried, and Drake was still nowhere to be seen. Kitsu bared her fangs before launching herself down the hallway.

"Where is Drake?" the vampress hissed.

"I'm guessing you're talking about that vampire who's going around calling himself Alucard? He's dead by now. My associate just took the elevator downstairs to finish him off," Leigh said, buying time as she began circling around the strange new opponent. "And you, I take it, are Kitsu?"

"Yes, my name is Kitsu," she replied, "and you will die before my name ever crosses your lips again."

"Oh?" Leigh said, looking off to the side, not far enough lose track of Kitsu's movements. " Kitsu," Leigh chirped, trying to provoke the vampress. "Kitsu, Kitsu, Kitsu! Can't stand to hear the sound of your name on the tongue of a mortal?"

"I will tear out your throat," Kitsu roared, "and send you to hell!"

In a fight, haste and rage can make a person reckless, but Kitsu moved with intent and experience. She had met and dealt with countless swordsmen in past lifetimes. She rushed in low, and prepared to grab Leigh's arms with her preternatural speed. Kitsu's superhuman agility would not allow Leigh the time to stop her attack. She was moving too fast to stop herself, however, and found herself with an elbow rocketing toward her nose. The vampress ducked, turning her charge into a dive. She avoided the brunt of the blow and instead took a glancing shot to the eyebrow.

As she crashed into a nearby chair, Kitsu found herself amazed; the young human in front of her had executed an almost perfect counterattack. As she scrambled back to her feet, she felt something tickling her shoulder. Looking to her side, she found that a lock of her hair had been neatly sliced at a nearly perfect forty-five degree angle. Her eyes widened as she looked at Leigh, expecting her to be smug with the attack she had just made. Instead, the girl was extremely focused, with a slight anger shining in her eyes.

Leigh shifted her feet into a loose and flexible stance. She had missed her chance to end the confrontation swiftly. The young hunter watched her adversary closely. She noticed that Kitsu's composure was more wary now, and she would not let such an upset happen again. It was going to be a long hard fight, and Leigh could only hope she had the stamina and endurance to finish it. A frown crossed her brow as she imagined her father, showing up to save the day only to find his daughter dead.

Kitsu changed her strategy as she started weaving back and forth. She ducked forward, quickly feigning an attack. Leigh fell for it and flinched, taking a step back as Kitsu ducked once more. But this time Leigh didn't flinch and refused to attack. Kitsu decided to exploit Leigh's reaction and feigned once more. She was ready for the knee that Leigh rocketed forward to counter the lunge. Kitsu stepped just inside Leigh's stance and took hold of her leg by the straps of her sheath. The vampress then slammed two quick punches into Leigh's defenseless ribcage.

The sheath holding Leigh's fighting knives tore off her leg, and the young hunter stumbled backward. She was only barely able to swing her sword back over her head, and she smashed the pommel into the vampiress's chin. Both combatants reeled back, trying to quickly regain their footing. The two were an almost perfectly even match. But as Leigh caught her breath, she realized that any damage she dealt to the immortal would be little more than an annoyance. Her own stamina was already greatly decreased from the earlier battle with Randolf.

Guns would make this so much easier, Leigh thought to herself angrily as she gasped for air.

Her anger was soon replaced with fear as her thigh began to throb. The knives were now in Kitsu's possession. Before the thought had even crossed her mind, Kitsu had already unsheathed the blades and thrown the scabbard away. Leigh knew firsthand how sharp the blades were. The same blades she had admired earlier now struck fear into her heart.

Kitsu hauled her arm back, starting to throw one of the knives. Not knowing whether or not it was another feign, Leigh prepared herself. She still found herself shocked by the speed of the dagger when it left Kitsu's hand. There was no way on earth she should have been able to block such an attack. The knife collided with Leigh's katana. As is did, a thought burst into Leigh's mind. Pain lanced through her body as the deflected knife tore across her shoulder, but still, she knew what was about to happen.

Leigh screamed and jerked backward in agony as the dagger left her flesh. She turned as if in pain. A whispering footstep at her back let her know that death was only a heartbeat away. Intentionally falling forward, she kicked a foot backward, giving her torso just a little more momentum. Leigh could hear the second dagger slice through the air above her head as she hugged her sword close to her body. Her body rolled smoothly around her weapon as Kitsu carried through her motion just above her. At the end of the roll, Leigh crouched down and jammed the sword up under her armpit before standing up.

The combined momentum of Kitsu's attack and Leigh's sudden rise allowed more than enough force to drive the katana through the vampress's abdomen. After piercing her abdomen, the sword lanced up into the vampress's heart. Kitsu's mind reeled from the mental and physical shock. How many hundreds of swordsmen had failed to kill her in the many battles of the past? She tried to make one final stab with her dagger, but her arm would not respond, and the blade fell uselessly to the floor.

Drake ..., Kitsu thought as her body began to die. If only he could manage to survive, her death would not be in vain. Heaven, nirvana, paradise, if only they existed, if for no other reason than the hopeful reunion of herself and the man she loved more than any other.

Leigh heaved the vampress over her shoulder and off the blade. One final slash from the sword bisected what was left of the body, and it turned to ash. The remains drifted to the floor without a sound, blanketing the hallway in a thin snow.

Despite her victory, Leigh could find no joy in her heart and found only relief instead. Had it not been for her sudden foresight, she surely would have died. Somewhere deep down, her faith in her training grew. Her mind had been totally clear when she had slain the vampire, but only because she had practiced similar scenarios hundreds of times with a trainer. Even still, she gave most of the credit to providence, amazed that her unconventional tactic had been so successful.

She felt flush, oddly aroused, and powerful; a conglomerate of emotions that she could not make sense of. Her first step away from the fight felt like the first step of a new life. Her legs were trembling as she took the next step and felt that she may fall over. Instead, she knelt down and retrieved her daggers and sheath from the floor.

Leigh sat her katana on the floor momentarily and slowly strapped her other weapons back on. She breathed deeply, trying to force herself to calm down. As she came back up to her feet, she felt her muscles pull and stretch and heard joints popping. Her wounds throbbed and ached, though none of them were immediately life-threatening. Even the tiny self-inflicted cut she'd made earlier on her neck itched beyond all belief.

She almost laughed when she thought about it. The itch seemed to dull the pain in the rest of her body by taking her mind off of it. Without a second glance at the quickly disappearing dust behind her, Leigh turned on her heel and headed toward the elevator. She hoped she wasn't too late to lend a hand to Kehl and Olivia. That is, she thought to herself, if she could still offer any in her current state.

CHAPTER 22

A PRICE PAID

The elevator moved far too slowly for Kehl's liking, especially since the current events had abruptly changed their pace. The last he had seen of Olivia was of her unconscious body being dragged down a hallway. If she really possessed information regarding Rana, Kehl could not allow the mysterious woman to die. Still, he only halfway trusted her and couldn't help but wonder if even this attack was all part of some elaborate plot.

After what seemed like hours, the doors slowly slid open. Kehl set off quickly, following the string of dim lights to the collapsed stairwell. His gaze lingered in the darkness of the perilous hole for a moment before he stepped into the emptiness. He landed just as Alucard had, and immediately leapt from the pile of rubble, landing in a crouch on the clean floor some distance away.

Off in the distance came a disturbing loud metallic thud—the vault had been opened. Kehl was already running, fearing that he was already too late. Small clouds of dust rose from his feet as he dashed through the blackness. He could hear the elevator beginning to return to the top floor far above. He couldn't help but wonder what had delayed Leigh, and if it was even her making her way down. A few more of the lights had blown out since his last visit, but he was able to find the vaults with ease.

The solemn row of vaults lay silent. They were still well lit, although the fifth one stood with its door wide open. Olivia was leaning against the wall opposite the door, her shoulders jumping up and down. Strangely, Kehl couldn't tell whether she was crying or laughing. Regardless, Kehl sped down the corridor and looked into the belly of the iron beast. He could see the huge dark man lumbering deeper into the vault, growling as he reached the gate. It seemed Olivia had unlocked the vault for him but had not revealed that there was a secondary door inside.

It made no difference to Drake as he wrapped his hands about the thick iron pillars and began to pull. The whisper of cloth made him turn his head just in time to receive a thundering punch to his temple. Kehl was smaller than Drake physically, but what he lacked in size he made up for in the power of his age. The blow sent Drake crashing headfirst into the bars, bending them slightly. Before Drake could react, two more punches thundered into the unprotected area just above the hips. Such a blow would have slain a normal human, but they did little more than annoy and wind the massive Drake.

Whirling about, Drake attempted to land an elbow, but unlike before, this fight was on Kehl's terms. Kehl ducked under the blow before launching a knee into Drake's gut. Utilizing his momentum, Kehl descended and used the added force in another punch that fell on Drake's jaw. The bone inside had already started mending itself when the fist left the flesh, but there was still pain, and lots of it. Bracing his back up against the bars, Drake viciously kicked both of his legs forward into Kehl's stomach. Kehl staggered back and had just enough time to see his opponent reach back with single arm and take hold of the door.

The seams at the shoulder of Drake's jacket popped loose as the muscles in his arms swelled with sudden and savage exertion. Behind him, the bars buckled and groaned. A section of the gate ripped away entirely, flying past Drake with deadly speed. The direction of the fight had changed as the bars connected with Kehl's forehead, knocking him down and rendering him almost unconscious. The chunk of metal slid across the floor and fell partially out of the vault door. Kehl would no longer be a bother for the next several moments, if not longer.

Mere feet now separated Drake and the Midnight Nocturne. He made quick work of what remained of the iron bars. As he neared the jewel, a sickening feeling spread through his gut, forcing him to stop. A quick glance behind revealed that Kehl was still too groggy to stand. Drake checked himself over and sought out the source of the strange sensation. It wasn't pain causing the odd feeling. As he returned his gaze to the shrouded Midnight, he suddenly wondered what his actions would cost him and whether that price would justify the end result.

But his misgivings melted away as he took the final step that brought him directly in front of the jewel. A shiver ran up and down his spine when he pulled away the shroud. It was everything he had imagined it would be, and more. It was a shame that it would have to be destroyed. Perhaps, he thought to himself, the broken shards could be salvaged.

He casually tossed the shroud away before scooping up the jewel. Its perfectly flat surfaces made his hand tingle, while the edges felt as if they would slice deep into his flesh.

Kehl managed to push himself shakily up to his feet just in time to see Drake take hold of the jewel. Without the slightest warning, the door to the vault slammed inward. It groaned as it was unable to shut with the chunk of metal bars blocking its path. Too dizzy to offer any resistance, Kehl lurched forward and attempted to snag the Midnight Nocturne. Drake backhanded him hard across the cheek. Kehl crumpled again onto the cold vault floor. There was just enough room to allow Drake to edge sideways through the partially closed vault door. Olivia was gone, but he didn't seem to notice; only the jewel mattered now.

Halfway out of the vault, he came face to face with Leigh. She was dirty and scraped up from slowly climbing down the pile of debris to get to the vaults. Drake could smell Kitsu's scent on her, as well as the bitter odor of burnt ash. Rage boiled in him as Leigh leveled the sword that killed his lover at him. He rushed forward with blinding speed, backhanding the flat side of the sword. The attack sent the blade flying from Leigh's hands and buried into the wall on the opposite side of the room. With his next step, Drake pounded his fist into her stomach, lifting her off the ground and ripping a scream from her lips. Before she could fall to the ground, he spun on the ball of his foot and brought the back of his heel around, dealing Leigh a crushing blow to the neck that sent her tumbling across the floor.

Leigh hit the wall hard. Her vision was blurry as she staggered to her feet and drew her fighting knives. She functioned only on instinct, her mind barely conscious, her movements sluggish. She stumbled forward, slashing at the air in front of her, much too far away from Drake to actually cut him. He laughed at her feeble efforts.

"I should kill you for what you've done to Kitsu," he said.

But in that instant, the words seemed to ring hollow to his own ears. The jewel was now more important than anything else in his entire life. His earlier dilemma of having to choose between the jewel and his lover was removed. This pitiful human in front of him was hardly worth his time. She was barely even conscious. Without giving the young hunter a second thought, Drake turned away from her and ran from the room.

With the vampire gone, Leigh had no reason to continue fighting. Her vision slowly darkened around the edges as she fell to her knees.

She tried to stand, but her body wouldn't listen to what her mind told it to do. She fell hard onto the unforgiving floor. Just before she blacked out, she thought she saw someone running toward her. She wondered with her last conscious thought if it was Kehl.

CHAPTER 23

CHASE

Kehl slowly reached a hand to his forehead, groggily brushing away several flecks of dried blood. Had it been minutes? Hours? Or only mere seconds that he had been unconscious? The world had blacked out after Alucard hurled the door at him. He could vaguely remember lunging for the jewel. Walking as fast as he could, he made his way out of the vault. Looking down the length of the room, he could see the hunched figure of Olivia bending over Leigh.

"What happened?" he asked.

"You failed me," Olivia answered simply, almost as if she knew that it would happen. "Leigh, however," she continued, "succeeded in destroying Alucard's escort."

Kehl could see that Olivia's eyes were locked on Leigh with real concern, as a parent might look upon a sick child.

"Where has Alucard gone?" Kehl asked as the last remnants of fog drifted from his mind.

"His true name is Drake, and I assume he is leaving the club," Olivia said simply, watching as Leigh moaned and began to stir.

"Go," she commanded Kehl. "Go, now."

The weight of his failure settled into Kehl as he ran from the room. He couldn't tear his mind away from Leigh. He also couldn't place aside the possibility that Rana was alive. Why were these things that should be so trivial compared to the Midnight Nocturne so prominent in his mind? He would have to clear his mind before he got back to his motorcycle.

* * *

When the elevator doors opened, Drake was already running. He planned to hold Olivia hostage when leaving the club, but she had mysteriously vanished. The scent of his lover's ash was strong in her apartment, and it made him dizzy. Behind him he heard the elevator descend. He was being pursued, and although already having defeated Kehl twice in combat, he was not so sure his luck would hold out in another fight. He glanced for a moment at the Midnight Nocturne held tightly in his hand before quickening his pace. Now that his lover was gone, all that mattered was power. The jewel had to be destroyed. By the time he cleared the apartment and was about to reenter the club, the elevator was already starting its return journey, no doubt with Kehl inside.

Far down the hallway, the doors of the elevator slid open. Kehl could see Drake slip through the door and out into the club. He raced across the living quarters and ripped open the door. Unsurprisingly, the dance was still going on, growing even more chaotic and intense than before. Drake quickly disappeared into the writhing mass of bodies.

The presence of the jewel only seemed to excite the crowd into more frenzied dancing, which made it more difficult for the large vampire to pass. He overcame this obstacle with his inhuman strength, physically moving people with his might when they did not allow him passage. When he finally made it to the coat check room, he found the massive front doors locked and closed. With one strong kick, he shattered the lock and knocked the doors open.

The bouncers were taken by surprise on the other side of the door. They tried to stop Drake, but he brushed them aside as if they were flies. He could already see his driver waiting in the parked car on the other side of the street. This was exactly why he had one of his servants follow the limo with a faster vehicle. The Midnight Nocturne was one of the most desirable jewels in all of history. Even though the events of the night had angered Drake, it was to be expected and he had come prepared.

Drake jumped the velvet rope and began sprinting across the street to his car. The driver spotted him and stood outside the car with the door open and the engine running. It was Drake's favorite and fastest car. It was also the one he was the most used to. There would be no better vehicle for him to make an escape in. He jumped in and threw the car into gear, spinning the tires before they caught hold of the pavement and launched the vehicle forward. Drake watched in his rearview mirror as the nightclub quickly vanished from view behind him.

* * *

After pushing through what seemed to be endless miles of bodies, Kehl finally made his way to the entrance chamber. It was empty, save for the coat check girl. She stood resolutely at her post. As Kehl approached, she calmly bowed down under the counter and retrieved Kehl's jacket, tossing it almost casually over the counter to him.

"Go get him," she chirped as Kehl looked at her with a curious expression.

His motorcycle jacket held not only armor plating but also a concealed pistol. The girl had just chucked it at him without so much as a second glance. *Never forgets a face,* Kehl thought to himself as he hastily pulled on the jacket and zipped it up. The girl then pulled his riding pants out from under the counter and tossed them at him as well. Shaking his head, Kehl stuffed the pants into his jacket and dashed out the front door. Surprised, he found his motorcycle leaning on its kickstand close to the entrance behind the ropes. The sound of squealing tires drew his attention to an exotic black sports car speeding recklessly down the lane. It had to be Drake, trying to escape with the jewel.

Kehl swung his leg over the seat of his bike and pulled the laser-cut key from his jacket pocket. The bike started up instantly with a roar as he turned the key. He kept one foot on the ground and gunned the engine. The bike whipped around toward the waiting road. A sudden burst of acceleration lifted the front wheel into the air, and the motorcycle launched forward. The speeding sports car had already vanished from sight in the few seconds it took to start the motorcycle. Kehl ducked low against the gas tank, pulling the throttle back as far as possible as he changed gears. He didn't bother turning on his headlight: he could see fine without it, and its beam would merely announce his presence to Drake.

Further ahead on the road, Drake couldn't shake the feeling that he was being followed. Something caught his eye as he looked through the rearview. After giving the mirror a double take, he saw nothing but inky blackness behind him. Red lights swam into his vision as he came up on another motorist. He jerked the steering wheel to the side and flooring the accelerator, barely avoided a collision. Immediately looking back into the mirror, all he saw was the swerving headlights of the car as it smashed into a building.

Just as Drake was about to dismiss the strange feeling, he turned his eyes to the passenger-side mirror. There in the small mirror he could see the headlights behind him silhouette a motorcycle and rider who was almost perfectly in his blind spot. The swerving must have been difficult for the rider to negotiate while maintaining a comfortable spot in the unseen areas behind the car. Drake had to smile. Although his car was heavier, it could easily outrun most motorcycles. Unless his pursuer rode an equally exceptional piece of machinery, he would make a clean getaway.

Shifting down a gear, Drake smashed down on the gas. The car accelerated quickly and threw him back into his seat. With a glance in his mirror, he saw that the motorcycle still close behind. Accelerating once more, he jerked the steering wheel and made a ninety-degree turn and into an alleyway. On the slippery snow-covered road, it would be nearly impossible for the cycle to continue its pursuit.

Drake decelerated, pleased to see the motorcycle's wheels slide out from underneath the rider. The kickstand threw sparks into the snow as the motorcycle flipped over onto its side and slid toward the building that formed one wall of the alley. But his joy was short-lived, as Kehl increased the throttle and propelled the bike forward as it impacted the wall. With a kick of his leg, the motorcycle was upright once more, damaged, but still in pursuit.

The exotic car fishtailed as Drake floored the accelerator, rocketing down the rest of the alleyway before turning back onto a main street. The cycle followed, staying close behind. To Drake, the bike seemed to be falling behind by the slightest of margins. Merging onto a bridge, Drake decided to try to outrun the bike. He pushed his vehicle to its limits, passing car after car as if they stood still. He no longer bothered to check his mirrors. The needle of his speedometer climbed above and beyond the one-hundred-miles-per-hour mark and kept rising as he smashed through a toll gate.

He didn't hear the gunshot over the roar of his engine, but he heard the bullet tear through the body of his car next to his seat before piercing the windshield. Swerving suddenly and erratically, he tried to make himself a difficult target. The next shot tore through his right shoulder, tearing out a nasty chunk of flesh that would take hours, maybe even days to fully heal. Barely able to move his hand, Drake opened a small hatch next to the shifter. He flipped a switch inside and immediately brought both hands to the steering wheel. The car jerked forward with a sudden burst of nitrous-powered speed.

Wind whistled through the hole in the front glass as he gained more and more speed. Weakened by the gunshot, the windshield began to crack under the sheer force of the wind. Scenery on either side of the cabin passed so quickly that everything seemed to blur into streaks. Drake passed what little traffic remained on the late-night roads as if they were immobile rocks. A police cruiser caught his attention but didn't bother to follow, as the car was now approaching two hundred miles an hour.

As a car swerved out of control in front of him, Drake gazed once more into his rearview. It seemed as though he had escaped the motorcycle. But a sudden beeping noise brought his attention back to the dash. Finding the correct gauge, he saw that his engine was growing dangerously hot. Gritting his teeth, he decided not to turn off the nitrous. If the engine blew, he would just have to abandon the car. His eyes darted frantically back and forth between the road and the heat gauge.

Looking back into his mirror, Drake had only a split second to see the underbelly of the motorcycle as Kehl pulled it up onto one wheel. The front wheel of the bike came crashing down hard on the rear end of the car. Built of lightweight materials, the trunk section of the sports car crumpled around the tire. Kehl readied his pistol and shot three quick rounds into the driver's side. The third shot tore through the driver's seat and caught Drake in the back, piercing his lung.

After returning his gun to its holster, Kehl jerked back hard on his handlebars, freeing his bike from the car. The front tire chirped as it touched the ground at the almost inhuman speed. As Kehl slowed his bike slightly, he decided to follow Drake.

Inside the cabin, Drake roared with anger as blood bubbled from his mouth and wounds. He slammed his fist down on the steering wheel, forcing his damaged arm to work. He threw the transmission into a gear that was far too low and slammed on the brakes, sending the car into a sudden violent skid. Kehl came into sight, framed perfectly through the passenger side window. A moment later, the motorcycle torpedoed into the side of the car. The impact was incredible. Without the roll cage surrounding the cabin, the motorcycle would have plowed completely through the car. However, metal tore through metal as Kehl slammed onto the roof of the car before flying through the air and landing hard on the road. His body slid off into the distance before finally coming to a halt.

Accelerating once more, Drake tore the motorcycle from the side of his vehicle and shot off into the darkness. His vision was already starting to grow dark, but he would make it home. He had to. Once there he would feed on one of his newly acquired servants. With Kitsu's death, all of her wealth and property became his. Although he mourned her passing, he would not hesitate in the least in utilizing her assets.

CHAPTER 24

PECULIAR

Leigh's eyes snapped open. The last thing she remembered was having her sword batted away like a toothpick. Sitting up, she looked about her, not recognizing the living quarters of Olivia. Suddenly the panic subsided as a massive headache descended on her brain. With a groan, she fell backward, grateful that she had woken up on one of the Olivia's sofas and not in the afterlife.

"Hello Peepers," came a comforting and familiar voice.

"Daddy?" she asked without looking, ashamed at her failure.

"I'm here baby," he whispered, patting her on the head. "I see you killed your first vampire by yourself today. She was an old one too, from the sounds of it, from feudal Japan or some such."

Leigh rubbed at her eyes, attempting to rid herself of the headache. "I think it was more luck than anything. She was so much stronger and faster than me."

"Tell me about the fight," Jesse said.

"It started out okay," Leigh answered. "I anticipated her speed and managed to counter her first attack."

"Good, good," her father murmured.

"It went bad from then on, though. She got inside my guard and hit me hard. I almost thought she cracked my ribs. And then she took my daggers."

"Ouch," Jesse said with an empathetic wince. "So how did you wind up killing her?"

"She threw one of the daggers directly at my sword. I couldn't have blocked it if she'd wanted to hit me anywhere else, but she didn't know that. The dagger cut me on my shoulder, so I feigned pain to draw her attack. She flanked me and would have taken my head off with another of the daggers, but I rolled forward. I reversed the sword in my hands and stabbed it backward as I stood back up. It never should have worked."

"But it did," her father said with a chuckle. "It sounds to me like your training paid off."

"It didn't against Drake," she replied darkly.

"Don't worry about him, or the jewel," Jesse said dismissively. "Kehl is after him."

Leigh frowned. "He's a vampire too, you know."

"And a very peculiar one at that," Jesse continued. "Just look what he did."

Reaching around the couch he picked up what appeared to be a rather shabby cardboard box. He tipped it forward slowly to show Leigh the contents. Curled up inside and wrapped in a towel was a tiny peach-colored ball of fluff. Leigh could see that the kitten's eyes were badly swollen. She couldn't understand how the poor thing could sleep with all the fleas that plagued it.

"He saved the kitten?" she asked with quiet amazement as she put her hand down in the box and gently caressed the top of the kitten's head. It yawned, stretched out its claws, and went right on sleeping. A warm, caring feeling spread through Leigh and combined with her headache and worry to make her feel queasy.

"Lay back down," Jesse instructed her as her brow screwed up.

"He tried to sweep me off my feet out on the dance floor," she said as she put a hand to her head and closed her eyes. "Can you believe that?"

Her father remained silent. This was unexpected news.

"And it's not really like I fought it. It's been two years since the last time a guy even so much as chatted me up. He even showed me how to dance." She shook her head and looked up at the ceiling. "I had no clue what he was until he vaporized a paper cross made out of a straw wrapper." After what she'd just been through, the paper cross gag was actually starting to seem funny. "Anyway, I should be more worried about the Nocturne now than about some stupid guy."

"Yes, you should," her father said. He spoke so quickly that Leigh wondered what had changed his dismissive view of the Nocturne from only moments before.

As she turned to examine his expression, she noticed that his head was turned off to the side and he looked though he was about to cry. It seemed there were things that he wanted to say but couldn't. She then quietly returned her eyes to the ceiling, acting if she hadn't seen his strange behavior. Somewhere in the back of her mind she realized that he had never reacted this way before. Her father had actually been happy when the last boy came to call. So long as dating didn't interfere with her training, Jesse really didn't mind what she did with her spare time.

For a moment, Leigh wondered if her father was only angry because Kehl was a vampire. Jesse actually preferred when a vampire and human fell in love together. It usually meant the end of the predatory nature of the vampire in the relationship, so long as the human wasn't turned. The human would generally stop aging so long as the vampire continued to feed. Given what was basically a never-ending supply of blood via their lover, the vampire no longer needed to hunt to feed. The constant feeding would weaken the human, however, leaving even the most robust people permanently exhausted. Needless to say, such a state would be bad for Leigh if she planned to carry on the family business. Maybe it was just the simple fact that Jesse didn't want to see his daughter like that, seemingly on the verge of death, yet never aging.

Thinking it through, Leigh found her theory hard to believe. If hunting the supernatural was truly so important to her father, he would never have retired, much less moved to England. Perhaps he knew something about Kehl's past. It didn't matter. She was on the job now and would have to push such thoughts from her mind.

"I patched you up as good as I could manage," Jesse said, as though the strange turn in conversation had never happened. "You're going to need some rest, though."

"Ha, that's not what you said when you were training me," Leigh said with a groan as she put her feet on the floor.

"This is different," her father said with a frown.

"No, it's not," Leigh said with a slight smile. "I can sleep when I'm dead."

CHAPTER 25

DEAD ON ARRIVAL

Kehl's eyelids drifted open and he saw the interior of an ambulance. He was badly dazed and could feel that his body was struggling to repair the massive trauma that it had been dealt. He could hear the volunteer rescue squad driver radio into dispatch with a status report. "I'm on the way back in with a DOA. Unit 349 out."

"No use rushing," the other volunteer said from the passenger seat. "He had to have been going way too fast. Did you see his bike?"

"Yeah," the driver said. "It was almost unrecognizable. I don't think I've ever seen a worse case of road rash."

"I'm surprised he didn't look like spaghetti pizza after that wreck," the passenger said.

The driver laughed in a faraway manner, unhappy to be carrying a cadaver. Unaccompanied in the back, Kehl sat up, groaning inwardly as unhealed ab muscles roared painfully in protest. As he flexed his fingers, Kehl could feel that at least his hands were healed, although his forearm muscles audibly popped in protest of movement.

His shirt and jacket had been ripped off, and his legs were still strapped into the gurney. Reaching down, Kehl undid the bindings as quietly as he could, freeing himself with ease. He only wished that retrieving the Nocturne could have been that easy. He could see the medics staring absentmindedly at the road, still thinking that they were carrying his dead body to the morgue.

New muscles knitted themselves together as Kehl attempted to stand. But his body still couldn't support itself. Stumbling forward, he tried to brace himself and accidentally tipped over a drawer of emergency tools. His attempt to catch the drawer only sent its contents flying out, making a loud racket. In the front of the ambulance, the passenger turned to see what was causing all of the noise. His eyes widened in disbelief when he saw Kehl supporting himself against the side of the ambulance wall.

"Holy shit!" the man screamed, causing the driver to jump.

"What? What!" the driver roared as he desperately tried to right the ungainly ambulance.

"You won't believe this," the passenger said, unable to move his eyes from Kehl. "He's alive!"

"Come on, man," the driver growled. "Don't screw with me like that. I almost wrecked the truck because of you!"

Momentarily taking his eyes off the road to look at his partner, the driver saw that he was still staring into the back. With a curse, the driver pulled the ambulance over to the side of the road and jerked his head back. What he saw next would make him tout the event as a miracle. The ambulance doors swung open loosely behind an empty stretcher. Further back down the road, he could see someone limping away, presumably the would-be corpse.

The driver then turned the ambulance around and pulled up beside Kehl.

"Hey buddy," he called out the window. "I ... I think you, uh, might need to get back in the ambulance."

Kehl shook his head and continued walking.

"I don't think he knows what happened to him," the passenger whispered.

"You were actually dead a few minutes ago," the driver called out.

"I've been dead for a lot longer than that," Kehl said, turning to look the driver in his eyes.

Something in the vampire's gaze stirred emotions deep inside of the driver, making him want to believe Kehl's words.

"Okay, buddy," the driver replied, "even if that's true, what do we tell dispatch? We reported that we were carrying a DOA. That's a very serious thing."

"Tell them that you managed to revive me and that I refused further treatment."

"But there will be police reports about your wreck," the driver insisted.

"Leave me be!" Kehl roared, baring his fangs at the ambulance driver.

"Okay, buddy," the driver said before speeding off, completely terrified.

Some ways down the road, Kehl continued limping his way back toward the Nocturne, unsure of how he would break the news of this newest failure to Olivia. His limp faded the further he walked, until eventually his stride returned to normal. He wondered what he must look like to the few passersby there were, a shirtless man walking through two-inch thick snow in the dead of night.

CHAPTER 26

LAST RIDE HOME

Looking to the sky, Kehl could see that morning was only a few hours away. He also felt his powers beginning to wane with the coming of day. He wondered if the full rays of the sun fell on him, would be destroyed? Since his turning, he had never once set foot into daylight, being well familiar with the legends. Thoughts of simply waiting in the street for sunrise to take him flickered through his mind. A loud roar from an engine broke him from his morbid thoughts. He turned as Leigh's tattered old Mustang came plowing through the snow, unhindered. The window closest to him rolled down as the car came sliding to a halt right beside him.

"Drake got you too, huh?" Leigh's voice said from the other side of the car.

Kehl made no reply as he leaned over and made eye contact with her. Her expression did little to conceal her worry for him. Some of his wounds from the crash were still clearly visible, and Leigh couldn't seem to stop looking at them.

"They said I should come find you and get you home, what with it being so late and all. I've got your cat too."

"You can have the cat," Kehl replied. "And the sunlight doesn't bother me." He was bluffing, not knowing for sure if the sun could indeed destroy him.

"Anyway, we don't even know where Drake is headed next, and even though you can keep going forever, I, personally, could use some rest." Reaching across the car, Leigh threw the passenger door open as forcefully as she could.

Kehl stared at her for a moment before climbing into the car. It was clear that she really wanted to get him away from the sunlight. The inside of the car smelled of old leather and the natural scent of its young driver. To Kehl, the scent was the sweetest of all perfumes. Long-forgotten feelings began to stir in his damned heart as he drank it in.

"So," he said as Leigh put the car in gear and started driving, "what happened to you down in the basement?"

"I don't know," Leigh said, slightly irked, though not at Kehl. "I really don't remember much at all. I've got a nasty knot on my neck that's probably going to bruise, but other than that, I don't know."

"Take a right up here," Kehl said.

"I managed to get Kitsu, but only barely," she murmured.

"Kitsu was there too?" he asked. "Take a left here."

"I don't know whether she was his master, slave, or a lover, but she was anxious to find Drake."

Kehl turned his head slightly to look at her. Her eyes showed slight swelling. There were also slightly bloodied bandages on her other shoulder. Being human would make her wounds heal much slower than his own. He found himself wishing for some way to help heal her, or at least to help alleviate the pain.

Over the next half hour, they talked about their fights with Drake, Kitsu, and the two newborns. Keeping a moderate pace, Leigh easily navigated out of the snow-blanketed city until they rolled to a stop in front of the open gates to Kehl's estate. The darkness prevented Leigh from seeing very far past the gates, and she found herself growing deeply curious.

Pulling the parking brake, she looked over at Kehl. "It must be nice …"

"It's lonely, really. I only have my books and my memories to keep me company. I wouldn't have need of such a large house if not for all of trinkets I've accumulated over the years."

"What about your employees?"

"Well, I have a staff, but not a permanent one. They usually come once or twice a week and do their work during the day when I'm either asleep or away on business."

"Business?" Leigh asked, giving him a very tired and curious look. "What business does a vampire have?"

"Well," he answered calmly. "There are various investments that need managing. It's good to keep a nice flow of money in and out so people in high places don't get too suspicious. I had to fake my own death thirty years ago. It was an awful bit of business involving a wrecked car and a lot of paperwork."

Leigh giggled softly, but her laughter seemed to drain what little energy she had left. As she grew quiet, her eyes slipped closed as her head lolled. An instant later, she snapped her eyes opened and looked around, trying to figure out what had happened. After blinking several times, she rubbed her eyes and looked over at Kehl.

"Did I just fall asleep?" she asked, embarrassed.

"Yes," he said with a sympathetic smile.

Blinking her eyes a few more times, she put her hands back on the steering wheel. "Sorry about that, I'm just so tired, and the heater is making me drowsy."

"You have nothing to be sorry about," Kehl replied. "How far do you have to drive to get back home?"

"Oh," she murmured, the fatigue deepening in her voice as she made the estimate. "Uh, probably a little more than an hour, maybe two if the snow gets worse."

"That's an awfully long way, and you look really tired," Kehl started.

Leigh surprised him with a grin. "Are you trying to get me to spend the day with you?"

"Well, you're awfully torn up. And it's a big mansion, so you don't really have to spend any time with me. I usually just sleep during the day, or sometimes I read in the library when I can't."

Leigh avoided talking about her injuries. "There's a library in there?"

"It's modest," Kehl said, somewhat shyly. "Just a few things I've collected over the years, really."

Leigh laughed and tried to rub some of the sleep from her eyes. "I usually just keep my books stacked on the floor in the bathroom."

"Okay, the fact that you actually just said that means that you are too tired to drive home," Kehl said smugly, closing the car door.

A bright, genuine smile crossed Leigh's lips. "Maybe you're right."

"Drive on in," he said, "or drive back home. But if you do, I'm coming with you to make sure you get back okay."

There was no way Kehl would let the young girl drive home through the snow and get herself killed in a car wreck. Leigh looked off into the darkness with some apprehension. It was a very long way for her to go home, and, honestly, she didn't trust herself to stay awake the whole way. What would be worse, getting in a car wreck, or spending the day with a sleeping vampire who just might get hungry? She was just about to risk the drive home when a renewed wave of exhaustion poured over her.

"Okay," she said, putting her car into gear and driving through the gates. "You convinced me."

CHAPTER 27
THRESHOLD

Leigh felt crazy for going through with it, especially when all of her instincts were telling her not to. As they drove past snow-covered shrubs Leigh imagined vampires or werewolves waiting in the darkness to pounce on her. The snow crunching under her tires reminded her of the sound of crushing bones from a horror flick. Suddenly, her fear vanished and she found herself grateful to have Kehl so close to her in her weakened state. Darkness spread in from the edges of her vision, and she felt her head nod forward yet again. With a sudden jerk of the steering wheel, she snapped her head back up. The Mustang slid sideways for a moment and brushed against a bush. Leigh cursed but corrected her course.

"Whoa!" Kehl yelped, reaching for the wheel.

"No, don't!" Leigh growled, making a very tired, yet successful swipe at his hand.

"Ouch," Kehl said playfully, rubbing at his hand.

"Oh, come on," Leigh said in her exhaustion. "That couldn't possibly have hurt you. You're a vampire."

Leigh absentmindedly stopped the car almost right in front of the mansion.

"Does too," Kehl said, suddenly thinking of the torture room buried beneath the mansion, worrying that she might find it.

Kehl opened his door and stepped out into the snow. He then made his way around to the other side of the car. As he opened the door, Leigh started to get out but looked as though she was about to collapse. Kehl offered his hand and helped her stand up. He could see that her physical conditioning alone kept her upright, even though she could barely maintain her balance.

"Aww," Leigh whined as her feet sank into the now six-inch deep snow. "These are the only nice shoes I have," she said, seeming almost drunk in her current state.

Kehl moved too swiftly for Leigh to resist, and with one quick motion, he literally swept her off her feet. Suddenly, Kehl's mind was outside his cabin, centuries before, carrying another woman across a threshold. He paused for a moment, wondering how he could be doing things like this after being informed that Rana may yet be alive.

Leigh struggled to understand Kehl's actions through the exhausted, punch-drunk haze clouding her mind. She couldn't decide whether he sought to take advantage of her or if he was just being kind so that the snow wouldn't ruin her shoes. What confused her even more was the fact that she found herself smiling, mystified that this could possibly be happening to her. She decided that once inside the door, she would not allow Kehl to touch her again. He had carried her to the door in the amount of time it took her to make her decision. After setting her down, he opened the door, which was usually left unlocked, and went inside. Seconds later, the foyer and entrance way lit up warmly and invitingly.

"Come on in," Kehl said.

"Oh!" Leigh said, suddenly feeling horrible about herself. "The kitten!"

Kehl nodded and walked back to the car, opening one of the doors and peeking in. Looking into the backseat, he found the small cardboard box with a bit of towel sticking out. He quickly retrieved the box and looked inside. Leigh must have covered the kitten in a towel to protect it from the cold. All he could see of it were its eyes. Oddly enough, they seemed slightly less swollen than before.

Kehl returned to the foyer and walked inside, closing the door behind them. The house was well lit and very comfortable-looking despite its monstrous size. It was nowhere near as sparse or as gothic as Olivia's apartment, although it bore its own sort of darkness. Leigh fantasized that the house hid some deeply hidden secret, not knowing how correct her thought was.

"It's warm in here," she said, noticing that the temperature inside was quite comfortable. "I didn't think that vampires needed heat."

"We don't, really," Kehl answered with a faraway smile. "I don't need the warmth, but it helps to not feel so alone. It also helps me to fight my ... urges. When it's cold, I find myself wanting to feed on something warm."

Their gaze met, and for a moment Kehl thought that he could almost see a pleading look in the young huntress's eyes. It was as though she wanted him to feed from her. Kehl decided it was only his own tired imagination. He did not know that Leigh was searching his own eyes for a hint that he wanted to drink her blood. She knew he was wounded and needed blood, but she was still uncertain of her own intentions. Would she let him feed on her essence and heal? Or would she deny them both of their most primal desires? Deep in her soul, Leigh wanted to feel his immortal kiss, even though it would cost her everything.

"So, let me show you to the guest rooms," Kehl said, interrupting her thoughts.

Leigh paused for a moment as she thought through his words. The guest rooms in a mansion this big were likely far away from the master suite, maybe even in their own wing. Perhaps Kehl wanted her to be as far away as possible so that they both might be more comfortable. She appreciated his concerns but didn't like the idea of spending the night in a strange mansion a long way away from its only other inhabitant.

"This way," he said, starting to go up a flight of stairs.

"Um," Leigh murmured, "you don't have a couch, do you?"

Kehl was confused. "You wouldn't prefer a bed?"

She shook her head. "I prefer to have something at my back. It makes me feel safe." *And not so alone*, she thought to herself.

"Very well," Kehl replied like a concierge. "I have couches in the library, living room, and in several of the hallways, not to mention in a few of the bedrooms."

"Which would be closest to you?" she asked before realizing what the question implied. "Just in case something happens during the, day I mean."

Kehl noticed her quick cover and could not help but read into it. Both of their minds were spinning from the weight of everything that had happened. He would not allow the situation to spiral further out of control. It took a moment for him to formulate an answer to her question.

"The library has some of the most comfortable couches, and they are close to my rooms."

Leigh nodded, grateful that Kehl seemed to dismiss her slipped comment. "I'd like that."

Kehl showed no signs of reaction. "Follow me then."

Kehl led her up a flight of stairs, deciding to let the house speak for itself as he showed her the way. The house was nearly eight centuries old at it's core, and even though there were numerous additions and renovations it remained a mysterious and romantic place. At times, merely walking its halls would sometimes make Kehl heartsick. Behind him he could hear Leigh pausing momentarily to examine a trinket or piece of art before hastily catching up. After several moments of walking, they arrived at the entrance to the library.

"Oh no," Leigh moaned as Kehl opened the last door.

"Something wrong?" Kehl asked, turning to her just as he brought up the lights in the library to a dim glow.

"I had expected something else. I don't know what, maybe an office with a couch and some books around the walls," she replied.

Kehl looked at the library with a clueless expression and then back at Leigh. "I'm sorry that it doesn't suit you. Here, this should make it a bit more cozy."

Kehl turned a knob on the same panel as the light controls and a massive fireplace on the opposite side of the library burst to life. Leigh was surprised to see such a thing in a library, but as her eyes adjusted to the light of the fire, she realized that the flames burned safely behind a glass barrier. It seemed more than a bit risky having a fireplace in a library, but it gave the room a very distinctive atmosphere.

"No, that's not what I mean. It's just too big for me to be able to sleep here. I fell asleep once at school in the library. When I woke up, it felt like all the books were glaring at me. It was like they were chastising me for being so careless. I didn't know you had an actual library."

Kehl laughed. "I'll take you to one of the guest rooms, then."

Leigh shook her head quickly. She cautiously posed another question. "Do you have a couch in your room?"

Kehl paused, feeling awkward when he finally answered. "Yes, I do."

Leigh nodded in a noncommittal way. "Can I leave the kitten in here for the night? I don't want to leave it alone, but that fireplace seems nice and warm. I think the box will do just fine as a bed for her tonight after being outside in the snow for so long."

Kehl nodded and motioned to a spot next to an overstuffed sofa. Leigh walked to the spot and sat the box down as carefully as she could before kneeling at its side. Halfway out of its towel blanket, the kitten looked up at her and mewed. Its tiny paws kneaded the fabric beneath its toes once it spotted Leigh.

"Here we go, baby," she whispered to the small kitten. "You'll be okay here tonight."

Leigh reached down into the box and gently adjusted the blankets to make the kitten more comfortable.

"Have you come up with a name yet?" Kehl asked as he watched her with interest.

"Kali Sunshine," she replied.

"I like it. How did you come up with it?"

"Even though she's sick, she is just so full of energy and light. She reminds me of the sun on a perfect cloudless day." Her voice trailed off as she gazed down at Kali and scratched behind her ear.

In the evening, she would have to give Kali a bath and try to get rid of those fleas. Maybe it was only wishful thinking on Leigh's part, but the kitten seemed to have gotten a little better since being brought from the club. Tiny half moons of bright blue eyes peeked out from under her swollen eyelids. Kali mewed again and purred contentedly.

Leigh found herself growing more comfortable with the strange vampire next to her. "Why did you save her?"

Kehl gazed away from Leigh toward the sofa. "I don't know. I felt pity for her, but I also admired her tenacity to cling to life. I didn't notice her at first because of the fight with Elizabeth. Would you believe that she actually came up and bit me?"

"That was a very sweet thing you did," Leigh said, caressing Kali's forehead.

"I don't know," Kehl murmured. "I didn't know Elizabeth, but she was so young. It wasn't until she told me about killing her own mother that I even decided to go through with it. I guess the only way I could deal with that was to help the kitten. I just hope the poor thing isn't past saving."

Leigh nodded slightly before pushing herself slowly to her feet.

"She will be fine," Leigh said with certainty. "She drank a whole cup of milk back at the club."

"You don't think she has rabies?" Kehl asked. "She did bite me, remember?"

Leigh giggled, "No, she doesn't have rabies. She was probably just trying to get your attention."

Leigh's dress still lay in ruins as she stood, and even though Kehl only gazed at her back, he could not help but feel both thirst and burgeoning arousal. With her hair falling over her shoulders, Leigh's wounds were concealed, and her body appeared perfect. He was both unprepared for and unable to resist this sudden loss of control.

He involuntarily took a step forward, his lips curling back into a silent snarl as he bared his fangs. His body was badly damaged and needed blood to fully repair itself. The weak mortal standing in front of him would be easy prey. Kehl took one more step and reached out his hand. Her shoulder was only inches away from his grasp. One more step and he would have her. She would experience the single most excruciatingly erotic moment of her life before he stole it away.

Unaware of Kehl's intentions, Leigh yawned and threw her head to the side to readjust her hair. The bandage at her back was immediately exposed to Kehl's vision. The sight of Leigh's blood snapped Kehl out of his frenzy, much to his own surprise. Freely flowing blood should only have deepened his thirst, but now that it came from Leigh, he found himself not only concerned for her but ashamed of himself.

He turned his eyes away out of sheer guilt, struggling to force the thoughts from his mind. The effort made his hands tremble. His body needed sustenance badly, but it was almost daylight. It was imperative that he got to rest soon. He would have to feed sometime soon though, if he wanted to keep himself under control. Under no circumstances would he take Leigh's blood, even if she offered. There were other sources and means available for his nourishment when he needed them.

"This way," Kehl said, clearing his throat and walking somewhat more swiftly across the library to show her the stairs that led up to his chambers. She followed after him, glancing back several times at the cardboard box. As they came to the base of the spiral staircase, Leigh looked up at the top and then back down to the bottom.

"I hope these aren't like the ones at the club," she said with a grin.

"No, they're perfectly strong," Kehl replied, quickly making his way up the first several steps.

"Not so quick," Leigh gasped from behind him.

Kehl nodded as he made his way more slowly up the stairs. Halfway up, he turned to see how Leigh was doing and suddenly felt ashamed of himself once more. Standing below him, still only on the second step, he saw Leigh laughing quietly at herself.

"This really hurts," she said with a pained giggle. "I guess I got beaten up pretty good."

Kehl could see the muscles flex in her jaw as she gritted her teeth and pushed herself up the stairs, only slightly slower than normal. He had forgotten what it was like for pain to linger so long and intensely after an injury. He continued the rest of the way up the stairs and waited patiently for her to make it up. He wanted to help her, but knew that she would want to make it up the stairs by herself.

"There we go," she said, taking the last step.

Kehl motioned to the door just opposite the stairs. "Okay, just through here."

Leigh tried to step forward and stumbled. Kehl had to use both arms to catch her as she tumbled toward the floor. With the back of her neck now exposed to him, he could clearly see the blood seeping through the bandages on her shoulder. He could also see the massive bruise spreading out across her neck. The fact that she could still even move spoke volumes about her strength.

"Damn," Leigh cursed. "I didn't mean to fall, and you weren't supposed to catch me."

The forcefulness in her voice surprised Kehl. "Oh, I'm sorry."

Leigh bit her lip as his hands left her body. She hoped it didn't look like she struggled to keep herself standing. Though her pride would not allow it, she still wished that he would keep his arms around her and not let her go. Leigh had been through some tough training, but nothing would have prepared her for the beating she had taken tonight.

Kehl cleared his throat before repeating himself. "It's right through here."

Leigh stretched her back as she stood up straight, half walking, forcing her legs to move toward the doorway. Kehl allowed her to go in first to the unfamiliar darkness. Leigh knew it was so he could catch her if she looked to be stumbling again.

"The light switch is to your right," Kehl said as she made it to the other side of the open door.

Leigh turned on the lights without allowing her eyes time to adjust to the sudden brightness. When she could see again, she had to close her eyes for a moment and take a second look. The room was less of a room and more of a combination of chambers. The area was bathed in blue, and she could see countless trinkets littering the area. Off in a corner, away from the bed, lay the couch he had told her of. It sat in front of a window, but the curtains were tightly drawn, and Leigh suspected that there were shutters on the other side.

Despite her training, which told her that not all vampires slumbered through the day in coffins, she still found herself surprised at the absence of one. The bed was draped in long flowing sheets of thick blue silk that would easily block the rays of the sun should the windows be unexpectedly opened during the day. Despite the lush surroundings, the bedroom still retained the air of a crypt.

"Well, here we are. Would you rather take the bed?" Kehl asked.

"I would be fine on the couch."

Leigh shook her head. "Thanks for the offer, but I still prefer the sofa." She still retained enough of her senses to resist asking him to share the bed with her.

"Okay, let me get you some blankets and pillows," Kehl offered, oblivious to the thoughts running through Leigh's head. "I will also find us some new clothes for tomorrow."

Leigh nodded as Kehl disappeared, off somewhere to find the needed items. His scent was strong in the room, and she found herself tempted to lie down on his bed instead of on the couch. Fantasies burst into her mind of what might happen should Kehl find her lying there. Shaking away the cobwebs that clouded her judgment, she made her way to the couch and sat down.

CHAPTER 28
CURIOUS DREAMS

A shuddering sigh escaped Leigh as she sank into the overstuffed cushions of the couch. Though it wasn't fancy, it had to be one of the most comfortable couches Leigh had ever encountered. Her drowsiness increased tenfold as she lay down. Moments later, she was nearly asleep. He eyes opened ever so slightly as she saw Kehl walking toward her with a stack of blankets and a pillow.

Her voice was only barely a whisper. "Can I trust you?" she asked him.

Kehl nodded, handing her the pillow before silently spreading the blanket over her body. Leigh could barely keep her eyes open as he looked down at her.

Without cause or reason, a savage hunger ripped through Kehl gut. It would be all too easy to feed upon her there, lying defenseless on the couch.

"Give me a call if you should need anything," he said, suppressing his sudden thirst. "Now get some rest while I try to figure out where Drake is headed."

Her lips moved, but hardly any sound came from them as she said, "Okay."

Mere seconds later, Leigh's eyes closed and she was asleep. She looked completely different in her slumber, and Kehl couldn't take his eyes off of her. Another wave of hunger tore through him as he forced himself to look away. He cursed softly and set off at a brisk pace toward the library.

Kehl found his reading nook, a small desk that sat alone in a corner, and sat down. On top of the desk sat a laptop, which he then carefully opened. He hadn't used it in ages and was grateful that it still managed to boot up quickly. A quick double click brought up a Web browser. His homepage was already a popular search engine. He rubbed at his eyes and tried to come up with a search string that might bring up relevant results.

A search for the name Drake only brought up Web pages about ducks, which almost made Kehl laugh. When he looked under the heading of the Midnight Nocturne, it brought up the night club's Web site. But there were also some old archival newspaper entries about the discovery of the jewel itself. Perhaps, Kehl thought, if Drake sought to destroy the jewel, he would need an expert on the subject.

He searched next for ancient Egyptian specialists in New York. This query brought up a surprising number of successful results. Too many, in fact, for Kehl to try to track down in a single night. As he looked out the window, he noticed that the sky was growing steadily lighter. It would be morning soon. For a moment, he lost his train of thought, just gazing at the morning light, thinking of how much different it seemed than the twilight sky.

As a thought occurred to him, he returned his gaze back to the computer screen. He remembered the Egyptian word for nighttime: Kauket. Entering the ancient word brought up several sites, one of which caught his eye immediately. It was the Web site of a New York–based Egyptian antique and curio shop owned by the Caro family. One specific document was for sale, a scroll said to reference the Kauket Stone. There was no doubt in Kehl's mind that this place was where Drake would be headed.

A quick click on the contact information link brought up the street address of the store. Kehl printed out the complimentary driving directions before returning to their home page. Along with their normal business hours, there was a special notice about closing early during the approaching day. That little bit of information confirmed Kehl's theory. He now not only knew where but also when he could find Drake. Normally open until 9:00 PM, the store was closing tonight with the setting of the sun.

His eyes drifted down to the clock on his desk as he tried to formulate a plan. He was surprised to realize how late it had gotten. It seemed he'd only been online for a few moments, even though it turned out to be nearly an hour since he'd logged on. Sunrise was now only perhaps a half hour away. As he rubbed at his eyes, he felt a fresh wave of nausea and hunger tear through his body. Dizziness swept through his mind as he took to his feet. His body was still badly damaged, and he needed blood.

It would be disastrous to go upstairs now. He would not be able to stop himself from preying on Leigh. Instead, he did something that was perhaps even more risky. After walking to the far end of the library, he opened the doors to his rooftop patio and walked through. The early morning light was already beginning to glow just above tree line. Chill and crisp, the air was nearly at subzero temperatures, but to his cold, undead body, the rising sun made the frigid temperatures feel like an inferno.

As he walked to the edge of the roof, he wondered how many years had passed since he'd enjoyed the simple pleasure of seeing his own breath in the morning sunlight. The clean air of the morning helped to abate the pain of his hunger. But the reprieve was short lived as the sun pierced the horizon. Surrounded by trees, most of the rays of light were blocked from reaching the mansion. A few beams of illumination did penetrate far enough to fall on Kehl.

A faint burning sensation rose from his chest as a single shaft landed on his bare torso. The skin where the light touched looked like it was steaming. Kehl watched closely as the ray of light intensified, the pain growing exponentially in just a few moments. Kehl endured for as long as he was able. He soon returned to the interior of his mansion, the hunger seemingly cleansed away by the brilliant, though painful, light of the sun.

* * *

Surrounded by shifting, ethereal images, Leigh walked through the land of dreams. The pains of her mortal body were long gone as the fantasy pulled her back to the basement of the Nocturne. She could see all the way down the empty corridor and even smell the dust. A loud clamor brought her eyes to the familiar fifth vault. Moments later, Drake was running toward her.

No words were spoken as the fight started the way it had before, with Drake backhanding her blade. This time her hands remained tightly wrapped around the sword as she whirled about, sending a vicious slash to his abdomen. She could feel the blade pass through his flesh, but as it cleared his body, it was if the cut never happened.

Drake laughed cruelly as his eyes burst into glowing red orbs. Twisting at his hip, he started to deliver the same devastating kick to her neck that he had before. Too quick for her to block, the blow hit her hard. She could feel herself stumble, but felt no pain. Looking up at the vampire, she no longer felt any fear. Leigh dropped her sword as she took hold of his leg and hurled him into the darkness with a strength she only possessed in her dream.

As she dashed after him, the dream shifted. Her surroundings melting away and changed around her. Small, blurry objects started to fall all around her. After a moment, they turned into brilliant snowflakes. Looking about, Leigh found herself on an endless expanse of snow-covered ground. She felt as though something was waiting off in the distance, something so important that wasting even a single moment getting there would be too much.

She set off at a dead run, finding that she could run atop the snow. Each step she took seemed to cover leagues of ground. Even with these miraculous new powers, she felt that no matter which way she turned, she only ran farther away from her objective. Finally coming to a stop, she sank to her knees in the snow. It was only when she gave up hope that she felt a presence behind her.

Leigh whirled about and found Kehl standing shirtless in front of her, heedless of the cold, barren landscape surrounding them. Sudden anger washed through her as she threw a punch at his chin. He didn't so much as blink as her fist connected. He stood perfectly still as another punch followed with the same result.

"You're a vampire!" she screamed, launching her knee at his crotch. "A god damned vampire!"

Kehl moved faster than her eyes could follow as he moved inside the attack, grabbing her leg and holding it still at his hip. With the other hand he took hold of the back of her neck, tearing a scream out of her, but not from pain. His actions brought her pleasure, but she continued to fight, knowing what would happen next.

He moved slowly this time, opening his mouth to reveal his brilliant white fangs. Almost tenderly, she felt him nuzzle under her chin, his breath raising goose bumps on her neck. Tears slipped from the corners of her eyes as she felt the pearly spears caress her neck. She suddenly wanted this, wanted him, and as his fangs sank deep into her neck, she pulled herself closer, pushing her body up against his as ecstasy tore through her.

Suddenly awake, Leigh bolted upright, gasping for air. She could still feel the echoes of the dream rippling through her mind. She was covered with sweat, but it had nothing to do with the thick comforter that Kehl had laid over her. Her body now ached in many different ways due to the erotic contents of her dreaming.

As she readjusted herself on the couch, she noticed that Kehl now slept in his own bed. He had not disturbed her during her slumber. She wondered if he had somehow invaded her dreams, since they had been so intense. All too soon the pain of her injuries returned, and she was forced to lie back down. Still dazed despite her sudden awakening, it didn't take long for her to fall back asleep and for oblivion to seize her mind.

The dream returned with sudden clarity and with more intensity than even her unconscious mind could handle. Her and Kehl's embrace continued, but now they lay nude, surrounded by blankets on a bed in a strange place. Pleasure streamed from her neck, but as she felt Kehl's hips move between her legs, a whole different sort of pleasure erupted into her lower body.

It seemed that she had only blinked her eyes before the dream shifted, moving to the same desolate wasteland as before. As she got up onto her feet, she noticed that she now wore a green satin dress. Turning around, she surveyed her surroundings, trying in vain to get her bearings.

The edges of her dress billowed out as she whirled once more. Before she could finish the rotation, her eyes met one of the most horrible sights she could imagine. She wanted to scream, but it was caught in the back of her throat as curiosity got the better of her. Two stark grey eyes stared back at her from a face that seemed to be made of flesh burned to ash.

She took in the entirety of the apparition as it spread its wings. It had the form of a man, save for talons and a set of brilliant fangs. Somewhere deep inside, she knew she no longer controlled her own dreams.

"I had no doubt," the creature said, lifting a taloned hand to her cheek.

Her voice was a small, trembling whisper as the claws slid harmlessly down across her skin. "Of what?"

"Oh, that he would be attracted to you, among other things."

With the earlier portion of her dream still fresh in her mind, a strange sensation tore through her heart. "I ..." she stammered, "... among other things? What do you mean?"

"Oh, he hasn't told you?" the creature asked in an amused, rhetorical tone as it turned about. "He hasn't told you what he did to his first lover?"

Spreading its arms wide, the creature summoned into the dream an ancient bed. Leigh could see dark blood stains spreading down the blankets. She didn't want to look, already suspecting what awaited her. She could not resist, however, and her legs carried her around her ghastly host to the victim lying on the bed. Leigh stood transfixed as she gazed down at the form of a young woman surrounded by a pool of her own blood. Even in death she could recognize the almost otherworldly beauty surrounding the unfortunate girl.

"What was her name?" Leigh whispered, stepping closer to the body.

"Rana Alexander," the creature replied as it watched Leigh with interest.

Leaning over the bed, Leigh cautiously ran a finger down Rana's neck just outside the bite marks.

"Was it intentional?" she asked, feeling her heart harden at the thought of ending up like the unfortunate beauty.

After a moment's pause, the creature responded, "Perhaps the question you should ask is whether or not he had a choice."

Suddenly the whole world seemed to depend on the answer to that one simple question.

Leigh turned her head to look at the monster, as though searching it's visage for an answer. "Did he?" she asked.

"No," it answered, devoid of emotion.

Leigh could feel the dream start to fade as she turned back to look at Rana. She seemed so peaceful and calm, even when surrounded by her own crimson essence. It was as though her sacrifice came willingly and with love. Leigh could not help but wonder if Rana had known and met her fate with acceptance.

CHAPTER 29

THE GIFT

Opening her eyes wide, Leigh woke up silently. Her heart raced deep inside her chest. Kehl still lay sleeping in his bed. Even so, she pushed herself away from the edge of the couch until she could feel cushions at her back. Leigh closed her eyes as she prayed that she wouldn't have another such dream. She no longer knew whether she could resist the urge to join Kehl in bed, even with the gruesome images of Rana still in her head.

Just as she was about to fall back to sleep, a moan from across the room awoke her. She could hear Kehl tossing and turning in his bed. Her legs felt like they were made of lead as she tried to get up from the couch. It was hard for her to move, but Kehl seemed to be suffering from something as well. As she remembered the previous night, Leigh couldn't remember Kehl having fed on anything, or anyone for that matter.

Kehl hadn't bothered to take off his pants and seemed to have crawled directly into bed. Leigh could see why he was having trouble sleeping. His whole body seemed to be covered in wounds that kept shifting and writhing as they tried to heal. Leigh cautiously leaned over his restless body and laid a hand on one of the wounds. His skin was hot to the touch, which was out of the ordinary for a vampire. It was almost as if he'd been outside, standing in the sunlight.

Why should she care? Why should the well-being of this vampire concern her at all? Leigh could find no answers as she removed her hand, unable to keep it from trembling. With a ginger touch, she pinched at the soft flesh just above her wrist. Her gaze turned toward Kehl's mouth as his lips parted, ever so slightly, revealing the fangs beneath. At first she turned away, walking back toward the couch. She stopped when she heard Kehl moan again.

She knew of the ecstasy that a vampire's bite could bring, but that was not why she returned to his side. Something pulled at her heart from deep inside her, something that she couldn't resist. In the back of her mind, she wondered if she still remained in a dream, amazed at her own actions. She'd never even really been in a man's bedroom before tonight.

As she knelt by the bed, she hesitated only briefly before extending her arm slowly before Kehl's lips. Another moan rose from his chest as she moved her wrist closer to his mouth. His instincts took over as his cold hand encircled her forearm and his fangs sank into her flesh. Leigh struggled to keep from letting out a shriek of pain as she took a handful of bed sheets in her free hand and bit down on them.

The pain was intense and sharp at first, like being stabbed with a dull knife, but seconds later it faded and softened. A pleasant, warm feeling began to spread up her arm in an alarming way. Leigh tugged on her wrist as she attempted to free herself, but Kehl's feeding combined with her earlier blood loss rendered her extremely weak.

Kehl continued to feed as the warmth spread throughout the rest of Leigh's body, relieving the pain of her injuries. As she lowered her gaze, she saw that the wounds covering Kehl's body were healing to the point of being only slight blemishes on the skin. Her rapid blood loss made her feel more tired than she'd ever felt before.

A fiery burst of pleasure raced up her arm and exploded into her torso, making her moan. It's effects were intense and immediate as her body tensed in ecstasy. Reality proved to be much more intense than any erotic fantasy. Sexual energy exploded through her body in a way Leigh never would have thought possible. It did not cease, but instead intensified. She took a fistful of the sheets in her hand as she whimpered with a pleasure that she hitherto did not realize possible. Much more of this irresistible sensation, and she would lose herself completely to its effects.

Leigh mustered every last bit of strength she could and tore her arm away from Kehl's lips. Thoroughly exhausted, she lay there against the bed, gasping for air, disbelieving what she had just let happen. As she looked at her wrist through bleary eyes, she noticed that the bite was much smaller than she'd anticipated. In fact, there was very little bleeding at all. Whether this was due to her being drained or to some anticoagulant delivered through the vampires fangs, she did not know.

Absentmindedly, she ran a hand over the bandages at her shoulder, shocked at first that she felt no pain. Groggily, she looked over at her shoulder as best as she could, carefully removing her bandages.

Underneath, the skin was smooth and silky soft, as if the blade had never torn through her flesh. Looking back at Kehl, she started frantically pushing herself away from the bed, fearing the worst. Had he turned her? No, it was impossible; her father had taught her about the dangers of turning someone, and that it was very dangerous to do so in a single night. She forced herself to calm down, slowing her breathing as she thought things through. The process demanded much concentration, and from what she knew, there could be no way for Kehl to turn her in his sleep.

Leigh looked once more at her wrist and almost screamed; the fang marks were all but gone—only two freckle-like scars remained. With two fingers, she felt for her own pulse, relieved to feel the strong, warm throbbing against her fingers. She closed her eyes and cursed herself inwardly, hardly believing what she just done. An old prayer found its way to her lips as she tilted her head back. The prayer was more for Kehl than herself, for somewhere deep down inside of her heart she felt no regret.

As she reopened her eyes, she saw that Kehl now slept peacefully, the wounds all but vanished. Her body wobbled slightly as she took to her feet and walked back toward the couch. She could feel herself losing consciousness as she at last lay back down. She fell into a deep, dreamless sleep.

CHAPTER 30

DAYDREAMS

An almost perfect oblivion spread down over Kehl's mind as the world faded from bright light into abject darkness. Bliss enfolded him as, unknown to him, Leigh's blood flowed through him. Its sustenance filled his sleeping mind with unconditional contentment. He was finally free of his past, of his damned current existence,. His mind was only aware of the nothingness that surrounded him. But such a peace can never last.

"Wake up!" came a familiar voice, although Kehl couldn't remember who it belonged to.

"Wake up!" it repeated. This time the voice brought with it a searing pain that forced Kehl to open eyes.

His vision was inverted, and at first he couldn't understand why he was upside down. As soon as he attempted to move, the reason was revealed. Pain exploded down from his legs as he realized that he was suspended by his ankles. Kehl craned his neck and saw that his wrists were chained to the base of a wall with strong shackles. Then came the hunger, the gut-wrenching, soul-swallowing hunger of not having fed in months. With it came memories. He remembered this place. Kehl looked around in panic. He was once more in the dungeon of the Alexander family.

"Hope I didn't wake you," Scott said, pressing the hot poker against Kehl's chest once more.

Kehl moaned in agony, unable to escape or speak. He tried to wake himself from the dream but was unable to. It seemed that he was not be able to alter its course as he tried to imagine a different setting. Amazed at how real the dream felt, Kehl decided that it must be a forgotten memory playing through his unconscious mind.

"Hungry, aren't you?" Scott spat, bringing Kehl back from his thoughts.

His eyes felt dried and shriveled as he turned them to gaze on Scott. Two years had passed since the death of Rana. Her younger brother was now a man, and he was full of hate for Kehl. He tortured the vampire on an almost daily basis, only pausing to invent new devices to use on him.

"Not thirsty," Kehl croaked through a dry and cracked throat. "I'm sorry."

"I told you never to say that!" Scott screamed as he slashed the burning tip of the poker across Kehl's bare chest, leaving a blistering gash. "Just for that, I'm going to feed you."

Kehl could feel his stomach turned as the young man vanished from sight. He remembered what was coming. Moments later, Scott returned with a large pail full of an inky thick substance. A small bit of the substance leaked over the top edge and oozed slowly down its side.

"I know I've told you this many times before, but I just can't pass up the chance to rub it in," Scott said, taking a small knife from his belt and stepping toward Kehl. "I make this stuff specially, just for you. You would be surprised at what things still contain some amount of blood. Dead animals, livestock drowned in the creek, vermin killed in the barns and houses. I find all of these things and collect their blood, just so you can have something to drink."

Scott sat the bucket of disgusting fluid down next to Kehl's head. He then retrieved a very odd looking device from a nearby table. This strange contraption was his own invention. Scott called it the feeder, an ingenious device that fit around Kehl's head and forced his fangs down into two holes drilled in a hollow wooden bit. Scott used leather tubing to feed blood into the mouthpiece. The contraption often leaked, but it excelled in force-feeding the vampire.

Attaching the bucket to a hook higher up on the wall, Scott wasted no time in securing the device around Kehl's head. He then almost casually stretched the length of tube back up to the bucket, to the tap at its base. A twist of the valve allowed a thick bubble of fluid to collect at the start of the tube. Kneading the fluid down the length of the hose, Scott squeezed it tightly toward the base and forced the disgusting mixture into Kehl's fangs.

Kehl gagged and heaved, although there was nothing in his stomach to throw up. The blood was cold and vile, tasting of nothing but death and decay. It was enough to sustain the vampire without revitalizing him, keeping him alive just enough to torture. A slow-spreading, burning sensation filled Kehl's body as the blood disbursed through his veins. Unable to help himself, Kehl could do little more than gag and wait for the bucket above to empty.

Kehl could remember having dreams of his torture before, but he could not remember ever having one so vivid or realistic.

"You're in for a treat today," Scott said as he disconnected the empty bucket. "I'm going to show you just what you did two years ago. Mother!"

On his beckoning, Maria Alexander moved into Kehl's range of vision.

"Hello, Kehl," she said as Kehl met her eyes.

Her face had grown gaunt, and her once-dark hair was now streaked with grey. Her gaze burned with a cold, calculating madness. After the death of her daughter, Maria used the incident to bring the entire town of Braunburg under her control. Her first act as matriarch was to banish her husband for his support of Kehl.

"We have a special gift for you today," she said, turning to call to someone Kehl couldn't see. "Bring her in."

Two people, one of whom Kehl recognized as Rana's older sister, carried a roughly hewn coffin into the room. Trysta seemed to have aged by decades. Her body retained only the barest traces of her once voluptuous form, and her hair peppered with silvery strands. She seemed to be carrying far more than just the weight of the coffin as she and her companion set it upright against a table in the center of the room. Taking two metal bars from the walls, they jammed them into the box, prying at the lid. Piece-by-piece, the top came off, revealing something that Kehl in all of his immortal days would have never desired to see.

Lying in the box was the shriveled corpse of his beloved Rana, her fangs still perfectly white in her open mouth. Kehl screamed, and for the first time since his imprisonment, he struggled against his bonds. The inside of the coffin had been torn to ribbons by her attempts to escape. With all of his might, he pulled at his restraints, but his weakened body did little more than rattle the chains.

"Do you see this?" Maria said calmly, pointing out numerous deep gouges into the interior walls of the coffin. "She awoke two days after you bit her, while we were preparing for her burial. She killed ten villagers before she was finally caught. We tried at first to restore her humanity, but when conventional means would not work, we resorted to more, shall we say, brutal methods. We attempted to torture your demons out of her body. In the end, she tried to take my life, so I buried her—alive."

Kehl's head began to spin, and he started to forget that he was dreaming.

"This is your legacy," Maria intoned, "the soulless shell of my daughter Rana."

Kehl's eyes closed as he turned his head sideways, trying to force the sight of the decomposed body of Rana out of his mind. Marie was quick to step forward. Digging her long nails into his cheeks, she jerked his head forward. She pulled a small dagger from somewhere in her dress and quickly drove it several millimeters into his groin.

Kehl gasped with pain and opened his eyes. Once more he could see the coffin, and this time he could not bring himself to look away. Silent tears streamed from his eyes, rolling down over his forehead. Moments later, he started to sob in deep, soul-shuddering heaves. Now he was not only responsible for her death, but also for her murders and subsequent burial. Although he took responsibility for what had happened, Maria should have had more pity for her offspring.

"She was your daughter!" he hissed.

Driving her knife deeper into Kehl's body, Maria growled as she spoke. "What did you say?"

Driven half insane with both physical and psychological pain, Kehl laughed maniacally as tears streamed down from his eyes. "You should have put her out of her misery."

"Why don't we wake Rana up and ask her what we should have done?" Marie said as she pulled the dagger free of Kehl's body.

Her words crushed what little defiance Kehl had managed to muster. Rana would no doubt remember everything that had transpired. He could not bear to see the knowledge of such things in her living eyes. Hoping to seem indifferent, he remained quiet, praying that Marie would not call his bluff.

"What, no disagreements then?" Marie asked, grinning like the devil himself. "Trysta, if you would be so good."

Kehl looked to his former sister-in-law and saw that the simple girl was broken under Marie's will.

As Marie tossed her the dagger, Trysta whimpered, "Please no, Mama, they've suffered enough."

Marie moved so fast that Trysta could barely flinch before her mother slapped her hard across the cheek. The force of the blow sent tears glittering from her eyes. As Trysta looked back at her mother, she knew the order would not be repeated. She wiped her eyes, refusing to cry as she drew the small dagger across her wrist and stepped toward

Rana's coffin. Kehl could see several fresh scars across her wrist and wondered if they were the remains of a failed suicide or if this entire macabre event was only a repeat of the past. Either way, Trysta's blood flowed easily from her wound as she held it over Rana's mouth.

For the first few moments nothing happened and Trysta withdrew her wrist, quickly wrapping it in a bit of cloth. A sudden hiss from the coffin made her jump back. The corpse exhaled breath in the same hiss like fashion. Before Kehl could fully come to terms with what was happening, Rana's eyes were open.

Though badly bloodshot and only barely restored by her sister's life-giving blood, Rana's eyes trained instantly on Kehl's. They widened in recognition and hatred as her small fangs shuddered and lengthened in her open mouth. Another lungful of air was all her body could manage as her eyes rolled back into her head and her body lay still.

"Rana!" Kehl screamed, bolting upright in his bed as he gasped for air.

He didn't recognize his surroundings when he first looked around, having sunk so far into his dream.. Looking over at Leigh, he saw that she slumbered peacefully, and for a moment he felt calmed. The respite didn't last long as his mind slowly let the taste in his mouth filter through to his brain.

Kehl cautiously touched his lips. His fingertips were covered in crimson. Kehl shook his head violently as he threw himself out of bed, unable to believe his own actions. He rushed over to the couch, carefully examining Leigh. She was stretched out on the couch with her arm extended. As carefully as he could manage, Kehl swept away several locks of hair around her neck.

He sighed a breath of relief after finding her neck free of any bite marks. As he slowly took a seat on the arm of the sofa, Kehl tried to compose himself. Perhaps he was still dreaming, trapped in the same nightmare after a false awakening. But with a glance at Leigh's arm, his questions were answered. He felt himself beginning to get dizzy from what he saw. There on her wrist, for all the world to see, were two pale scars. Although the wounds were already partially healed, Kehl held no doubts that he'd bitten her.

Lethargically, he pushed himself up to his feet, still dazed by the dream. Walking slowly over to the portrait of Rana, he struggled to clear his mind. He sought some measure of sanity in her image, but it raised only more questions. He looked over his shoulder at the sleeping form of Leigh. His eyes widened ever so slightly as he tried to make sense of what had just happened. His understanding came slowly. If Kehl had fed on Leigh during their slumber, he would have surely bitten her on the neck. The wound on her wrist would only make sense if Leigh had offered it to him of her own free will. In his current state of mind, Kehl could think of no sweeter gift that could have been given.

CHAPTER 31

JESSE BRYANT

"You have failed me, Jesse," Olivia said. Her voice was devoid of emotion. "Your daughter was not supposed to be interested in Kehl whatsoever."

"I cannot control her emotions, Mistress," Jesse said pleadingly.

The nightclub had long since cleared out for the night. It looked all the more deserted during the day. All of the nighttime staff had gone home, leaving only Olivia, Jesse, and a few other people there. Only minutes ago Olivia had questioned Jesse on the status of his daughter. Not pleased with his summary, Olivia delved deeper, utilizing her dominion over her servant.

"Kneel!" she commanded.

Bowing his head, Jesse complied.

"This was not part of the plan," she said as she began pacing. "You assured me before that there would be no way possible for her to develop feelings for him."

"Yes, my lady," Jesse said, his eyes locked to the floor.

She raised her voice in anger. "You should have told me last night that she had burgeoning feelings for Kehl. Why did you withhold this information from me? Why did you do it?"

Once more, silent tears leaked from the corners of Jesse's eyes, though his expression betrayed no emotion. "I simply feared for her life," he said evenly.

"Am I so harsh?" she growled.

Jesse's tears slowly stopped. "No, Mistress," he said, standing. "I will rid her of these troubling feelings."

"Very well," Olivia said, still with her back turned. "Do not let your actions interfere with the plan."

"Yes, Mistress," Jesse said before swiftly leaving the room.

She should have expected this. Leigh was young and attractive, and even though Kehl was centuries older, he still retained his youthful handsomeness. According to Leigh's recognition of Kehl as the person who nearly wrecked her car and her subsequent anger, the plan should have rolled along smoothly. Unfortunately, her most trusted servant had withheld crucial information, possibly damaging the plan beyond repair by leaving the two alone together overnight.

A wedge would have to be driven between Kehl and Leigh for the future events to properly take their course. Olivia knew that Leigh had found Kehl walking along the side of the road, but when morning came without word from either of them, she'd naturally grown concerned. Confronting Jesse about the situation then revealed the existence of Leigh's true feelings.

Drake would also have to be found, but for other reasons. To Olivia, the jewel was but a pittance when compared to her greater goal. For now it was daytime, and she knew that he would not risk travel, especially in possession of the jewel. It would be far too risky for him to encounter a foe while weakened by the daylight.

Olivia walked deeper into her rooms and tried not to think about the troubles plaguing her plans. There still had to be some way to complete her masterpiece. But without Leigh's help, it would be impossible for Olivia to accomplish the task on her own. Even her most trusted servant now defied her. She felt herself unraveling as she neared her bedroom.

It was all too much. Placing one hand on the wall and another on her stomach, she let out a shuddering breath. No matter how deeply she searched inside of herself, she could not completely convince herself that her plot would succeed. Some tiny part of her rebelled and could not be squelched. She continued on into her chambers, refusing to let herself break down completely until she stood before her mirrors.

Just like countless mirrors in the past had offered innumerable women sanctuary, so too would hers. Looking into their perfectly clean surface, she saw her reflection, noting with pleasure the sudden steel that hardened behind her eyes. It was almost as if her conscious mind and the image of the hardened woman standing in the mirror had changed places.

Reaching to her shoulder, she slipped off one strap of her dress and then the other, letting the garment fall to the ground. She looked herself over in the mirror. Her skin was smooth white, and her wounds from dealing with Drake were already faded. She admired the dark red and black trimmed lingerie she had selected the week before. All thoughts of failure were now gone from her mind. Her reflection brought a smile to her lips. She found herself grateful to have been blessed with short, unobtrusive fangs that, even having fooled a fellow vampire, were no less sharp than his own.

"Mirror, mirror, on the wall," she heard a familiar male voice behind her say.

"Hello, Richard," Olivia purred without flinching or turning to look at him.

"My lady," he replied, and Olivia knew he bowed behind her. "What do you see in the mirror?"

Olivia remained silent as he moved forward and wrapped his hands about her waist. Richard slowly moved his hands up and down her abdomen, his lips brushing across her shoulder. Olivia immediately took firm grip of Richards hand as it slid up toward her breast, digging her thumbnail deep into his skin. Although her arms were slim and shapely, Olivia's grip was excruciatingly strong.

"You know better, Richard," she whispered as he grunted with pain.

In the amount of time it took for him to draw in a single breath, she freed herself from his arms and circled around behind him. She pressed her body firmly up against his back, wrapping him tightly in her arms.

"You will never have my body," she murmured seductively into his ear. "But I will give you this," she continued, now sliding her own hand down his abdomen from behind.

Olivia immediately and savagely buried her fangs as deeply as possible into his neck. Richard shrieked in agony, his body jerking spasmodically. Olivia held her servant tightly in her arms as the pain gave way to unbridled pleasure. She only allowed his ecstasy to last the briefest of moments before withdrawing her fangs.

"I will never be yours," she whispered in his ear. "You are mine," she said forcefully, releasing him from her arms.

Richard fell to his knees as she continued. "Find other places to sate your lust, because next time I will not be so generous. Leave me, now."

Richard pulled himself together as best he could and scurried from the room.

As she stepped back into her dress, Olivia pulled its smooth fabric back over her body. A tingling feeling at the back of her neck gave her the impression that she was being watched. She whirled about with a vindictive finger, ready to chastise Richard for lingering. To her surprise, no one stood behind her. Only the emptiness of her room met her gaze.

Who did she expect to see there, hiding in the shadows? Leigh, Kehl, Jesse, Richard? Or someone else from her past? Her mind was awash with emotions. Her body still ached from the unhealed wounds dealt to her by Drake. She would need to feed in earnest soon. The blood she'd taken from Richard was only a pittance compared to what her body required. She stomped one of her feet in frustration, accidentally using a little more of her strength than she intended. The force of her foot impacting the floor made a thud that reverberated though the walls of the old factory.

A sudden and urgent knocking at the door made her start.

"Mistress?" came Richards voice.

Through the door she could hear the concern mingle with hurt and confusion in his voice. Drinking up his emotions as if they were the sweetest blood, Olivia mastered her emotions in an instant.

"Yes, Richard?"

"Is everything all right in there? I heard a loud bang. It sounded like it came from your chamber."

"Everything is fine," she purred through the door. "I was only relieving a bit of tension."

Richard remained silent for a moment before he spoke again. "I'm sorry if I angered you earlier, Mistress."

Tightly closing her eyes, Olivia gritted her teeth as she arched her back up against the wall. Richard's submission to her aroused both her body and her hunger, compounding her frustration. The taste of Richards blood made it harder to resist feeding on him again. She would need to find another source of sustenance, or she would lose another valuable employee before her plan was complete.

"Is there anyone else left in the club, Richard?"

There was a slight pause as he tried to think of anyone that would be left.

"I think the deejay is still here packing up his equipment. I don't know his name or any particulars though. I haven't even paid him yet."

"What can you tell me about him?" she asked, the question revealing her motives.

Richard sighed. "He is not unattractive. Trim and slightly built, from moving his equipment around by himself I'm guessing. He has longish brown hair, and is probably about as tall as I am."

Olivia bit her lip in anticipation before asking for more information. "What color are his eyes?"

"Grayish blue, I think. I only looked closely at his face when I hired him for the job," he answered.

"He will do," Olivia said through the door. "Send him here, and tell him that I want to give him an extra tip for giving us such a good show last night. Refer to me only as the owner. Do not mention that these are my private chambers."

Richard remained silent for a moment and then asked, "Shall I be ready to dispose of a corpse?"

"I will call for you if I require your services," Olivia answered noncommittally. In truth, she'd not decided what she was going to do to the deejay yet. "Now, go and find him for me."

It pleased Olivia that she heard no pause as Richard turned on his heel and swiftly walked away from the door.

Gray eyes, she thought to herself.

So much like the eyes of her creator, but would they be enough to save her unwitting prey? She buried herself in fantasy and lost track of time. Several minutes later, a soft knock at the door behind her brought her back to her senses. She moved close to the door, leaning up against it ever so slightly.

"Who is it?" she called, already catching wisps of the stranger's scent through the door.

"Uh," the deejay murmured, surprised at the female voice answering him. "I'm the deejay from the party last night."

A grin crossed his face on the other side of the door as he imagined what his tip might be. He cleared his throat and tried not to sound excited. Permanently between girlfriends, he found the idea of an affair with a wealthy female night club owner very attractive. If he could deejay there every night, he'd be set for some time.

"I'm here for my tip," he said.

Olivia smiled widely as she wrapped her hand around the doorknob and opened it just enough to allow him in while still concealing herself. She watched him as he walked into the room and looked about, confused at first. Richard's words were true; the man was far from unattractive, even when dressed in only blue jeans and a T-shirt. Closing the door, Olivia let the sound of its shutting draw his attention to her. He seemed to be anticipating this almost as much as she was.

In that moment, she was everything he'd ever wanted in a woman, although the feelings were not completely his own. It was so very simple for Olivia to snare him in her trap and assert her will upon him. Olivia watched him as he slowly stepped forward, his gray eyes locked on hers. His gaze shone with intent rather than with the glazed stare of the controlled; such was Olivia's finesse that she left just enough of his free will to enjoy the encounter.

He did not fall into her arms but took hold of her forcefully before pressing his lips to hers. His directness surprised Olivia, although she did not resist him in the least. Her lips parted slightly as they kissed. She let her tongue snake out to softly invite him in. He answered in kind, his tongue dancing slowly with hers in a tenderness that contradicted his earlier enthusiasm.

The deejay pushed her back against the wall and pulled the straps of Olivia's dress down over her shoulders. Obediently, she shrugged it off and kicked it to the side. She brought her hands up and under his shirt, dragging her nails down the firm muscles of his chest and abs. Olivia backed away from another kiss. Her fingers found his waistband and tugged at it slightly. The deejay eagerly dispensed of his shirt, tossing it off into a corner. He then grabbed Olivia around the torso, pushing her up against the wall yet again. Olivia could feel his hands creeping around to undo her bra and smiled even as their tongues writhed against one another. The strapless lingerie fell easily away from her body as the deejay turned his lips away from her mouth and down her jawline.

How much time had passed since she'd let a mortal this far through her defenses? His lips traveled down over her shoulder before dipping lower. As his soft kisses passed over where her beating heart should be, Olivia flinched ever so slightly. Gently taking him by the chin, she pulled him up high enough to look her in the eyes.

"I think I shall have to keep you," she murmured, noticing a small spark of defiance somewhere deep inside of his gray eyes.

After kissing him softly on the lips, she made her way along his jawline to his neck. She could sense his quickened pulse throbbing just beneath the skin. Olivia thought to herself of how much she deserved this momentary distraction as she carefully sank her fangs into his neck. The deejay, not only under her control but also under the influence of lust, gave no indication of pain other than a quiet gasp. His body shuddered with pleasure as Olivia's arms wrapped ever tighter around his body.

Ecstasy tore through her body as she continued to feed. The warm blood coursing through her veins filled her with the false sensation of life, if only for the briefest of moments. When her prey lifted his hand to softly caress her hair, however, she nearly lost hold of her euphoria. Rage broiled up inside of her at this sudden sign of tenderness, but as his hand started trembling, she was unable to sustain the anger. It felt to Olivia as though they were slowly becoming the same person.

When the deejay's legs began to grow weak, Olivia started to ease him down onto the floor. He was growing weaker by the second and would not be able to endure much more. His breath came in shallow gasps as the vampress pulled back and looked down on her prey. She could tell that he remained conscious only by the smallest of margins. His gaze was steadfast, however, and he kept his eyes locked firmly on Olivia's. She trailed her fingertips down to the two shallow wounds at his neck, pausing momentarily as she touched his blood.

"Yes," Olivia whispered as she ran a finger down his chin. "I will have to keep you."

CHAPTER 32

LUNG SHOT

Drake jerked awake with pain throbbing through his arm and chest. Aware of the still-healing wound at his chest, he groggily looked down at his arm. He was shocked to see a bright spear of sunlight lancing into the car and searing his flesh. He jerked his hand back. The beam of light filtered in from the outside through a hole from the wreck the previous night. After drawing in a brief, ragged breath, he immediately convulsed, painfully coughing up blood.

A quick search around his waist found the Midnight Nocturne just where he last remembered leaving it before passing out. Somehow, despite his wounds, he seemed to have managed to make his way home and into his garage. He unfortunately forgot to close the garage door. Luckily, the tint on what remained of his exotic car's windows filtered out enough of the sun to keep him away from harm.

With the push of a button, the garage closed after a few moments, plunging the car into more comfortable darkness. Drake sat there alone for some time, coughing sporadically until he had cleared enough of the fluid from his lungs to breathe more freely. As he opened the car door, standing up proved to be almost impossible. His lung must have collapsed sometime in the very early morning after he had made it home. It seemed that it had yet to fully heal and expand to its proper capacity.

Still clasping the jewel in his hand, he peered into the abandoned garage. The limo driver had returned home as ordered and left the Hummer parked neatly in its expanded bay. His car was now badly damaged, rendering it almost completely useless. As it was, he was lucky to be alive—one mere centimeter closer to his heart and the bullet would have most likely proven fatal.

In accordance to his instructions, only one of Kitsu's maids remained in the building for the daytime so Drake was relatively alone. He'd not planned on the possibility of being so badly wounded, and no one remained at the house to care for him. With a glance down at his chest, he could still see a large chunk of flesh missing, though most of his bones had reconstructed.

Still short on breath, Drake leaned back onto the car and pulled a cell phone out of his pocket. He quickly flipped it open and hit a speed dial number before putting it to his ear. On the other side of the line, the phone rang three or four times. With an audible click, the call went to voicemail.

"Thank you for calling Caro's Curiosities, Antiques, and Egyptian artifacts. We are currently unavailable to answer the phone right now, so please leave a message and we will get back to you as soon as possible."

Drake quickly punched in a four digit extension to access a private mailbox with no greeting message.

"I have the jewel," Drake managed to say before coughing into the crook of his arm. "I might be a little late tonight for our appointment, but I need you to be ready for what we discussed. There may be a problem. Kitsu will not be able to make it."

Drake coughed once more as he snapped the phone shut and walked across the garage. As he made it to the door to the house, he doubled over, sending a splash of crimson onto the floor. He had been shot before, and decidedly in worse places, but something inside was taking longer to heal than usual. He would most likely have to feed before he could venture out again that evening.

The garage was connected directly to the main house, and Drake made his way slowly but surely to the bedroom. After pulling off his ruined shirt, he crawled carefully into the now-lonely bed and lay down on his side. He let go of the Midnight Nocturne for the first time since leaving the club last night. He threw it into a chair just off to the side of the bed. For the first time, the weight of losing Kitsu and the seriousness of his wounds came crashing down on him.

The bed was strong with Kitsu's scent, and the gunshot wound suddenly felt like it could still kill him. He turned his head to look over at the Midnight Nocturne lying innocently in the chair. It seemed that the jewel already had some sort of effect on him. It had been able to suppress even his affection for the mate he had chosen to spend all of eternity with. If this was only a sampling of what the effects would be once the jewel's power was released, then Drake could hardly wait to get his hands on it again.

With his attention locked on the jewel, Drake didn't notice when Kitsu's maid curiously crept into the room. She was every bit as beautiful as her former boss. But unlike her mistress, however, fate had seen fit to make her into a servant. Her beauty contradicted her role in society. She had bright brown eyes and shoulder-length brown hair streaked with random colored highlights.

"Sir?" she whispered, craning her neck to see him where he lay on the bed. "Sir, are you all right?" she asked, walking slowly around the bed and kneeling before Drake, obscuring his view of the jewel. "I saw blood in the garage and followed it back here."

Drake remained silent for a moment before speaking. "Kitsu is dead."

"Oh no," the girl whispered. She was completely human, with no bonds to her mistress to inform her of her demise.

"Will you serve me in her stead?" Drake asked immediately, not giving the girl enough time to fully think through what she'd heard.

She bowed instantly and said, "It is what Kitsu would have wanted."

"Then come to me now," he said, motioning with his hand.

The girl paused at first, reluctant, perhaps suspecting what was to come. Her new master was very badly wounded. After returning to her feet she crawled up into the bed with fear in her eyes. Drake beckoned for her to lie down next to him. Slowly, she lay down beside him, huddling herself up as tightly as she could, afraid to so much as touch him.

"Don't be scared," he whispered. "It only hurts for a moment, and then you will feel almost excruciating pleasure wash over your body."

The maid nodded mutely and seemed to shrink even further away into herself. Drake groaned as he pushed himself up on one elbow. The girl's skin felt silken as he gently ran one of his fingers down her cheek. He could see the tiny crystalline orbs welling up at the corner of her eyes. She had so quickly been confronted with not only the death of her mistress but with the prospect of her own death as well. But Drake knew that anguish well—very well.

Drake leaned in slowly, as if to plant the softest of kisses on the girl's neck. He bared his fangs. The maid shrieked as his large fangs pierced her skin and sank into her jugular. As she gasped for air, a warm sensation enveloped her in the blink of an eye. All at once, every nerve in her body seemed to scream with ecstasy. Arching her back, she pushed her body up against Drake's.

Her blood surprised Drake as he fed almost ravenously. It was sweet and seemed virginal. She shrieked once more, but in a much more subdued, pleasured manner, and she wrapped her arms around him. Drake did the same, feeling the girl dig her nails into his back as he pulled her close. She shrieked no longer, only moaning occasionally as her strength began to fade.

Moments later, her arms fell limply down onto the bed. She was unconscious and almost completely drained. Drake roared as he pulled away from her neck, fighting his instinct to drain the girl dead. His body wasted no time as it went about mending itself. A rough hacking cough brought up the last remainder of blood in his lungs, although it still seemed he could not draw a full breath.

His wounds ached and writhed, causing him almost more pain, and they began slowly healing. As he turned his eyes back to the girl lying listlessly on the bed, he felt a twinge of worry flash through him. The wounds from his bite would not remain open enough for her to bleed to death. However, should anything go amiss during the day with her body so weak, she would surely die.

After having fed, exhaustion gripped Drake as he slowly reclined back onto the bed. Drake inched away from the girl and closed his eyes, hoping that if she woke next to him she wouldn't be frightened. Brief, glimmering images of Kitsu flashed in front of his eyes, only to be replaced by the Midnight Nocturne. Its appearance brought up many questions into his mind. Why should he have pity for the maid lying next to him? Why did he not hasten to destroy the jewel instead of staying here in bed like a weakling? Drake turned his head to the side. He locked his eyes on the Midnight Nocturne. It seemed so innocent, sitting there alone on the seat, appearing to be little more than a rock, save for the minute sparks of light thrown from the tiny stones inside. One more question ran through his mind before he passed out: why had Olivia betrayed him earlier that night?

CHAPTER 33
CURIO

Far into the wealthy stretches of the city sat a rather inconspicuous antique store. Founded in the forties, the store specialized in hard-to-find Egyptian artifacts. Ever since its founding, the store was run by the same family through the generations. The family had crossed over from Egypt legally, though many had considered them thieves and traitors for selling away the national treasures of their homeland. Had anyone back home known the true reasons for their departure, they would never have been able to escape with their lives.

Behind the somewhat drab two-story facade existed a rather large warehouse structure that contained what amounted to several million dollars' worth of ancient Egyptian artifacts. The current proprietor, and last of her family line, was Aja Caro. Today she was closing up shop early in the afternoon in preparation for her special guest.

Her lengthy jet-black hair lay in a hasty ponytail as she moved around with spider like grace. She was pure Egyptian from head to toe, with deep caramel skin and a thin yet surprisingly curvaceous body. Dark brown eyes gazed out from her catlike face as she kept her eyes on the shadows. The shop had grown dark with the rapidly ending day, and Drake was due anytime.

After setting down a small pile of papyrus papers on the stone top of an alter, she carefully leafed through them. Many centuries ago, her family once protected the history of the jewel that she now sought to destroy. Somewhere along the line, one ancestor in the Caro family changed their agenda. Instead of protecting their knowledge, they sought to exploit the powers that the jewel could give them. Achieving the impossible, her family had opened of the tomb of Akhenaten and retrieved the jewel. Aja smiled wickedly as she looked next to the papers at the bloodstained alter. She knew the story well.

Her family had worked through the shadows, manipulating the pharaohs, holding the fear of anarchy over their heads. For many years, the Caro family retained their power, until at last one pharaoh managed to steal away the Midnight Nocturne through a bloody campaign that lasted many years. The man's final act as pharaoh was to seal the jewel back inside the tomb of Akhenaten. The task cost him his life, but it brought the Caro family crashing to its knees almost instantly. As a final good-bye to their fallen foe, the Caro line erased the pharaoh completely from the pages of history with its last remaining influence.

Aja could not be more proud of her heritage and enjoyed the influence that both her name and beauty had given her over the modern world. Even tonight she planned to exact just such an influence on Drake. She held supreme faith in the legends, and if Drake was successful in his mission, he would become the most powerful man on the planet. Being the compatriot of such a man would grant her many privileges and would also restore her family to power. Perhaps now that Kitsu was no longer his companion there would also be the possibility of taking her place at his side.

Thus, she had dressed herself in something that was ceremonial in the way of the ancients. Her choice in clothing left little to the imagination, and she had even toyed around with the idea of performing her duties topless. A golden sash covered in hieroglyphics wrapped around her shoulders and fell over her breasts, barely covering them and revealing hints of her dark nipples as she moved about. Just under her chest she wore a golden corset that terminated in long cotton pants that had a slit extending all the way up to her hip.

Aja moved off to a storage cabinet. She opened it and retrieved a jar of plain, muddy water. Though it had an unassuming appearance, the murky liquid was actually quite valuable, as it was holy water from the Nile itself. She then picked up a large and ancient stone bowl and carried it over to the alter and sat it down. After opening the jar, she poured the water into the bowl, making sure to get as much of the settled mud out as possible.

She brushed her fingertips across the surface of the water, swirling it slowly. Already Aja could hear the whispers in her head as the water seemed to continue rippling by itself, even after she removed her fingers. There was power in the water and in the mud. Both substances had been crucial in the creation of the Nocturne, and they would be just as important in its demise.

Something fell and made a loud noise farther off in the warehouse, sending Aja's hand flying to the blade concealed in her corset. Her first thought was that Drake had arrived early, appearing suddenly and without announcement as he usually did. She felt no fear, only a sudden lust to destroy whatever the thing was that had startled her. She forced herself to be calm as she closely examined her surroundings. Off the distance, she saw that a rat had knocked over a somewhat worthless artifact.

Drake was usually a punctual visitor, always showing up on time, but today he was running late. When Aja had received his message, he had sounded pained. Perhaps he'd been wounded while retrieving the jewel. The Midnight Nocturne was no ordinary gem, and Aja knew all too well what happened to those unfortunate enough to be around it for too long. She found the chance to be near it invigorating and arousing.

A sudden knock at the front door drew her attention away from her tasks. She ignored the interruption at first and went back to the cabinet and removed a roll of clean papyrus. Moments later, the knocking resumed, much louder than before. Aja set her jaw, angrily storming off toward the front door.

Before pulling the blind back, she made sure the closed sign was in the window. Outside, a wealthy looking middle-aged man stood, politely waving. A wide and inviting smile crossed his lips as Aja made eye contact with him.

Aja exaggerated the movements of her lips she mouthed out the words, "We're Closed."

"Just a peek?" the man asked, loud enough for Aja to hear him through the door. He pinched his fingers together in the air to signify that he only wanted a quick glance around the shop.

The stranger then caught sight of Aja's costume. His eyebrows rose as his gaze locked on her nearly exposed breasts. Aja shook her head and closed the blind before walking off. Under normal circumstances, she would have allowed the man in, even while dressed in her current attire, unwilling to pass up the opportunity to acquire another wealthy client. Thankfully, the man seemed to have given up as the knocking vanished a few moments later.

A dark cloud passed over her mind as she turned around to gaze at the door. Walking back to the window, she cautiously opened the blind. The open street beyond the door lay completely empty. The mysterious stranger had vanished as quickly as he'd appeared.

She found herself suddenly growing very suspicious of the rather untimely visitor. Somewhere deep in her mind, she began to wonder if his appearance signified more than just a chance encounter.

* * *

Richard walked away from the curio shop, feeling rather goofy as he ducked around the corner. He pulled a cell phone from his inner jacket pocket and, feeling horribly like a character from a bad spy movie, quickly dialed a private number. The phone rang only once before it was picked up on the other end. A sigh of relief escaped his lips before he gave his report.

"Kehl was right, the store is closed, and I couldn't get in but there is still definitely someone here. There is woman inside that looks like she's dressed as an Egyptian priest. Either she's into some kinky kind of stuff or this is the right place."

"Very good, Richard," Olivia said. "I just got off the other line with Leigh and Kehl. They will be on their way soon. Get yourself out of there. You're much too valuable an asset to lose in a pointless fight with a vampire."

Richard nodded, although he knew she couldn't see him. "Yes, Mistress."

As he continued down the sidewalk at a casual gait, Richard no longer felt like a fool. He looked up toward the horizon to see the last bit of the sun slip away. As though on cue, a dark exotic car with heavily tinted windows sped down the street and slid into the side alley behind him. He paused for a moment, taking note of the car before he made another phone call.

* * *

At this point, Drake didn't care who saw him pull into the rear parking lot of the small curio shop. The influence of the Midnight Nocturne once again flowed through his veins, making him arrogant as well as powerful. Opening the door, he stepped smoothly out into the vacant back lot of the store. His body was now fully healed, and he felt invincible. His perceptions had changed through the day, making the buildings in front of him seem small when compared to himself. He was eternal and soon to be omnipotent in a world full of weak mortals.

He strode swiftly up to the door. He opened it more fiercely than usual and entered. An old, dusty aroma tickled his nose as he made his way into the warehouse. Drake was familiar with this building, having spent much time conversing with its owner about the Midnight Nocturne. He found his way to Aja and her alter easily enough.

She gave no greeting, asking instead a simple question. "What are we going to do without Kitsu and her servant?"

"Will it make a difference without them here?" Drake replied dismissively.

"It makes all the difference, you idiot! I told you that we need the blood from two vampires and at least two mortals."

Almost before she could blink, Drake's hand was at her throat, cutting off her air supply. Aja's eyes went wide as she tried to meet his gaze. She struggled, but only to make a show of doing so. Drake would not kill her, for he couldn't destroy the jewel without her. Making use of this knowledge, Aja had intentionally drawn his anger to demonstrate her false submission.

"First, don't ever," he growled, "ever take that tone with me again. And second, I am expecting interlopers. At least one of them will be a vampire and the other will be a human girl, if she survived the beating I gave her earlier."

His hand left Aja's throat only after his eyes had raked over her body. Aja was beautiful, but Drake also knew that she could be dangerous and manipulative. Questions of whether or not he should let her live after tonight filtered through his mind. Memories of Kitsu also drifted into his thoughts, and he suddenly realized that he would need another plaything.

Rubbing the pain away from her neck, Aja nodded. "I apologize, I won't be rude to you again. I will need the jewel, however." Her voice was raspy from the brief strangling.

Drake looked down at the Midnight Nocturne and worried about what Aja would be capable of with it in her hands. His self-confidence got the better of him as he held the jewel out, as though it were any other trivial token. Aja, after all, was merely human and could be controlled, if not by the violence that cowed her moments before then by the simple promise of power.

Aja shivered as she gazed upon the jewel for the first time in her life. Stories of its unsurpassable beauty did little to describe its true glory. Reaching out, she gently caressed its dark surface, drinking in the tiny sparks of light that could be seen even in the dim light. Well attuned to the arcane, she could feel the raw power trickling from the stone and up her arm. Tingles exploded throughout her body setting her hair on end.

"How soon will you be ready to start?" Drake asked.

Her voice came as though from miles away. "I can start right now, if you wish. Once started, the ritual is virtually unstoppable."

"Virtually?"

"There are no methods known to me of stopping it, but that doesn't mean it isn't possible. As yet, there are many things that remain hidden in the ethereal mists of the world. Who knows what will be unlocked if we succeed tonight?"

"I do," Drake answered. "The floodgates inside of my damned soul will be unlocked, releasing my rightful power."

Or, Aja thought, *this could be just another Pandora's box.*

"I want you to start the ceremony now," Drake said evenly.

CHAPTER 34
BLOOD IN THE NILE

As Aja wrapped her fingers around the jewel's dark, smooth surface, she could feel the ancient magic stirring inside. Power that she never knew existed welled up inside of her, begging to be used. She walked slowly, as though in a trance, back to the shrine she had prepared earlier. Gently and carefully, she used both hands to lower the Midnight Nocturne into the bowl of water.

Almost immediately, the small rays of light streaming from the jewel increased in intensity. Laying the stone long-wise in the bowl allowed enough room to completely submerge it. Small bubbles were already beginning to rise up through the muddy water. Aja quickly removed her hand, as the water approached its boiling point after only a few seconds. Using the power unlocked by the jewel, Aja started to chant in the long-dead language of the ancient Egyptians.

Gradually, the water around the jewel ceased its boiling, although the surface still rippled with the discharge of energy. Aja held her hand over the jewel and unsheathed her dagger. Without a second thought, she brought it down swiftly to cut a thin slice across her palm. From behind, Aja could hear Drake stir as her blood began to flow. Squeezing her hand into a fist, she promoted the flow of blood, while at the same time arching her back as if from pain.

Drake stirred once more, only this time he moved forward with such speed and intent that it took Aja's breath away. One of his strong hands wrapped about her bare waist in an embrace that was anything but comforting. The other hand reached out and grabbed her wrist before the blood could drip onto the jewel. Aja could feel Drake's heavy, labored breathing on her shoulder as he became obviously excited behind her.

"Not yet, or I won't be able to finish," she moaned, masking her concerns that he would prevent the ceremony under the most seductive voice she could manage.

His breathing slowed until she could no longer feel it upon her shoulder. Drake pulled her arm back and held it just above her shoulder, licking away the first of her blood, savoring both its flavor and the salty taste of her skin on his tongue. As he backed slowly away, Drake made up his mind concerning Aja's fate: she would be his for all of eternity.

Able to discern that something regarding her fate had just happened, Aja barely managed to keep her hand from trembling. After extending her palm over the bowl, she allowed three crimson drops to fall onto the surface of the water. The bowl immediately resumed boiling, reacting to her blood more violently than it had to the jewel. Forgotten words crossed her lips once more as Aja managed to calm the raging water to a point where it was almost still.

"Your turn now," she whispered to Drake as she stepped aside.

Without a word, Drake stepped forward, looking at Aja rather than the jewel. He kept his eyes locked to hers as he brought his arm to his mouth and drew his fangs across his wrist. Only as he held his arm out to let blood on the jewel did he turn his eyes away from Aja. She was certain now that Drake wanted to keep her.

"That's two of us now," he mentioned, surprised that his blood seemed to calm the water in the bowl.

Aja nodded. "Now we need the blood of an unwilling immortal."

Drake turned with a grin to look toward the back of the warehouse as a tremendous crash came from outside. "It sounds as though one may have just arrived."

A few moments later, the back door of the storeroom slammed open loudly. At the same time, the sound of breaking glass echoed from the front of the shop. Aja immediately disappeared into the shadows while Drake chose to remain in plain sight. Aja knew the interior of her business better than anyone, and though she was not the most skilled in a fight, the shadows would offer her a major advantage.

Drake hardly needed to move a muscle as he leaned his head to the side to avoid a thrown dagger as it rocketed silently from the darkness. He was about to laugh at such a foolish attack when he heard a sharp intake of breath behind him. In the darkness, his keen eyes could see Aja's form slide away from a sarcophagus. The thrown dagger had buried into the stone coffin directly next to her head. Barely turning around in time, he only glimpsed the fist flying toward his jaw.

Kehl closed the ground quickly, smashing another punch just below Drake's ribs. The larger vampire flinched, but did not lose his footing, even as Kehl attacked again. Drake landed a backhand across Kehl's cheek, knocking him up against a freestanding portion of Egyptian wall. It teetered unstably for a moment before settling once more.

On the other side of the wall, Leigh leapt back, afraid that the wall would collapse. The amount of danger she was in only grew as Aja leapt from her new hiding place. A chance flash of light off of the curved Egyptian blade was the only warning afforded to Leigh. Knives already in hand, she threw her arms up, narrowly deflecting the attack.

Leigh whirled about with a high elbow and scored a lucky shot to Aja's brow. In the blink of an eye, Aja disappeared back into the darkness. Leigh looked about, trying to decide what would be her best defense. Running into the shadows while in unfamiliar territory would be disastrous. At the same time, remaining motionless would allow her opponent the time to navigate through the darkness and flank her.

On the other side of the crumbling wall, the combat was less complicated and dealt more with sheer brute force instead of guile and cunning. Both Drake and Kehl were bloodied, their knuckles split, their cheeks cut, and each was already sporting at least one broken rib. Drake lifted Kehl off the ground with a punishing uppercut and wasted no time in throwing himself forward in an attempt tackle his opponent into the wall.

As soon as his feet touched the ground, Kehl leapt up and back, slamming his knee into Drake's exposed chin. The force of the blow sent Drake flying over top of Kehl's body and headfirst into the wall. Unable to endure the impact, the structure crumbled and fell around Drake, burying most of his torso in ancient, dusty rubble. Kehl scrambled to his feet as he watched for any signs of movement. It seemed that Drake was unconscious for the moment.

Kehl quickly spotted the altar standing in a well-lit area with the bowl on top. As he rushed over, he spotted the Nocturne lying in the bowl, seemingly forgotten. Reaching down into the bowl with his bloodied hand, he wrapped his fingers around the jewel. Only the fact that his blood flowed in the water of his own decision prevented the ritual from continuing. Pain rushed up his arm as bright white light burst from somewhere under the water. His fingers wrapped tight around the jewel, and he tried to pull it from the water. But it was no use. An unseen force held the Nocturne submerged in the bowl. Kehl narrowed his eyes and attempted to look down directly into the white light. Pain exploded in his mind as the light seared into his eyes, blinding him. He roared with pain and exertion, finally managing to tear the jewel from the water.

The clay bowl exploded with incredible force, sending shards of rock ricocheting about the room. Several pieces buried themselves in Kehl's chest and arm as the blast blew him backward. He fell to the floor as the Midnight Nocturne slipped from his hand and slid away. Kehl looked around, unable to see. He struggled desperately to find the jewel. He grew still as he heard the sound of ancient stones shifting against one another.

Drake pushed himself to his feet from underneath the ruined wall, laughing as he rose. He was unharmed by the exploding bowl thanks to the protection of the rubble. The jewel lay close by at the base of the collapsed wall. He picked it up easily before walking over to where Kehl lay on the floor. Drake turned him over roughly with one foot, looking down into Kehl's face with a smirk on his lips.

"You just can't win," he said, stepping on Kehl's chest and pushing several of the stone shards deeper into his abdomen.

Despite his temporary blindness and current wounds, Kehl retained enough presence of mind to take grip of Drake's leg with fearsome force. Drake did not struggle against the attack. Instead he laughed loudly. Kehl would have broken his leg if the next thing Drake said had not stopped him cold.

"Why are you trying so hard?" Drake growled, grinding his shoe into Kehl's chest. "She was supposed to sell me the Midnight Nocturne last night. It had been planned for quite some time."

Kehl's vision started to clear at last. His grip, however, loosened on Drake's leg as he tried to process this new information. As he looked up through the mist, he could only see Drake's silhouette.

"Liar," he gasped, though there was no reason for him to trust Olivia.

"Believe what you want, but she double-crossed me. I was denied entry at the door to the club. This jewel is the one thing I have desired most for the majority of my eternal life. Maybe you should ask Olivia why she chose to play games with me. And also ask her why she put you and that young girl between me and the jewel."

Kehl's hands fell away from Drake's ankle. This new information confirmed his earlier suspicions that he was involved in some larger plot. But why would Olivia endanger not only Leigh and Kehl, but also the jewel? A vague web of events started forming in Kehl's mind. It seemed that everything that had happened up until this point was just meant to put him in harm's way.

"What of the two people that you sent to the club last night?" Kehl asked, trying to buy time for his eyes to recover.

A confused expression crossed Drake's face. "Who?"

"There were two of your victims who turned into vampires last night," Kehl answered.

"Ridiculous. Kitsu and I only fed amongst our servants. We never hunted in public—it would be suicidal. How do you think we managed to survive for so long? You must have done something similar yourself, no?"

A deep silence fell over Kehl as he tried to think clearly.

"Aja!" Drake called. "The bowl is destroyed, but I still have the jewel. We must take our leave immediately!"

Kehl heard no answer as he painfully rolled himself over on his shoulder, only the sound of receding footsteps. As he closed his eyes, Kehl could feel the world spinning. If the stone shards were not removed soon, they could easily take his life. He could only hope he would survive to confront Olivia about the worrisome things Drake revealed to him. He would also have to find some way of retrieving the jewel.

Lost in his thoughts, a surprising sight tore him from his concentration. Leigh was running to his side.

"Leave me," he managed, feeling as though he might lose consciousness. "They have the jewel; you have to stop them."

Leigh knelt by Kehl's side and took hold of one of the shards as best as she could. "I may have destroyed Kitsu, but I cannot handle Drake alone. Besides, I wouldn't be able to live with myself if I let you die after everything that happened last night."

No sooner had she finished speaking then she quickly pulled a long, curved sliver or the bowl from Kehl's body. Kehl moaned but managed to keep himself from flinching as she took hold of another piece.

"Look," she said, in a comforting tone, "I don't know why all of this is happening, or why I feel the way I do."

Kehl could see she was nervous. She was stammering as she absentmindedly pulled another shard from his body. "But I think if we get through this alive, I might want to get to know you better. As a person, I mean, and not just as an associate or a vampire for that matter."

"And not as something that you may be forced to kill one day?" Kehl asked with a grunt, just before Leigh pulled another shard out.

Her answer came slowly and not without a clearly noticeable hint of self-doubt: "Yes ..."

"You mean you like me even though I'm a blood-sucking monster?" Kehl said, attempting to bring a bit of humor to the situation, despite the circumstances.

"I think so," she murmured, looking away. "All I know right now is that I can't let you die."

Years of training screamed that she should let him die, but strange feelings deep down inside of her compelled her otherwise. In her heart, she found no means to resist these urges. As she looked down at Kehl's chest, she couldn't help but wince. Her somewhat gruesome work was not yet done. Her fingers slippery with blood, she grasped another bit of the bowl and tried to pull it out of Kehl's body. The fragment proved elusive as her fingers slipped off its surface.

Kehl winced as the piece shifted inside his body.

"Sorry," Leigh said, wiping a bit of his blood off of her hands onto her pants.

Kehl couldn't understand why Leigh was trying to save his life, and for some reason he wished to tell her about Rana, that she may still live. But he thought better of whining to the woman who was currently trying to save his life and remained quiet. Leigh noticed his silence and decided to say something to keep his mind working.

"You know," she murmured, "I had a very strange dream this morning."

Kehl's eyes widened, and he suddenly wanted to stop her from continuing. He was powerless to do so. He tried to come up with something to say and failed.

"There was this man who looked like a demon, his skin was all burned away," she said. "He talked about you some, and then I even dreamed about you."

Kehl closed his eyes and shook his head quickly back and forth. "I'm sorry."

Leigh laughed softly. "Don't be. They weren't bad dreams at all, really. Just strange. I know it must sound stupid. Forget I even mentioned it."

In reality, Kehl would be unable to forget for a very long time that this mortal girl had dreamed of him. His world had become infinitely more complicated in the last several moments. Everything seemed to be tied together in a huge knot that he was unable to undo. He was almost grateful that Leigh continued tending to his wounds in relative silence. When she finally removed the last of the large shards, she paused with the tip still piercing his skin as a sudden coldness filled her voice.

"Do not ever try to feed from me without my consent," she said forcefully.

Kehl nodded, unaware of the weakness behind Leigh's words. She didn't even completely know him yet, but somehow she felt that if it ever came down to it, she wouldn't be able to kill him. A moment passed as she fully removed the final piece. Already somewhat healed, Kehl groaned as he forced himself to sit up. He could now clearly see Leigh looking at him with something more than mild concern.

"I should be all right," he said, looking down at his partially healed abdomen.

His wounds were slowly knitting themselves back together, though not as quickly as they could be.

A sinking feeling tore through his wounded gut and forced him to divert his eyes from Leigh. "We should probably get after them," he said.

"Definitely," Leigh replied, wrapping her fingers about Kehl's arm, offering to help him up.

Kehl waved her away and pushed himself to his feet. "It's a good thing you sabotaged their car," he said with a grin.

Leigh clapped her hands together and laughed.

CHAPTER 35

A SMALL SACRIFICE

Outside the antique shop, Drake witnessed what two tons of old-fashioned muscle car could do to a modern featherweight car. The Mustang sported one shattered headlight and a badly bent bumper, while the rear end of Drake's car was badly crumpled and bent. The rear wheel was crushed in at such an angle that it rendered the car undrivable. As Drake looked around, he noticed that there were no other vehicles in the lot.

"Where is your car?" Drake growled to Aja, furious with the loss of yet another vehicle.

"I don't have a car," Aja replied. "This is New York City. I take the bus or walk. It's cheaper that way."

Drake looked down at the jewel in his hands and thought for a moment.

"You said we needed the blood of four different people, right? Maybe we don't need another bowl. You said that the ritual was irreversible. Do you think maybe just the blood would be enough to finish it?"

"I don't know," Aja murmured, deep in thought. "It's possible, I suppose."

As she turned her eyes toward Drake, Aja could see that he'd already made up his mind. His brow furrowed in concentration as he turned to face the door. In the blink of an eye, the door burst open and their two opponents rushed through.

Kehl took a flying leap from the steps. Expecting such an attack, Drake did nothing to defend himself as Kehl descended with a bone-rattling punch across his temple.

Aja had to duck out of the way as one of Leigh's daggers hissed past her ear.

"I don't want to kill you," Leigh said, even as Kehl pressed his advantage. "Please, just give us back the jewel."

Aja glanced quickly at Drake, wondering if the jewel was worth risking her life for. Before she could find her answer, Kehl dealt his opponent a crushing blow just under the ribs. Drake flinched, but managed to jerk the sharp end of the jewel across Kehl's wrist. It tumbled from his arms, but he'd succeeded in drawing some of Kehl's blood against his will. Without thought, Aja lunged for the jewel, stretching her arms out as far as she could.

Time seemed to slow down as the Midnight Nocturne fell perfectly into her hands. Unbridled power tore through her body. The sensation was much more intense than before. Perhaps the ritual, though incomplete, had indeed managed to weaken the jewel by some measure. It was not until she took to her feet that she noticed that Kehl and Leigh now stood several paces away. It seemed that they were afraid of something, although Aja couldn't imagine what.

She glanced curiously at Drake and noticed that he too bore a somewhat fearful expression.

As Aja looked down at the jewel, she saw that her nails were now grown to talons that shimmered with a silvery light. The backs of her hands were covered with a dusting of fine black fur. Quickly deciding that it must only be some effect of the jewel, she resolved to utilize this newfound influence over her foes. When she spoke, her voice had a grit to it that she'd never heard before. It even felt as though her teeth were elongated and fang-like.

"The keys to your car," she commanded.

Leigh scrambled for her keys and quickly threw them over to Aja. She turned her gaze back to Kehl and realized that whatever fear she may have struck into him was completely gone now. He lunged at her in an attempt to reclaim the keys to the Mustang. Drake capitalized on the sudden opening in Kehl's defense and stepped forward to ram a knee straight into his gut. Kehl doubled over as he fell to the ground, gasping for air and gripping his abdomen.

"Get back!" Drake roared at Leigh.

With her eyes still locked on Aja, Leigh scrambled backwards.

"Here," Aja said, handing Drake the keys. "I don't know how to drive a stick."

Drake remained silent as they edged around the car and got in.

"Not only do you not own a car, but you don't know how to drive?" Drake asked sardonically as he inserted the key and turned the ignition.

The engine turned over but would not start on the first attempt. Drake looked out the window and noticed that Leigh seemed to be watching him very intently. It was as though she was waiting for something to happen. With a loud curse, he gave the ignition a second, violent twist. Outside of the car, Leigh watched as both of the custom installed airbags on either side of the car exploded. The intense fear vanished instantly from her mind as both Aja and Drake were knocked senseless by the impact of the blast. Never having much faith in car alarms alone, Leigh had instead designed her own theft deterrents.

A satisfied smile crossed her lips as she reached down and helped Kehl up.

"They're out cold," she said.

She opened the passenger side door and found Aja completely unconscious, the Nocturne lying harmlessly on the floorboard between her legs. Leigh was unprepared for the impact the jewel would have on her when she took hold of it. Raw, electric power shot up her arm and into her head, filling her mind with brilliant and blinding white light. She recoiled and tried to let go of the jewel but her fingers would not release it. She touched her free hand to her forehead, trying to clear her mind enough to drop the gem. As if in response, her vision completely faded away, leaving her awash in the naked power assaulting her mind.

Images flashed in front of her, glimpses of looking at herself in a dirty mirror. Her face seemed younger and different. Scenes of herself standing nude in front of mirrors encircled her, and while she had no memory of such events, the same feeling of familiarity remained. These were her memories. The people she saw in the flashes of memory were herself.

I understand now, came a sudden voice that sounded somewhat like her own.

Immediately, another presence exploded into her mind. Although Leigh couldn't explain why, it seemed older and far more powerful than herself. It filled her mind with a darkness that wrapped her up in its dominating will. She suddenly felt very cold and alone, as well as incredibly angry at someone from her past. A sudden scream tore through the darkness, ripping the vision to shreds before restoring the bright white wash of power through her mind.

Then she was back to reality. The white light vanished instantly from her mind so quickly that it made her head spin. Her eyes darted frantically about as she tried to regain some sense of her surroundings. Kehl stood directly in front of her, staring at her like he'd seen a ghost. He held the Nocturne as far away from Leigh as possible in one of his hands.

"What happened to me?" Leigh asked.

"You took hold of the jewel and fell back into my arms. Your eyes rolled back into your head before I managed to pry it away from you. You don't remember what happened?"

"I don't know. I don't know!" she said, shaking her head furiously back and forth. "It just took control of me. I felt people inside my mind, but at the same time it felt like I was looking at my own reflection. It's hard to explain. A voice even said 'I understand now,' whatever that means."

Kehl looked at her carefully. He felt like he was beginning to understand what was going on now, although some major pieces of the puzzle were still missing. He still did not feel that it was time to talk to Leigh about these things. Whatever just happened had clearly done quite a job on her mind already.

"Don't ever," Leigh said, rubbing her eyes to stop herself from crying, "ever let me touch that thing again."

Kehl glanced down at the Midnight Nocturne, narrowing his eyes. There was no doubt that the jewel was weaker now. The energy it held inside seemed to bleed into the very air surrounding it. And yet, Kehl seemed to be immune to it, perhaps due to the earlier blast when he removed it from the clay bowl. He then looked back at Leigh, still curious as to what must've happened in her mind to make her fear the jewel so much.

"Look out!" Leigh screamed suddenly, pointing behind him.

Her warning came too late as Aja, her face bloodied by the impact of the airbags, hurled one of Leigh's daggers at Kehl. Still turning, Kehl had no time to stop Leigh as she dove in front of the blade. She shrieked in pain as the dagger buried into her arm. In the car, Aja slumped back against the dash and passed out once again, a satisfied look on her face.

Lowering Leigh down with one arm, Kehl pulled the dagger free of her arm and tossed it aside.

"Why did you get in the way?" Kehl asked as they both examined the wound.

"You've been hurt so badly these last two days, I only wanted to spare you some pain," she answered softly as she looked deeply into his eyes.

Kehl smiled sympathetically. "Thank you, but that wasn't necessary."

"I think it looks a lot worse than it is," Leigh said softly, flexing her arm with a wince. "It must have missed most of the muscle and just stuck in the skin."

Kehl looked down at her arm. There were two clear wounds, one much longer than the other. It did appear that the blade had merely stuck into her skin, entering on one side with the point pushing back out about an inch away. The wound bled badly, and they would have to bandage it soon. Kehl hoped that she had a first aid kit somewhere in the Mustang. Her incredibly blue eyes were filled with confusion and pain. His first instinct was to comfort her, to hold her and assure her that all was well. But how would she react?

"We need to get you some bandages," he said.

"Yes."

A comforting smile spread across his faces as he lifted her back to her feet. More concerned about Leigh's wound than about the blood running down her arm. He didn't notice as a lone drop fell onto the jewel. The blood boiled when it made contact with the smooth surface of the jewel. Then all at once it crystallized, completely frozen. Kehl heard the Nocturne buckling, and he looked down to see deep cracks spread across its surface. He saw Leigh's blood on its surface and understood what was about to happen.

"Get away!" he shouted to Leigh.

"Why, what's happening?" she asked.

"Get behind the cars, now!" he yelled.

Leigh did as she was told, peering over the hood of the car to watch Kehl. Brilliant light of all different colors burst from the quickly expanding fissures as he lifted the jewel high. A sudden shockwave of force burst from the jewel, traveling out in all directions. Kehl felt it pass through every molecule of his body and screamed. Leigh screamed as well and fell to her knees behind the car, offering no protection at all.

The calm of the alleyway behind the store shattered as gusts of winds suddenly picked up, sending pieces of trash blowing about. Kehl tried with all of his might to release the Nocturne but to no avail. Another, more powerful blast exploded from the gem, sending a visible disturbance through the air. Kehl roared with pain. He was rooted to the spot, unable to move as a third blast erupted and threw Leigh up against the wall of the curio shop.

"No!" he screamed as her body fell limply to the pavement.

Yet another explosion forced him to his knees, even as he held the jewel aloft.

Shaking his head, Kehl forced himself to concentrate. He had managed to pull the jewel from the bowl earlier, maybe now he could stop its destruction. He roared defiantly at the jewel, smashing both it and his hands into the ground. Pain exploded in his arm, returning sensation back to his previously numb fingers. But his grasp still remained firm on the quickly deteriorating jewel. He pounded his hands into the ground once more. He cracked the pavement with the force of the blow, driving the jewel down into its surface.

After jerking it free, he lifted his hands high into the air. With all of his might, he hammered the jewel one final time into the unyielding asphalt and finally freed his hands from its surface. One last burst of energy surged from of the jewel, lifting Kehl up into the air. His mind filled with blinding light as the world around him vanished. Explosive pain tore through every cell of his body, and it felt as though he was being torn to shreds. The sensation passed as quickly as it occurred, leaving him floating in the blank white world of his mind.

CHAPTER 36

UNWELCOME GUEST

Was this death? As though in answer, a calm sense of peace settled over Kehl's thoughts and body. He seemed to be floating in an endless illuminated space, completely numb to any sensation other than bliss. Kehl closed his eyes, wondering that if after all of the years of being undead he would finally be able to truly rest.

"Kehl," came a familiar voice.

"Rana?" he asked. "Is that you?"

"Yes, darling, it is me."

"I'm finally dead, aren't I?"

There was a slight pause before she answered. "Open your eyes."

Kehl did as he was told and forced his eyes open. He found himself standing outside of his and Rana's cabin. He turned around to look out across the valley and found himself looking down on the village of Braunburg. It was unchanged from how he remembered it in his young adolescence. The clear blue sky stretched out to the far end of the valley as bright sunlight fell down to warm the air.

"Is this heaven?" he asked, feeling as though he was about to cry.

"It is," Rana answered. "For me, at least."

"What do you mean?" Kehl asked, turning to the source of Rana's voice.

She stood before him in the simple green dress from the day they had met for the first time. She was radiant. Her age was unchanged from the night of her death. In his chest, Kehl felt a strange sensation: the pounding of his heart. He touched his own cheek and felt warmth. A happy laugh came from his lips as he felt the sensation of life pound through his body for the first time in centuries. With a quick step forward, he wrapped Rana in his arms and pulled her tightly to him. She returned his embrace, although it seemed with somewhat less enthusiasm.

"What's wrong?" he pleaded.

"You can't stay, Kehl," she answered sadly.

Stepping back, he held her softly by the shoulders. "What do you mean I can't stay?"

Rana was unable to look him directly in the eyes. "It's not your time to be here yet. I don't even really know if you will ever be able to come here again."

"What? No, it can't be," he replied, shaking his head and turning away from her to gaze at the sky. "Haven't I suffered enough? It's not enough that I was born with this curse? That I did what I did to you. I suppose even this is all just another nightmarish dream."

"No, Kehl, it's not. This *is* heaven, or at least my version of it."

"And you, of all people, are telling me I can't stay?" he murmured, turning to look at her.

Tears filled her eyes and Kehl already regretted his choice of words. "I do want you to stay, but it's not my decision to make," she said.

"Then God doesn't want me here."

Rana shook her head furiously, "Don't say that, I couldn't have brought you here without help."

"If you say so," Kehl said, rubbing at his eyes.

"I do. You were brought here so I could tell you something. I think it may even be some sort of apology for everything you've endured."

"So what is it that I have to know?" Kehl said, growing impatient.

"You have a soul."

"What?" Kehl asked softly. "That's impossible, isn't it?"

"No, you were born with the curse in your blood and soul. You weren't created by another vampire. When a person is turned by a vampire, they lose their soul. It's what happened to me, when you bit me."

"I can't tell you how sorry I am, Rana. I had no choice."

She held up a hand in a kind way. "I know, Kehl. I've known since the beginning. Don't you remember what I told you in your dreams that night? I said that I would love you until the end of time, and I will, but there is something else that you need to know."

"Is it about the jewel?"

"No, it's about the Mistress, Olivia," she replied.

"I know that everything is just part of her plot, but I haven't confronted her about it yet."

"It's not that. It's about who she really is. I told you that sometimes people lose their souls when they are turned. What you don't understand is that Olivia is me. Or rather, she is my body without a soul."

"What?" Kehl asked. "No, that's not possible."

"It is very possible. Look at me closely."

Kehl did as she requested and watched as subtle changes started to take place in her features. Surprisingly, little changed. Her eye and hair color slowly changed, as well as some slight differences in body shape. Her face, however, was unrecognizable. He wondered if Olivia had resorted to plastic surgery to change her appearance.

"Did she have operations done on her face so I wouldn't recognize the body?"

"No," Rana answered. "It wasn't necessary. My mother tortured my body for so long that it eventually altered its features. She has the same vampiric gift of healing as you do, so there were no scars."

"I can't believe that I didn't recognize you."

"It's not me in that body, Kehl. Olivia is a soulless vampire filled with nothing but hatred for you. She would set the world on fire if she knew that doing so would destroy you."

All of the pieces of the puzzle were finally starting to fit together. The dream Kehl had experienced earlier that day had revealed the truth about Rana's soulless body. Kehl would have never expected it to return from the grave, seeking vengeance.

"If I created her," he asked, "I should be able to control her, shouldn't I?"

"Not in this case. I think at some point during my mother's torture, she forced you to free my body from your control."

"Oh," Kehl murmured, grateful that Rana's appearance quickly shifted back to her own.

"It did keep her from killing you herself, though. She can't harm you since you are essentially her creator."

"How do you know all of this?" Kehl asked her softly.

"I've had help," she said with a smile. "Also, I cannot fully be at peace while my body is still animated, so I've been watching over you."

"Thank you, that means a lot to me, knowing that you've been watching," he said. "I've missed you so much."

"I know you have, and I want you to stop torturing yourself so much."

Kehl remained silent as a tear slid down his cheek.

"I want you to let me go, Kehl."

"I can never forget about you."

"You don't have to forget me, my love, just let go of your grief and anger."

"I'm not sure I can."

"You have to, darling. Things are going to get harder now that the jewel no longer protects the world. You wouldn't have been able to visit here before now. I don't even know if it will ever happen again; this is all just the beginning, for better or worse. Things are going to change for you too."

"I won't be allowed to come here again?" Kehl asked as a sinking feeling spread through his gut.

"I don't know," Rana answered. "Our time is running out now. You can't stay much longer."

"So that's it then? I have to say good-bye and lose you all over again?"

Rana smiled sadly. "At least this time we can say good-bye properly."

For a moment, Kehl thought about arguing but knew in his heart that it would only waste the precious little time that remained. The two embraced tightly. Although a great sadness welled up inside of Kehl, he found that he could not cry. Love itself seemed to radiate from Rana, filling him with its all-consuming warmth.

"This is it then?" he whispered softly into her ear.

Instead of saying anything, she nodded slightly before nuzzling up against his neck.

"Please, Kehl, destroy Olivia and put all of this behind you."

"All I can do is try, my love."

Rana nodded again. "You have to get ready now, darling."

"It's time, isn't it?"

"Yes."

The world went completely white again for the briefest of moments. The presence of Rana vanished instantly, leaving only a cold void. Kehl dropped his arms to his side and turned his eyes upward. He wanted to be angry that he could not stay with Rana, but he was unable to sustain the emotion. A slight smile crossed his lips as the new memory of being human and being with his Rana once more crossed his mind and gave him strength.

CHAPTER 37
PURPOSE

Pain exploded through his body as Kehl returned to the real world all too quickly. He gasped for air as he collapsed over top of the remains of the jewel. Both of his hands felt as though they were badly fractured from his earlier struggle. The jewel itself now lay in a near perfect circle of nine identical shards. It took several moments for Kehl to gather his thoughts and take stock of the situation. The warm, all-consuming joy that he'd felt earlier was now gone, replaced by the familiar emptiness of being one of the damned.

The situation was very different now. He knew exactly what was going on and could now act with purpose and determination. For the first time in centuries, he felt as though he had a purpose, a reason for existing. Although his hands were still badly wounded, he knew that the first thing he must do was find his partner and make sure she was okay.

"Leigh," Kehl murmured as he looked over toward the wall where her body still lay motionless.

He pushed himself to his feet, disregarding his injured hands and the remains of the jewel. Quickly finding his way over to where Leigh lay, Kehl knelt at her side. He saw that she was still alive but could not tell how bad her injuries were. Hopefully the blast had only knocked her unconscious and left no other permanent wounds.

"Leigh," he said softly, lifting her head with one of his partially healed hands.

Her eyes opened so quickly that it startled him.

"Where am I?" she asked, her pupils slightly dilated.

"In the alleyway behind the warehouse. There was a blast when the jewel exploded. It knocked you up against the wall. I thought you were a goner for a moment there."

"Oh," she said, noticing the trail of the tear on his face. "Are you okay?"

"Yeah," he answered with a grin. "I just thought we'd lost you there a moment ago. I couldn't really check for a pulse."

Kehl held up his badly damaged hands with an odd sort of grin on his face. Leigh's eyes widened in shock.

"Your hands!" she cried. "What happened?"

"The jewel was going to explode in my hands. I couldn't let go of it."

"So how did you get rid of it?" Leigh asked as she took his hands gingerly by the wrists, pulling them close to have a better look.

Kehl winced in pain. "I pounded it into the ground and freed my hands, but it still shattered. The blast knocked me out for a few seconds. I had a vision, but I can't explain it just yet. Now that I know you're okay, we need to get the fragments together."

"Where are they at?" she asked.

"Over here," he answered.

They helped one another stand, and Kehl guided her over to where the fragments still lay. Leigh looked down at them apprehensively. They lay in a small circular crater in the pavement, surrounded by what looked like a halo of salt. Only time would be able to tell what forces were now loose upon the world.

"What's going to happen?" she asked, not taking her eyes from the remains of the Midnight Nocturne.

"I'm not completely sure."

Kehl glanced over at Leigh's Mustang and noticed that both the seats were now empty.

"It would seem that Drake and Aja escaped."

"He's gotten what he wanted now," Leigh replied. "It's strange though, I thought that everything would be different, but I feel exactly the same as I did before. All except for a headache from being smashed up against the wall."

"I don't feel any different either," Kehl added, "but things are definitely going to change."

Kehl cautiously reached down into the small crater and brushed his fingertip against a single fragment. Its touch sent an electric tingle up his finger and into his arm but did not affect him in any major way. One by one, he picked up each shard and carefully placed them gently into his pocket. He worried for a moment about the pieces coming into contact with one another, but after a few moments, they seemed to be fine. The real trouble would come when he tried to confront Olivia about her true intentions. She had risked the fate of the entire world in an attempt to destroy him.

The question of the future loomed in Kehl's thoughts. Without the jewel, the possibilities were almost too big even for Kehl's immortal mind to deal with. Whatever problems arose would have to be dealt with in their own time. This situation with Olivia required his full attention.

"Did you see what happened to Aja when she touched the jewel?" Leigh asked, making her way to the driver's side of the Mustang. Along the way she picked up her throwing daggers and returned all but one to their sheath.

"Yes," Kehl replied. "It looked like she started turning into to something very nasty."

Leigh nodded before she sat down in her car. Using her dagger, she cut away the remnants of the spent airbag. Kehl sat down in the passenger seat and took hold of the bag on his side. With a grunt, he jerked it out with sheer force. His hands were now almost completely healed.

"It looked like she almost changed into a werewolf," Leigh continued. "But I have never felt an aura like that come from a lycanthrope."

"Nor have I," Kehl said, looking down at his hands as he gave them a flex. "She took me by surprise. There must be something very powerful inside of her."

"Oh good, they left the keys," Leigh said to herself as she gave the steering column a quick glance. "Good thing for my airbags, eh?"

"Yeah," Kehl said with a chuckle. "I didn't think old cars like this came with them. I've actually owned one or two."

"Oh, they didn't," Leigh replied. "That was my own doing. I figured that would make a perfect trap. If you don't hit the kill switch on the floorboard, the car won't start. If you try to start it a second time, the airbags deploy. To tell you the truth, I didn't know that they would work. I guess they did all right."

Leigh pushed her foot deep into the floorboard before she gave the key a quick turn.

"Come on, baby," she cooed, hoping that the earlier shockwaves hadn't damaged her car even more than the earlier crash.

True to the golden days of Detroit, the engine roared to life without a single complaint.

Leigh sighed with relief, accidentally lowering her guard to the weight of their current situation. She fell back into the deep bucket seat of the Mustang and closed her eyes. Their inability to stop the destruction of the Nocturne may have changed the entire world around them in major ways. And though she thought herself insignificant to the world as a whole, her very identity was now under pressure.

The voices in her mind had been hers. She recognized the reflections of other women as her own. Combined with the events of the last twenty-four hours, she was feeling too thinly spread. It felt as though she were being pulled apart from every possible direction and being torn down the middle. Only her love of her father drove her on now. She must find out once and for all why he was tangled up with a woman like Olivia.

As she looked down at her arm, she realized that the wound from earlier was still bleeding. Several red drops had already fallen from her arm and onto her seats. Next to her, Kehl was already rummaging through the glove box looking for a first aid kit. The glove box was a mess, but he managed to find a roll of gauze that would do the job until they could find better supplies.

"Here, lift your arm up," Kehl said softly.

Leigh did as she was told, and Kehl started wrapping her arm with the bandage. "I have to talk to you about that vision I mentioned earlier," he said.

"What about it?" Leigh asked, feeling more tired than she could ever remember being.

"I found out some information about what's going on."

"So there was a larger scheme of things?" Leigh said, too tired to doubt his experience.

"Yes, the vision basically just confirmed what we were both suspecting. The whole situation with Olivia just doesn't seem to make sense. Inside the antiques store, Drake told me that she had made an offer some time ago to sell him the jewel. How else would Drake have even known that she kept it in the vaults underneath the club? He also denied creating those two newborn vampires we were forced to kill."

"That does make sense," Leigh replied. "My father has also been acting strange ever since we took this job. I can't be sure, but I think that Olivia has some kind of control or leverage over him. He was once the most famed vampire hunters in the world, but I think he may have finally fallen into some sort of trap."

"You and your father are close, aren't you?"

"Yes, very."

"Then maybe the leverage is you?" Kehl replied. "She might have threatened to kill you or do something worse if your father didn't follow orders. That's the only weakness that I can imagine him having."

"That is definitely a possibility," Leigh said as Kehl finished tying the bandage off. "Thank you."

"You're welcome."

"What do we do about the jewel?" Leigh asked, her fatigue finally starting to show in her voice.

Kehl shrugged. "There is nothing else that we can do. It's over. Whatever powers were released when it was destroyed are here to stay, for the time being at least."

"You're right," Leigh replied. "I think the only thing we can do right now is confront Olivia about all of this."

"I agree, but I think maybe you should stay away just for a little while. At least until we find out what's going on with your father."

"No can do. If she has my father under her control, then I want to deal with her myself. Your idea isn't completely bad, though. How about this: you enter the club through the main entrance, and I will try to sneak in and find Olivia or Dad."

"You're really worried about your father, aren't you?" Kehl asked.

"Yes," Leigh said, feeling tears well up in her eyes as her voice cracked.

Kehl wanted to tell her that everything would be okay.

"You know something, don't you?" she said, noticing his reaction. "What do you know?"

Kehl remained quiet as he shook his head.

"I swear you will be walking back to the Nocturne if you don't tell me what you know in the next five seconds."

Kehl knew that the threat was empty, but he didn't want to start an argument when Leigh did deserve to know the truth. Kehl bowed his head and let out a deep breath. When he spoke, he tried to make his voice sound as calm as possible. "I was told in my vision that Olivia is a vampire," he said simply. "And I think your father must have been bitten."

"That's not possible," Leigh said, staring out the windshield and out into space. "I would have noticed the signs."

"It is possible, and in fact, I am completely certain of it. I don't know whether I died or what, but for a few moments I was with someone who died a long time ago, someone who I trust absolutely. Drake also told me he didn't bite those people at the club. It fits in perfectly with everything else that's been going on, especially with your father's odd behavior. Olivia must have bitten him someplace where you couldn't see."

Leigh shook her head and slammed her door closed. Kehl followed suit but closed his door more gently. She then grabbed the shifter and threw the car violently into reverse. Kehl held tightly to the armrest and waited until she had time to guide the car out of the alleyway and back onto the main road before telling her the rest of the story.

"Olivia is a vampire," Kehl said hesitantly. "And I know for sure, because I created her. When the last shockwave from the jewel hit me, it sent my soul to heaven, or at least someplace like it."

Leigh shook her head, letting the engine rev before shifting hard into gear.

"It was there that I found out that Olivia is the soulless body of my dead wife, Rana Alexander. She was my first love, and the only woman I have ever been with, even after all these centuries."

Looking out the passenger-side window, Kehl let his mind wander as he continued. "I was not always a vampire. I was born human and aged normally for the first twenty-one years of my life. In my younger life, I cannot remember a time before Rana. We spent literally every day together, carving out a life for ourselves. Eventually I requested her hand in marriage, and she accepted."

Leigh pushed the accelerator down fiercely, ignoring the speed limit. The scent of burning rubber invaded the interior of the car. Kehl didn't mind her reaction, although it did surprise him. It seemed as though she was getting either very angry or very jealous.

"The curse in my blood manifested itself, and I changed into a vampire on the night of our wedding. Everything happened as though in a dream. Unable to help myself, I fed on her blood. I've lived with the guilt of what I did that night for so very, very long."

He paused for a moment to look at Leigh and gauge her reaction. Her eyes were still locked firmly on the road.

"Sometimes when a person is turned into a vampire, they lose their soul. It's is also very difficult and dangerous to turn someone with a single bite. For some reason, it happened with Rana. Her body reanimated as a vampire, full of nothing but hatred and anger directed toward me. She killed several people in our village before they managed to subdue her. Her mother tortured us both to the very edge of death and insanity. At first they buried Rana's body alive and then later exhumed her for use in my torture. I assume it was many years later that the body came to terms with its identity as a vampire and named itself Olivia. Eventually, the Alexander family died off or forgot about us down in the dungeon. Obviously, we both managed to escape through our own means."

Silent tears slipped down Leigh's cheeks as she listened to his story. "I really don't know how to respond to all of this," she said, wiping away her tears while trying to keep her eyes on the road. "I believe you, but I'm not sure that I want or need to hear all of this."

Kehl looked back at her and saw the tears in her eyes. He paused for a few moments before he decided to continue. He would not have her think him a monster.

"I didn't know that Olivia existed until this whole mess happened. Her family tortured me to the point of insanity. I don't even know how long I rotted in their dungeons, only fed by the cold blood of dead vermin and old corpses. I know that I deserved every moment that I suffered through. You must believe me, I never wanted this life. All I wanted to do was marry Rana and grow old with her."

"So how did Olivia come by that scroll?"

"I am guessing that her 'ancestor' Berenger was actually her father, Rallos Alexander. I knew that he'd served in the crusades, but he never mentioned anything about being a spy."

Leigh let out a heavy breath as she tried to process all of the new information. "It's been a very busy night, physically and emotionally."

"Yes," Kehl agreed. "Now that we are past all of that, I want to help you save your father from Olivia."

Leigh threw on the brakes and sent the car skidding onto the shoulder of the road. Tears welled up in her eyes as she looked at him. Kehl started to touch her shoulder, but she batted his hand away. He was hardly able to imagine what must have been running through her head. There were the ramifications of what happened tonight, as well as the enslavement of her father and even some budding romantic emotions. When Kehl reached out a second time for her shoulder, she did not resist.

Leigh wanted to ask him why he picked her, out of the entire crowd the night before, to dance with. Her initial feelings of attraction toward him still remained very much intact. She felt strangely drawn to Kehl in some inexplicable and irresistible way. But were the feelings her own? The earlier presence of others in her mind made her doubt even the strongest of her feelings. And now that he wanted to help her, she found her feelings for him were growing stronger than ever. So strong that it made her heart pound inside her chest.

"I can get out, if you need space," he said softly, taking hold of the door handle.

Leigh spoke quickly, her voice cracking. "No, no ... please stay."

Kehl nodded and silence blanketed the car. They sat there for several moments. The engine of the Mustang purred on as though nothing was wrong with the world. As time passed, Leigh started to believe more and more that her father had indeed been bitten. It hurt too much to even think about it, and when she broke the silence, she changed the subject.

"Why did you dance with me?"

"I don't know," Kehl answered honestly as he looked out the window once more.

"Do I remind you of her?"

"No. Not at all."

"Thank god for that."

Kehl chuckled distantly.

"Was she pretty?"

"Yes, she was the most beautiful woman in our part of Europe."

Leigh smiled in a far away manner and watched as a car drove past them on the highway. Normally she wouldn't consider herself a pretty woman, but for some reason when Kehl was around her she felt beautiful. Perhaps it was the way he looked at her so intently when they talked. She was more accustomed to being talked at by demanding employers.

"Thank you for dancing with me," she murmured.

It only took a second for Leigh to pull herself together, but even when she calmed down, her thoughts were still conflicted. She would have to find some way to keep a lid on things until she liberated her father. With a much gentler motion than before, Leigh put the car in gear and made her way back up onto the highway. She tried to drive smoothly but wound up missing second gear.

"Remember that dream I told you about?" Leigh asked.

Kehl looked at her as his brow crossed in thought. "The one with the demon?"

"Yes," Leigh replied hesitantly. "He told me about Rana too. I just wanted you to know that I do believe you."

They both grew quiet once more as the nighttime cityscape passed by outside. Leigh felt herself calming down as she came to terms with all the feelings raging through her heart. She would need to be completely focused if they were to have any chance of success. She could not, however, find the words to express to Kehl what was going on in her head, so she remained silent.

Several minutes later, Kehl broke the silence. "We don't have much of a plan."

"It might be better to keep things basic and to play it by ear. We don't really have any idea of what's going to happen once we get back. You should be able to handle yourself just fine. I can find my own way in. If not, I have the katana and a couple of guns in the trunk if I need them."

Kehl thought momentarily about asking her for a gun, but then thought better of it. It was nighttime and the club would no doubt be in full swing by the time they arrived, complete with guards and weapon checks. The plan was overly simple, but it did seem to be for the best. He wondered if he would find any resistance at the front door. If Olivia truly was a vampire, then she would have definitely felt the reverberations from the jewel.

"Okay, you find your father while I confront the Mistress. Do you want to meet up if we survive this?"

Leigh thought about his question for several long moments. "Yes," she replied. "I would still like to spend more time with you. And not just time on the job."

Kehl nodded and looked out the windshield at the dark streets rushing by. It felt so strange that this young mortal woman was so interested in him. The last two days were quickly changing everything about his world. If they made it through this final, most dangerous trial, perhaps he would finally be able to escape his past.

CHAPTER 38

UNCERTAINTY

Olivia sat on the edge of the couch in her quarters watching TV. She'd felt the shockwaves reverberating all the way from the curio shop. The destruction of the jewel was being reported on the news as a mild earthquake with an epicenter somewhere in New York. Every news channel was abuzz with information. Tremors were said to have been felt all the way around the globe, which was strange for such a weak earthquake. It was torture for her to not know whether or not her plan had succeeded.

No doubt remained that the jewel had been destroyed, but even the fate of the world took second chair to her vendetta against Kehl. She'd called Richard earlier and directed him to return to the antiques store. Nearly an hour had passed, and she still hadn't heard back from him. Even so, her hopes were high that her revenge was now complete. She now felt more powerful than ever before, even though there was no way to validate her feelings.

"Today the world was shocked by what seemed to be an exceptionally powerful and odd earthquake," a newscaster said. "Though there were no fatalities reported in the mild quake, there were reverberations reported from as far around the world as mainland Japan. Experts are baffled by what may have caused the tremors. Many are strongly suggesting that the epicenter may have been someone in the northeastern states, possibly somewhere here in New York City."

A sudden ring from the phone on the table next to Olivia startled her so badly that she almost leapt from her chair. Olivia immediately grabbed the remote to her TV and turned it off before picking up the phone. Only several people on the entire planet knew the number to this phone, and Richard would be the only one calling at a time like this.

"Mistress," came Richard's obedient voice.

"Yes, Richard, what happened?"

"I followed your directions and returned to the antique store. The jewel has been destroyed, but there was no one around."

"So Drake managed to destroy the Nocturne?" she asked.

"Yes, it would seem so," he said, falling silent for several moments.

"Is Kehl dead?" Olivia asked

"If Drake didn't kill him, then it's very possible that the blast tore him to pieces. It was incredibly powerful. I'm surprised that there isn't more damage to the city."

"You don't know if Kehl is dead?" she screamed, getting to her feet. "Why didn't you call me earlier?"

"With all due respect, Mistress, I followed your orders implicitly. I was not here earlier to see what happened. I did try to search for any of his remains, but I found no traces of ash. There were high winds at that time, so any traces would have blown away."

Olivia rubbed at her eyelids, trying calm down and think things through.

"Did you see what happened to Leigh?" she asked.

"I do not know if she survived either."

"And Drake and Aja? Are they still alive?"

"I honestly don't know. Drake's car is still sitting there wrecked in the parking lot, but the Mustang is gone."

Olivia sighed heavily and thought quietly for a moment. "I suppose I'm going to have to be prepared for guests. I can only guess at who it will be."

"It would be advisable to prepare," Richard replied.

"Thank you, Richard. You followed your orders as closely as you could. Get back to your car and return here as quickly as possible."

"Yes, Mistress."

Hanging up the phone, Olivia looked at the darkened TV and wondered what was going to happen. The club would no doubt be packed tonight, as it was still the weekend. She would have to alert the guards and have them armed to the teeth. She would also need Jesse standing ready. If Kehl still drew breath, there was only be a few people on the planet who could defeat him now.

"Jesse," she called softly.

The door to her living quarters opened quietly as Jesse entered and walked down the hallway to her side. Casting his eyes downward, he knelt by her side. "Yes, Mistress."

"There is the possibility that both Drake and Kehl will be here at the club tonight. I will need you to watch the shadows and deal with Kehl if he arrives."

"What about Drake?" he asked.

"If Drake does come back, which I doubt, then I will deal with him personally," she answered.

Jesse's voice was somewhat strained as he spoke. "What am I do if I encounter Leigh?"

"You will send her directly to my quarters."

"May I ask why?" he said, pushing himself to his feet as if a heavy weight lay on his shoulders.

Olivia's eyes widened as she turned to look him in the eyes. Jesse's gaze was filled with an intense pain. He struggled against her control, breaking free further than he'd ever managed before. Olivia bared her fangs before giving Jesse a backhanded slap hard against the cheek. The blow was more powerful than she'd intended, and he staggered and fell to his knees.

"I understand, Mistress," he said, submitting once more to her almost total control. "I will not question you again."

Jesse bowed deeply to her, weeping in heaving sobs.

"If you ever question me again, I will find your daughter and kill her right before your eyes, and then I will turn you into my ghoul. Do you understand?"

"Yes, Mistress, please forgive me," he whispered.

"You are forgiven," she said tersely. "Now go and prepare for tonight."

Jesse rose to one knee and bowed his head. When he stood, he silently made his way down the hallway and left her chambers. Kehl would no doubt be a most deadly adversary, but Jesse was more worried about his daughter. No matter how absolute Olivia's control became, a small ember of hope burned inside of Jesse's heart that Leigh and Kehl would emerge from all of this victorious.

CHAPTER 39
FALSE DREAMS

Drake looked down at the unconscious form of Aja, wondering what manner of beast the jewel had revealed inside of her. Now back inside the antique shop, there was finally some time for him to think. Awoken by the first blast from the jewel, he had pulled Aja from the car and carried her into the building before the next explosion sent them both flying through the door.

Not knowing what waited outside, Drake chose to remain in the relative shelter of the shop. For all he knew, Kehl might have been changed by the jewel into a demigod. After giving the situation a few moments to cool down, he found himself starting to worry about his partner. He gazed down at her attractive, angular face and found himself hoping that she was okay.

He gently brushed away a lock of her black hair, touching her for the first time not in anger. Her lips were parted slightly. Her breath was heavy. The memory of his earlier arousal touched upon his mind. Suddenly he found his gaze resting on the rhythmically throbbing skin of her neck.

He was still hurt and felt the hunger rising strong in his gut. Leaning down close to Aja, he parted his lips, wondering if this was the right thing to do. Whatever was inside of her seemed like it was more powerful than himself, so much so that it frightened him down to his core. With the jewel destroyed, there would be no way of knowing what she might become. If he bit her and allowed her to bleed freely, he could kill two birds with one stone. His vitality would be restored and whatever monster slumbered inside of Aja would never awaken again.

Her delicate scent rose from her body and made Drake hesitate. The natural clean smell of her skin mingled with the remnants of a fragrant perfume from earlier in the day. He lingered close to her for a moment as a thought sprung up into his mind. What if he just walked away from her and let her finish her life? Now that the jewel was destroyed, he felt as though he'd regained some small measure of his humanity. After fighting Kehl during their last encounter, he came to the understanding that he had been used as a tool by Olivia.

As Drake considered his actions over the last two days, his behavior seemed uncharacteristic even to himself. He'd been completely consumed by the need to destroy the jewel. The endless quest for more power was now over, after what he felt was an anticlimax. His great wish to destroy the jewel had occurred while he was unconscious in the Mustang. And most of all though, he found himself missing Kitsu. He knew now that her loss was completely due to his own overzealous ambition. It was also a loss that he would never fully recover from.

Pushing himself to his feet, Drake rolled his neck, surprised to find that he wasn't really all that tense. A rumbling sound erupted from nearby. It was the sound of a car starting. That meant that at least one of his two former adversaries was still alive, maybe even both of them. It didn't matter; the jewel was gone now, and Drake felt nothing but failure in the aftermath of his greatest single dream.

A deep sadness crept into his heart, the kind that he'd not felt since the death of his wife and children. He had expected a sudden all-consuming burst of power that would greatly magnify all that he already possessed. But now, weary from combat and the rush of emotions from the last several days, he only wanted to return home and rest. As he walked toward the door, he took one last glance back at Aja. She would be fine, provided that she woke up. As he strode out the door, he took a look around the alleyway. The Mustang was indeed gone, separated from his now very wrecked car. The alley itself looked no different, save for perhaps a little more debris lying about.

The snort of a sardonic laugh rose from his throat as he thought about the immensity of what had happened here only minutes before. He would have thought there would be some evidence other than the remains of his car and a very small looking crater. A few steps brought him to his vehicle as he examined the damage. The frame of the car seemed to be intact. Only the rear corner was crushed badly. One of the wheels was protruding at an obscene angle. With a growl, he kicked viciously at the tire. As his foot connected, the car rocked up onto its opposite side with the force of the blow.

Drake frowned and looked at the car, then at his foot. He had been strong as a human, very strong, and though his vampirism magnified that strength, he could not ever remember being this strong. As he looked at the car, he could now clearly see the exposed underside of it. Like most exotic cars, it was built around a lightweight, tubular frame.

Taking hold of the automobile he tried to lift it. With less exertion than he expected, the car rose off of the ground in his hands. He started laughing. The earlier disappointment was bleeding away as he adjusted his grip. What he was about to do, even with his newfound strength, was not going to be easy. Exotic cars, even as light as they are, were still heavier than any normal human could lift.

Roaring with strain, his muscles bulged as he picked the car up to his waist. Planting one foot backward, he then lifted the car over top of his head. Its weight made him stumble slightly, but he managed to keep his balance. This wasn't the power he had craved, but it would have be good enough. He frowned as he realized that it would never be good enough to replace Kitsu.

Throwing the car back to the ground, it landed hard, shaking the earth under his feet. As Drake looked around the alleyway, he half hoped that someone had seen him. He took out his cell phone and called for his driver to come pick him up. It seemed that he would now have to find a new purpose for his undead life. He was truly his own master now, and there were new strengths for him to test out. The whole world was out there, waiting for him.

The jaded sense of needing nothing but money and power was completely gone now. After walking away from the antiques store, he made his way to the street to wait for his driver. As he stood there, gazing at the city around him, he seemed to be experiencing the night for the first time. He would live his life to the fullest from this point on, if not for himself then for the memory of his former wife and daughters. And for Kitsu.

CHAPTER 40

PLAY IT BY EAR

Several blocks away from the Nocturne, Leigh pulled her Mustang over to the side of the road.

"All right," she said as she unbuckled her seatbelt. "I'm going in on foot from here. The valet should recognize my car when you pull up. There is no way to tell what will happen then. If anyone asks about me, just tell them I got hurt in the blast and had to go to a hospital. They might not believe it, but it should be a good enough cover for a short while."

Kehl nodded. "What do I do if I encounter your father?"

Leigh fell silent for a few moments. If Kehl's story was true and her father really was under Olivia's control, it was likely the two would end up fighting. Just the thought of them coming to blows made her cringe. She didn't want to think of who would win; she only hoped that if it did happen, her father and Kehl would both survive.

"Kehl, please don't kill him," She asked, staring hard at him. "If we can neutralize Olivia, we should be able to free him from her control."

Kehl nodded and remained silent. He was thinking through several possible strategies. Jesse was a legend in his own right and a force to be reckoned with. Not only was he one of the most feared and respected hunters in the entire world, but he'd also dispatched vampires much older than Kehl himself. In all actuality, it would be very hard for him to even survive this encounter without using lethal force.

"He will not be harmed, if I can help it," Kehl said, reaching over and touching Leigh's shoulder.

"Thank you," Leigh said, taking hold of his hand.

She leaned over and kissed him gently and wordlessly on the cheek. She turned red when Kehl gave her a surprised look.

"What?" she cried. "You're going to have your hands full with my father, and I'm thankful that you're not going to hurt him."

Kehl smiled and opened his door. Leigh shivered slightly as she did the same and stepped out into street. The night seemed to have gotten colder since they left the antiques shop. They both watched for a moment as a few lazy flakes of snow fell slowly to the ground. It was a beautiful night, despite the strange and violent things taking place.

"Damn," Leigh said with a shiver as she glanced over at Kehl and scurried around to the trunk of the car. "You vampires aren't affected so much by the cold, are you?"

Kehl stood perfectly still and looked up at the sky. He actually seemed to be enjoying the inclement weather.

"The chill of winter is nothing when compared to the chill of the grave," he replied as he joined Leigh behind the car.

She already had her key in the trunk lid. After giving it a quick twist, it popped open. Just like the rest of her vehicle, the storage compartment was highly modified as well. Bright LED lights provided ample illumination for the two dozen or so weapons neatly packed away in foam liners. There were several sawed-off shotguns, one assault rifle, half a dozen pistols, and a couple of flashbang grenades.

Lying haphazard among the impeccably organized weapons were the blades Olivia had given to Leigh. Kehl watched Leigh intently, finding himself impressed as she geared up so quickly. First was the katana. Taking a small piece of rope, she tied a slipknot around the guard and then to the scabbard before securing it around her torso so it lay on her back. Next she slipped on the smaller blades, and then finished with a brace of pistols at the small of her back, just under the sword.

"That's a lot of equipment to be sneaking around in." Kehl said.

Leigh shrugged as she strapped an ammo belt around her waist. "I'm used to it. It's nothing compared to what I used to train in. Do you want anything out of here before I close it?" she asked, indicating that he was welcome to take anything he needed from out of the trunk.

Kehl looked down into the trunk, scanning all of the assorted weapons intently before he calmly reached down and pulled out a single flashbang grenade.

"That's it?" Leigh said, looking at him carefully. "Are you sure?"

Kehl nodded and stuck the grenade down into the same pocket with the shards of the jewel. After a careful few moments of arranging, he managed to make it look as though only the fragments filled his pocket.

Leigh narrowed her eyes and looked at him curiously. "If that flashbang goes off in your pocket like that, it's going to act like a real grenade with those jewel shards in there."

"Maybe, but the flashbang would be an easy way to disable your father without hurting him. With the shards around it, I should be able to talk myself into the club fairly easily without being searched."

Leigh nodded and closed the trunk of her car, hesitating with her hand still on the lid. She suddenly stepped forward, cupping her hand around the back of Kehl's neck before pulling him down into a kiss. Taken completely by surprise, Kehl stumbled back a step when she released him. Thoughts exploded into his mind like fireworks, memories from the past, the possibilities of the present and of the future. He opened his mouth to say something but could not find any words.

Leigh laughed and smiled. "That was for teaching me how to dance. I just wanted you to know how much I enjoyed that. Just in case, you know, if …" she said, trailing off.

"We don't see each other again," Kehl finished for her, thinking that those words sounded better than *If we don't make it out.*

"We had better see each other again!" Leigh said, giving his shoulder a punch. "You're going to have the valet ticket for my car!"

They both laughed.

"Here's the keys. I deactivated the security system after the bags were blown, so she should run just fine for you."

Kehl smiled and nodded. "I'll be careful with her."

"You better be, or I really will hunt you down and make you suffer. This is my favorite car in the world; don't forget it."

Kehl smiled and waved as Leigh disappeared into the darkness surrounding the road. Opening the door, he climbed back into the car and gave the ignition a turn. The engine roared back to life once more. Things were so complicated now, and even though he maintained a cheery demeanor with Leigh, his mood was nothing but dark. There were going to be some very hard fights and many difficult questions to answer tonight.

As he checked the road behind him to make sure no one was coming, Kehl noticed a car speeding down the street. He watched as the vehicle tore past him on the street and just barely caught sight of the driver. He instantly recognized the figure of Richard in the driver's seat. It seemed that he was paying more attention to the cell phone at his ear than to the road. Kehl felt it safe to assume that the phone call most likely concerned either the jewel or himself.

Carefully putting the car into gear, Kehl guided it back onto the street and continued on his way to the nightclub. Three blocks away from the club, a voice tore into his mind. Its presence forcefully pushed his own thoughts out. Kehl smashed on the brakes, accidentally sending the car into a swerve. It slid wildly for a moment until he regained control.

Sorry, the voice said, *that thing that happened earlier, they said it was an earthquake, but it wasn't, was it?*

No, Kehl thought.

I didn't think so ... I'm on the next corner, if you could pick me up.

Kehl wondered why on earth Anne would be standing out on a street corner in the middle of the night, especially in this part of town. Just when he started to wonder if she was a street girl, her voice came screaming into his head.

No, I'm not! God, you and your damn assumptions. Look, just pick me up and I'll explain.

Feeling something wet at his lip, Kehl brushed a hand under his nose and found it covered with blood. Things were definitely different now that the jewel was destroyed. Before, her voice came in an almost whisper to his mind. Now it pushed his thoughts out of the way like a bulldozer. He saw her waiting up ahead as he wiped away the last of the blood from his lip.

She was dressed differently now, with long black stockings, a black skirt, and a black hooded sweater. It seemed like she didn't want to be noticed. Between her special skill and her dark clothing, Kehl had no doubt she could probably make her way through even the roughest parts of town undetected. He brought the car to a rest directly beside her.

Barely giving the car time to stop, Anne quickly pulled the door open and slid in.

"Wow, this is a nice car," she said appraisingly. "Most of my friends like the small import cars, but this car is freaking sexy."

"It's—" Kehl started.

"Not yours," she finished for him. "I know it belongs to Leigh."

Kehl looked at Anne, not remembering telling her about his partner, nor even of thinking about her recently.

"How did—"

"I know?" Anne asked, finishing his sentence for him again. "My little 'gift' has become even more of a curse ever since that earthquake. I'm sorry for finishing your sentences for you, I've just been a little freaked out ever since this started. I don't even have to try to read people's minds anymore, it just happens on its own now. It's like their thoughts bleed right out of their minds automatically. It all just started happening right around the time that earthquake hit today."

Turning to face Kehl, she narrowed her eyes. "But it's not happening now. Why is that?"

"I am actually attempting to meditate, so you can focus on your own thoughts and tell me why you were out here in the middle of the night."

"Well, that was thoughtful, or rather, not thoughtful," she said with a pained laugh as she rubbed at her temples. "God that sounded stupid."

"No, not at all," Kehl said. It surprised Anne that he really didn't harbor any insulting thoughts.

"Something else happened too," she said, looking out the window into the darkness. "I found out about something, and I don't know how to explain it to you."

Kehl put the car in gear and guided it back onto the road. He couldn't help being curious even though he didn't need for things to be any more complicated.

"Leigh touched the jewel before it was destroyed, didn't she?" Anne asked.

Kehl nodded. "I had to take it away from her."

"I thought so. Wow, there really isn't enough time for this," she said, looking up the street as they neared the nightclub.

"It looks like there is a line to the valet station, so there should be a little bit of a wait," Kehl replied.

"Okay, here we go," Anne said quickly. "When Leigh touched the jewel, it linked our minds for a moment."

Kehl kept his eyes on the road as she continued.

"I don't even really know if *linked* is the right word to describe what happened. It actually felt like I *was* Leigh for a moment. And for a moment I felt whole, for the first time in my life, like I was complete. And suddenly everything made sense—why I've always felt alone, even when I'm with my friends. But it didn't last. A darkness came into our mind and swept Leigh away. Then it focused on me."

"It was the Mistress, wasn't it?" Kehl asked.

"Yes, it was," Anne replied quietly. "Do you remember the bite marks that I showed you when we met in the club?"

"Yes," Kehl answered, as he watched the line of cars ahead. "It was Olivia who gave them to me."

"Is that how you got your abilities?"

"No, I can remember having them before she bit me. I was maybe ten or eleven at the time when it happened. One night I decided to take a walk through Elizabeth's garden while I was visiting. I remember looking at a particular orchid that only bloomed at night and thinking of how wonderfully simple it would be to exist as a flower. Then I felt impossibly strong arms wrap around me from behind. Before I could even react, she had sunk her fangs into my neck.

"My first instinct was to play dead, so I focused through the pain and created that thought for my attacker. The result was instantaneous; she dropped me like a spent toy. I was able to send a message to Elizabeth that I needed help, just before I passed out. Elizabeth always said she blamed herself, but I never understood why until today. Just like I never knew for years just who or what had attacked me. For some reason the bite never turned me into a ghoul or a vampire like you. The only explanation I can come up with is that my psychic powers made me partially immune. When Leigh touched the jewel, it brought me into contact with not only her mind, but with all of the people she was close to, especially you, since you've bitten her."

"I haven't bitten her intentionally," Kehl answered in a low tone. "She offered herself to me in my sleep. I had no control over what happened."

"Anyway, she is linked to you by more than just emotions now. It was when the jewel exploded in your hands that I found a link to another person: Olivia, whom you created centuries ago. Then your mind filled with a bright light that pushed me out and into Olivia's mind. It was there that I found out the truth. Elizabeth had invited Olivia to her home that night, and that's why she'd blamed herself for so long for what happened to me. I wish there had been some way for me to stop Elizabeth from killing her mother and from Olivia eventually turning her into a vampire."

"There was nothing you could do," Kehl said softly.

"I know, Olivia probably would have turned me instead. And all of this is really because of you."

"I'm sorry."

"No, you really don't have to be. I didn't mean it's all your fault, I just meant that we are all connected because of you."

"And because of Olivia's plot," Kehl replied.

"Yeah, that too."

Kehl brought the car to a stop at the end of the valet line. There was no time now to try and understand everything that was happening. He would have to force himself to deal with all of these things later. For now, all that mattered was resolving this conflict and saving Leigh's father. Even this young girl had suffered under Olivia's twisted machinations.

"You're right about that," the girl said.

Kehl's returned the void to his mind. "Can you give me any information about what's going on inside?"

The girl closed her eyes and tried to send her mind into the club. Now that her powers were magnified, it seemed only all too easy. Just as she visualized the inside of the club, her thoughts became draped in an inky blackness. She screamed and opened her eyes wide, gasping for air.

"What's wrong?" Kehl asked, looking over at her, not knowing what to do.

"It's Olivia," Anne replied. "She is more powerful than before. It's like she completely took control of my mind and threw me out. She might even know who I am now."

"I shouldn't have asked you to do that," Kehl said, looking ahead to check on the line.

Anne shook her head. "No, it's okay, I can tell now she didn't find out who I am. She's searching the club now, looking for the source of the probe."

"Could you try reading the guards at the front door?" Kehl asked. "If you're up to it?"

"Definitely," Anne said with a nod.

Anne cast her mind to the front of the line and touched upon the thoughts of four guards. They were all on the highest level of alertness. She could clearly read Olivia's orders at the forefront of their thoughts. Surprisingly, they had been informed to allow Kehl access.

"There are four guards at the front door. They are on alert to look out for you but have orders to let you pass unharmed. I'm not completely sure, but they think that Olivia may have a trap set for you."

"That would most likely be Jesse," Kehl said. "What are you going to do while we are inside?"

"I'm coming with you," Anne answered without a moment's hesitation.

"What about the guards?" Kehl asked. "I don't think they will let you in."

"Oh, I have a few tricks up my sleeve," Anne replied. "They will never even know I was there. In fact, I may be able to get you in without being searched."

"What will you do once you're inside?"

"I will try to keep Olivia busy while you make your way to her."

"Are you sure you can handle her?" Kehl asked.

"Honestly," Anne replied, "I don't know. Since she bit me before, she may have some sort of dominion over me. It's really not that important. If you can find some way to stop her, I should be okay."

Kehl nodded once again, pulling the car forward a bit more. They were only one spot away from the valet station now. There was no time left. As he calmed his mind, he looked over at Anne. She was breathing quickly, watching the entrance to the club intently. He wondered if she was ready for what lay waiting in the club.

"Yes," she said, without taking her gaze off of the doors. *I am ready.*

CHAPTER 41
LEAP OF FAITH

Moving silently through the night, Leigh made her way undetected through the dark streets. Only one more building lay between her and the nightclub, but she would have to be careful. Even though she approached from the side, she'd already spotted one guard patrolling around the exterior walls of the Midnight Nocturne. She had no doubt there were more on duty, stationed somewhere out of sight.

She stuck to the shadows, pressing her back up against the building as she peeked around the corner. She saw a guard making his way down the sidewalk opposite of her building. She cursed silently as she saw the street beyond was brightly lit. At least it let her keep an eye on the guard as he walked further down the street until he vanished from view.

Leigh moved as swiftly as possible without making noise, dashing to the corner of the alleyway. With her eyes locked on the back corner of the club, she waited to see if another guard would round the corner. After several moments, she spotted the same guard returning in the opposite direction. She waited for him to pass again before taking another look across the street.

Unfortunately, there were no entrances on this side of the club. Turning her gaze upward, she spotted several security cameras mounted to the wall. She'd forgotten about the extensive security system that Olivia had at her disposal. Shrinking back into the shadows, she watched as the guard turned back around and headed the other way.

Her gaze slowly found its way to the ground as she looked at the road that circled the club. It seemed to be very narrow path, more like a small lane than an actual street. It must have been a utility road for the building from its days as a factory. Leigh turned her eyes skyward. An idea came to her as she noticed the building she stood under was roughly the same height as the nightclub.

Leigh made her way back around the building as she looked for the entrance. She found the main doors padlocked and all of the windows thickly boarded shut. As she continued on around the building, she found a half-dropped fire escape ladder. Further down the alley, she could see the entrance to the club.

The light from the front door spread out all the way to the dirty street in which she stood. It was a little more conspicuous than she would have liked. After several moments of watching, however, no one turned to look her way. She heard the familiar roar of her own car, and she saw it pull up to the entrance. For a split second, she swore she could see another person in the car. When she blinked, however, the person vanished and only Kehl was getting out of it. Dismissing the strange vision, she set back about her task.

Damn. I don't have much time, she thought to herself.

As she looked up at the badly rusted fire escape, she hoped that it wasn't so badly deteriorated that it would not hold her weight. She carefully backed up several paces into the darkness, her eyes locked on the ladder. After four quick strides, she jumped as high as she was able. One of her hands slipped as she caught the lowest rung and she nearly lost her grip. She gritted her teeth and groaned as quietly as she could, refusing to let go.

Carefully avoiding the ice, she took hold of the rung with her open hand and pulled herself up. The ladder was rusted solid and didn't give an inch as she climbed up. But it was a different story as she started to climb the stairs. The whole structure felt like it could collapse at any moment. She tried not to look at the wall. She could see the mounts shaking in the bricks.

"Not again," she whimpered.

She made her way to the top as quickly as she dared. After pulling herself up, she vaulted onto the roof and ran to its edge. Off in the distance, Kehl was walking into the club. For some reason, she could barely make him out, his silhouette seemed fuzzy. Maybe, she thought to herself, she was just getting tired.

As she turned her gaze back to the roof of the Nocturne, she was grateful to find it mostly free of snow. It appeared to be some ten to twelve feet away and just a little bit lower than her current spot.

Leigh cast her gaze back over her own rooftop, finding it to be mostly clear save for some abandoned lawn furniture and a couple of heating vents. The outer wall of the roof only rose perhaps a foot above the rest of the surface and would make a good spot to jump from.

As she turned her eyes down over the side of the building, she looked for the security guard.

He was near the far end of the building, right where she needed him to be. Quickly jogging back to the middle of the roof, Leigh briefly checked all of her equipment. Even though she knew everything to be secure, it never hurt to be sure. If she dropped a knife or a dagger, the guard below would instantly be alerted to her presence. After taking two deep breaths, she set off as fast as she could across the snow-covered roof.

The chill winter air cut across he cheeks as she picked up speed. A thought flashed into her mind halfway to the edge of the roof: what if the snow was packed into her shoes and made her slip on the very edge? She'd always been interested in parkour but never thought that she would be trying it out in the middle of winter on a snowy night.

From what she knew of the sport, the idea was to move quickly and accurately, reacting in the best possible way as the terrain presented itself. She didn't need to worry about slipping until the slip actually happened. All worries vanished from her mind two steps away from the jump. Her foot landed solidly on the ledge, giving her a firm foundation as she pushed off from its surface. In midair, she took care to keep her torso upright as she tucked up her legs so her feet wouldn't catch the edge of her target.

Her knees absorbed some the shock of the landing before she rolled over her shoulder and back. With any luck, the maneuver would have minimized most of the noise. The rest of the sound was hopefully muffled by the bass from the club. Slowly crawling over toward the edge of the roof, Leigh peered down at the guard. It seemed that he hadn't noticed anything as he continued along on his patrol.

She moved away from the edge of the roof and stood up. As her eyes searched up and down, she spotted a skylight not far from where she'd landed. She tiptoed quietly over to it and looked down inside the club. The window offered her a wide view of the darkened entrance room that led directly to Olivia's quarters. Had anyone been inside, her landing would have been instantly noticed.

Further examination of the skylight revealed that it was latched from the inside. But something appeared odd about the glass pane closest to the latch. As she looked closer, it seemed that it had been repaired many years ago. Leigh took out one of her knives and poked curiously at the caulking. Her heart nearly skipped at beat as she found the glass plate loose. She quickly cut away as much of the caulking as she could. After inserting her knife under the plate, she pried it up as carefully as possible and pulled it free. Without a sound, she set in on the roof next to her. Warm air poured up out of the hole in the skylight as she reached inside and unlatched it.

    The metal frame was already frosted over as Leigh took hold of it and pulled as hard as she could. At first the window refused to move. Forced to use both hands, Leigh pulled as hard as she was able. After straining for several moments, she finally managed to open it slightly. The opening she made would only allow her perhaps a foot and a half of space to get through. It would have to be enough.

    Leigh lay down on her side in front of the window, moving up to its side as she peered over the edge. The room below seemed completely dark and abandoned. She carefully lowered her legs down into the hole and turned her body as she slipped inside. As she grabbed hold of the window sill, she checked to make sure there was room to land.

    The floor was still about seven feet below her, with some of the furniture dangerously close. She saw no other alternative than to let herself fall. Leigh mirrored her landing on the roof, absorbing most of the impact with her knees before rolling away with the remainder of her momentum. She narrowly avoided crashing into the same chair that she'd sat in the previous night.

    As she rolled up onto her feet, she quickly assessed her surroundings. The apartment was indeed empty. A sudden crash from the doorway made her dive into the shadows for cover. To her surprise, the lights never came on. Leigh expected to hear shouting, but was instead surprised to hear drunken laughter drifting into the room. The door slammed closed and Leigh could guess what was going on.

    The clamor grew closer until she could make out the impassioned moans of a man and a woman. As she peered out of the kitchen, she saw Richard kissing a woman who looked very much like herself. Both of them were already halfway undressed and nearly down to their underwear. Leigh winced, unable avoid noticing Richard's rather obvious excitement. Seconds later, she looked away as he successfully removed the woman's bra.

    "We've got to make this quick, Richard," the woman said, gasping for breath. "My husband likes poker, but he won't be at the card tables forever."

    Richard looked over the woman's perfect body and couldn't help but think of Olivia and her earlier scorn. The memory aroused him in a strong way, and if this woman wanted it quick, he could make it quick. He jerked his head toward the couch, indicating that he wanted her to lean over it. It was supposed to be his job to keep an eye out for Kehl or Drake, but he could not deny his lust any longer.

Leigh quietly moved from her hiding place while keeping an eye on Richard. Before she took two steps, she saw Richard's gaze turn upwards to the ceiling. It took him a moment to realize the skylight was open. He'd never known Olivia to open that window. He opened his mouth to curse but never had a chance to. Leigh quickly stepped forward and smashed the bottom of one of her knives hard against the back of his head.

Richard fell unconscious on top of his lover as Leigh made a hasty and silent retreat. Behind her, the woman laughed and giggled, thinking it was all part of his game. Hopefully she would think he'd only passed out from too much alcohol. Leigh quickly made her way down the hallway in the direction of Olivia's quarters. She kept her eyes locked directly on the couple as she moved.

In the ensuing commotion, an empty champagne glass fell to the floor and shattered noisily. Richard's limp body fell to a sitting position with his back against the couch. The woman stood up, clumsily clutching at her clothes. She looked down at Richard with a mixed air of amused satisfaction and disbelief as she recomposed herself.

"I thought you'd had one too many," she said to Richard, laughing a bit. "At least the anticipation got me going just before you passed out."

Leigh's jaw dropped in the darkness beyond as the woman dressed and then walked casually out of the room, leaving Richard with his pants down. *Oh well*, Leigh thought, *it wasn't like the jerk didn't deserve it.* She then turned her attention back to the door leading into Olivia's chambers. Slowly wrapping her fingers around the doorknob, she gave it a gentle turn. She was unsurprised but slightly annoyed to find it locked.

Looking back down the hallway at Richard's unconscious body, she cursed silently. She'd already seen more of his body than she was really comfortable with. Too bad the only way that she would be getting through this door was with the keys that were undoubtedly in his pants. Leigh sighed heavily as she reluctantly made her way back down the hallway, keeping her gaze far away from Richard for as long as she could possibly manage.

When at last she had to look down at his body, she felt a wave of disgust sweep through her. It wasn't that she didn't like men. In fact, she found herself wondering what Kehl would look like in this same position. That thought at least made the experience bearable as she knelt down. Unable to keep from looking at Richard's body, she now knew why he had been so confident and forward. She fought back the urge to punch him where it would hurt the most.

Instead, she grabbed his boxers and jerked them fiercely up above his waist so hard that the waistband partially separated from the rest of the garment. A lethargic, snore-like groan escaped Richard's lips, but he showed no signs of regaining consciousness. She searched deep into the pocket closest to her and tried to find the keys. Unfortunately, she found none on that side. Moving to his other side, she checked the other pocket, it too was empty. She cursed out loud as she looked intently down at his unconscious form; this was going to be harder than she had anticipated.

CHAPTER 42

DARK CORNERS

Kehl and Anne were at the coat check desk at the entrance to the club. The check girl looked like she'd been up all night the night before. Kehl wondered if it had something to do with what happened to Rastis and Terrance. Tonight the guards were searching each and every guest, and as Kehl and Anne seemed to have made it past the guards, she didn't bother asking them for their weapons.

Kehl looked over at Anne as they made their way into the main room of the club. Her brow was furled as if she were angry. He wondered if she was fighting a battle at that very moment in her mind.

"I think we should find you a seat," he said softly to her.

She nodded distractedly as he looked about for a concealed table that would be close enough to one of the exits. A quick escape might soon be called for. After a moment, he found a table in an almost completely dark corner. The only illumination on the table was the exit sign shining from a door next to it. No one would see her there unless they already knew where she was.

"Here we go," Kehl said, leading her over and pulling out a chair for her. "If things get bad, you should cut and run."

Anne could only nod as she rubbed at her temples with her fingers.

Kehl turned out toward the dance floor, keeping himself to the shadows as he made his way around the packed room. Halfway to the employee entrance, he saw the door open and a man he could only imagine was Jesse step through. The man immediately turned his head and looked directly at Kehl. Kehl diverted his eyes and quickly took to one of the sets of stairs leading to the catwalks.

He attempted to make himself as inconspicuous as possible, strolling casually past the digital picture frames. He glanced at them briefly, as though he was genuinely interested. Halfway across the catwalk, he saw Jesse swiftly climbing up the stairs on the far side.

As Kehl looked back the way he'd come, he realized his retreat was blocked by a young couple. The pair was entangled in one another's arms as they made their way up the stairs. Kehl shook his head and turned back around to look at Jesse. There was no possible way now for him to avoid this fight, short of jumping down into the crowd below.

To Kehl's surprise, Jesse stopped a few feet away from him and stared at him with a strained look in his eyes.

"You are Kehl, aren't you?" he asked.

Kehl nodded and remained silent.

"I don't usually kill vampires without first learning their history. Unless, of course, they are an immediate threat. I apologize for having to do this, but I have no choice. I cannot disobey the Mistress. Her control is absolute. If I even tried to disobey her, she will turn my daughter into a vampire. Then she would turn her wrath upon me. I can only hope that this apology has not been too much defiance."

As if cued by his words, his expression screwed up into one of profound agony. In almost an instant it was gone, replaced by a gaze completely devoid of emotion. Jesse suddenly dashed forward just as all the lights and picture frames of the club died completely to be replaced by strobes and lasers. Kehl's eyes adjusted instantly to the darkness, but not quickly enough to avoid Jesse's sudden attack.

Kehl felt an explosion of pain burst into his skull as Jesse's shin smashed against his ear. He felt several pops in his neck as his head snapped sideways. He tried to shake away the pain and only nearly managed to block Jesse's next attack. That first blow had been almost as powerful as one from Drake. No mortal could possibly possess that much power.

After getting enough of his wits about him to retaliate, Kehl whipped his leg around so fast that Jesse would have no time to block it. Pain shot through his leg as he made contact with Jesse's shins. Kehl danced back a few paces and tried to work out the agony in his leg. He knew now that his opponent wore shin guards, at the very least.

He dashed back quickly, launching a punch that he knew Jesse could easily block. When his opponent did indeed block it, Kehl pulled the blow just as it landed. The hard surface under his shirt revealed Jesse wore arm guards as well. Before Kehl managed to retreat, Jesse launched forward with a devastating knee that sank deep into his gut, just below the solar plexus.

Kehl fell to his knees on the catwalk, gasping for air. He knew now why Jesse was one of the best of the vampire hunters. Kehl's eyes gazed down through the darkness. He saw that the crowd still danced on, oblivious to the conflict in the darkness above them. In the still frame captions of the strobe lights, their fight must have seemed like wild dancing.

Kehl coughed a little bit of blood up into the palm of his hand. As he looked up, he noticed Jesse take a spiked wooden kubaton from his belt. When used properly, it was one of the most dangerous and effective weapons in close combat. The main body of the weapon was little more than a six-inch long stick with a diameter that let it fit easily into the hand. Two three-inch wooden spikes protruded outside the fist on either side of the middle finger. A single blow to the heart or head would be more than enough to finish someone, vampire or human.

Kehl pushed himself back up to his knees. He only had just enough time to catch Jesse's fist as it rocketed directly towards his chest. Kehl had made the mistake of using both of his hands to stop the attack. Jesse capitalized on the opening in Kehl's defense and backhanded him hard across the face with his free limb.

Kehl's hands slipped away from Jesse's fist as he drove it home. The wooden spikes drove deep into Kehl's chest, penetrating deeply into his flesh and nearly spearing his heart. Drowned out by the bass, no one heard Kehl roar as he suddenly pushed himself up onto one knee. A heartbeat later, he stood up and landed a devastating uppercut under Jesse's jaw.

Jesse released the weapon and staggered back from the force of the blow. Kehl jerked the kubaton from his body and snapped its spikes off before breaking it in half. As he tossed the pieces over the side of the catwalk, he met his opponent's gaze. He was going to have to take this fight a whole lot more seriously now. If one of those spikes had managed to pierce his heart, he would now lay in ashes.

Reaching down into his pocket, Kehl tried to find the flashbang. Jesse immediately recognized that he was trying to find a weapon and attacked. Kehl lifted his knee to the side to block the incoming blow. Before Kehl could regain his balance, Jesse was upon him with a flurry of blows to the face and body. Kehl successfully managed to block most of the attacks and even managed to land a few of his own. Kehl could feel that Jesse was quickly beginning to fatigue.

Aware of his own growing weakness, Jesse quickly removed his forearm guards and renewed his attack. His blows were less powerful now, but without the weight of the arm guards, they came with blinding speed. An entire lifetime of combat experience told him just where to strike. Kehl was hard pressed to hold a stable defense even with his preternatural abilities.

Kehl let his lower defense fall for only a moment, but that's all it took for Jesse to slam a kick into his ribs with an armored shin. The kick sent Kehl crashing into the catwalk guardrails, nearly knocking him over. The vampire pushed himself back to the center of the walkway as anger filled his mind. Kehl bared his fangs and lunged forward, backhanding Jesse hard across the cheek.

Jesse staggered from the blow, its force nearly enough to knock him unconscious on. Kehl left him no time to recover as he slammed a series of blows into his ribs. Jesse fell back further, still trying desperately to recover. Light flashed from Kehl's fangs as he approached, telling Jesse that the gloves were now off.

For the first time in a very long while, Jesse felt the fear of death creep into his heart. He found the feeling to be at once to be extremely draining yet exhilarating. The weary hunter threw himself forward, attacking with every last ounce of his remaining strength. Every one of his blows landed successfully, though they seemed to have no effect on Kehl.

Kehl was consumed with the most anger he'd ever known. All of the events of his entire life seemed to have been leading straight to this one single night. With each of Jesse's blows, his anger increased exponentially, and he felt less and less pain. He lashed out blindly in his rage, exploding through Jesse's defenses with a savage flurry of attacks.

Blood stained his fists as they came away from Jesse's face. He felt the old man's ribs strain to hold the force of his punches. Kehl flanked Jesse and kicked him off of his feet, sending him crashing to the catwalk. Hatred filled Kehl as he looked down at the barely conscious form of Leigh's father.

As thoughts of the young huntress filled his mind, however, his hatred for her father vanished. As he looked down, Kehl realized that if he had continued for only a few moments longer, Jesse would not have survived. He'd nearly broken his promise to Leigh. Kehl sighed with relief as he watched Jesse's head roll to the side as he lost consciousness.

Kehl turned to look behind them and noticed that the couple had made their way away from the catwalk. The dance floor was now in a frenzy, and he doubted that anyone would find Jesse. From his vantage point, Kehl looked for Anne in the far back corner. He could see her sitting with her elbows resting on the table. Her fingers were rubbing at her temples as if she had a bad headache.

As he approached the steps leading back down to the main dance floor, he spotted two guards making their way to his location. He ran swiftly down the stairs, only just making it to the bottom as they intercepted him. Both reached into their jackets to retrieve weapons as they yelled over the music for him to stop. Anger exploded into Kehl once more.

The club was crowded, and Kehl knew that they would never risk firing at him with the entire crowd standing behind him. Easily swatting away one of the guns, he stepped forward and punched the other guard hard enough to knock him off his feet. The remaining guard tried to fight back even as his partner fell to the floor. But he was inexperienced in fighting vampires, and Kehl made short work of him.

CHAPTER 43
ERASED

Across the floor from Kehl, Anne fought a battle on an entirely different sort of battlefield. Her eyes were open and staring at the table, but her physical surroundings were the least of her worries. She'd been psychic since before she could remember, but conducting a battle on a metaphysical plane was something completely new to her. So far, she'd only managed to keep her opponent from invading her mind.

She'd felt the presence the night before during her time in the club. It had been strongest when Olivia had made her announcement. But then it had only been more of a presence of will, a subtle but strong dominating aura. Before the destruction of the jewel, Anne would have described Olivia's influences as passive. Now things were different, much different.

Olivia's powers of influence were now quite a force to be reckoned with. Anne cast her mind across the club to keep the focus away from her physical body. So far her tactics were proving to be successful. Her mind swam through the ocean of minds dancing out in the center of the room. Most of the patrons' thoughts were similar, either thinking about sex, dancing, or drinking.

She dared not venture through the air above the dancers heads, for then her mind would be fully exposed. Still, there had to be some way for her to assist Kehl. She would have to think of something soon. A few of the dancers out on the floor had noticed something odd happening on the catwalks. When she'd looked up with her physical eyes, she'd seen Kehl fighting with a man she didn't recognize.

Then a sudden attack came from Olivia, stabbing down through the other minds in the room toward hers. Anne twisted her consciousness away, darting away like a frightened fish in a very small pond. That was when a plan started to form in her mind. Adept at influencing a single mind, she wondered if she could affect several at a time. She slipped as close as possible to surface of the crowd as she dared, letting all of their surrounding thoughts wash over her mind.

To a person less experienced than herself, the sensation would have been maddening. Even she had some difficulty keeping her own identity as wave upon wave of thoughts swept into her. Acting like an amplifier, Anne threw all of the psychic energy running through her mind back out as strongly as she could. In immediate response, the dance picked up in her section of the floor, making some people dance more intimately. Others started jumping where they stood.

Just as quickly as she made her attack, Anne felt the presence of Olivia recoil. Flitting away into a different section of the floor, she repeated the process. Once more, the crowd erupted in response, forcing Olivia to retreat closer to her own physical body. A sudden driving attack from the vampire caught Anne completely off guard, although it fell far short of its mark. Anne sent her thoughts to yet a different section and tried something different.

Only staying in that position for a mere moment, she sent a burst of thought upward before quickly moving to a different spot. Repeating this several more times, she soon had the entire dance floor in upheaval. Olivia's attacks now fell down through the crowd like rain, but they proved to be unfocused and ineffective. Soon Anne felt herself starting to tire from mental exertion. Fortunately, Olivia also seemed to be growing weak from the rebelling thoughts of the now-riotous crowd.

Anne retreated to her own body. She felt dizzy and sick to her stomach but still managed to stand up quickly. Barely able to maintain her balance, she stumbled away from the table and walked out of the nearby exit. She welcomed the cold isolation that the outside night air offered her. Walking down the alleyway, she felt herself stumble slightly. She barely caught herself against the wall as she completely collapsed. Sliding down into the snow, Anne cupped her face in her hands and started to cry.

Whatever she was fighting inside of that club was a piece of herself. No matter how hard she tried, she could not deny that one simple fact. Was it that part of her that drove her to help in the destruction of her own best friend the very night before? She wanted to go back inside and help Kehl, but try as she might, she was unable to get her thoughts back together.

She didn't notice the darkness creeping in around the edges of her vision. Nor did she notice the numbness starting to spread through her body. Her mind automatically dismissed the sensations as effects of the cold winter night. As she took her hands away from her eyes and looked about the alley, she tried to bring herself back to grips. After getting back on her feet, she brushed off as much snow as she could manage from her clothes.

"My, my," came a deep male voice from the shadows.

Anne whirled about to see a darkly clothed man approaching her from the shadows. His face was thin and angular, and his nose showed signs of having been broken in the past. Why hadn't she noticed him there, lurking in the shadows? Her powers were now exponentially greater than before she should have known. Anne shook her head and backed away a few steps. The man continued talking to her.

"I just came down here to try and sell a few grams tonight, but it looks like I'm going to get something so much better."

He was now only a few feet away from her. Anne tried to focus her thoughts enough to send an attack out, but she couldn't. The numbness in her legs was now spreading up her thighs. Her arms were also starting to feel heavy and lethargic as she looked up into the face of the dealer. It felt as though she looked at him through a long, dark tunnel.

"The last time I had a piece like you they threw me in jail," he said, drawing even closer. "You aren't going to run?" he asked, looking down into Anne's glazed eyes.

Anne shook her head, though not in response to his words. An inkling of what was going on had finally come to her. It wasn't the cold that made her numb, it was Olivia slowly taking control over her body. Anne brought her hands to her forehead and screamed in fear, pain, and anger all at once. The drug dealer looked down at her curiously and then further down the alley.

It didn't seem that she'd drawn any attention to their presence. After finding the coast clear, he took Anne viciously by the shoulders and pulled her deeper into the shadows. With a violent shove, he pushed her face first up against a wall. Just as he started undoing his belt, he heard something he never expected: laughter from Anne. The sound made him so furious that he took a handful of Anne's hair and smashed her head against the wall.

Her laughter stopped for only a moment as Anne's body slumped briefly against the wall.

"What the hell is wrong with you?" he said, forgetting his belt for the time being.

"Oh, nothing is wrong with me," she said, looking back over her shoulder.

Blood dripped down one side of her face from a jagged cut on her forehead, and her cheek was badly scraped from the wall.

"The question is: what is wrong with you?" she demanded, turning herself around.

"What the hell are you talking about?" the man yelled at her as he stepped back.

Looking him directly in the eyes without the slightest hint of fear, Anne narrowed her gaze. A sudden needle like pain lanced into the rapist's mind.

"What the fu—" he stammered as he suddenly recoiled.

Another stab of pain lanced up from the bottom of his brain right behind his eyes. He roared with anguish and brought a hand up to his forehead as his eyes screwed shut. Another attack sent him staggering backward until he hit the opposite wall. Then the pain suddenly vanished. As he opened his eyes, he wiped away what he thought to be tears. A look at his fingers showed them stained with bright crimson blood.

"What the hell are you doing to me!" he screamed.

Without a word, Anne walked just in front of his recoiling form. Her hand shot up with incredible speed and took hold of his jaw. Her nails dug deep into his skin and drew blood. Jerking his head to one side, Anne took one thoughtful look at his throat and then seemed to think better of it. In that moment's hesitation, her opponent gathered enough presence of mind to try punching her. Just as he swung his arm, an incredible pain rushed up it like a bolt of lightning.

"What are you?" he cried wretchedly. "Please don't kill me."

"And you won't rape another woman as long as you live?" Anne asked in a quiet voice.

"No. Oh god, no. Never again, I promise."

Anne nodded slowly as if considering his promise.

"Okay," she said. "I don't believe you, but I'll let you live."

A rush of air burst from his lungs as the man sighed in relief. He doubled over, holding himself up on his knees. One of his hands slipped slowly down to a knife he kept concealed in his boot. Anne's eyes widened before his hand ever even got close. A sudden pain burst from the very core of the man's head, exploding outward.

"I said I would let you live," Anne whispered through his tormented screams. "But I didn't say how."

It was only a moment's work for her to completely erase his mind. The human refuse fell completely mute as his body landed limply on the ground. A slack, vacant expression filled his unblinking gaze. Never again would he even be able to even think about having his way with unwilling women.

Approaching footsteps brought Anne's attention to the entrance of the alleyway. A guard on patrol had heard the man screaming and now ran to see what the commotion was. For Anne, bending this newcomer's perception was not only easy, but was harmless. The guard bent down as he shouldered his firearm, checking the pulse of the fallen man.

After failing to get the recumbent man to his feet, the guard contacted someone inside the club with his radio.

"This is external foot patrolman alpha. I've got an unconscious man on the outside perimeter. Looks like he had a little bit too much to drink, over."

"Roger that," came a crackling voice over the radio. "Take him around back. I will call an ambulance to come pick him up."

"Yes, sir," the guard replied, giving his radio a beep to signal the end of transmission.

Anne watched in amusement as the guard pulled the rapist down the alleyway and around the back corner. Of course, she wasn't really Anne anymore. Anne would have never done such an incredibly cruel thing to another human being. Olivia now enjoyed full control of not only the young girl's body but also full use of her psychic powers. Inside the body, Anne's individual consciousness could do nothing more than watch her own actions helplessly.

The experience was as maddening and as disorienting as the most twisted of nightmares.

I could do the same thing to you, Olivia's voice said in Anne's mind.

A wave of fear, sadness, and anger washed through her mind. Laughter echoed back through her own ears and into her consciousness.

Oh, don't worry, little one. I have much, much better plans for you.

Anne tried as hard as she was able to not let herself wonder what those plans would be.

I know about the secret feelings that you have for Kehl.

No ... Anne thought.

Oh, yes, my darling. But don't worry, It's not your fault. All three of us have been pulled into the darkness surrounding Kehl.

'Three? Anne thought as Olivia took them back into the club.

Oh, don't play coy, Olivia said, sending jagged spikes of pain into Anne's mind.

Anne screamed silently, shrinking back into herself.

I know that you read Kehl's mind. Whether you wanted to or not is irrelevant. You know of Leigh and her feelings for him. You must know by now of my true identity and at least have some suspicion of my plans to destroy him.

Anne forced her thoughts to remain silent.

Now, Olivia continued, *I will make you the very instrument of Kehl's destruction.*

No! Anne screamed through her thoughts.

Laughter poured through her head once more as she thought of the tall, handsome figure of Kehl. She imagined herself driving a dagger through his back and reeled inside of herself. Her thoughts turned back to the recent death of her friend Elizabeth. Would she now do the same to the first man who'd ever been able to understand and appreciate her gift?

You are making me think these things, Anne said, forcing her thoughts out as sharply as she could.

Olivia's control easily absorbed the weak attack before clamping down even more tightly upon Anne's mind. Anne found it harder and harder to maintain her individuality among Olivia's thoughts. She found herself rationalizing her actions with desires that she never would have imagined. She'd always been jealous of Elizabeth's wealth. Why wouldn't she orchestrate her demise? Kehl was a man she would never be able to make fall in love with her. If she could not have him, then there was no way she would let Leigh steal him away.

Yes, Kehl deserved to die. She would only know peace when his immortal life at last came to its final conclusion. And when his death came, so too would hers. They would unite in the afterlife. That was the solution to her empty, unfulfilled life. The thoughts were so attractive, so compelling that for a few moments her mind actually entertained them. Darkness enveloped her consciousness as she gave into what were truly her darkest fantasies.

She now saw herself not only as a participant in the murder of Kehl but as the very mastermind of the plot. She would taste his blood. No, she would bathe in the very essence of his life. These thoughts were not her own, yet they seemed so familiar that it felt like they were. With every passing second, her sense of individuality slipped further and further away.

I thought you were dead, Olivia whispered in Anne's head. *How convenient it is that you should return to me on this, of all nights.*

CHAPTER 44

THE MEANS TO AN END

"At last!" Leigh gasped quietly, holding the key to Olivia's chambers aloft.

The sounds of a scuffle outside of the door cut her excitement short. She dove into the shadows and quickly concealed herself. There was no way of knowing whether it would be Kehl coming through the door or Olivia herself. Hopefully, whoever it happened to be would assume that Richard had passed out from too much wine in the middle of sex.

A loud slam came from the other side of the door, making Leigh shrink even further into the shadows. Silence washed over the room immediately afterward. Instinctively, Leigh's fingers tugged at the strap securing her katana, allowing her to adjust the scabbard to a more tactical location. After loosening the slipknot that held the blade in its sheath, she pushed her thumb up under the guard and freed the blade exactly three quarters of an inch from its home.

As the door opened, Leigh coiled her legs into a ready crouch and prepared to strike. When the silhouette of a man passed in front of her, she quickly drew her sword, bringing its gleaming edge to his throat. To her surprise, the man showed no signs of even the slightest of fright. Had her blade traveled even the slightest bit further, it would have slit open his throat.

"Leigh?" came Kehl's familiar voice.

Letting out a deep sigh, Leigh took the sword away from his neck. As his eyes turned to meet hers in the darkness, she forced herself to keep the blade ready.

"Did you have to fight my father?"

"Yes," Kehl answered quietly, without hesitation.

"Well," Leigh said, urging him on, "what happened?"

"He beat the hell out of me on the catwalk," Kehl replied with an uneasy grin. Leigh immediately raised an eyebrow.

"Did you use the flashbang?" she asked.

Kehl could see the katana jump slightly in Leigh's hands as she finished her question.

"No, I didn't have to. I left him unconscious on the catwalks."

The sword jumped once more, but this time Leigh only returned it to its sheath.

"So long as you didn't hurt him too badly," Leigh said before lashing out with a surprisingly strong punch to Kehl's shoulder. "That's for even hurting him at all."

Kehl rubbed his shoulder. Pain still echoed through his body from the fight with Jesse. The fact that Leigh trusted him with the life-and-death struggle with her father meant a lot to him. His thoughts were interrupted by the sudden sense of a presence behind him.

"Hey. Am I late?"

Kehl and Leigh both turned around to see Anne standing behind them in the open doorway.

"Who is this?" Leigh asked, looking up at Kehl.

"This is Anne. Things have been so hectic in the last two days that I completely forgot to mention her."

Leigh's eyebrows rose as she turned her head to look the newcomer over from head to toe.

"She helped me find Elizabeth before she fully turned," Kehl explained.

"Elizabeth is my best friend. Or rather, was my best friend," Anne said with an odd laugh.

Kehl felt that her comment seemed out of place. Maybe it was only a reaction to meeting Leigh. It might even be jealousy. Leigh was several inches taller than Anne and a bit more shapely. Kehl could only imagine the suspicions washing back and forth through the two women's minds. Strangely, he didn't feel Anne's presence inside his mind.

Narrowing his eyes, Kehl looked at her closely. She looked to either side, as if to see what he looking for.

"What?" she said nervously. "What's wrong?"

"Are your powers working?"

Anne turned and shut the door before looking him directly in the eyes.

"I am trying to keep as low of a profile as possible so that Olivia doesn't know that I'm here."

A slight movement caught Kehl's eye. A he turned to look, he saw Leigh's hand return to her sword.

"What kind of powers do you have?" Leigh asked.

Anne sighed. "Psychic. I can read and influence the minds of other people."

Leigh frowned and looked down the hallway toward Olivia's quarters. She wondered if Anne knew of her jealousy or of her developing feelings for Kehl. He should have told her about Anne. With everything that was going on, she felt that she needed to know everything. She shook her head slightly and tried to push the thoughts from her mind.

"We're wasting time," she said, setting off down the hallway.

By the time Kehl and Anne caught up with Leigh, she already had Richard's key inserted in the lock to Olivia's quarters.

"Shouldn't we have a plan or something?" Anne asked, looking around Kehl's shoulder as Leigh unlocked the door.

"I think I'm as ready as I'm going to be," Leigh replied. "How about you, Kehl?"

"I guess so. But I think we should fan out once we get inside."

Leigh nodded. "I'll hit the lights once we are in position."

"Hey guys," Anne said.

"Shh," Leigh hissed, opening the door quietly.

Anne whispered this time. "Guys …"

No response came from Leigh or Kehl as they swiftly and silently made their way into Olivia's living quarters. Anne sighed and stepped through slowly, closing the door quietly behind her.

"Guys," she said in a normal voice as she flipped on the lights. "I was trying to tell you that there is no one in here."

Leigh sighed angrily as she looked at Kehl with an exasperated look on her face before turning back toward Anne.

"You know, I haven't known you very long, but I'm not sure how much longer I can put up with you."

"Ah, what's going on in your mind, Leigh?" Anne replied mockingly. "Are you … jealous?"

Leigh advanced quickly on Anne, and as she did, Kehl noticed the younger girl's eyes narrowing in concentration. The situation was getting out of hand, and he would have to act quickly. As he stepped between them, he threw his hands toward both of them. Leigh's elbow stopped against his palm as she attempted to draw her sword. An icy pain rushed up his other arm, momentarily numbing him as it raced toward his brain.

"Stop!" he growled as loudly as he dared. "Look, this fight between you two is pointless." Leigh sheathed her sword. The icy pain slowly vanished from his arm. "There are more important things going on here, and if you two are going to do nothing but squabble, I may as well take on Olivia alone."

Leigh let out a deep breath of air and nodded as she turned away from the other two. When Kehl turned to look at Anne, however, she bore a pleased smirk. Kehl was unable to comprehend what her intentions were with such a spiteful comment. A suspicion crept into his mind that perhaps Anne was yet another one of Olivia's agents. Maybe her powers were only a lie, fabricated out of information that only Rana would have known. The true source of the voices in his head could have easily been Olivia herself.

Kehl would have to decide in the next several moments whether or not to trust Anne. Her earlier anguish of the death of her friend had, at the time, seemed genuine enough. Even the presence inside his mind had seemed to belong so distinctively to Anne. Perhaps these were only the aftereffects of the jewel's destruction making her lash out. If it proved true that she could not control herself, he would not be able to trust her.

"I'm sorry, Leigh," Anne said, taking her companions completely off guard. "I am actually jealous of *you*," she continued. "I wish I could have taken your place out on that dance floor when you two first met."

Leigh turned around and looked curiously at Anne. "There is nothing for you to be jealous about," she said before turning her gaze toward Kehl without meeting his eyes.

"I think maybe there *is* something for me to be jealous about," Anne said aloud, locking her gaze on Kehl.

When he turned around to meet her eyes, Kehl found them full of a deep anger.

"What is she talking about, Kehl?"

Kehl started to speak but found himself unable to utter even the barest of syllables.

Anne raised her eyebrows, never taking her eyes away from Kehl. "Why don't you tell her how you feel about her?"

"Enough, Anne," Kehl said, cutting her off. "We need to be able to focus on our objective, and we cannot do that with you constantly bringing up our private thoughts."

Leigh nodded in agreement. "As much as I would like to know what Kehl is thinking, right now is definitely not the time."

Kehl turned his gaze toward Leigh, but she refused to meet his eyes. There was a sadness there, resting behind her plaintive visage. Though he didn't know it, Leigh wanted nothing more than to know Kehl's thoughts. At the very risk of his own life, he had safely neutralized her father. She wanted so badly just to kiss him for that great courtesy. She just wished that everything would stop for the briefest of moments and allow her to properly express her gratitude.

"I am sure that you already know, but Olivia has control of my father. On top of that, her deepest desire is to destroy Kehl. We have to confront her tonight, or we may never have another chance."

"Please try to focus," Kehl said, reinforcing Leigh's statement. "If we are going to do this, it would be nice to have your help, especially with your talents."

"But if you are going to act like this," Leigh continued, "then we really are better off without you."

Both Leigh and Kehl expected an angry outburst from Anne, but to their surprise, she remained silent. She closed her eyes and frowned in concentration. She seemed at once to be incredibly distant even though she was standing right in front of them. When she at last reopened her eyes, she looked out hazily through thinly narrowed eyelids.

"Richard is about to wake up," Anne said, her eyes suddenly growing wide. "Richard is about to wake up! We have to hurry."

Leigh took a deep breath and looked at Kehl, waiting for him to make a decision. As Kehl turned his gaze toward the closed door, he wondered if Richard was indeed starting to stir. Quickly glancing back at Anne, Kehl saw an expression on her face that he couldn't completely comprehend. There was an urgency in the way she met his gaze, yet it seemed that a veil lay across her eyes, hiding something. If he would have to guess, he would almost say it seemed to look as though she was plotting something.

"He's awake," Anne said in an urgent whisper. "And now he is headed this way."

"All right, we'll bring you along," Kehl said. A sinking feeling settled inside of him. "Just tell us where Olivia is."

"There is a door just around the corner from the kitchenette. It's easily overlooked if you don't know it's there. I think Olivia keeps it partially concealed with her own powers."

"I don't know about this," Leigh said, staring at the door leading back to Richard. "I hit Richard pretty hard. He should be out for hours."

As if to contradict her suspicions, the door rattled as if a body had just fallen against it from the other side.

"Damn," Leigh exclaimed, her hand instantly dropping to her katana.

"Quickly," Kehl growled as he swiftly walked across the room and found the door.

Hastily opening it, he stepped through, followed immediately by both Anne and Leigh. The room was completely dark, allowing only the slightest illumination from the living room to penetrate its depth. Anne quickly closed the door behind them, plunging the trio into complete darkness. Kehl immediately lowered himself into a defensive position. Even with his heightened nocturnal vision, he could not pierce the inky blackness of this room.

"Leigh, Anne, stay as close to me as you can," he said.

A moment passed without any answer.

"Leigh? Anne?" He called, a chill spreading slowly through his body, even as he spoke.

A peal of female laughter floated through the air to meet his ears. Realization flashed through his mind as he suddenly recognized the trap.

"This was Anne's doing, wasn't it?" he asked the owner of the voice.

"However did you guess?" came a voice that was all too familiar; it was the voice of Olivia.

"She tried to fight me, and I took control of her. Can you believe that she would challenge a vampire as old as we are, Kehl?"

Her words came as a surprise. He now knew that Anne was not originally a part of her plot. He suddenly felt that he should have tried to help her earlier when she'd been acting odd. It would have been all too easy for Olivia to take control of the young girl, having bitten her once before in her lifetime. Too distracted to defend himself, Kehl left himself wide open for the coming mental attack.

A sudden lance of pain in his head brought forth memories of Rana's voice. He remembered her soft voice saying his name over and over again. Then he found himself lying on his wedding bed, only with his and Rana's roles reversed. He felt the pain of his own bite through the manifestation of the vision. Then he suffered all at once the terrible pain that both he and Olivia had experienced in that miserable dungeon so long ago.

The combined weight of the physical and mental memories made his head feel as though it was about to explode. He fell down hard onto his knees, pressing his palms against his temples as he struggled to push Olivia out of his head. Her presence in his mind vanished quickly, though Kehl suspected it had more to do with her wanting to toy with him and less to do with his feeble resistance.

"What have you done with Leigh?" he asked, shaking away the memories.

"Leigh?" Olivia asked. "Leigh! Why does that girl mean so much to you, when you've only just met her? I had originally planned to have either her or Drake kill you, but unfortunately I underestimated not only your charm, but also your strength."

"You didn't answer my question," Kehl said, unsure of how to handle Olivia in this state.

"Do you really want to know what I've done with her?" she shrieked. "I am merely using Anne to keep her, oh, shall we say, entertained?"

A sudden scream tore through the air. He immediately recognized Leigh's voice. Kehl bared his fangs as he looked off into the darkness. He was completely ready to lay down his own life in order to save her. But it required all of his strength to merely rise slowly up to his feet and address Olivia.

"This fight is between you and me," he said in a low growl. "Leave her out of it. Leave them both out of it!"

Olivia laughed as Leigh's screams turned to anguished sobs in the distant blackness.

"You have feelings for her, don't you?"

"I ..." Kehl murmured, shaking his head as he felt Olivia diving into his thoughts once more. "I don't know."

"Oh, but you do. They are only the start of something that could be much stronger, but they are still there. You three make an interesting triangle, do you know that?"

"What are you talking about? That was just you making Anne act up earlier."

"You forget. I am now privy not only to your thoughts but also to those of Leigh and Anne. What Anne said earlier may have been dictated by me, but make no mistake, she does indeed have the blooming sensations of love for you."

Kehl sought desperately in his mind for some plan to confront Olivia. He could think of nothing that seemed to be of any use.

Perhaps he could break through the illusion created by Anne's mind. He struggled to focus, trying to find some link back to the young girl who had so bravely volunteered to help him.

"Do you actually think that your pitiful efforts will do any good?" Olivia asked.

"I have to try," Kehl replied, knowing it was useless to try to conceal his thoughts from the combined powers of Anne and Olivia.

"I could just destroy you right now through Anne. She can easily dive into the deepest parts of your mind. I've already tested her powers out on someone tonight and destroyed them without her so much as blinking an eye. I wish I'd known of her existence before tonight. I could have just destroyed the jewel myself and then used her to kill you."

"But you can't kill me, I created you," Kehl said, trying to buy some time.

"I can't kill you myself, no, but through Anne I can do anything that I want. I could paralyze you with her powers and have her walk up and stab you right in the heart."

"So why don't you just have her do it and be done with it?" he asked.

As if in answer, both Leigh and Anne appeared before his eyes. They were both blindfolded. Their hands were bound and held high above their heads. Kehl struggled to run to them with all of his strength, but he couldn't move an inch.

"You see, Kehl, simply killing you would be too simple."

"Leigh!" he screamed, as whatever held him back suddenly released him. "Anne!"

Leigh's image shimmered and vanished, leaving only Anne. Her body was upright but held standing like a limp doll. As soon as his hands touched her body, she fell into his arms. As he ripped away the blindfold, he saw that her eyes stared blankly off into the darkness.

"Anne," Kehl said more softly.

Awareness returned to her eyes as she suddenly blinked. She frightened Kehl as her head started jerking violently from side to side. She stopped after a moment, her eyes widening as tears ran down her cheeks. Her pupils were badly dilated as she turned her gaze toward Kehl.

"Kehl?" she asked. "What's happening to me?"

"It's the Mistress," he replied. "Olivia, she has control of you."

There was no way for him to know whether or not he was talking to the actual Anne or just another illusion. With Anne's now prodigal powers under her control, Olivia was nearly unstoppable.

"Kehl," Anne pleaded. "Save me, please."

Her body seemed to weigh nothing at all as he lifted her into his arms. Her eyelids opened wide once more before her eyes rolled back into her head. As gently as he could manage, Kehl shook her slightly.

"Anne!" Kehl said, shaking her still limp body. Her head rolled from side to side loosely as her lips parted.

Kehl, came Anne's voice in to his mind. *Kehl, I am so sorry*

"What for?" Kehl asked aloud. "What are you sorry for, Anne?"

All too late he felt the hand withdraw from his pocket. Kehl saw the grenade pin from the flashbang looped around Anne's finger. He immediately let go of her body. There was no time to watch her body vanish into the darkness at his feet. His hand buried deep into his pocket as he struggled to find the device.

"This is what you deserve, Kehl," Olivia said, suddenly appearing in front of him.

"Now, not only are you going to die, but you are going to take me, Leigh, and Anne with you when you go. This is what I have struggled for, what I have lived for, ever since I awoke into this nightmare that you created for me."

"No!" screamed Kehl, all but ripping his pocket from his jacket.

With no more time than it took for him to blink, Olivia was upon him, her arms wrapped about him like steel chains. She buried her head against his shoulder. As he stared into the darkness, he saw Leigh and Anne appear, both of them conscious but unable to move. He tried to turn away, but he was held firmly by Olivia's arms. If he couldn't manage to escape, he would not be able to spare them from the now inevitable detonation.

"Do you know what the worst part was?" Olivia asked as time ticked by. "Even without my soul, I still loved you."

Kehl roared with all of his might just as the grenade detonated. Launched by the force of the explosion, the shards exploded from Kehl's pocket. Kehl was unable to hear himself screaming as the small jewels tore through his body. His eyes, unfortunately, were spared the blinding effects of the bomb. He saw the fragments tear through Olivia's body and saw them fly across the room to pierce Anne's shoulder. He couldn't see what was happening to Leigh.

Torn to shreds by the bulk of the shards, what remained of Olivia fell away from Kehl. Unable to remain standing, Kehl crumpled to the floor as well. Nausea washed through his mind as he struggled to stay conscious. As he rolled onto his undamaged side, he felt his wounded flank. A large chunk of flesh was missing, and he could feel the entry wounds from fragments now lodged in his body.

"Leigh!" he yelled, unable to hear the sound of his own voice. "Anne!"

A gurgling sort of laughter in his mind brought his attention to the impossibly mangled body next to him. Somehow, Olivia was still alive, despite being next to the blast. Bits and pieces of her were already turning to ash. With death approaching quickly, she looked nothing like her former self. At last, Kehl thought to himself, Rana would know peace.

Olivia's voice came as a half-gurgled whisper into his thoughts. *I finally have my revenge,* she said.

Her eyes slipped shut a moment later as her body completely turned to ash and crumbled to the floor. As Kehl looked around, the rest of the room became easily visible. Leigh lay completely still across the floor. He tried in vain to pull himself closer to her, but every motion sent incredible amounts of pain through his body. The knowledge that they all were going to die, however, drove him relentlessly on.

"Leigh," he said once more, at last managing to push himself just a bit closer.

All too quickly an icy numbness spread up through his legs. He suddenly found himself growing incredibly tired. Darkness crept into the edges of his vision as he pushed himself the tiniest bit closer. His eyes came to rest on Leigh's motionless form. A thin line of blood ran down the back of her neck. Kehl used the last of his strength and pushed himself up onto one arm. The last thing he would remember before passing out was the sight of a long shard of jewel lodged deeply into Leigh's neck.

CHAPTER 45

ONE FINAL DREAM

"Kehl," came a soft voice through the darkness. "Kehl, wake up."

Opening his eyes, Kehl saw a sight that even after centuries remained extremely familiar. The endless dead fields, filled only with dead trees and reigned over by darkened skies. As he got to his feet, he found himself free of wounds. Turning around, he looked about for some explanation as to why he once more found himself in this strange place.

"Why am I here?" he asked, wondering if he would once more meet the secret other half of his soul.

"You are here, Kehl, because without me, you will die." The answer seemed to reverberate from the landscape itself.

Kehl grew silent for several moments. "Would you be able to help me save Leigh and Anne?"

The world around him seemed to shake as if trying to tear itself apart.

"I do not know if it can be done," the voice answered. "Both of the young women are tied directly to Olivia, the monster that we created so very long ago. Our bite not only gave her body the gift of eternal life but also tore her soul asunder. Even if we manage to save them, there will always be some small amount of darkness inside of them. Also, if we do this, the chances of our own survival will be greatly diminished."

"It's a risk I am willing to take," Kehl answered without a moment's pause.

"Very well," the voice replied. "It will be necessary for us to fully unite."

Kehl did not need to turn around to know that the mirror image of his soul now stood very close behind him.

"I have been waiting for this moment for so long. There are powers sleeping deep within you, things you can scarcely comprehend. For so long, you have denied yourself access to this part of your soul. If you would have embraced your nature centuries ago, we would never have found ourselves in this situation."

Kehl remained silent as the source of the voice walked around in front of him. He saw once more the image of himself with eternally burning flesh, massive crow's wings, steely talons, and elongated fangs. A shimmer of doubt ran through his mind as he wondered about the consequences of joining with this dark inner part of himself. but he pushed his worries away. He would not be responsible for the deaths of two more innocent souls.

"Come," said his reflection. "Drink of me."

Kehl took a single step forward and reluctantly wrapped his arms about the creature's torso. The skin flaked away easily under his fingers, but the flesh beneath felt as hard as steel. His other half mirrored his actions, and dug its claws painfully into his body. As Kehl bared his fangs, he tried to ignore the sounds of his image doing the same. The thought of what he was about to do sent shivers down his spine and made him want to vomit. He now lay all that remained of his humanity on the line.

If only I can save Leigh and Anne ... he thought to himself, sinking his fangs down into the charred flesh.

He immediately felt the sharp stabbing pain of being bitten in his own neck. There was no sense of ecstasy but rather the opposite. A deep coursing agony engulfed his body as their embrace tightened. Raw power suddenly erupted through his body, surging through him in a way he'd never experienced before. His body started to shiver with the sensation. As he pulled his fangs away from the creature, he threw his head back and roared with fury.

His muscles bulged in sudden contraction, his neck twisted in with a sudden shock of pain. Inside of his chest, the undead blood boiled, threatening to free itself of the prison of his veins. The image standing before him burst into a cloud of ash before coalescing into dark tendrils that dove toward his neck. They drove their way into his wounds forcing their way into his body. His blood, already boiling, suddenly turned to ice.

Raw, unbridled power surged through his heart and mind, threatening to wash away his own thoughts. Pain erupted in his back as wings burst from his shoulders. A flame from within ignited, burning his skin away from the inside out. The agony and torment plaguing his very soul manifested in a rending scream that bust from his lips as he fell to his knees. Darkness enveloped him, blanketing him in its inviting completeness. His body shook with uncontrollable shivers as he wrapped his arms about himself to ward off the all-consuming cold.

"We will only have a few moments," he heard a voice say inside of his mind. "You will be completely under control for only a short period of time, Kehl. You will know exactly what to do."

The chill in his body immediately turned to the most inviting warmth. A sleep-like peace descended on his mind, washing away all of the previous pain. His struggling ended as he gave in to the peaceful, irresistible sensation. He closed his eyes and let himself fall into the arms of merciful slumber.

CHAPTER 46
BROKEN PROMISE

Kehl's eyes immediately opened into the world of the real. The pain still lingered at his side, but it was only an echo of its former self. Every bit as grievous looking as before, his wound still freely leaked away precious life blood. He planted one hand firmly on the ground and pushed himself up to his knees. As he slowly got himself up onto his feet, it felt as though his muscles were only stiff from a bad night's sleep. His eyes, still every bit as gray as before, now seemed to emit an unearthly light.

As he looked down and saw both Leigh and Anne laying helpless on the floor, he felt a sudden blood lust wash through him. His body swayed under the effort of resisting the strongest hunger he'd ever known. He consciously forced himself to resist as he took two unsteady steps forward.

"No," he told himself aloud. "I am stronger than this."

Pushing his thirst away, he knelt down beside Anne. For being so close to the detonation of the flashbang, her wounds were nowhere near as bad as his own. Only two wounds were visible—a grazing wound at her hip and hole bored through her shoulder. Kehl cupped his hand under his damaged hip and gathered a small amount of his blood in his palm. He balled up his fist and allowed only a single drop to fall into each of Anne's wounds. Both of the jagged injuries immediately ceased to bleed and began to close. The young girl would have scars, but nothing she wouldn't be able to live with.

Weariness took its hold upon him as he pushed himself to his feet. As he walked toward Leigh, he stumbled and fell to one knee. The pain in his side seemed so very far away now, so very distant. He regained his footing and moved closer. Looking down at Leigh's unconscious form, he remembered gazing down at the lifeless body of Rana on their wedding bed. This time would be different; he would not allow this young woman's blood to stain his hands. As he knelt by her side, he vowed to do whatever it would take to save her life.

Ever so gently, he took hold of the small, jagged remnant of the Midnight Nocturne lodged in her neck. As gingerly as he could manage, he pulled it free. Dark red blood gushed from the wound as Leigh seemed to grow pale. As quickly as possible, Kehl scooped her up into his arms. In that moment, with her life hanging in the balance in his very arms, Kehl could do only one thing to save her.

"I'm sorry, Leigh," he whispered, brushing away a stray piece of hair that had fallen across the stream of blood.

Parting his lips, he first gently kissed her neck before lining his mouth up with the wound. One fang sank directly into the jagged hole left by the gem, the other buried into her jugular. As her blood filled his mouth, it set Kehl's senses on edge. Her scent filled his nostrils as his arms tightened around her body. In his weakened state, Kehl succumbed to his hunger, pulling Leigh's essence into himself without thinking.

Leigh moaned as she weakly took hold of one of his arms. Her hand squeezed him slightly, but it proved enough to bring him back to his senses. Kehl pulled himself back reluctantly before looking down at her neck. Instead of one jagged hole there were two. The wound left by his bite looked somewhat more serious that just the single wound from the jewel fragment. Miraculously, though, only a tiny trickle of blood now seeped from her body.

His fangs naturally produced coagulants that allowed him to feed on prey for extended periods. Only one thing now worried him about her wellbeing. There was the smallest chance that she would become a vampire herself. But Kehl pushed the doubts from his mind and focused on her recovery. Given enough time, the wounds would completely seal themselves and be no more than a pale reminder of this whole ordeal.

"A reminder," he murmured to himself as he looked off into the darkness. It would be a reminder that he had broken the most important request Leigh had ever made of him.

"Kehl?" came her voice from his lap. "What happened?" she asked sleepily.

"The flashbang went off, and I still had the fragments of the jewel in my pocket. The explosion killed Olivia," he said, remaining silent for a moment. "You were hurt pretty bad."

"I remember the detonation, and then it felt like something stabbed into my neck."

Kehl watched as her hand reached up to her neck and felt first one wound and then the other.

"Oh my god," she whimpered, looking at the blood on her fingers.

"I had to," Kehl said. "I had to take the jewel fragment out of your neck and seal the wound or you would have died."

Leigh took in a sharp, shivering gasp and started to weep silently in his arms. Before Kehl could tell her that he was sorry and that she would be okay, the door behind them exploded in. Jesse leapt through the door to see his daughter lying in Kehl's arms, crying. His eyes met the fang marks on her neck. Rage poured through his body as Kehl turned to look at him with blood still staining his lips.

Free from Olivia's control, Jesse moved quickly, with every ounce of his speed and strength. He lashed out with a powerful swing of his leg, smashing his shin against the side of Kehl's head. The force knocked Kehl on his side and sent Leigh tumbling to the floor. Kehl landed on the ground and struggled to escape, though he only managed to push himself up onto his hands and knees. Jesse's leg whipped out once more, this time smashing into Kehl's wounded flank. Kehl screamed as crimson droplets fell from his mouth onto the floor.

"How dare you!" Jesse cried, kicking Kehl again. "How dare you do that to my daughter!"

Kehl shook his head feebly from side to side as he slid back to the floor.

"At least the Mistress promised that she would not lay her fangs on Leigh. If I had known that you would do it, I wouldn't have fought her control. I would have killed you myself!"

"Daddy," Leigh whispered.

She was completely unable to move, weak from her loss of blood. With some effort, she managed to turn her head and look at her father. In her current state, she was unable to comprehend his actions. Leigh had never seen her father act like this, not even in his darkest moments. She saw the hole torn into Kehl's side, and she knew that he would not be able to withstand much more punishment.

"Don't kill him," she asked as tears ran down her cheeks. "Not yet. Please."

Jesse clenched his jaw so hard that they felt like his teeth might break. His own words whispered throughout his mind. He didn't know exactly what had happened; perhaps Kehl had bitten his daughter with some unknown, innocent intentions. Unable to make up his mind, Jesse lashed out with yet another kick. The blow sent Kehl rolling away, and he lay still.

Leigh gasped as she watched her father. Completely unable to help Kehl, she closed her eyes and hoped that her father would stop. Hot tears rolled down her cheeks as she tried to not think about Kehl dying. If her father killed him before they had the chance to talk, she would never be able to forgive Kehl for breaking his promise.

"Peepers," came her father's voice. "Peepers, are you alright?"

Jesse dashed over and knelt by Leigh's side and lifted her into his arms. Leigh opened her eyes and looked up into her father's worried, loving gaze. The faraway distant look in his eyes was finally gone. He was at last free from Olivia's control. Her worry for Kehl allowed Leigh the smallest of smiles. With what little strength remained in her body, she wrapped her arms about Jesse.

"Are you all right?" Jesse asked again, more urgently.

"Yes," Leigh said, looking over toward Anne.

The young girl stirred as she pushed herself up into a sitting position. She touched a hand to her forehead and winced in pain. Her eyes darted about the room as she tried to get her bearings. Her last memory was of sitting alone in the snow, crying her eyes out. Now she found herself sitting in a darkened room with aching pains racing through her hip and shoulder.

"What happened?" she asked, looking over at Leigh and then at Jesse. "And who are you?"

"I'm Jesse," he answered, "Leigh's father."

"Ah," Anne replied. "I should have known that."

Anne was so completely disoriented and confused that her psychic powers were entirely useless. Delving deep into her mind, she tried to recall what had happened. She remembered the darkness wrapping about her mind and the all-consuming power. The memory of Olivia's possession of her spread slowly into her conscience.

"Oh my god," she said, cupping her hands over her mouth. "I am so sorry."

"So, you know what happened?" Jesse asked.

Anne nodded slowly. "Olivia took control of me and my powers and used me like a puppet. She brought me back here and forced me lead Kehl and Leigh straight into her trap."

"And what happened after that?"

"She finally confronted Kehl with her true intentions." She motioned to their surroundings. "The club, the Nocturne, all of it. Everything was only part of her plans for destroying him. Unable to kill him directly on her own, she set up a plan so that he and Drake would have to fight to the death. If that part of her plan failed, she had the best vampire hunter in the business in reserve, along with his daughter."

Jesse and Leigh looked at each other.

"The one thing she didn't count on, the one thing that she didn't plan for, was the chance that Leigh and Kehl would be attracted to one another."

"Is that true, Peepers?" Jesse asked.

Leigh hesitated for a moment before she answered her father. "Yes, I don't know why it happened, but I found myself falling for him. It wasn't a trick, either. He actually talked to me instead of using any powers. He showed me how to dance, of all things. We couldn't stop Drake from destroying the jewel, though."

"That doesn't matter at all," Jesse said. "I'm just grateful that you are okay."

Across the room, Anne sighed deeply and buried her head in her hands. She felt so young and unable to deal with such heavy concepts. She felt violated after Olivia's possession and couldn't help but feel that some amount of darkness still lay inside of her heart. There were also her own burgeoning feelings for Kehl and a subtle, baseless jealousy toward Leigh.

Lying in her father's arms, Leigh felt as though she might fall asleep. Her body badly needed a rest. But the need for sleep was quickly replaced by a gut-wrenching sensation that made her bolt upright. The first thought in Leigh's mind was that the pain might be the first sign of changing. Her fingers clenched into a fist against her stomach, and she groaned deeply. A chill ran through her body. Her back arched as she pushed back against a very worried Jesse.

"What is it?" her father asked, wrapping his arms about Leigh as she writhed in his arms.

"I don't know!" she screamed as her body started to shake. "Where is Kehl? I can feel him in my blood!"

Jesse turned to look for Kehl, expecting to see his unconscious body lying on the floor. Instead, he saw a darkened silhouette standing in the shadows. Grey eyes, ablaze with ethereal light, pierced the distance between them. Jesse found himself completely paralyzed by the gaze, as though it held him by his very soul. It seemed that Kehl wasn't even there at all, as if only his soul remained.

Leigh still struggled violently in her father's arms. "What's wrong?" she asked pleadingly. "What's wrong with Kehl?"

Kehl's ghostly eyes turned to watch Leigh's suffering, and for an instant the cold light in his eyes softened. Leigh twisted and turned in her father's arms, but she could do little more than catch glimpses of Kehl's intense eyes. The pain in her stomach and blood intensified, forcing her to curl up in a ball.

"Is he okay?" she asked.

"I don't know," Jesse replied, taking his eyes off of the vampire for only an instant to look at his struggling daughter. "I'm more worried about you right now. What's happening to you?"

"This pain," she moaned. "It's his pain, in my blood. It's my pain!"

Her words made little sense, and Jesse could not understand her. He'd heard similar things said during a turning, but his daughter showed none of the other signs. Her mind seemed to be sharp and alert. Her body seemed to be growing warmer rather than colder. Unable to figure out what was happening, Jesse found himself able to do little more than comfort her in her suffering.

When he looked back at the vampire a second later, Kehl had vanished. Jesse scanned the room, searching for any trace of his passage. In the same instant, Leigh fell completely limp in his arms. More confused than ever, he looked over at Anne, who merely shrugged and shook her head. After a moment, he glanced back down at his daughter and brushed away a bit of stray hair.

Leigh gasped in lungful after lungful of air, her body feeling weaker than ever. Shadows danced in her mind, leaving only the sense of absence clear in her thoughts. She tried to validate the feeling as merely her body needing blood, but she knew that wasn't the truth. Something had happened to Kehl, and he had vanished without a trace.

Her father's words only confirmed her feelings. "He's gone, Peepers."

"No," Leigh said, shaking her head. "He can't be."

"He just vanished into thin air, darling. He's gone."

Her tears continued to fall as she lay in her father's arms. She knew that his words were true and that Kehl was no longer there. Why would he just leave her there alone? Perhaps he knew that her father would take care of her. Maybe, she thought to herself, she was only trying to come up with alternatives to his death.

"What time is it?" she asked her father, a sudden burst of hope blossoming into her mind.

Jesse didn't understand her question at first. "What?"

"I said, what time is it?"

"I don't know," he answered. "Almost morning, I suppose."

"Can you take me to my car?" she asked, looking off into the darkness.

CHAPTER 47
REQUIEM

Most of the snow still remained on the yard when Leigh finally pulled the Mustang into Kehl's estate. In the breaking dawn, the mansion seemed transformed, brought to life by the light. Her father sat in the seat beside her, watching her every action carefully. He'd been reluctant to let her drive, but her strength seemed to have grown with every step she'd taken to the car.

"Are you going to be all right in there alone?" he asked.

Leigh turned and looked at him with a glazed look.

"Yes," she answered quietly.

Opening her door, Leigh stepped out into the snow, remembering how Kehl had carried her across it the night before. She made her way to the door and was surprised to find it open for her. At first she thought that it might be Kehl answering, but unfortunately it turned out to be a man she did not recognize. He was young and bald. He was full of energy even though his eyes seemed to be sad.

"Hello," the man said in a polite manner. "You must be Leigh."

"Yes," Leigh answered hesitantly. "I'm sorry, but who are you?"

"Merely a messenger," the strange man replied.

"A messenger for whom?" Leigh asked, intentionally leaving out Kehl's name.

"For the former owner of this estate," the man answered. "For legal purposes, that I am sure you are aware of, he lived under an alias, but his true name was Kehl Sanria."

Leigh remained silent for a moment, trying to come to terms with the possibility that Kehl was actually dead. The thought made her sick to her stomach. She wiped away the tears forming in her eyes as she tried to sort out her feelings. She did not love him, she told herself. She hadn't known him long enough, and she was only suffering from a brief infatuation. But that didn't sound right in her heart. She wondered if only there had been enough time, would they have truly fallen for one another.

"Is there any way I can go inside?" she asked, pushing her sad thoughts aside for the moment.

"Yes, of course, but there is a small matter of business that we need to take care of."

"Could it wait until I get my cat?" Leigh asked.

"No, I'm afraid not, and there is no use going to get the cat."

Leigh's jaw dropped at his reply. Anger flared into her mind, her first thought being that this strange man had done something to her new pet.

"What's wrong with the cat?" she asked.

"Oh, nothing is wrong with the cat. I just didn't want you to waste your time."

Leigh was now utterly confused, "What are you getting at?"

"Only that this entire estate, and all of Kehl Sanria's accumulated wealth and assets, are now yours to do with as you please."

Leigh blinked, not quite comprehending what the man had just said. "What? I still don't understand."

"This is all yours," the man said, spreading his arms to indicate the estate. "Kehl was very wealthy and kept me on retainer nearly around the clock. He called me yesterday morning, and had me write up his will, should anything happen to him last night."

Leigh felt her heart break as she fell to her knees. Behind her, Jesse threw his door open and ran from the car. He nearly fell in the snow as he rushed to come to her aid.

"What's wrong, Leigh? What did he say to you?" he asked, shooting the messenger a murderous glance.

"I was only telling her that this mansion and everything in it now belongs to her. Also a rather large fortune is now hers, as well."

Jesse looked down at Leigh. "I think it's another trap."

"It's no trap," the man replied. "In the library you will find a portfolio of all the deeds and titles to everything on this land. Also, there is a list of secure bank accounts and access numbers and quite a few sets of keys."

"I guess there is something you want her to sign?" Jesse asked skeptically.

"No," the man said, stepping forward and offering Leigh a hand up. "There is no need for a signature, everything is already taken care of. Mr. Sanria could afford not only the best legal support, but also the most resourceful as well."

Looking up at the strange bald man, Leigh took his hand and allowed him to help her to her feet.

"With that," the man said briskly, "I will be on my way."

"So soon?" Leigh asked. "We don't even know your name."

She was curious, but more than that she wanted to know if he had information about Kehl. Somewhere deep in her heart, she held out the small hope that maybe he still lived. Her eyes widened as she waited for the bald man's answer. It seemed to take him a moment to formulate an answer.

"My name is not important," he replied, stepping past them and into the snow.

"Do you need a ride to where you are going?" Leigh asked, turning to watch him walk briskly through the snow.

"No, thank you," he said. "A car is meeting me at the gate."

"Would you like a ride to gate then at least?" Jesse asked.

The strange man looked down the driveway in a thoughtful way. It seemed to both Leigh and Jesse that he would be happier walking, but to their surprise, he turned around and agreed to the ride.

"I would appreciate it," he said. "You could not imagine how much walking I've done in my short years."

Jesse and Leigh looked at each other. The man standing before them appeared to be in his late twenties at the most. A sudden suspicion rose in Leigh's mind, but before she could ask the man if he was a child of the night, like Kehl, the sun broke over the horizon and cast bright morning light on all three of them. The bald man smiled at her as if he had known her thoughts.

"I'll take him," Jesse offered, looking at his daughter with his eyebrows raised.

Leigh nodded. "I think I need some time to myself anyway," she said, smiling sadly.

Jesse nodded and quickly went around to the driver's side of the Mustang. Moments later, he and the bald man were making their way up the driveway and Leigh was left alone on the doorstep of her new home. Leigh turned around and looked at the doorway, wondering how she would ever be able to live here comfortably, reminded constantly of Kehl.

Maybe she would learn more about him through living in his former mansion. As she stepped into the house, she closed the door behind her. She walked slowly through the only part of the house that she knew, absentmindedly making her way to the library. Her thoughts were full of Kehl; her heart longed for him to be here with her, by her side.

In the library, she found the portfolio on a coffee table in front of one of the couches. Without looking too closely at any one paper, she leafed through it without picking it up. A small mewing sound suddenly drew her attention. Curled up against one of the armrests of the couch was Kali. Leigh sat down next the small kitten and scratched its head gently.

"How did you get out of your box?" she asked, amazed at how much better the kitten looked now.

Although Kali's eyes were still a bit swollen, she looked much healthier. Scooping her up, Leigh lay back on the couch and sat the kitten on her stomach. Kali seemed content to lie there and go back to sleep. She watched the kitten until it fell asleep, which in turn, reminded Leigh just how tired she was herself. Her body had yet to fully replace the blood she'd lost several hours before. As she closed her eyes, her final thoughts were of Kehl and how much she missed the man she had only just met two days ago.

Epilogue

Almost exactly a year separated Leigh from the unfortunate events surrounding the Midnight Nocturne. She was only just growing comfortable in her new home when she'd started receiving job offers from around the country. If nothing else, the destruction of the jewel had been good for business. Currently, she was on her way to Europe by airplane. She'd been hired to investigate a series of murders in a relatively small town. As she looked out of the airplane window at the ground far below, she tried to piece together the relatively minuscule bits of information she'd been given.

A dozen people were dead already, and they'd all died in the same manner. Someone or something had drained the victims of almost every ounce of blood before ripping their bodies to shreds. Rumors were circulating through the town about the source of the attacks. Nothing conclusive could be found in the wild speculations of the superstitious.

With a sigh, Leigh rested her head back against her seat, her eyes turning absentmindedly up toward the luggage rack. A year ago, she wouldn't have had any competition for this job, but things had changed. Instances of vampirism and lycanthropy were sharply on the rise. Other accounts of supernatural happenings were also coming in from around the globe. There was now a demand for hunters of almost every kind. Her new employer had informed her that there were not only other hunters in town, but even a small team of them as well.

The profession was cutthroat, both literally and figuratively, and Leigh knew she would have to watch her back. While she was no longer in the trade as a source of money, others definitely were, which was a concern for those in this job. The local government had offered a sum of several millions to track down and eliminate the source of the killings. In a situation such as this, her fellow hunters could quickly turn into enemies. It was not only her lack of greed, however, that separated Leigh from her compatriots.

Firstly, her employer was not a member of the local government, and he was hiring her with his own means. Secondly, he'd provided her with some choice information that was not only unavailable to her competition, but was also extremely important to Leigh and the situation at hand. And thirdly, he had a firsthand account of what they thought to be the killer.

A husband and wife had hired Leigh to protect their son, the witness, from both other hunters and the killer, should they decide to come after the family. Leigh's heart ached in her chest as she remembered seeing the pictures the boy had taken. He was a young teenager, and one night after the first several killings, he'd decided to go out and find the murderer himself.

Armed with only a digital camera, he had crept out into a dark and rainy night. Leigh could only imagine how he'd managed to sneak up on so dangerous a foe. There were twelve photographs in all, but only the last three seemed to contain any evidence. The first shots were little more than blurry images, taken from too high and wide of an angle. As the shots progressed, however, the misty, rainy night came into sharp contrast with the wet buildings in the photos. Leigh could even make out the edges of the plastic bag around the borders of the lens that the teenager had used to protect his camera from the damp.

Leigh leaned forward in her seat, reaching down into her carryon bag to retrieve the three pictures. She leafed through them in order. The first photo was of an ordinary-looking twenty-something couple as they walked by a fountain in what looked like a small town square. Leigh had studied the picture for hours and had found nothing out of the ordinary, although she felt that she was missing something.

The second photo had obviously been taken very hastily. It was crooked and slightly blurry. What it showed in its glossy surface, however, was clear. Lying in a relatively small halo of blood on the cobblestone street of the square was the young couple. Their bodies were torn to shreds, and had Leigh not seen them in the previous photo, she wouldn't have even recognized the bodies as human remains.

Her heart started to race as she slowly flipped to the last image. It was this picture that had made her take the job. Even now, halfway across the ocean, it felt as though she was looking at the devastating piece of photography for the first time. Framed perfectly in the last photograph was the ghostly silhouette of a man standing above the bodies. His gray eyes seemed to burn through the glossy surface of the paper and directly into Leigh's very soul.